'I'm going to kill them in

A boy sits in his front living-room contemplating multiple murder. And so begins an extraordinary and compelling story of an Irish teenager buffeted by Church, state, school and family. The story that he tells is manic, touching and hilarious and marks the arrival of a new and exhilarating Irish writer.

FOR I HAVE SINNED

Colm Herron

DAKOTA

Published in 2003 by Dakota

ISBN 0-9546453-0-8

Printed and bound by Biddles Ltd, Woodbridge
Park Estate, Woodbridge Road, Guildford, Surrey

To nobody

You're the only one I can tell. There's some name for you and I'm trying to think what it is. Anyway, I'm going to kill them in the College chapel. They'll all be together there and they won't be expecting it. Just after the *O Salutaris* I'll let on to be sick but I won't go to the sick bay, I'll go out of the chapel and round behind the Main Study. That's where the toolshed is, that's where the pitchfork is. I'll get back in before the end of Benediction and walk up the middle aisle and tell Father O'Donoghue to put the host back into the tabernacle and then I'll get the three commandants to stand up against the wall together in a straight line. That's what I call them. The commandants. Everybody's going to do what I tell them. Nobody will try to take the pitchfork off me because I'll be holding Bernard's old dummy handgun. They'll know I mean business all right. Maybe *you* don't think I mean business. Maybe you feel like laughing when you think of somebody like me saying he's going to do something like that. Well, you won't be laughing anymore when I'm telling you about them lying there with their dead eyeballs sticking up out of heads and their blood splattering all over the place. I won't wear a mask because I want them to know who's doing it. I'll leave The Pogue to the last because he's the worst so he'll have to suffer more with the waiting, watching the other two getting it first. I'll wait for him to beg for mercy and then I'll I shove it up him. As soon as he's dead I'll ask one of the other teachers to go the president's office and phone the police so's I can give myself up. They can't hang me. They're not allowed to hang you when you're only thirteen. They send you to reform school. Well, that's okay. Reform school's okay. Borstal couldn't be anywhere near as bad as this place.

7

I didn't do it. I didn't do it yet anyhow. I'm going to put it off for now but somebody'd better be praying for those cunts that Mammy doesn't die before I leave the College. When you think about it, if I killed them and her still alive it would break her heart, she'd die of shame so she would. She's just an ordinary wee woman, well, not to me, to me she's a saint, but she's dead proud of us and she's always praying that none of us ever get into bother. She's got high blood pressure and varicose veins in her legs and heartburn and other things wrong with her too and I don't know how long she's going to live. How could anybody know that for sure? She could die anytime so I hope for their sakes they're sorry for their sins because bad and all as they are I don't want them to go to hell. The bastards. You probably think I'm backing out. Well I'm not. What's the point of making Mammy suffer, killing her too when she hasn't done anything wrong? No point. No point at all. So I'm not backing out. Definitely not. I'm just postponing things, that's all.

The plan is drastic all right. I'm not going to argue about *that*. But once I thought of it I knew it was the right thing to do and I wouldn't be able to look at myself if I changed my mind. Then I took a walk out the Northland Road and I started to calm down a bit and then I wanted to forget about it but not for long. I said to myself, Are you some kind of a chicken or what? When I thought it up first the day before yesterday I was sitting in the house and I had this desperate headache and I was all tensed up because I knew for sure I was going to get the shite knocked out of me again the next day by Father Couchman even though I had the Divine Right of Kings off back to front. I have ways of making you confused. That's Couchman's motto. (Just to let you know, he did beat the shite out of me. Yesterday and today. Twice today. I was the first to be asked and then he asked me again just before the bell. He didn't mix me up the second time but he knew I was switched off because I wasn't expecting to be asked again. I knew the answer but I didn't know the question and I stammered - Wa-wa-what, Fffffaller? and he gave me six for not saying Pardon.) Why does he hate me? You tell *me*. *I* don't know. But I'll tell you one thing. I never saw anybody as sleekit at making you go wrong. It didn't take me long to jube on that he gets some kind of a big thrill out of doking me. I know and he knows I know and the two of us know there's nothing I can do about it. He's the one with the power and I'm just a wee skitter.

It's not just Couchman. The other two are even worse. They're fucken monsters, the three of them. God forgive me, I shouldn't be using that kind of language but that's all they are. Fucken monsters. Anyway, there was me, in the sitting room my lone. I was supposed to be doing the rest of my ekkers but I wasn't fit. I was thinking about what my big sister Mairead said one time about drowning being the easiest way to die. I can't leave the College. Mammy couldn't take it, she couldn't take it. And I'm not going to run away anymore. I thought how quiet down the quay would be on a Sunday night and nobody would see me going in when it was dark. And then I thought, Why should I go to hell just because those bastards won't leave me alone? Because that's where I'd be going, make no mistake about it. Nobody has the right to take life away except God, He gives it and He takes it away, and anybody who does it goes to hell unless the balance of their mind is disturbed. Well I'm not mad so why should I go to hell when I haven't done anything wrong? I'd be down there screaming in agony and those three hoors would be up here beating the shite out of other boys whenever they felt like it. So I thought, Why shouldn't they be the ones to suffer? I don't mean in hell. I just mean to be killed very slowly. I don't want anybody to go to hell, you're not supposed to, not even that shower of shitehawks.

There's a funny thing about The Couch. He used to really like me. In fact I was his pet. He used to be all over me. It was sickening. The whole class knew and they used to give me looks as if it was *my* fault, as if I was licking up to him. He came down to my desk and wrestled with me in fun. Wrestled with me. A priest. There was this sweet smell off him when he was up close and it was hard to breathe right. He started fake arguments with me, really childish. I thought it was funny, a priest going on like that. He said things like - You know what I think,

Cornelius Murphy? I think you make faces at me every time I turn my back on you. And I said - No, Fffffaller, I don't, honest I don't, because I didn't, and he said - You'd think butter would-n't melt in his mouth. Look at him. Butter *would* melt in your mouth, *wouldn't* it, Cornelius? So I said back - I dunno Fffffaller. What could you say? One day he gave me his wristwatch and asked me if I'd like to wear it and after he put it in my hand he said I stole it and he pushed and pulled at me to get it back and I wasn't even trying to hold on to it. Now it's - You've stopped working Murphy, you're only a lout Murphy, this is what you're going to get until you start pulling your socks up Murphy. And his big strap comes down, three on each hand every time I have him. I *am* working. That's the thing about it. I work harder at History than I do at anything else. But no matter what I do he's going to get me. Until the time comes. Then he'll know what's sticking to him. Cunt.

He's not the worst of them. The Pogue's the worst. Him and The Couch and McRide run the place as far as I can see. Father Meehan, he's the President, he's hardly ever out of his office. Plenty other boys get it too. Tommy Ellis left in April. He let on to me his daddy wanted to move him to the Christian Brother's Tech but everybody knows he left because he couldn't stick it anymore. They were giving him a desperate time. They never lay off him, not one day. But it's funny him going to the Christian's. Imagine leaving the College to go there. Out of the frying pan into the Christian's. Gander McLaughlin told me Tommy stopped going to mass. When he's sent out on a Sunday morning he walks right past the Cathedral and goes on down to the quay. Gander went down with him one time. He says the two of them just stood there, seeing who could skim the Foyle the most times with stones and watching some boat heading out to sea. Then they went home when mass was over. That's real-ly serious. I mean, if you lose your faith that's you finished. I wonder did Gander dob mass that day or was he at one earlier one. I don't want to ask him in case he wasn't.

You remember the yahoos in *Gulliver's Travels*, you know the ones that looked like human beings only they were really disgusting animals that hadn't a brain in their head. Well that's what the commandants treat nearly our whole class like. Yahoos. The ones that get an easy time are the geniuses because they know near enough everything and anything they don't know they learn right away and never forget it. They never forget anything. They can take in facts the way you and me take in air. I'll tell you now what they're like. They see a new list of irregular Irish verbs and they pee themselves on the spot they're that excited. They have this kind of dried up look and they're really pale and serious and of course the whole lot of them are complete pukes. They don't play football and they walk spla-footed and they never run or if they do it's a sort of a sideways run and they never stand beside you in the jacks and they don't crack jokes and they don't laugh if *you* crack one, even if it's a scream. But you want to see the way the commandants go on with them. They go on as if these freaks are great people and the rest of us are nothing but lazy bastards. *I* know some people are born brilliant and everybody else has to stew like mad to do well at school. *I* know that and I'm only *starting* to get educated. But these teachers, the people who are *supposed* to be educated, *they* haven't caught on yet. They think very clever brain equals very class person and very ordinary brain equals very lazy lout. And here's another thing. They keep telling you the state of your soul's a million times more important than the state of your brain and then they beat the shite out of you for not being smart enough. So did you ever wonder what's going to happen you if you're not holy enough? Don't say. But you want to know the worst thing of all? They *control* you. I'm telling you. *They control your life.* Like on a Monday morning when I'm going up the College walks, I can't even imagine half-twelve on the Saturday ever coming. And I'll tell you what's a million times worse. On a Monday morning I can't even see *Tuesday* coming. But on a Sunday morning I can see Monday all right. It sits there all day and all night waiting for you. On a Sunday you know for a fact that any crack you had on the Saturday from half-twelve on might as well never have happened. Sunday should be called Dreadoomday. That's a good one. Dreadoomday. It's the worst day of the week. Now isn't that funny? It's the worst day of the week and it's the only day we don't have to go to St. Paul's. And the boredom. Jesus. You're not allowed to go on the swings or banana slides or play football in Brooke Park and your ears are deaved with the Protestant bells all day long. Long's the right word. And why do they always sound as if there's been a disaster or something? They're like funerals queuing up to get into the cemetery from morning to night. Anyway, do you see this thing about time at the College? *Doing* time at the College I *should* say. Do you know what my first year was like? A life sentence with no time off for good behaviour. Did you ever get the feeling you'll never be the age the Seniors are now? One class with The Pogue is longer than sitting in the Strand picture-house from half two till half ten watching *Shane* plus *The Bowery Boys* plus *The Three Stooges* plus Movietone News plus the trailer plus the ads three times each. Me and Stoopy Shiels and Charlie Murphy did that once. Three times, I mean. I'll tell you sometime how we got away with it. But it's just as if the commandants are all the guards in a concentration camp rolled into three and they control the time dimension as long as they're inside the College walls. They can do whatever they want with time and with you and nobody stops them. And you just can't see it ending. Ever.

What a nightmare! It all started with not keeping my mind on the Billy Bunter book. And the thing was, it was so funny. One minute I was laughing away to myself at Bunter hiding the fudge cake up his shirt and the next minute all I could see was Sally O'Donnell lying on her stomach on the grass in Tillie's field. Now I don't know about you but there's something about Sally lying on her stomach on the grass that makes me go out of my mind down there. She was wearing this wee short silky skirt (I'm talking about *really* short) and she was swinging the bottom part of her legs and sometimes one of her heels touched her bum and sometimes it didn't. Well, that did it. I threw Bunter on the floor and got the bolster out from under the pillow. I know what you're thinking. I could have said aspirations like I did nearly every other time. But I didn't. Okay? I didn't. I took the cover off and whispered to Sally it would be all right and I lay on my back and pulled her over on top of me and held her tight. After I finished I lay there and didn't even try and let on to be sorry because there was no point. I lay there and my body was just sailing along but the rest of me felt as if it was sinking.

I didn't fall asleep for a good while. Maybe I did but I don't think I did. I know before the nightmare started I was thinking it didn't seem fair for one wank to bring you the same punishment in hell as the dirtiest brute in the world that was riding day and night for about forty years. But then the next I knew I was in the lift of Austin's department store in the Diamond. That's the lift I got lost in when I was four. I'll never forget it. I stepped right into it because I thought Mammy was coming behind me. But then the big iron door with the slanty bars clanged closed and Mammy wasn't there. Nobody was there only me. I shouted and shouted but there wasn't any answer. I screamed and shook the rattly door but nobody came. I couldn't find any handle but there was a whole lot of buttons on the wall and, in the middle of my hysterics, I pressed the bottom one because it was the only one I could reach up to. Then the whole world seemed to jolt and jerk and the lift shot down the ways. Whenever it stopped the shock nearly knocked my wee teeth out. But wait till you hear what happened then. The door clattered open and all I could see was this man shovelling coal into a big furnace. Honest to God. He stopped what he was doing and came over to the lift. I know *now* he was only trying to help but do you see *at the time,* he made me a hundred times worse with his black face and his big stary eyes shining out at me. But now in my dream I was a good lot taller so I pressed the top button because I wanted to go up the ways. I pressed it quick because I didn't want anybody to be coming in and seeing me bare and the stains still sticking to me. But the lift didn't go up this time either. It went down. I looked out through the grills and saw different departments full of burning people. I got a great view of the first floor down because the lift went slower there and I definitely saw Hitler and Mussolini and

13

Geronimo and the Mau Mau. It slowed down again coming to the floor below that and you know who was there? The commandants! Hell rub it up them! But then I started getting really worried because the further down I went the hotter it got. When I hit the bottom the door opened and right away I found this desperate sickening smell. God, you should have heard the screams of these ones. And the sight of them! I never thought I'd see anything like it. There were millions of couples and every one of them was naked and they looked completely disgusting because they were doing away at it to each other. You could tell it was hurting them something fierce but they couldn't stop because they were stuck together and the more they did it the more the skin got burnt off them by the flames. Then somebody took me by the hand and when I saw who it was I nearly died. It was this humpy old hag that was half bald and her face was covered with scabs and her mouth and nose were all snotters. She kissed me very hard and when she was doing it she bit off my lower lip. I didn't feel any pain but I saw the lip hanging out of her mouth and the blood dripping from it.

- Mmm, she said. - You're sweet. I've been waiting for you for ages.

Her chest was hanging down like two busted balloons and there were more scabs on different parts of her and a whole lot of them were coming off too soon and as well as that there was a terrible smell of shite off her and when I looked down I saw her legs clattered with it.

- You were meant for me, she cackled. - Now I'm going to love you forever and I mean forever baby! and she pressed my body against hers. As soon as she did that my skin started getting all bubbly and I could hear the sizzle of it.

- Oh God, I said and that's when I woke up.

Father McElhone made me feel better. He knew I was in a wile state but he was still very annoyed about what I did to myself. When he came round a bit he told me to take my rosary beads to bed with me in the future and hold them in my hands until I fell asleep. He told me if I was tempted I was to look at the crucified Christ on the cross that was attached to the beads. He said Jesus loved me even though I was unworthy and had offended Him and I must put my trust in Him. And then just as he was giving me absolution I got this fantastic feeling. It was like a terrible weight was being sucked out from inside of me and golden air was taking its place. I'm going to daily Mass and Holy Communion since. That's three weeks steady. I'm walking past girls usually without looking near them but sometimes I have to think fast if I *have* to look at them. Like when Sally stopped me yesterday and asked me if I was sick or what was wrong I wasn't out much and she was wearing these white shorts so I made my eyes go a bit googy so's I wouldn't see her down there. I told her a fly got into my eye. That might seem a bit drastic but it worked. I haven't given into one bad thought since my last Confession three weeks ago.

Me and Stoopy and Gander were coming up Creggan Hill and Gander said - Christ, wud yeez luck at yon fur an arse.

He was on about Sally. She was a bit in front of us and she had a cream skirt on her that came down to just above her knees. I tried not to look but I looked anyway. Jesus. She had this kind of a swing I never noticed before. Maybe it was the skirt but whatever it was her bum seemed to be about a quarter ways up her back and one side of it was rolling one way and the other side was rolling the other way. And her legs were longer. They were far longer than they were before. You should have seen them. I took it all in far quicker than I'm writing it now because I knew if I looked too long I'd be away with it. Stoopy gave me a dunt.

- Whass wrong way yer eyes, Spud? Are ye goin skelly or what?

- Nothin, I said and started rubbing away at them, as if they were sore or something. God, I better stop doing this. Maybe I can start saying aspirations without moving my lips.

She stopped to cross the road and looked around to see were there any cars coming. That's when she saw us. She waved.

- Hello, Conn, she shouted and my heart near exploded. Stoopy and Gander went - Wooo! Wooo! Wooo!

I think she blushed a wee bit. I know *I* went like a beetroot. But I didn't answer her. I couldn't. I couldn't speak. So I just waved back. She started a wee trot that made the whole inside of me do the jitterbug. She was getting away from us because she knew Gander and Stoopy might get a bit dirty.

- Ye realise what ye're goin tay do now, Spud, don't ye? said Gander. - First chance ye git ye're goin tay hiftay git er up the Cnoc na Ros lane. Ye know she's got a notion a ye, don't ye?

- Sssssays who? I said.

She disappeared round the corner as if she was doing the hundred yards.

- Says Annemarie, said Stoopy.

Stoopy's supposed to be going with Annemarie and Sally and Annemarie go about together.

- Sure any gawm kin see it, said Gander. - Ye don't need Annemarie tay tell ye that.

- Ye're jokin, I said but I was singing away inside.

- No harm tay ye, Spud, Gander said - but d'ye wannay know whass the matter way ye? Ye're a fucken disaster, thass whass the matter way ye. D'ye think fur wan minute she's goin tay keep fancyin ye if ye don't start mickin a move?

- Gawn away an sssssscratch yerself, I said but I didn't really know what I was saying.

- Gawn *you* away an scratch *your*sel, Murphy, he said. - I'll tell ye somethin now fur nothin. D'ye see yer man from Demesne Gardens, yer man that thinks he's got the big prick–

- Head the Ball Boggs, said Stoopy.

- Right, Head the Ball Boggs, said Gander. - D'ye nivir see im luckin at er? Sure he slabbers at the mouth iviry time. D'ye see whin he sees er the way she is now, he'll hiv er up that lane an the drawers off er an all before she knows whass happenin.

Then he gave a dirty big laugh.

- Mibby he won't need tay tick them down at all, he said. - Mibby she'll save im the bother.

- Or mibby fur all *we* know *she* won't need tay either, said Stoopy. - Mibby she's nothin on under that wee skert, Stoopy said.

- Hi, wait d'yeez hear this wan, Gander roared. - How d'ye know Sally O'Donnell doesn't wear any knickers? I'll tell ye why. Cause ye can see the dandruff on er shoes.

I suppose you're wondering why I didn't give Gander a bat in the mouth when he started getting crude about Sally. Well, first of all, if I'd done that he'd have taken me apart. He really is a hard lick. Second of all, that's the way Gander goes on this past while in front of other boys and there's not a thing you can do about it. If it was just me and him he wouldn't have said it. Okay, he comes out with a whole mouthful sometimes when there's only the two of us but he'd never go on like that about Sally. He just has to be a bigmouth when there's other people there. Don't ask me why. *By* the way, I'm not worried about Head the Ball. You know what he does? He wears these sort of light green flannelly trousers all the time that show up anything that's under them. Stoopy says they're so tight you can see the track of a fly walking up his leg inside of them. And when there's girls around he starts pulling them up tighter so's to show off his toolbox even more. He's nothing but a slag and Sally wouldn't look near him.

She kept coming into my head after that I got home. She's not like they were saying. She's not cheap. I think she might let you kiss her but she's not cheap. Stoopy says you have to give them a good feel or they get fed up with you but he's nothing but talk. I bet you anything he's never even kissed Annemarie. I don't think he even *goes* with her. Anyway, this here's getting me down. The whole thing about the way they go on now, I mean. Up till around Easter if you went with somebody all you did was stand outside their house talking to them or maybe sit beside them on Deeney's steps shouting away at people playing football or gable tennis. One thing you didn't do was touch them. They'd have run into the house and maybe even told their ma on you. Now they nearly *expect* you to take them round the lane.

I know the name for you now. *Alter ego*. It means *second self* and it means *very good friend* as well. Father Rodgers wrote it on the blackboard today. Arthur told me one other time but I forgot. Arthur's my biggest brother. So, anyway, that's what you are. The one I can tell things to. I used to tell Gander things sometimes but then something happened him. I don't know exactly when and I don't know exactly what either and I don't want to ask him. You couldn't ask him the way he is now. We used to be really good muckers. We never lay out of each other's houses. He came up to our house nearly every night and we played table tennis on our front room table and sometimes we told each other jokes and stuff. He was never dirty then and he didn't curse either, except for flume and frig. One time when he was telling me something about his wee brother Harry that died last year he started crying and I put my arm round his shoulder. I didn't know what to say, I just let him cry on. He cried a good while. Down in his house we sat on the sofa reading his Annuals for hours. His ma was dead on and a whole lot of times she brought us in glasses of lemonade and chocolate digestives on a tray. She said I was a nice modest wee boy and after that Gander called me Modest Murphy sometimes. I didn't care. It was better than Cornelius Pius Alphonsus which is the only hateful thing Mammy and Daddy ever did on me. I'm called Cornelius after my great-uncle Corny that got his head cut off when he looked out of a train window that was open too near a tunnel the time of the Black Flu and Pius after the pope and Alphonsus after the bishop. Gander's real name is Stanislaus and his ma called him that in front of me once. He just said - Aw Ma and she laughed. She's really good-looking. And nice too. She's the nicest woman I ever met except for Mammy. Gander was learning the piano and he let me play with his meccano when he was practising his pieces. He taught me how to sing *Danny Boy* with him playing it. It wasn't one of his pieces but he

18

had the music of it and he still played it even though he didn't have to. It's one of the best songs I ever heard. I learnt it all but I can only remember the first verse now. This is it.

O Danny boy, the pipes, the pipes are calling
From glen to glen and down the mountainside.
The summer's gone and all the flowers are dying,
Tis you, tis you must go and I must bide.
But come ye back when Summer's in the meadow
Or when the valleys hushed and white with snow.
Tis I'll be here in sunshine or in shadow
O Danny boy, O Danny boy I love you so.

That's all I remember. The next verse gets really sad so it does but it's still a class song.

Remember I was telling you about how Gander changed. I remember now when it was. It was the day before we went back to the College after the summer holidays last year and the two of us were sitting there feeling a bit desperate, reading two of his Annuals. *Trying* to read would be more like it. We were in a bad way all right. Then he started.

- Member ye wur tellin may about yer da dyin whin ye wur wee? Tell may this. What'd he die of?

- I dunno.

- Ye know what I was thinkin? I was thinkin, fur all ye know, mibby he's not dead at all. Mibby yer ma jist made it up about im bein dead.

- Naw, he's dead awright, I said. - Wa-wa-why wu-wu-wud sh-sh-she let on he wa-wa-was dead if he wa-wa-wasn't dead?

- How day I know? Mibby he jist cleared away off somewhere and nivir come back and she didn't wannay let on tay ye. Mibby she'll tell ye whiniver ye git ouler.

- Wa-wa-wise up. I towl ye he's dead.

- Wise *you* up. What micks ye so sure? Did ye *see* im dead?

19

Sure ye wur oney a baby the time he died.

- Wa-wa-well if ye really wa-wa-wannay know, thur's a picture of his fffffuneral in our sssssideboard drawer.

- Sure that cud be somebody else's funeral fur all ye know. It's oney important people git pictures ticken at thur funeral. Was yer da vurry important?

- I dunno.

- What did he work at?

- He wa-wa-was a bus driver.

- He wasn't vurry important then. Bus drivers aren't vurry important so they aren't. Did he lave yeez any money?

- I dunno. I don't think sssso.

- *My* da's rich. He sends us a wile lotta money from Stoke-on-Trent. He bought that piana fur may so he did. Well, it was fur me *and* Harry but then Harry died. He was too young tay start lessons anyway.

- Wa-wa-whin's he comin home? Yer da.

- Nixt Christmas.

- Wa-wa-was he home this Christmas?

- Naw. He's over about sixty men and he cudn't git off.

- Sssso how's he goin tay bibble tay come home *nixt* Christmas? Wa-wa-will he sssstill not bay over sssssixty men.

- What the fuck d'ye mean?

- I mean, if he cannay tick off. If he's still over sssssixty men lick ye say, he'll sssssstill not bibble tay tick off.

- I didn't say he can nivir tick off. Did *I* say he can *nivir* tick off? Did *I* say that? Anyway, I towl ye. He's comin home at Christmas and he's gittin may a bike this time.

- Sh-sh-sure ye've got a bike.

Gander stood up then. I thought he was going to lift his boot to me.

- Fur fuck sake, wud you mine yer own fucken business Murphy. What the fuck's it got tay do way *you*, anyway?

He was standing looking down at me like some sort of a madman and that's when I really started stammering and he started mocking me. He called me Machine-gun Kelly and told me I was the biggest stupe in Derry because I couldn't say the simplest word without going on like a mental case. I got really annoyed about that even though I'm used to people slagging me about my stammer. Some of the College teachers make me feel like a real dunce so they do. A whole lot of times just when I'm about to get a word out they say - Next boy. You sit down Murphy, we haven't all day.

I don't think I told you about any of that stuff about the stammer. To tell you the truth I try to forget about it as much as I can. I think maybe it's a part of the reason I do all this writing. Because you can't stammer when you're writing. Okay, that sounds a bit mad but you really are like a different person whenever you're writing. You're completely free and all. Imagine being able to put down anything, anything you want. And you can write things without thinking or you can sit for an hour thinking before you even start and nobody's telling you to get a move on. Some nights I think I'm going to waken up in the morning and the stammer will be away. Nobody saying the next word for me anymore as if I'm stupid. No teacher looking at me as if I'm a freak. No more losing my breath and hurting my chest trying to get something out. Maybe when I get my first ride the tenseness will disappear forever. But that won't be till I'm married and I'm not sure if that'll ever happen because why would a girl marry me if I don't go near her for fear of committing a mortal sin? Maybe I'll meet a beautiful girl with a stammer that's scared of hell the way I am and we'll just kiss and hold hands for years without being impure until the first night of our honeymoon and then I'll get stuck into her like a piledriver and we'll go out of our minds and wake up like different people in the morning.

But even though Gander really scundered me that day I sort of forgave him because I knew he was in a bad way about his da not coming home for Christmas and all. Of course I never told him I forgave him because that would have meant he'd done something wrong and *he* didn't think he'd done anything wrong. I just tried to go on as if nothing had happened but *he* knew something had happened. It was like he was only partly the same person and he'd taken a jump forward but I was still back where he used to be. He's not too bad when it's just me and him except he goes on as if I'm a twerp sometimes. And

21

now there's these two morons from Bishop Street. He's been hanging around with them this past while and he thinks they're class acts. They're two of the biggest goofs on God's earth but you'd think the way Gander goes on there's nobody like them. You know something? It makes me wonder if our friendship was really friendship when you see the way he goes on with them. It's a funny thing about friends. You know the way when you were a bit smaller and you and some wee boy were so friendly you were nearly like Siamese twins. And then suddenly you stopped being pals and you didn't even have a row. For no reason at all the two of you were away with another wee pal each. But then when you're twelve of thirteen you get a bit of sense and you know what a real friend is. Or you think you do. I really liked Gander but I'm not too sure now if I do or not. It's nearly as if he got a bang on the head and his brain was affected. All him and these two bastards ever think about is sex. Well, I suppose it's all I ever think about too except for football but at least I'm trying not to think about it. The way it is with them, they're trying to see how filthy they can get. I mean as far as they're concerned, girls are either useless or they're great rides. If you say to them about some girl - She's brilliant lookin, they'll say - Sure they're all the same between the legs. And you want to hear them about other people in Derry. The way they go on, most of the men are either sheep shaggers or fruits. One day Gander and the goofs were on about this man I know and they were saying he had to be pulled off a lamb up Sheriff's Mountain. One other day when we were coming back from a game of bootie in Brooke Park Gander was in front of me with the same two pricks. I was about five yards behind them and I could hear him telling the whole of Creggan Hill about these two men he saw one night down the Lucky Lane. I'm not joking, he's about five times as loud as he used to be.

- Jesus, yeez wanted tay see them, he roared. - They wur lick two fucken dogs so they wur.

And then he said a whole lot of things I'm not going to write down. But you know what I was thinking when he was mouthing away? I was thinking, Isn't that funny? I was thinking about the time in his front room when me and him were acting parts out of *My Darling Clementine*. I was Doc Halliday and he was Wyatt Earp. In the middle of it Gander got down on his back on the floor and said to me - Right, Conn, let on I've got a bullet in the bottom of the belly an Doc Halliday's half drunk but he still has tay use his doctor skills tay git the bullet out.

So I knelt down and mimed fixing him up but then he gave me a shock.

- Naw, Conn, pull down may trousers an underpants an do it right.

He saw me staring at him and he said - Mawn, Conn, do it right. Please.

The thing was, I wouldn't have minded doing it. I was starting to get all warm and wobbly and weak. And Gander's very good looking. A few times in my house and his house, when there was nobody else around, I felt like pressing him up against the door or the wall but I never did it. I know he knew it because one time he caught me staring at his trousers *that* kind of a way. But the day I'm telling you about, the day he wanted me to feel him, what I really felt like doing was lying flat on top of him. But I didn't do it. I didn't do anything because, first of all, I was in the state of grace and I knew it would have been a mortal sin and second of all, his mother might have come into the room in the middle of it. Geemidy God, can you imagine it? But do you know what happened? The most amazing thing. Just after I got up and walked away from him his mother landed in with a tray of lemonade and biscuits. Can you imagine what it would have been like if I hadn't stood up to temptation!

Anyway, the Wyatt Earp thing was about a year ago. After that, me and Gander went on as if it never even happened. We were just the best of pals. Until that day I was telling you about.

Everything was dead simple when I was wee. Most of the time anyway. Do you see if I'd known the way things were going to turn out, I wouldn't have been so mad keen to get older. Okay, when you're seven or eight people keep telling you to get lost or to shut up or if they're not telling you that they're going on as if you're not even there. And big boys shove you around and treat you like some sort of a reel. But now I'm fourteen and the same sort of stuff's still happening to me plus now there's sex and Saint Paul's. Do you see sometimes when I'm walking past some wee boy that's standing at a puddle kicking dirty water all over himself or something like that, I nearly feel like going over to him and saying - Good on ye. Keep it goin. I mean, there he is, muck to the eyeballs and nobody paying the least heed to him. He'll probably get a bit of a doing when he gets home but he doesn't give a hoot. Or it probably doesn't even cross his mind. But do you see me, all *I* do is worry. Well, most of the time. Do you see sometimes when things are going really well, I mean *really* well, I start to get sort of fidgety trying to remember the last thing I was worrying about to see if I got it sorted out or if I should still be worrying about it. Gander's dead right. I'm a bit of a disaster so I am. Even when I was wee I got myself into a state for a while wondering about how many balls I was supposed to have. I'm not joking. I was about eight, I think. It wasn't anything to do with sex or anything. Those days I never even thought about sex. I never even *knew* about sex for God's sake. But this time anyway I got it into my head I had three balls. I'm not exactly sure why I thought that. I know I used to examine myself sometimes when I was getting my bath or after my number two. You know, when I was too young for it too be a mortal sin. And I went round for months just taking it for granted I'd three balls. I knew dogs had just the two but that was dogs. I don't know how I made the mistake. I suppose I must have kept counting one of them twice seeing as they were in this kind of a purse and you couldn't take them out or anything. I wasn't that interested anyway. But then this day, I decided to do a really careful count. Don't ask me why. I remember I got into a bit of a sweat when I could only find two. I started to think that I might have *shed* one of them or something. But then I remembered one day I was up in Brooke Park and I heard these two big boys having a fierce row and one of them was saying to the other one - Ye know whass wrong way *you*, fuckface, don't ye? Yer fucken balls hivn't dropped yit, that's what's wrong way *you*. So I started wondering when my other two were going to drop. Or was the big boy just being dirty? I kept thinking there must be a wee opening in the purse that I hadn't come across and maybe the first one fell out when I was sleeping. I thought of Mammy making the bed and finding it and screwing up her face and saying to herself - Ah, so it's started way wee Conn already, and throwing it in the fire and not saying a word to me about it. Anyway, I counted them every day after that and I still had the two all right. This was around the time I was starting to get crafty and I decided it was better not to ask just anybody about it. I mean, I was hardly going to say to one of my pals - By the way, (really casual and all) - how many balls hiv ye at the moment?

I've got three big brothers and two big sisters. I knew my sisters wouldn't have a monkey's. I wasn't a hundred per cent sure what all they had (in fact, to tell you the God's honest truth, I hadn't a baldy clue) but I was pretty sure they'd no balls. I knew if I'd asked any of my brothers I wouldn't have found out. Arthur and Bernard would have told me not to be disgusting and Frankie would have called me a dirty wee brute and walked away on me. So I plucked up the nerve to ask Father Sheerin. I didn't stop him in the street and ask him of course. I used the old head. I went to Confession. When I got into the box I pulled the scarf I was wearing up over my mouth so it was a kind of mask and also it muffled my voice. If he asked me about that I was going to tell him I'd a gumboil. The confession box is dark but priests are in there that much they have eyes like cats. You can't see them properly but they can see you all right. Clear as day. As soon as he slid over the shutter I said - Bless me Faller fur I hiv sinned.

I only said that because I was nervous and that's what I always said when the shutter opened. But I caught myself on right away and said - Sorry, Faller. I hivn't sinned.

There was a silence and then a whole lot of breathing through his nose. I could see the two slits glowing away and getting bigger so's he could see me right and I could also feel them going right through me. I knew I shouldn't have come. So I decided to go. But when I was getting ready to make a run for it I heard the pepperminty voice and I sort of froze.

- Why have you come to Confession? Why are you wasting my time?

I tried to blurt it out but it wouldn't come. I closed my eyes tight and tried again.

- I didn't know who tay ast, Faller.

- Ask what? How long is it since your last Confession?

- Two weeks, Faller. How many balls is a boy sposed tay hiv?

There was a long long silence as if he had gone away but I knew he hadn't gone away even though I wished that was where he was.

Then he said - Are you trying to be funny?

- No, Faller. I used tay think I had three. Now I hivn't. I jist wanted tay fine out the right number.

- And what, may I ask, is your name?

(Why is it, when somebody gets all quiet and polite, it means they're just about to go in and out through you?)

- Conn Murphy, Faller. (I know what you're thinking. You're thinking I was stupid. Well, it's all right for you. You weren't there. Not *really* there. Not the way I was. The last thing you expect in a confession box is for the priest to start asking your name and all. They're not supposed to. I don't think they're even *allowed* to. Anyway, there was me, feeling like a frozen snotter, still wearing this stupid scarf and pressing it even harder to my mouth so's to disguise my voice even more. *After* I'd told him who I was. Maybe I *am* stupid. Or mad. Maybe I need one of those electric shocks in the brain.)

- Well, Master Conn Murphy, said Father Sheerin, - I know your mother and your brothers and sisters. I also know your teacher. (I'm pretty sure that last part was a bit of a bluff.) - And if you ever again profane the sacrament of Penance I'll tell them all and I'll make sure you get the hiding you deserve. Say ten Our Fathers and ten Hail Marys and ten Glory be to the Fathers.

You never heard a shutter slamming the way that shutter slammed. I got out very quick. I had two things on my mind. Second of all, I had to look up *profane*. But first of all, I would say the penance he gave me, even though I didn't have to. I was only eight but I wasn't stupid. Well, you know what I mean. I knew you only had to say your penance if you'd gone to Confession. But I hadn't told any sins so it wasn't a real confession. So Father Sheerin was wrong. Twice. He didn't answer my question and he shouldn't have given me a penance to say.

Stoopy Shiels's da's got a shop down William Street and he used to give the two of us a half a crown each sometimes and we usually spent it going round on the buses with a quarter pound of dolly mixtures each. Stoopy loved on the bus because nearly everywhere he had to go that he couldn't walk to he had to be taken in his da's car and he hated that. I don't know why but he hated it. The reason I liked the buses was because Daddy was a bus driver and that's what I wanted to be. Sometimes I'd be sitting there thinking he might have driven the very bus we were in. When I was on my own I always tried to get really close to the driver and I watched every single thing he did. I loved the uniform and especially the brilliant hat with the shiny peak. Daddy's is still hanging up high on our hallstand even though he's dead nearly thirteen years. I was allowed to wear it one time, just for a minute, and I got this very funny wavery sort of feeling. Whenever Mairead took it off me I kept touching the parts of my head the hat had been pressing against. The driver's door was so far off the ground I would nearly have needed a step ladder to get up to it. I could probably make it now because I've grown a good wee bit since then. My Uncle Cyril, who's also a bus driver, lifted me up into his cab one time and it was great. You should have seen the size of the steering wheel. Massive. I tried to turn it but it wouldn't hardly move for me. And then the controls and speedometer and all. Brilliant. The pedals were away down far. You wanted to see the footbrake. It was bigger than a man's foot so it was. And the accelerator was just a wee shiny thing the size of nothing. But the best of all was the smell you felt inside you. Like a mixture of petrol and leather that was sat on millions of times. I never let on to Stoopy about any of that so he hadn't a clue what I was thinking when we were sitting there eating away at the dolly mixtures. He also didn't know I was going to be a bus driver when I grew up. But I'm not too sure about that now. I think if I get the marks I'd like to be a teacher and tell children stories. You know, teach them things by telling them stories, not teach them things by roaring at them and beating them stupid. We went down Carlisle Road in the Waterside bus a good lot. That's the street a whole lot of girls went for a sailor. You couldn't hear what they were saying right with being inside the bus but that way you noticed other things. Like how the sailors always headed straight for the good-looking girls and talked to them as if they were really interesting or something. And the ordinary-looking girls and the fat and ugly ones stuck together and not even the ugly sailors would go next or near them. So these wagons would be talking away to each other all the time and looking around to see if anyone was coming for them but trying to let on at the same time that it didn't matter. Sometimes a sailor suddenly put his arm round a girl's waist and they walked up towards Bap's. That's the ice cream place in Ferryquay Street. The right name is Battisti's but nearly everybody calls it Bap's. I used to always wonder what was wrong with the girls, had they taken sick or what, that they needed the sailors to hold them up when they were walking. They didn't need to lie sideways up against somebody the rest of the time. Stoopy always said they went off with the sailors so's they'd get a free knickerbocker glory. I know now that girls wouldn't have got dolled up with their black eyes and red lips and all just for ice cream. I know now what kind of a knickerbocker glory they were really looking for. Probably after they came out of Bap's the sailors brought them to some place and they did whatever they wanted with them. What do you think Dutch sailors do with girls when they've got them up a lane and they don't understand a word of Derry? Sure what else would you expect from sailors, especially

28

English ones, with their show-off hats and their disgusting tight trousers and their stupid bell-bottoms? They come over here from their pagan country and they ride away at any stupid Derry girls they can get. Sheila says all you hear in their comedy programmes is double-meaning dirt. Sheila's the next oldest after Arthur. I really hate the swanky accents Arthur and Bernard got the time they were over there. You'd think to listen to them they were reading the news. You should have heard them last week. They'd this big row with each other about the sauce. It all started with Arthur telling Mammy to stop buying Flag sauce because the Union Jack was on it. So she got the only other brown stuff in the shop and that was HP. The next day Bernard was taking his dinner and he was looking all round the table.

- Wheah's the Flawg sauce? he said.

- In the bin, said Arthur.

- WHAWT! WHAWT! roared Bernard. - WHY?

- I'm not hawving the British Flawg putting me off my dinnah any longah, said Arthur.

- Thawt's a lawgh, said Bernard when he spotted the HP sauce. - I suppeose you'd rawthah hawve the British Houses of Pawliament giving you indigestion. Deon't you kneow whawt HP stawnds faw?

- Whawt?

Bernard put on this really snobby sneer. - God give me patience! he said. - Why deon't you look at the picture on the label? Houses of Pawliament, you clot!

By this time the two of them were slabbering at the mouth. Then they started to fight and Mammy started to scream and roar and called them two big hallions. It was funny watching them. But scary too. Because nobody big ever fought in our house before that. If they'd gone on I was going to run out. But it sort of faded away. When I think back on it now, all they were doing was pushing and shoving at each other the way people do when they don't really want to fight and they don't want to give in either. After a wee while they let on they were stopping for Mammy. I think the two of them are cowards just like me.

When me and Stoopy used to see all that stuff going on in

29

Carlisle Road I was too young to understand what was really happening. But it's disgusting when I think about it now sometimes. I mean, girls were born in the image of Our Lady and they're supposed to be trying to be like her. Instead of that, these ones were letting sailors do anything they liked with them. It's no wonder Mary keeps appearing, warning people about hell, when there's girls would do anything to get a sailor. There's a convent in Pump Street just round the corner from Carlisle Road and a whole lot of different Derry girls go to Children of Mary meetings there. I know that for a fact because my sister Mairead and my cousin Patricia are two of them. They wouldn't be seen dead in Carlisle Road when the boats are in. It's wile when you think of the Children of Mary inside the convent praying and singing hymns and listening to the nuns and outside there's these other girls going on like prostitutes. I still see ones about sixteen heading down towards the quay different nights. You always know where they're going because they're all painted up and they've on these cheap-looking bright-coloured blouses and skirts up to their bums nearly. Imagine, those girls were only about ten or eleven when me and Stoopy used to watch the sailors and all in Carlisle Road. These ones you see now, if you ever look at them talking to the sailors, they go on dead slaggy, twisting away at their mouths in a kind of a dirty smirk as if they're saying - Right, I know what's on your mind and it's okay with me. What are you waitin for? Bring me up a lane now and do me.

They really are tramps. Somebody should take a whip to them so they should. Last Saturday night just after me and Gander got out of the second house in the Palace we saw this girl coming up from behind the Guildhall. That's where the quay is.

Gander said - D'ye see yon wan in the red? She's a real bloan so she is. Annie somethin ye call er. Luck, d'ye see er?

- Right enough? I said. I didn't want to know any more.

- Aw aye, said Gander. - Trevor Smith towl me she went tay the Corinthian wan Friday there an right in the middle a the dance fleur she tuck off the top part of er two piece suit an she was fucken bare from the waist up. She's barred since. She'll

30

nivir git in agin so she won't.

She was coming towards us. She had on this short red clingy frock that it was far too cold to be wearing. She seemed to me to be shivering. She was beautiful. I thought of her in the Corinthian and I started footering away for the rosary beads in my trousers pocket.

- A right fucken hoor that wan, said Gander - She used tay keep half the fucken fleet goin.

I don't like Trevor Smith. Gander's been hanging about with him since he dumped the two Bishop Street dodos and he shouldn't be because Smith's far too old for him. He's a Prod and he goes to Foyle College and he's one of these real sophisticated bastards. An animal.

Annie was right next to us and I was trying to look everywhere but at her. This other one caught up with her and said - What's the bars? Did ye mick yer mark the night?

- Naw, I did not, said Annie.

She sounded dead rough and I felt better. I wouldn't think about her as much now.

- Nether did I, said the other one. - If ye wannay know what I think, I think them Norwegians is fur fuck all.

The two of them headed up Shipquay Street.

- Them two'll bay luckin fur it the rest a the night, said Gander. - No siller in his right mind'd go near them. They've bin usin their fucken radar tay spot them since the Corinthian thing.

- Who's the other wa-wa-wan? I asked, just to be saying something.

- How the fuck day I know? said Gander.

- Wa-wa-was sh-sh-she in the Corinthian that time too? I asked.

- Whass wrong way yer head? How the fuck wud I know that?

- But you sssssid–

- Mawn tay fuck. I'll bate ye a riss tay the top a William Street.

Prick.

There's one sailor I know and he's not like any of the others. Dwayne Hepburn you call him. He goes with my cousin Kathleen Murphy and he's built like a battleship. He's got this great big smile up the one side of his face and he makes you think nothing wrong could ever happen when he's along with you. One day me and Kathleen and Charlie Murphy my other cousin were sitting with him in Fiorentini's having an ice cream sundae and this drunk man started saying things to Kathleen and Dwayne stood up and he said - You got a problem, buddy? and the man took one look at the size of him and was away like a shot. You want to hear Kathleen's ma Stella about him.

- D'ye see that man a Kacchleen's. He's biggern any two Derry men put taygeller. And what about his smile. Lick an open dour so it is.

He's got really slick shiny black hair and goldy brown skin a bit like William Holden. Whenever he's not wearing his uniform he has on his white suit. You just know he's a Yank whenever you see him. And he's got this brilliant drawl too, not put on or anything. He says things like Sure and That'll be just swell and This old dame I'm telling you about was lousy with rocks, *lousy* with em. It took me a good while to work out what some of the things he says mean. Like when he says Big deal or Very big deal, one day it means one thing and then the next day it means the very opposite. I imitate a whole lot of times and I hardly know I'm doing it. You know, he'd be talking to me sometimes and I'd be going Yeah? and Yeah! But I'd never imitate him in the chapel. God, you want to see him at mass! I was at mass twice with him and Kathleen and when he was coming back down from getting Holy Communion he was nodding away at people he didn't even know and smiling all round him like some kind of a mental case. Kathleen was broke to the bone and so was I. When I saw him coming back from the altar the second day I kept my head down and let on to be praying.

Aunt Stella got on to him one day I was there about these other Yankee sailors prowling around Derry.

- These guys belong to NATO, Ma'am, he said back to her. -

They're here to protect these gals.

- Thass the least a thur notions, said Stella.

- Ma'am, if you only noo. Most of these guys are lonely, said Dwayne.

- Aw, is that what ye call it? We've a different name fur it in Derry so we hiv.

- Well, all I can say is, you wanna see some of their lockers. Pictures of moms and lil sisters and sweethearts back home. They're pinin, Ma'am. Pinin.

- I'll tell ye wan thing now, Dwayne, she said. - Ye kin say what ye lick, but most a them's no good. I pray iviry night fur them poor Derry girls. D'ye see our Kacchleen. I'd rather our Kacchleen was dead than she lost er virginity. So thur ye are. Ye kin say what ye want.

Dwayne was looking at her, really puzzled. You could see he didn't know what to say.

But Stella really likes him behind it all. She says to every-body - He's a practisin Caccholic and ye don't git many a them from outside a *this* country so ye don't.

He's strange sometimes. Most of the time he's like a film star and then other times he's different. He told Charlie that when he was only very small he got polio and meningitis at the one time. He said he got over the two of them completely because one killed the other or something like that. I'm not sure what exactly but whatever it was happened it was some kind of miracle, he said. Then when he grew up a bit he realised God had meant him to live on so's he could bring His love to people he met. Imagine a Derry Catholic going on like that. People would say he'd a screw loose.

Me and Stoopy went through the Diamond on the buses plenty of times. At the start we used to look at the War Memorial but after a while we didn't bother. The statues are definitely class but there's things I don't get and nobody ever explained them to me. I understand some of the things. There's a sailor in his bare feet pulling on his raincoat and he seems to be in the middle of a storm. So that's the navy. Then on the other side there's this fierce-looking soldier leaning forward with his fixed bayonet and he's about to finish off somebody. He must be the army. Even though it doesn't show the Jap or the Nazi or whoever it's supposed to be you know the soldier gets him all right. It's dead dramatic actually. He's like one of those war heroes in American comics. I swear, if you look at him long enough he nearly seems to come alive. Right at the top, up really high, there's a statue of an angel with wings, half-naked, with bird shit running down her legs. She has a bunch of leaves in one hand and a sword in the other. A sword. An angel with a sword. I mean, it says in the Catechism that angels are pure spirits created by God. Well, we all know spirits don't have any bodies so how can she be holding the sword in her hand without it falling through her? Anyway, a sword's for killing so what would a pure spirit be doing trying to kill somebody? That's what I'd like to know. I asked Arthur because he's always trying to educate me and all he would say was, it's symbolic. I felt like saying - Thanks a million, Arthur. That's everything cleared up now. (But of course I didn't). I used to think she might be the airforce, you know, with her wings and all, but that seemed stupid so I never said it to anybody. But it doesn't even show an airman so I can't understand it.

Since I wrote that last bit I was up in the Diamond again and I stood looking at the angel and she's standing on top of a snake that's spread out on top of a ball. That's probably the Earth. So maybe the snake stands for war. Or maybe it stands for anybody that's against England. I bet you anything it was the English that put the War Memorial up. I'm starting to get sick to the teeth looking at it to tell you the truth. They probably got brilliant sculptors to do it so's they could get people from here to fight for them again in one of their wars. They're nothing but a shower of slabbers. You want to hear Dwayne about them. Dwayne loves everybody, even the English, but he says that doesn't mean he has to like them. He calls them assholes. He said that in front of Aunt Stella and Kathleen. I thought they'd be shocked but they weren't. Stella laughed her head off and Kathleen smiled and looked down at the floor. He told me and Charlie this one when Stella and Kathleen weren't there. The English sailors in Derry say that the Yanks are overpaid, oversexed and over here. So the Yanks tell the English that *they're* underpaid, undersexed and under Eisenhower.

The first time I ever saw the War Memorial I was only very small. I was with Mammy at the time and I asked her what it was and she told me. So I asked her what it was for and she said it was to help us to remember the people that were killed in the wars. One other time going through the Diamond I asked her again what it was for and she told me the very same thing. That's the time I said - Will we stop here for a wee minute and say a prayer for Tom and Guy?

And she gave me a push and said - Don't be silly. Ye don't do that here. Pray fur them in the house or the chapel. I knew by this time that even though she was a saint she didn't actually know too much. I never liked her not being able to answer my questions right. It wasn't because it annoyed me not getting the answers. It was because it annoyed me her feeling stupid. So I didn't ask her why you didn't stop and pray and why it wasn't called a People who died in the Wars Memorial or some name like that. I mean, you have to admit, there's something weird about it all. As far as I can see, people walk past it and drive past it nearly the whole year round without looking near it and there's noise all round it steady. Even the summer seats have their backs to it. Nobody joins their hands and says a prayer or anything. But then on certain days there's bands playing and Prods dressed in uniforms and bowler hats going up to it with wreaths and then everything has to stop and everybody's dead quiet and you're not allowed to open your cheeper even.

Tom and Guy were my cousins from Chicago and they stayed in our house in 1935. They were twins. I know it was 1935 because it's written with their names and all on the back of the photo. Daddy took it and you can even see his shadow in it. They're standing next to the rose bush in our back yard with Mammy and Uncle Billy and Auntie Martha. They were about the same age as I am now. Mammy told me they used to climb up on Brooke Park wall like wee monkeys and her and Martha were on the nerves for fear they'd fall and break their necks or something. They were killed at Pearl Harbour in 1941. They're always on the list when we say the trimmings at the end of the rosary. I asked Arthur if there were any war memorials in Germany or Japan and all he said was - Thawt's a good question. (Arthur's a real encyclopedia in case you didn't know.) I'll bet you any money there's not. I'll tell you why now. Because they were stuffed out of sight by the Yanks.

Charlie Murphy's ma's Uncle Jimmy was in the First World War. She told us he was in a place called Messine's Ridge the time thousands of soldiers were slaughtered by the Germans. There's a street in Derry called Messine's Park and that's the only place here was bombed by the Germans. It was in 1941 and twelve people were killed. One of Jimmy's friends that played in the same football team as him was with him at Messine's Ridge and he was killed. Bobby something from out the Waterside. He was a Prod. Charlie says when he was dying he tried to say something to Jimmy and Jimmy whispered the Act of Contrition into his ear and then the Hail Holy Queen after that because he still wasn't dead and then he couldn't remember any more prayers. They just went out of his head. The two of us think Bobby probably turned on the spot and went straight to heaven. Jimmy wasn't right when he came home. Auntie Bridie says some of the wains in the street used to laugh at him and shout after him on account of the way he went on. He had the shakes and every time he went out of the house he had to have this man called Danny Doherty along with him. He walked behind Danny holding his shoulders with his two hands just as if he was blind. But he wasn't blind. It was the nerves. He wasn't too bad as long as he had Danny with him. Charlie says they went to Conn Bradley's in William Street every night of the week except for Sunday and Jimmy drank in the house that night. Pubs are closed on Sundays. Then when

Danny died Jimmy didn't go out of the house for ages. But one night his ma got a taxi to come for him and his da and they went to Bradley's. That's the night the cops arrested him. There was a big row because some mouth at the next table told Jimmy he was a traitor for fighting for England. Jimmy broke his glass and stuck it in the mouth's face and then the cops came and he took on the whole lot of them and half crippled them. That's how he ended up in Derry jail. They said he was a criminal lunatic and he was tied up in chains nearly all the time. Charlie says there's nobody else on his ma's side you'd call mad. He says it was definitely the war did it. Anyway, round the time Charlie was born Jimmy was shifted to the asylum in the Strand Road but he was still kept in chains there. He's not long dead. I'd say he must have been a real class footballer because there's a picture of him up on the wall in Charlie's house. He's right in the middle of the front row, down on one knee, and there's a massive cup and a football in front of him. That means he was the captain. Bobby's standing behind him and his face is all blurred. When I was weeer I used to think it was funny, his face being blurred and all. I actually thought it only started getting blurred after he was killed.

Auntie Bridie, that's Charlie's ma, told us one time that when a whole lot of Catholics were leaving Derry to go and fight in the First World War they were standing in the Waterside railway station waiting for the train to come. On down the platform a crowd of Derry Prods that were going to the war as well started singing *The Sash My Father Wore* and the Catholic soldiers jeered them and sang *A Nation Once Again* and there was nearly going to be a fight. I asked Charlie if Jimmy was one of the Catholics and Bobby was one of the Prods but he didn't know and I don't want to start asking his ma.

I did a really stupid thing up at the War Memorial last August. I was going to Woolworth's to get chicken paste and fish paste because there was a whole crowd of us going camping the next day. When I got to the top of Butcher Street there was this big Prod parade blocking the way. So I moved round to the corner of Bishop Street because I knew it would be easier to get across the road from there. There was music everywhere and the drums would have nearly deafened you. After a wee while they started playing *Derry's Walls* and I said to myself, What's your hurry? This probably sounds funny but I really like that song. It's got a brilliant air and a fantastic beat. I actually know a whole lot of the words. Gregory Robinson from Marlborough Street taught it to me without even realising. Gregory's a really bitter B man and coming up to the Twelfth he gets worse. He sings away at Orange songs even out in the street sometimes. Round about the start of August me and Stevie, that's his nephew, were playing tippitie across the road and Gregory was cutting his hedge and singing away like a goodun to the beat of the clippers. It was so catchy I picked most of it up dead easy and kept going over it in my head after Gregory went in. But anyway, there was me standing at the corner of Bishop Street singing into myself along with the band. A big fat woman in front of me was singing it out really loud and she sounded like a crow with a frog in it's throat. But I wasn't going to tell her to keep it quiet or she might have taken it the wrong way.

> *The time has nigh come round, boys,*
> *Two hundred years ago,*
> *When rebels on old Derry's walls*
> *Their faces dare not show.*
> *When James and all his rebel band*
> *Came up to Bishop's Gate*
> *They nobly stood upon the walls*
> *And forced him to retreat.*
>
> *The cry is No Surrender!*
> *And come when duty calls,*
> *With heart and hand and sword and shield*
> *We'll guard old Derry's walls.*
>
> *For blood has flowed in crimson tide*
> *On many a winter night.*
> *They knew the Lord was on their side*
> *To help them in the fight.*

They nobly stood upon the walls
Determined for to die
Or fight and gain the victory
And raise the crimson high.

The cry is No Surrender!
And come when duty calls,
With heart and hand and sword and shield
We'll guard old Derry's walls.

I never learnt the end of it so I can't write the last verse. But
when they finished playing it there was just a steady beat from
this one drum. All the bandsmen and the marchers were
stopped and there was a man on his own out in front standing
there banging away. It just kept on and on. I nearly expected one
of the men in charge to go over to him and say - Okay, that'll do
it now. But everybody just stood there like statues for ages and
all you could hear was DOOOM! DOOOM! DOOOM!
DOOOM! It hurt my ears and got inside my head and my chest
and my stomach and then I began to feel this strangeness and
scariness around me and Austin's and the Corinthian ballroom
and the other buildings looked different, as if I'd never seen
them before. That's when I did my moron act. There was a space
of about five yards between the band and the man in front and
I was suddenly running across the gap. Did you ever do something and it seemed like somebody else? Well, I swear to God, I
was watching myself running across that road. I saw the other
drummer coming out of nowhere and making a dive at me and
I saw me stopping. He went straight for my face with the drumstick and before he could get me I was behind the railing that
people watching the march were leaning on.
     - Back! Back! Back, ye wee Fenian bastard!
     He didn't have to tell me. I was backing away that much I
nearly knocked two women down over the head of it. But there
was this madman, leaning over the railing, stabbing the air with
his stick and shouting - I'll teach ye respect, croppy! I was really scared, really really scared but I was something else too.
Angry. I didn't know then why I was angry but I know now.

39

The drummer had an accent exactly the same as Jackie McElhinney's out of my class and Jackie's a boarder from Coleraine. Do you know what I mean? This man was just in for the day and he'd have put my eyes out if he could have for crossing the road in *my* town. Who did he think he was! But then the next thing that happened was even worse. A cop came over and stood between the drummer and the railing and asked him dead friendly to get back into the band. He wouldn't at the start and the cop kept coaxing away at him. But he stood really cheeky and kept stabbing in my direction as if he had a knife or a sword in his hand instead of a drumstick. Then I heard him saying to the cop - Are *you* goin tay deal way the wee croppy then? I couldn't hear what the cop said back but the next thing was, the drummer wasn't there anymore and the cop was standing beside me.

- Name?
- Conn Murphy.
- Address?
- Sssssssss–
- All right. That'll do. Now listen to me, young fella. One more move out of you and you're going to get yourself arrested. Do you hear me?
- Yes.

Saved by the stammer. Sometimes it's handy to have it.

My heart was thumping like mad. Mammy is always warning us we'll never get a government job if we ever get arrested for anything. That's the only kind of job has a pension unless you go on for the Church. Imagine a big cop coming to our door and saying to her - I have a warrant here for the arrest of your son Cornelius Pius Alphonsus. It would kill her. But it wouldn't have happened because he didn't know my address. All he knew was my name. Anyway, from the sound of him he was just in for the day himself. He'd go back to whatever culchie place he was from and probably forget all about me.

I stood there after he went away and my heart was banging away in my ears and I thought for a minute everybody must be looking at me. But they weren't. The drumbeat had stopped and they were looking at these men that had black suits and black bowler hats and coloured sashes on them. There were about six of them and they were standing nearly with their backs to me, facing the War Memorial. Then one of them marched over to it and put a giant wreath down against the bottom of it. I heard a whisper from behind me.

- Bastards.

I turned round and this big tall man wearing a peaked cap looked down at me and sort of half-winked. He whispered on and I wasn't sure if he was talking to himself or me.

- None a them fuckers ivir fought anyhow. They'd run a mile fore they'd fucken fight.

I couldn't understand why he was blaming them for not fighting. *I* wouldn't fight. Maybe *he* would but *I* wouldn't.

We sang the new school song for Wee Rosie yesterday. We get the half day nearly every time he comes which is about once a year. But there's a whole thing we always have to go through first. We have to stand in two lines facing each other all the way up the walks and Father Drummond the dean waits at the gate looking in the Letterkenny Road and when he sees the Rolls Royce coming round the bend from the Daisyfield direction he puts his hands up in the air and we all start clapping and cheering as if it's Stanley Matthews or somebody that's coming. The black limo drives slowly past us and all you can see is the wee head nodding up and down in the back seat and this slow wave of his hand. Then he goes in to talk to the president and about six hundred of us are waiting outside. Bulldog Drummond and McRide and a whole black bunch of them are prowling up and down between the lines like a crowd of lion tamers and we're all standing really quiet, not looking near them in case they go for us. In the meantime the prefects are round the corner from the president's office waiting for Rosie to come out so's they can kiss his ring and ask him can we have the half day. And he usually says yes because of our good behaviour and the great welcome we give him.

41

Well, yesterday he gave the nod. It was half ten by the time we all got into the College chapel. I worked it out that I'd still have Couchman for History last class in the morning but I put that out of my head. I got a seat near the back and looked around me. I really like most of the College boys I know and I could see a whole lot of them near me. There's something dead exciting about us all coming into the one place, especially if we're getting off classes. Just when I was sitting there thinking of the picture me and Charlie would probably be going to in the afternoon, the College seemed a good enough school to be at. Nearly. Some of the SAS got into the row behind me. That's what Mister O'Donnell calls them. It stands for Slitheramuck Asylum Seekers. O'Donnell Duck's a real snob and dead sarcastic. He says they came to Derry years ago looking to see if they could get into the asylum but somebody sent them the wrong road and that's how they ended up in Saint Paul's. The SAS say they didn't do bad. They say in their big countrymen's voices - Man dear, sure this is as good a fuckeen madhouse as ye'll find anywhere, but they don't say it too loud. There's no such place as Slitheramuck, of course, but I'm not too sure where they're actually from. Somewhere up the country. Anyway, there they were, heads down and rubbing their hands together as if they'd won the pools and sniggering away before we even got started.

Rosie was sitting on this big throne at the side of the altar reading the Bible, or maybe it was his office, but he was taking plenty of wee jooks round him to see what he could see. He's a funny sort of a person. He's got a big massive belly and very rosy cheeks like these Irish colleens you see on postcards and you get a surprise every time he starts speaking because he's got this wee wee voice. The Bulldog was standing on the top step with a face on him that would have cut cowl iron and he was watching every move down below. Probably expecting us to float into our seats like angels. Then Schuberts started on the organ and we all stood up. From the sound of the notes he seemed to be trembling but we'd been practising the new school song for about fifty years and we had it off pretty good so it was hard to understand what he was nervous about.

Thee, O mighty God we praise.
Give us strength to live our Faith
And bring Your love to those around us
Like the great apostle Paul.

Help us see that life is fleeting,
Praise the marvels of the Lord,
Embrace Your Mysteries and Your glory
And seek to spread Your love divine.

So let us band to serve the Lord,
Respect his servants, those who teach,
Drink their knowledge humbly, truly,
And keep His standard raised on high.

Wee Rosie didn't clap but he looked pleased. He got up out of his throne and came over to the podium carrying sheets and sheets of paper. The coloured lights from the stained glass windows landed on his gold vestments and whenever he moved even a tiny bit he sort of rippled and flashed. I heard the whispers from behind me.

- He's got his good suit on the day, lads.

- Jasus, wud ye luck at yon wadge he's carryeen.

- Methinks His Lordship's got the complete fuckeen works of Dickens way'm this time.

- Lucks lick wur in fur a workeen lunch, men.

The whole bench behind me shook. I had to keep in the laughing myself. I was over the moon about the big wadge especially. It was looking like The Couch would have to wait.

The wee tinny voice started.

- My dear boys of Saint Paul's, I must congratulate you on your rendering of your new school song. You have been well trained and well prepared by Mr Hughes who must also be commended on his composition skills. The words are, for the most part, original and so, I am informed, is the music. The song, as I'm sure you know by this time, has service as it's theme. It is another, much longer, way of saying what Christ said to his apostles: Love one another as I have loved you. And this, as you are all aware, is your College motto: *Amate alius alium ut vos amavi.* I had occasion to speak to a second year student when I was last here and I asked him if he knew what the College motto was. My dear boys, the student, if that be the correct description of the person I am referring to, did not know. All he could remember was the first word - Love - and he was unable to give me its Latin translation. Needless to say, he was not wearing a College blazer. Had he been he would, of course, have known the motto, for it is prominently inscribed upon the badge. As I look around me today I do not see much evidence of uniforms. I ask you, boys, to encourage your parents to buy you one. That is, if they can afford to do so. Uniforms are a most important element of the discipline which is so essential for a Catholic educational establishment such as Saint Paul's. Discipline is, indeed, of paramount importance, not only in your quest for academic excellence but, even more essentially, in your search for heavenly reward. You must be disciplined in your obedience to your superiors. You are most fortunate in having excellent teachers who, by their dedication and professionalism, are living the exhortation of Christ himself: *Amate alius alium ut vos amavi.*

My dear students, you were enrolled in the army of Christ on the day you received the Holy Ghost in the sacrament of Confirmation. I hope you are playing your part in this great regiment of that army, the regiment of Saint Paul. Some of your own countrymen have suffered for the Catholic faith. Perhaps it is God's plan that some of you here today will suffer too. I pray that you may have the strength to live your faith and, if necessary, to die for it. But, my dear boys, if, through carelessness and weakness, you put your faith in jeopardy, do not be surprised at the disasters that may come later. Here in Ireland we usually find that faith does not go unless morals have already gone. Paganism and the idea that Original Sin does not exist are both responsible for the cult of materialism. The age in which we live is governed by the material things and the spiritual things are often counted to be of no value. It could well be that unless you remain firm in the service of Christ you could imperceptibly begin to pay more attention to the material and less to the spiritual. My dear Catholic boys, our time on earth is short. It is merely a probation period. In the present materialistic age it is appropriate to ask: What doth it profit a man if he gaineth the whole world and suffereth the loss of his own soul?

The voice came from the row behind me.

- Thath an eathy wan tay anther. The whole world.

The whisper was too loud. It was more like a hoarse shout. And you couldn't miss the snigger that came right after it. But he was really unlucky. He picked the wrong time. I'm not joking, it was probably the only five seconds there wasn't a cough or a sniff or a sneeze or a shuffle. Rosie heard. Everybody heard. I closed my eyes to put everything out of the way and all I could see were stained-glass windows flying through the air and smashing into each other and sick-looking worms moving about waving their arms. I opened my eyes again. The Bulldog and the Bishop were standing there together. I couldn't look at their faces.

- The fuckeen disaster's here already.

Somebody from the Slitheramuck brigade whispered that but everybody knew anyway. I shut my eyes tight again and got this flash in the coloured darkness of the Bulldog picking up the podium and throwing it like a spear. The silence went on and on. I know a thing or two about time standing still with having the Pogue and The Couch and McRide nearly every day of the week. But this was even worse. Every time you thought wee Rosie might be going to start speaking again he just kept on saying nothing. He must have taught here before he was made a Bishop. He definitely knows how to handle time. No mistake about it. When he spoke at last the whole chapel jumped together.

- I have an announcement to make. I hereby rescind my order concerning today's half holiday.

I heard the clatter of voices from behind me.

- Whaddy say? Rewhat?

- What the fuck's he talkeen about?

So Rosie explained what he meant.

- The clever young man with the gift of repartee will no doubt be pondering the consequences of using that gift illadvisedly while he and his fellow students sit through afternoon classes today.

- I hope ye're fuckeen happy now, Macker, came the quiet hiss from behind me. - Ye'd think ye'd a fuckeen learned tay fuckeen whisper bay this time, ye stupid cunt ye.

- Up you and up yours, sir, came the very loud whisper back.

- To continue, my dear boys. What doth it profit a man if he gaineth the whole world and suffereth the lawth of his own soul?

Dead silence again, except for somebody nearly choking. I felt as if my stomach was being taken out bit by bit with a pair of dirty tongs. Then he went on as if everything was completely normal.

- There is one form of service to God which spurns the gaining of the whole world and that is the service of the priesthood. The Sacrament of Holy Orders was established by Christ to ordain priests so that they could carry on His work. The College is, of course, a junior seminary which prepares you in no mean way for the seminary proper, if that is where you choose to continue your studies. Christ needs more workers in his vineyard. I sometimes think that it is possible the reason there are not more vocations from Saint Paul's is the very high regard that the boys have for the priests here. Some of you may feel you are unworthy of the office, that you are not holy enough, or even that you are not clever or gifted enough. If we looked at the priesthood from that point of view it is an honour of which very few would be worthy. If we were only able to get those who are absolutely perfect as priests then the number of priests would be so small that the Church would dwindle and die. Therefore I appeal to you all to pray for a vocation and pray also that your minds and hearts and souls may stay open to respond to the promptings of the Holy Ghost. Remember, it is not always the person with the greatest brains who makes the most successful priest.

- Or bishop, came the whisper from behind me but this one was so quiet you needed to be right there to hear it.

- To conclude, my dear boys of Saint Paul's, the greatest gift

46

you have and will ever have is membership of Christ's Church. But with that membership comes responsibility. In the words of the final line of your college song: Keep His standard raised on high. May God bless you and guide you always, boys. And remember to say a little prayer for your lord bishop.

- He's got some fuckeen nerve on im. I'll say that fur im.

Except for that whisper the place was as quiet as a grave. There were about six hundred of us with our hands joined or our fingers crossed or our eyes closed, hoping he'd say something like - How many of you boys really thought I was serious when I said I was taking away your half day? Hands up, come on now. That many? O ye of little faith! Go now and sin no more. And a happy half holiday!

We should have known there was as much chance of him saying that as there was of him lifting his skirt and doing the cancan. He went back up to his throne and The Bulldog sat facing him on the other side of the altar. All I could see in front of me were these heads bobbing up and down and jerking this way and that way, wondering what was coming next. Then Father Meehan, the president, the invisible man, came out from the sacresty followed by an altar boy carrying a censer. Benediction. I looked at the chapel clock. It was twenty past eleven. Last class in the morning starts at ten past twelve so that meant I was hammered. We'd get The Couch. Or rather he'd get us. Half way through the *O Salutaris* I felt the vomit in my throat. I swallowed it back down but it kept coming up. I knew I hadn't long. I got up and stumbled past the other boys in my row. When I got to the end of it I genuflected to the altar and made for the nearest door, the one that leads to the corridor. Father Rodgers was standing there. Roy's dead on. He's one of the best teachers in the college.

- What's the matter, Conn?

- Ffffaller, I'm sssssick.

I put my hand to my mouth.

- You'd better go outside and get rid of it all first. Then you can go to sick bay. The quickest way outside is that door over there. You see where Father Mc Bride and Mister Mahoney are standing?

47

I looked and sort of half ran till I got there. Mr Ride and The Pogue were leaning against the door like two corner boys.

- Hold it, said Mc Ride and held up his head. - Where, may I ask, are *you* off to?

I tried to swallow down the vomit that was coming.

- FFFFF-Fa-Fa–

- Back to your seat!

My insides were like water.

- But Fa-Fa-Fa–

- Did you not hear me? Back to your seat!

It happened before I could do what he said. It shot out and splattered all over the front of his soutane. The Pogue pulled a bar and swung the door open and flicked his head back as a sign for me to beat it. I beat it. I left a trail of vomit from the door to the lawn. Then I stood there with my hands on my knees boking up nothing. I was weak and sore but I was really happy. No Couch. No afternoon classes. I'd make sure of that. Nobody could say a word. I'd go to the the pictures with Charlie and maybe Stoopy the next day when we'd *all* have the half day. We always get the half day on a Saturday anyway.

I could hear the *Tantum Ergo* just and no more. There was a while to go yet. It was dead hot. The sun was really burning. I took off my blazer. There was vomit on the back of the collar. Funny. How did vomit get on the back of my collar? I walked round to the side of the Main Study where it's always cool. I leaned back against the wall and took a fit of shivering right away. There were hundreds of birds high up in the trees and a whole lot of them were barging and screaming at one another like mad eejits. It was nearly like they were holding a meeting and somebody let these rowdy ones in. I slid down the wall and sat on the ground and my jaw started trembling and my teeth started chattering. I got up and went round the back to the gardener's toolshed. The door was open and there was an old desk inside. As I was going in I nearly fell over this spade and pitchfork that were lying up against the door holding it open. I sat down on the seat of the desk and pressed my cheek against the lid of it. It felt nice and warm and rough. It was good in there away from everybody. My back was scratchy because there was sweat dribbling across it sort of slanty. I liked that. When it got to the middle it changed direction and ran down my spine. I sat up straight and turned round and rubbed the scratchy bits against the back of the seat. When I was finished doing that I looked at some of the things scrawled on the lid or dug into it.

> Wolves forever
> Mullsy is a queer boy
> Can you not focking spell
> J Sheerin June 50
> Rock around the cock
> St Pauls is Balls

Fair play to you, I thought, whoever wrote that last one. God, I wish I knew why You allow it. Priests too, some of them. I don't understand. Mammy doesn't understand either.

- What priests hiv ye got the year, Conn? They say Father McBride's a very good teacher.

I wonder who *they* are. Probably some of those geniuses that run like crabs. He doesn't touch *them*. He's only a bastard. Mammy thinks the priests in the college are just like the ones in the cathedral. She doesn't know and I'm better not to tell her.

I remember the time I went to the College first. It seemed great having a whole lot of different teachers and doing grown-up subjects. The excitement of it, copying down my first timetable from the notice-board. Going from room to room and only having each teacher for forty minutes unless you had a double. Then that schoolbag got heavier and heavier and heavier till it was a ton weight. I used to think I was smart at the elementary school. I'm not smart now. And my stammer's getting really bad. I had Roy Rodgers for History my first year. He was great. Then we got The Couch. The day he gave me my first whaling Gander said to me outside - Looks like the honeymoon's over, Spud. Gander annoyed me sometimes even before I'd the row with him. He'd nearly always something smart to say. And he never gets hit in History. He says he learns it on the bus to school and he never gets it wrong. I get it wrong all the time and I really stew it. I can't understand The Couch. Well, maybe I can. For the first month or so I had him he was all over me and then he walked in one day and he nearly killed me. Nobody deserves to be hit the way he hits me. I remember the smell of him that day. I still hate the smell of him. He's small and he's got a really thick body. His big eyes pop out at you. Before he turned on me he was like Peter Lorre. You know, quiet but dangerous. After he turned on me he was James Cagney to a T. Public Enemy Number One. Anyway, I'd learned the next five pages or so as usual. It was about the Divine Right of Kings. I really hated that part of the book. It seemed to go on for ages. He asked me a really twisted question and I got it wrong. He took me out. I knew from watching other boys being doked that you had to hold your hand out dead straight or it would be worse for you. We stood facing each other at the front of the class. I was amazed because he was only a wee bit taller than me and I'm small. I held out my right hand straight and strong and tried to look ashamed. I had this feeling that I'd let him down after him being so friendly with me and all. His cane touched the palm of my hand. It was tickly. He was taking too long. I looked up at him to see what was wrong. He was looking sideways at me. You should have seen his face. He was going on as if I'd done something terrible on him. He nudged my hand up a wee bit higher by tapping my knuckles nice and easy with the cane from underneath.

- Higher, Murphy, Higher. Are you stupid or what, you little yap? And straighten yourself up. You're like an old man.

I wasn't a yap. You're not supposed to call a second year a yap. Yap's the name Seniors call first years. They called us yaps in our first year and ducked us at the water tap behind Junior House if they caught us. They never caught me. It was the first time he ever slapped me and he was going on as if I was well used to it. But I didn't know how to stand or what way he liked you to hold your hand up. Maybe he thought I should have known from watching him doking other boys. But it's different when you're up there. It's dead scary. I put my hand higher up. I heard the swish and the whistle of the cane as it came down. It was terrible. It was just as if he'd torn my hand open. It folded up on me. I thought - How dare you! What have I ever done on you? This is MY body. You can't do this on me.

- Straighten it up! he shouted.

There were spittles around his lips. I straightened it up and he nudged my knuckles again from underneath because my hand had lost its position. I heard the whistle again. He was nearly jumping off the floor. He got me on the thumb, just the thumb. I must have moved it. I cried out of me. I couldn't help it. It felt as if somebody had hammered a nail into it. I bent over and put my hand between my left arm and my side, very near my oxter. I didn't mean to do that. I just did it.

- Hold up your hand, you little thug!

The other boys he'd slapped before seemed to know how it was all done. They understood him and he understood them and they just got it over with. I wanted to get this over with but I couldn't take the pain. I knew if I ran out I'd be expelled and the whole place would be laughing at me.

My hand went up again. I was still crouched over a bit but my hand was out for him a sort of a way. Suddenly I felt something like a stone hitting the ball of my left leg and I went down on one knee with the pain. It was the cane. He'd hit me on the leg with the cane.

- For the last time, hold your hand out right! And get up! Up, you little coward! Now, hand out right. I'll not have you wasting my time.

For the last time, he'd said. Okay, I could take one more. I held up my hand, looking at him all the time to try and tell from his eyes and his mouth if I was pleasing him. I don't remember hearing the swish or anything. When he hit me this time my hand just collapsed and I cried. I didn't mean to. I couldn't help it and I was really ashamed. I couldn't see him with the tears but I heard him.

- Stop snivelling. You'll learn, won't you, Cornelius?

- Yes, Ffffaller.

I turned and went back to my desk.

- Where do you think you're going?

I couldn't believe it. This wasn't right.

- Come back out here!

That's when the stammering really started. I jerked up

51

towards him, stammering away.

- Ffffffff-fa-fa-fa-fa-faller. I thought–

- You thought! You thought! I'll teach you to think. You'll go whenever I tell you and not before. Now hold out your other hand.

- Please, Fffff-fa-faaa, I said.

It just came out. I couldn't help what I was saying.

- Please Father what? he said.

- Please Ffffffffar. I'll know it fffffur the marra.

- I'll far you, Murphy. Up with your hand. You've wasted enough of this class's time.

When he finished with me I went back to my seat nearly doubled up. The three on the left hand were worse but they were quicker. I don't know why. I sat there and I didn't know where to put my hands. First I felt like the tips of all my fingers and thumbs were gone because I couldn't feel them. I could feel the pain but I couldn't feel the fingers. Next thing, I felt as if all the bones in my two hands were crushed. My face was all sticky and wet with tears from my eyes and water and snotters from my nose. In the middle of all that I heard Junior Begley being asked a question and then being slapped and The Couch saying
- Taken like a man, Begley.

Mammy told me one time that when priests are getting ordained the bishop blesses their hands with holy oils. I don't know what to think. She sends me out early some mornings so's I can get the ten to nine bus and be in College chapel for part of mass. Sometimes you even get all of it before the bell rings for first class. I was there three mornings Father Couchman was saying Mass. I remember the first time. It wasn't long after he started hitting me. It was funny because I was the only one there in the chapel except him and Seamus Devlin that was doing altar boy. Just after I came in Devlin brought the water and wine over to him for the Offertory and nearly bowed double but Father Couchman didn't look near him. He was turned away from me most of the time too, facing the altar, but he must have noticed me because I was kneeling in the middle of the back row. He seemed to be nearly saying the Mass to himself. He did-n't have that sing-songy kind of a voice a whole lot of priests have. He looked calm and happy as if this was what he really wanted to be doing instead of hitting boys. He was wearing a purple vestment and there was a cross down the back of it that had these brilliant Celtic designs like you see in some prayer books or in pictures of the Book of Kells. There was green and gold and yellow and orange and white and I don't remember what else. It sparkled away. I was hardly paying any attention to the Mass. I was watching every time he'd turn round to see if he'd see me. I was thinking too that this was a lovely chapel and that it was great to have a place you could go where Jesus was. He was so lonely there in the tabernacle and it only took a minute to come in and say hello to Him and say a wee prayer. And it was so cool and peaceful, like a different world. At the consecration Father Couchman held the body and blood of Jesus above his head. Each of the times he genuflected to Jesus I bowed my head and whispered to myself that I was sorry for the bad things I'd thought about him and I said a prayer that that I'd always know the History from then on and not make him do brutal things ever again. On me anyway. When he gave the Blessing at the end of Mass the only two to receive it were me and the altar boy.

We had him second. When he came into the classroom he had on the black soutane and there were chalk stains on it. He went down on his right knee on the platform the way he always does, with his back to the class, and he looked up at the crucifix above the blackboard and called out the first half of the Hail Mary and we answered with the second half. Then he got up and gave a kind of a sigh and reached away inside his soutane and took out the cane. Then he said - Right, where are we?

I remember that was the day I sat there thinking - I'm not getting the early bus again. I've had enough of doing *everything* I'm told.

But I still get it once or twice a week.

I'll never forget the three days before Hallowe'en last year. I'm shivering when I think about it now. The Couch had turned against me not long before that and I didn't think I could take the beatings anymore. I asked Mammy for the loan of her alarm clock three nights that week and I set it for five in the morning each time. I'd the back room because Bernard was away back to England for a while. When I woke up the first morning I went over and over the Divine Right until about eight. The first morning I did it I took a break every now and then to say a prayer. I looked up sometimes at the picture of the Holy Family that's above the bed. I think Jesus is about ten or eleven in it. Every time I tried to look at Him my eyes kept going to Joseph. I liked the way he had his hand round Jesus's shoulder. You could see he wasn't just doing it to look good. He really protected his Son. I knew that. Sometimes I was angry with God about Daddy and other times I prayed to God for him. I could have told him everything and everything would have been all right. I've got his picture in my prayer book. You want to see him. His eyes are so peaceful and he looks so strong and clever. He's closer to me than Jesus is. Sometimes Jesus is really far away. Joseph's dead. And Mary. The Hail Marys don't mean anything most of the time. They can't *do* anything.

Before it got light I heard the birds out the back. One minute they were slagging away at each other and the next minute they were showing off. Funny, they didn't annoy me. One of them sounded so close I thought he must be on the window sill. So I half-opened the blind and there wasn't any bird there. But the sun was starting to rise. I knelt on the floor and leaned my forehead against the window pane and watched. Then I felt my cheeks all wet and my nose starting to run. I wasn't sad. I knew the History and I wasn't sad but I was still crying like a wee girl. Imagine, tears and snotters and me thirteen. I went out to the bathroom and blew my nose and cleaned my face. I was very quiet because I knew there'd be rows and ructions if I woke anybody up at that hour. When I came back it was very cold in the bedroom. I heard the whirr of the milk float and when it stopped I heard the glink and the glunk of the bottles. That'll be Charlie Deery, I thought. It was twenty past seven on the alarm clock. I went back to the History and by the time it was eight I really knew for certain I knew it. Then I went in and called Mammy and she got them all up. That day The Couch gave me six for getting a question wrong. Then he gave me twelve the next day and six the day after that. It's funny how much you can take. That was the week I started the diary. I'm glad I did.

Trevor Smith's a dirty animal. He's the Prod I told you about that Gander started hanging about with. I think he's a queer. And he's supposed to be going on to be a doctor when he leaves Foyle College. So what do you think of that! Sometimes when we're sitting on Gallagher's wall he pulls Gander down on his lap and Gander just sits there like a big girl and doesn't even try to get away. Well, yesterday he'd Gander on his lap and he was holding him dead tight around the belly. He was going on as if he was only acting the cod but me and Charlie didn't know where to look. Anyway, this time Gander decided he'd take a blind swipe at him. He got him in the side with his elbow and he definitely hurt him. Smith shouted - You wee fucker and got his head in an arm lock and marched him up Cnoc lane as if he was raging mad. He kept roaring - Right, lift your feet, as he was dragging him up the lane. Gander was roaring back - Lay me go ye dirty big bastard. But after they got round the corner you couldn't hear them at all. They didn't come down for ages and there wasn't a mute out of them. Me and Charlie just stood there jooking up the lane now and then trying to rattle on about other things. I was nearly out of breath and all I was doing was standing there. Whenever they came down Smith had Gander in the arm lock again but anybody could see the two of them were only acting this time. Smith went home nearly right away and so did Gander.

There's a whole lot of questions I wish I could ask some-body but I'd only be afraid I'd get into bother. Mickey Doherty from the Waterside got suspended two weeks before his Senior exams last year for asking Father McBride what God would do with all the dead black babies that never got baptised if the

Pope ever announced there was no such a place as Limbo. McRide told him to apologise for being cheeky and Mickey said he didn't need to because it was a serious question. So your man threw him out of the classroom and told him not to come back to the College until he was ready to apologise. Mickey's ma and da were on to him all the time to do it because he didn't have to actually mean it. But Mickey wouldn't and he never got doing his exams and he's living over in England now. He was going to go to Queen's University too. I said to Gander and Charlie a couple of times about it not being fair that pagan babies didn't get to heaven when it wasn't their fault they were pagan and the two of them told me to run away and wise up. They'd no answer, you see. But then last Sunday I was up in the gallery with the choir at twelve mass as usual and this time Wee Rosie was giving the sermon instead of an ordinary priest and he gave me the shock of my life. I don't like listening to sermons because they're nearly all for big people but I'm supposed to because Arthur examines me on them when I get back to the house. Anyway, Rosie was going on in that wee voice of his and I was sitting there thinking he really sounded as if Father Sheerin or somebody had been half strangling him in the sacresty before he came out and suddenly something he was saying made me listen hard.

- Beware of the person who, in his ignorant pride, will question the teaching of the church. He will sow the seeds of doubt in the minds of others. He does not appreciate, nor does he wish to appreciate, that the Bishops are the successors of the Apostles, commissioned to carry out the teaching of Christ. His faith is weak and he is intent on passing on this weakness. Hold your place in the Army of Christ, my dear brethren, as soldiers always on guard. Where you have an individual who is suspect make certain he is cut off so as to make his influence of little or no value. You should always remember that you are free to exercise the power that is yours to make people who say these things disappear from public life.

I sat there with my nail sort of stuck in the letter M on the back of the pew in front. Honest to God, I was scared to look down at the pulpit. The state I was in , I was nearly waiting for him to say - The person I am referring to is at present in the cathedral with us. He is, in fact, hiding in the gallery destroying Church property with his dirty fingernails.

I felt dead stupid after I got home because Arthur told me Wee Rosie was really talking about left wingers. He saw me looking at him funny and he said - Not footballaws, Conn. Seocialists, and then he laughed away to himself. Sometimes I think I might be a bit mad. Gander told me a whole lot of times I'm not right in the pan and *he* doesn't know the half of it. Like when I finished the College retreat last month, I nearly had my mind made up that the only way I could stay out of hell was to get married as quick as I could and go to bed with her and stay there. That's what I mean about mad. There were two retreats on at the one time, one in the College chapel for the Seniors and one in the concert hall for us. It's not really a concert hall. It's four classrooms with partitions between them and they're only opened if there's something big on. It was sort of funny going to Mass and Benediction there, you know, when you thought of the things The Pogue and McRide did to us sometimes in the very same place. The priest's name was Father Sylvester and the second day it was about Sex. Most of us there had got a private spiff from Father O'Donoghue already. He's the spiritual director. The time I was in with him I was so nervous I hardly knew what he was saying. What he did was, he took us out of class one at a time during our second year and talked to us for about half an hour about The Facts. You had to sit right opposite him in his wee study. I remember I kept my hands joined on top of my trousers the whole time. You wanted to hear some of the things he was saying. It was dead embarrassing so it was. To tell you the truth I wasn't even listening half the time I was trying that hard to look intelligent and all. The ridiculous thing is, I was looking forward to it for months and as soon as I landed in there all I wanted to do was get it over with. He's a nice priest, really friendly and all, but I couldn't wait to get away from him. I nearly fell off the chair near the end when he asked me right out of the blue - Have you any questions, Conn? It wasn't even in my head to say it but I heard this voice asking - Wh-wh-wh-wh-wh-what about twins, Ffffffaller?

Then right away there was this massive gap in the middle of my chest because for all I knew he might have been just after telling me the whole thing about twins. But no. He closed his eyes and then made a spire shape with his fingers and then locked them dead tight together and said - Very good, Conn. Very Good. Twins. And then he told me about twins. Do you know this? I still couldn't tell you the first thing about twins. Stoopy says you have to stick it in twice in the one night but he's stupid. That's why this sort of spiff is so important. You can ignore the kind of shite ones like Stoopy come out with and not be spending half your time going round wondering if it's true. Well, you could ignore the shite if you'd the sense to listen to O'Donoghue. But that's the thing about being face to face. You sort of freeze. Mammy tried to tell me The Facts last summer when we were on holidays down in Greencastle. She got me to go a walk with her one day and when we were out she started talking about babies. I knew after a minute the two of us were in a bad way so I let on to her Father O'Donoghue told us everything and there was nothing I didn't know about all that stuff. I mean, imagine letting her go on. She'd have been telling me what Daddy did to her. I couldn't have stuck that. But she wasn't for giving up. She said it was her responsibility to make sure I knew, with Daddy dead and all. She told me I couldn't afford to be ignorant. She said the oldest ones in the house thought the nurse had me in her bag when she went up the stairs just before I was born. I gave a big loud laugh and said - Ssssso they thought delivering a baby meant the nurse bringin it tay the house. God!

I thought of Arthur and Bernard and I was walking on air. I was thinking - What a pair of gawms. I mean, what a shower of stupes.

I don't remember now exactly how I did it but I got her to give over about The Facts. She said - As long as ye don't learn the wrong way listenin tay dirty talk from boys out in the street.

I thought, She's right about that. Gander and Stevie and Stoopy are always going on as if they know everything and I'll bet you not one of them has the foggiest. But Charlie has. He's the one that told me most of the important things. Isn't it amazing how you're at Saint Paul's for six or seven years and maybe another four years at University learning subjects you're not that interested in and how long do they spend teaching you about the subject you spend nearly the whole day and half the night thinking of? A half an hour. Half a friggin hour. I'm dead lucky I've somebody that's not a dirty brute or anything to explain things to me. If it wasn't for Charlie I wouldn't even know the baby comes out of the woman's belly button. But he nearly lost the bap with me when I asked him how you get the stuff into her. He said - All I kin say is, ye're wan mental spa.

I was getting a bit desperate because I'd a feeling nobody else was ever going to tell me and I wasn't going to ask *them* because they'd only tell everybody I was stupid. So I went on the attack.

- Right, sssssein ye're ssssso sssssmart, I ssssssuppose ye're goin tay tell may ye putt it intay er belly button?

- Listen tay may a wee minute, Conn, he said - Nivir let on ye didn't know this and don't you *ivir* be askin may agin. The stuff goes up er bum. Lat's why ye're supposed tay go at er from the back.

- Sssssso then, I said, - wa-wa-why day the wa-wa-wans ye ssssssee coortin press away at each other fffffrom the fffffront?

- Jesus Christ, Conn, day ye know nothin? Sure they'd luck lick animals if they did it the right away in fronta people even way thur close on. Iss oney when thur in bed they do it right.

I wasn't going to let this go.

- Day ye really mean tay tell me the man gits up on the wa-wa-wummin lick a dog?

- Course he does. Why the frig day ye think iss called ridin?

The whole thing's disgusting. But at the same time it's mad in a sort of a way. I was lying in bed the night after Charlie told me the whole thing. I remember I was fiddling away with the rosary beads when I busted out laughing. I just started to think of all those well-dressed men going about Derry with their black umbrellas and lifting their hats to near every woman they meet and then I thought of their wives with their eyes up to heaven and their chubby cheeks and them lighting away at candles and whistling away at their novenas in the chapel and then the umbrellas and the hats in the hallstand and the novenas inside the prayerbook on top of the sideboard or somewhere and you know what's going on upstairs, don't you? They're at it like dirty dogs, in their pelt, banging away up in bed. I mean, it really is funny when you think of the different breeds of dogs. The people that fight in the Bucket of Blood pub up in Bishop Street are like the mongrels and the labradors live in those big mansions out the Limavady Road. Can you imagine a pekinese riding an Irish wolfhound? Well, that's wee Mr Coulson from down the Avenue in bed with Mrs Coulson. And I'll tell you something else. Do you see when I see a man or a woman walking funny, I know they've been at it the night before. Jesus. I can't understand why married men don't go mad all day thinking about what they're going to be doing that night. I mean, there couldn't be *anything* to compare with it. I look at them sometimes and I'm wondering how many times a minute it flashes into their minds. Or does it ever flash *out* of their minds? Even if you subtract the times for working and eating and drinking and going to the toilet and washing yourself and different things, that still leaves *hours and hours* for doing it. But all I see is them looking dead cool and calm and not even checking their watches to see how long it's going to be until they get home. Shopkeepers leaning their elbows on the counter and chatting away to some woman, cops walking all slow and important with their hands behind their backs, workmen leaning on their shovels and talking to each other about this big hole in the road, milkmen driving their wee floats about two mile an hour, teachers – *teachers*! – talking real serious to other teachers outside classroom doors and nodding away at each other, roadsweepers doing their rotten job that's never going to end. I'll bet you every one of them's at it inside their heads. They must be. But then you look at the young married girls clattering along the street in their high heels and long tight skirts and then later on the shoes come off and the skirts come off and their husbands are at them half the night and you just have to stop thinking or you'd explode. And I'll put you on any money the girls are trying *not* to think about it all day. They must have to go through some terrible things after they get married. One time me and Stoopy went into the dressing room in the Brandywell after Foyle Harps finished playing Trojans. We were bringing in a ball that was left behind on the pitch. All these men were standing naked drying themselves and you could see their pricks all red and raw-looking, like snakes with the skins halfway off them hanging out of steamy hairy pits. Jesus, it would have made you want to vomit. Imagine being a girl on the first night of your honeymoon and seeing that thing and then having to let him do whatever he wants with it. I know girls are very romantic and they love all this stuff about a big wedding and having their own house and babies and all. But I just think they'd be saying to themselves after one night - What can you do? Nothing's worth this but I'm stuck with him and that thing he has. I can't get a divorce or anything like that. People would never give over about me if I did. And, as well as all that, my mammy and daddy would be mortified. No, I'll just have to let on everything's fine and dandy. I suppose all the rest of the men must be the same and sure there's nothing to take their place.

So the secret doesn't get out and other girls keep walking into the same trap. But what I can't understand is, do you see when there's a wedding on in the Cathedral, there's always these women standing at the back admiring away at the bride when she's coming down the aisle and dabbing their eyes and noses with wee hankies and smiling all happy at the same time. And probably most of them are married and they know what's waiting for the girl that night. It would make you wonder if the whole lot of them's mad. Smith was telling us one day about this Austrian princess that never got over the first night. She took one look at your man's thing and went out of her mind and spent the rest of her life in an asylum.

It's obvious anyway girls aren't told The Facts right. If they were they'd all be going on to be nuns or if they were Prods they wouldn't get married at all. Except for the sailor hunters, I suppose. Any girl that enjoys sex must be a bit of a tramp. But do you see this thing about girls being told? Can you imagine a nun down at Thornhill taking them out one at a time and telling them about the snakepit? I mean, can you *imagine* it? No chance. She'd spend the whole half hour beating about the bush. You know, dead technical stuff about eggs and fertilising and all. Sure how could a nun know anything about it anyway? I'll tell you one thing. If she'd been in that dressing room with me and Stoopy she'd have been carted out head first so she would. Head first.

But that retreat in the College I was telling you about. Your man Sylvester was brilliant. There's something dead exciting about sitting there with hundreds of other boys waiting for the priest to talk about The Facts. You know what I mean. You don't feel all tight and breathless like you do on your own with Father O'Donoghue or somebody like that. And even though it's dirty he's going on as if it's holy and you can think about things he's saying without committing mortal sin. In fact, you're *supposed* to think about what he's saying. That's the funny thing about it. It's legit. It's man to man stuff. Plus Father Sylvester was different from any other priest I ever saw in my life. He was at least seven feet tall, I swear, and he'd a pinky polished-looking face and he'd jet-black hair. His white robes shone like the sun and there was this golden kind of design on the front of them and he'd a massive crucifix tied to his waist with a big rope. He walked about the stage very slow and sure of himself, a bit like an actor. And you wanted to hear the voice of him. He'd a lovely Irish brogue and sometimes it boomed and sometimes it whispered but even when it whispered it was still loud enough for you to hear. It was a sort of a sing-song-for-little-children voice that made you feel a wee bit silly. But still, I'll bet you anything now there wasn't one boy in the hall that wasn't glad to be listening to him. The commandants were away for a three day break (sharpening their teeth, Gander said) and we were here for *our* break. Well, that's what *I* thought anyway. Why do things never turn out the way they should?

Sylvester started off with some joke about three smashers walking down the street, just to relax us, I suppose. Well, I want to tell you this now. It was the stupidest joke I ever heard. But we all laughed our heads off anyway. After that he said - But seriously, boys, seriously. He dragged out the seriously the second time he said it for a good wee while and waited for the laughing to die down. Then he got on with it.

- My dear young Catholic boys of Saint Paul's, there is one gift, one very special gift, which God has given each one of us. And that is the gift of procreation. As we all know, God the Father made Adam from the dirt of the earth and then took a rib from him while he was asleep. And with that rib, my dear boys, God created the first woman, Eve, because in His great wisdom He knew that it was not good for man to be alone.

There was a real hush whenever he said that. This was big time. The trouble is, I can't tell you the next bit because I missed it. I heard this whisper from the boy on my right hand side.

- Murphy!

I looked at him and he was looking straight ahead but still whispering out of the side of his mouth. I don't know his name but I know him to see.

- Murphy! How did Eve find out Adam was bangin another wummin?

I stared up at the stage and whispered back - How?

- She counted his ribs when he was sleepin. Ye get it?

He's a real slick character whoever he is. I was nearly going to say to him about the thing I was thinking of. You know, just to let him see I was broadminded too. But it would have taken too long. And it was more like a serious question. Definitely not a joke. Anyway, knowing me, I'd have got caught. I'll tell *you* anyway. Do you see Cain, Abel and Seth, the three sons Adam and Eve had? Who'd they do it with? You know, procreate. Well, there was only one possible person and that was Eve. You realise what that means, don't you? *They rode their mother*. Okay, I know what you're going to say. You're going to say Adam and Eve probably had daughters too only it's not in the Bible. Right, that's true. If they put everything that happened into the Bible the books in it would stretch from here to China and back. So let's say there were girls in the family then. *So that means it was their sisters they rode.* Sure who else was there? It's no wonder it's only the Prods get taught the Old Testament. Did you ever notice, all our R K exams are about Our Lord's life and the Acts of the Apostles? And at mass the Gospel's always about Jesus and the Epistle's always some letter Saint Paul wrote. Not a word out of the Old Testament. The only way you'll get taught that is if you start going to Sunday School.

Anyway, I missed a wee bit out of the sermon the time I was listening to your man telling the joke. The next thing I remember was Sylvester saying:

- The power of procreation is, my dear boys, a wonderful power, an awesome power, a frightening power. When it is used properly, with love and respect within the Sacrament of Matrimony and purely for the purpose of procreation, God is pleased. But when it is used for evil and selfish pleasure, outside of holy wedlock, God is mocked. But God, my dear boys, God will *not* be mocked. No, God will not be mocked. He knows your most private thoughts. He can see you in the most secret of places. He hears every single word of dirty talk. He sees all your suggestive looks, he knows about every immodest touch, whether by yourself or with another.

Sylvester meant business all right. He wasn't beating about the bush anyway. If you ask me he was taking it apart. It really seemed to me nobody in that hall was breathing anymore. Nobody except Sylvester. He was booming away and there wasn't a thing he didn't know. I'll tell you this for nothing. That same boy must have heard a quare lot of confessions. You could tell to listen to him he knew he was talking to a crowd of dirty wee brutes. But do you know what I started thinking after the thing he said about it being all right to do it whenever you're married and all? You know, *God is pleased*. I started thinking about the women that get churched a while after their baby's born and I started wondering why they wait till the chapel's near empty after mass before they sneak up to the side of the altar rails with their candle. Charlie says getting churched means getting made clean again. I never heard it mentioned in our house but when Mammy and them are talking about some woman that's going to have a baby they always say she's expecting. They never say she's pregnant. Say *pregnant*. It sounds dirty, doesn't it? Pregnant. It definitely sounds dirty. Even Charlie sniggers when he says - I see Mrs Doherty's pregnant or - I see Mrs Ward's pregnant.

But I want to tell you about the sermon. Do you know the way it was? It was sort of a thrill to hear it all out in the open, nearly like being allowed to look at dirty pictures in the chapel. But at the same time you had a notion what he was leading on to.

- Your bodies, my dear Catholic boys, are the temples of the Holy Ghost and must be kept pure and free from shame. Now you wouldn't expect the Holy Ghost to dwell in a temple that's full of corruption ,would you? Remember this always, boys. If some person tries to encourage you to indulge in filthy acts with them, that person is not thinking of your good. Oh no. That person is using you for their own pleasure. People may say wonderful things to you. They may flatter you and tell you how great you are but they are only using you. Always remember that. After they've dragged you down they will move on to someone else. Jesus Himself said - *Woe to him that scandalises. It were better for him that a millstone were tied around his neck and that he were thrown into the depths of the sea.* Then he stopped talking and all the faces looked up to find out why. He was standing there dead still, like a massive white statue. Then after about a minute his face lit up into a big smile. He said - Now can any clever boy give me the definition of a noun?

My hand was up like a shot along with a whole lot of others. - Faller! we started to shout. - Sir! - Faller! - Faller! - Sir! He leaned down to speak to a boy up near the front. I couldn't hear what the boy said but then Sylvester straightened up and spoke to us all again.

- That's right. Good boy. A noun is a person, a place or a thing. Well, my dear boys, I asked that question for a certain reason. An occasion of sin is rather like a noun. An occasion of sin is a person or a place or a thing that may cause you the loss of your immortal soul. I want you to think about that, boys. Stay well away from any occasion of sin, anything that scandalises you. It may be bad company. It may be dirty books or dirty magazines or dirty films.

He was right there. I mind the time *Duel in the Sun* was on in the Palace and it was really filthy. So I heard anyway. Charlie

65

told me Catholics weren't allowed to go to it. He said the priests banned it from the altar. I didn't hear it at the mass I was at but Gander heard it. Trevor Smith saw it and so did Stevie Robinson but I didn't have to tell you *that*. I made an excuse I had to go somewhere the day Smith was talking about it up at Gallagher's wall and when Gander started to tell me the next day I told him he shouldn't even be thinking about it and he called me Father Murphy from old Kilcormack. But one other day Stevie told me bits out of it. I'm not going to repeat them but even in the middle of it I had to laugh because he's a real scream.

- Jesus, Conn, ye wanted tay see the tits the dame in it had on er. I cannay mine er name but I nivir saw anything lick them. They wur out lick yon so they wur.

And he made two big circles in front of his chest.

- I swear tay God I was near away way it, he said. - I'm tellin ye. I was sittin way a root on may that big I could near see over the man's head in front a may.

- Remember what Our Lord Jesus said. *Woe to the world because of the things that cause people to sin! If your hand or your foot scandalise you, cut them off and throw them away. If your eye causes you to sin, gouge it out and cast it from you. For it is better to enter heaven with one eye or one hand or one foot than to have them all and be thrown into the fires of hell.*

I missed a whole lot after that. What was it he said? *Cut them off and throw them away.* I wasn't thinking about Trevor Smith or the Palace. No, not the person or the place. I was thinking about the thing. He didn't actually mean to cut it off, of course. That was only a metaphor. He meant for you to stay away from it. Now, how do you do that, I'd like to know? The way I felt sitting there, I wished I could wake up the next morning without it. Who wants a millstone dragging them down anyway? Not me. For the first time since I was about nine I'd be able to go on like a normal human being instead of walking around Derry googy half the time. Sally would really see my personality then. I'd chat away to her, dead smooth and all, and keep looking her up and down right to her face the way Burt Lancaster did with Eva Bartok in *The Crimson Pirate*. She'd blush like mad and then I'd take her by the hand and walk up the lane with her and be really romantic.

But sure you need it, don't you? You need it for when you get married. You need it and you're stuck with it till you get married. Maybe I can leave the College next year and get a job in the BSR. That's the Birmingham Sound Reproducers. They've got a factory in the Creggan and they make turntables for playing records on. What am I talking about? What does it matter what they make? They pay you, that's what I want to tell you. I'd start saving for a house the first week. Sally's the one. All I have to do to keep her is to give her the odd coort up the lane and get to Confession that night (or the next night if the chapel's closed by the time we're finished.) Sally's the one all right. I used to think last year that if I ever got famous I'd try and marry Jo Stafford. I know she was only a kind of a dream but, to tell you the truth, I still think about her a good lot. I never saw her picture yet but all you have to do is listen to her singing *Shrimp Boats Is A- Comin* and you know she's really beautiful. She's not fat or anything and every inch or her is a brilliant tan. Jesus mercy, Mary help. She's got dark eyes and sometimes in bed I think of her wearing this dressing gown. Nothing else, just the dressing gown. It's dark blue and she opens it up and she says - Are you coming, Conn? and I say - You're darn tootin, Miss. (I have to go away for a while and work out if I gave into that. I'll be back as soon as I can).

I'm getting worse at concentrating on my prayers. Do you know what I was thinking in the middle of my penance? The real reason I fancy Sally is that she fancies me. But there's this other girl lives in Marlborough Road and she's completely perfect except she's a Prod. Tina Lyttle. Sally's like Debbie Reynolds but Tina's like Marilyn Monroe. I hardly ever think about her if I can manage it because I know if I do I'll probably go like a rock. She never comes near my house to swap. She thinks I'm nothing. She doesn't even look at me when I bring the American comics over to swap with her. She opens the door and she knows I'm there without looking at me. Two Saturday mornings ago she was checking to see if there were any pages missing from the middle of any of mine and she was wearing this cowgirl outfit. I mean, you should have seen it. I could nearly swear she didn't go out all day so that means she just got up out of her bed and put on this amazing cowgirl skirt and waistcoat. And her boots were nearly up to her knees, oh Jesus, and the position she was holding the comic you couldn't help seeing the rest of her legs going away on up inside her skirt. Suede, I think the skirt was. Soft suede. And her legs were brown. I was swapping *Demons of the Dark Vault* and *Gotham City Ghouls* for *Blondie and Dagwood in Trouble* and *Lil Abner*. I know now she just wanted shot of them. They're useless. Her da's a cop but that's not Tina's fault. He took our names twice for playing bootie in Marlborough Road and he raided our house with a whole lot of other cops when I was about two. Daddy wasn't dead very long and Mammy was fit to be held because the only reason they could have been raiding was badness. They found Bernard's old dummy handgun and they thought it was a real one. We still have a good laugh about that sometimes even though it was years ago. Imagine him doing that and him living nearly next to us. Sheila says he could easily have asked not to be on the raid seeing as he was a neighbour. He's nothing but a big stupid cunt. Anyway, the raid's ancient history but the taking names is a real sickener right now. He only caught us the two times because there's nearly always somebody keeping dick and every time we hear the shout - Big Lyttle! we scatter. He did the same thing each time he caught us. He made us stand in a line up against our gable wall and asked us our names and addresses even though he knew us rightly and he wrote everything down dead slow. Mammy's still on the nerves from the second time because it was only three weeks ago and we could still get summonses sent out to us. She says Harry McAllister got a summons for playing bootie in the street and that's why he had to go to America because he would never have got a job here but I heard it was because he gave cheek and told big Lyttle he was going to break all his windows after he finished breaking his legs. She goes on a whole lot about Tucker Kelly from Rosemount as well. She says he was got taking a bulb out of a lamppost and he can't even get a job sweeping the streets now. Arthur was there one of the times she said that and he said - The eonly reason Kelly cawn't get a job is thawt he doesn't recognize the Stawment govahment.

So I decided to be really smart and say - Wa-wa-why does he not recognize them? Hiv they changed or wh-wh-what?

- No, thawt's the wheole trouble, Arthur said. - They hawven't changed.

Doris Day has a song out called *Secret Love*. I nearly always think of me and Tina when I'm singing it because Tina's my secret love and sometimes I pretend to myself that I'm her secret love too. But it's stupid because she'd never turn. I wouldn't get married to her if she didn't turn. I mind ones telling me a priest in the cathedral read out a girl's name from the altar one time and he said she was excommunicated because she got married to a Prod in some registry office. They're living over in the Waterside since because there's a lot less Catholics there. That'd be me finished. Imagine having your name read out for every-body to hear and being cut off from God. It would give Mammy a heart attack. And just imagine having Tina morning, noon and night and knowing the whole time you're going to hell. No, Tina's out, Sally'll do fine well. Morning, noon and night. Holy God. I'll be too wrecked to get up for work. Unless we go to bed early. That's it. Get her to bed early. Sweet Jesus.

Stevie Robinson's Uncle Gregory's a B man and he chased a whole crowd of us into the cathedral last Hallowe'en. Here's what happened. We were playing down in Marlborough Street and some mad eejit put a lit banger through Gregory's letter-box. Well, you should have heard the explosion. Gregory came out and we all ran. You have to run when you're innocent or you'll get the blame. Adults are stupid. Do you see if they see somebody standing there just after a stone or a ball puts their window in or something like that, who do you think they

69

blame? Right. The only one it couldn't be. Even a tube knows the guilty ones run away. I mean, if you do something really drastic on somebody's house you don't stand there waiting for them to come out and beat the shit out of you or hand you over to the cops. You vamoose pronto. So the reason we all ran was , we knew Gregory would hang, draw and quarter anybody left standing. He was still after us when we got to Creggan Hill. That's over a hundred yards. Now, normal big people don't follow you that far. They run about twenty yards to see if they can catch some cripple. As we ran down the hill like madmen with the clothes sticking to us somebody roared - Into the cathedral! B men don't go into the cathedral!

So about fourteen of us headed in the cathedral gate. I didn't really believe he was still behind us because the cathedral's about another hundred and fifty yards from the end of Marlborough Street but you couldn't take any chances with Gregory. We clattered up to the doors of the cathedral and then slowed down and started to walk dead casual in case there were any priests about. But there was only one and he was up on the altar. Father McNally. This was the last night of the October Devotions and the place was crammed. I stood in the crowd at the back and my whole body was thumping and then I saw him coming in one of the doors. His face was red and so were his eyes. I swear it.

- That's it, I thought. - He's not even a normal B man.

I grabbed a Catholic Truth Society booklet from the stall beside me and opened it. It took me ages before I realised that I was holding it upside down but I was afraid to turn it the right way up in case Gregory would catch on. But at the same time I was afraid to keep it the way it was in case he'd see it was upside down. He'd probably got great eyesight. That crowd are all trained to be marksmen. And right enough, after a wee while he started moving towards me through the crowd of muckers that always stand up at the back even if there's a thousand empty seats on up. At that very moment Father McNally took the Host from the tabernacle to put it in the monstrance and all the muckers collapsed down onto one knee. So did I. I knelt down on the hard tiles and I prayed. Jesus Himself was exposed

70

on the altar. Out of the side of my right eye I was watching Gregory. He was the only one standing up. He must feel like a right eejit, I thought, not being able to kneel at the Exposition, stuck up there like an Orange lily. And I knew he was going to have bother getting near me because the muckers were taking up a lot of extra space now with them half kneeling and all. But you can never be sure about B men, especially one that chases you round half of Derry, so I bowed my head and prayed. And before I knew it, he was gone. Gone! But then I thought, It's probably a trick. So I stayed kneeling where I was, praying away and thinking away. If I waited till the end of Benediction and then went out along with the crowd in the dark I was bound to be safe. My right knee was hurting very bad but I didn't get up because I wanted to offer up my suffering in thanksgiving and also that God would take away the small chance that Gregory might still get me. At the end I sang the *Adoremus* with my whole heart and all the muckers were staring at me. Then I moved out. I was just like a speck in the crowd but there he was, standing at the Creggan Hill gate and I couldn't turn back because by the time I saw him I was too close to it and I was being sort of carried along. Only two people at the most could fit into that opening and Gregory was taking up one of the spaces and he didn't give a shit about people bumping into him and pushing past him and saying - Excuse *me*. I just had time to whisper - Soul of Christ sanctify me, Body of Christ save me, and then I was right up beside him. I stared straight ahead and walked straight ahead and then I sailed up Creggan Hill. My faith had got me through.

I never liked Gregory after that but Stevie's dead on. Stevie's his nephew. He's one of my best pals even though he goes on like a dirty brute. I don't take him serious because he just likes talking big. He's never even *gone* with a girl. He's actually dead shy with them. That's probably because he's googy and he's got a real ugly bake. But you want to hear the voice of him. He sounds like a wee oul man. He looks over your shoulder with his skelly eye and he says - Always remember the motto, Conn. If she moves, ride er. My voice is just starting to break now but I've been pals with Stevie from he was about nine and his voice was never anything else but broke. One of the things I really like about him is, he's Derry City mad, especially when they're playing Linfield who're the most Protestant team in the world. Them and Glasgow Rangers. But he nearly gave me heart failure that day three years ago me and him were over in Brooke Park. What happened was, we were playing a game of rushie and in the middle of it we heard a bell ringing in Christ Church which is right next to the park. It was the first time we'd ever heard a bell there during the week so after a good while he picked up his Derry City hat and scarf that we were using as goalposts and we went down to see what the score was. The church door was half open and Stevie said to me - Mawn in an see what the crack is.

I said no.

Stevie asked me why.

I said we weren't allowed to.

- What d'ye mean, ye're not allowed tay? Mawn on in. It'll not kill ye.

- But wur not allowed tay, I said.

- Jesus. Will ye go tay hell or wha? he said.

I couldn't tell him for sure if he was right or wrong there but I'd a feeling he was right. So I just said - Caccholics aren't allowed tay go intay a Protestant church.

- Sure wur not supposed tay go in ler either, he said.

- What d'ye mean? I said. - Sure you're a Prod.

- Aye but I'm a *Presbyterian* Prod. This place is Church a Ireland Prod so it is.

- Whass Presbyterian? I asked him.

- Fur fuck sake wud ye gimme a rest, Murphy. Whass this, whass that, whass the other thing! It jist means wur not Church a Ireland.

- But I thought yous wur all the wan, I said.

- Sure wur *all* all the wan, he said. - D'ye wannay know wha may da siz? May da siz iss the same as people bein mad about futball an supportin different teams. So mawn. Let's go.

I shook my head and stood there holding the ball. Stevie looked funny going in the church door with the Derry City scarf and hat on him. After about five minutes he came out again.

- Ye know wha *you* are, Murphy? he said.

I said nothing.

- Ye're a fucken coward. An I'll tell ye somethin else ye are. Ye're a bitter pig as well so ye are.

I still didn't say anything. I forgot to even ask him why the bell was ringing. I knew soldiers of Christ were bound to get called names like that but it was the first time it ever happened to me and I didn't know what to say back.

And then he said - Right, let's head intay yer pliss.

- What are ye on about, *my* pliss? I said.

- What d'ye think I'm pointin at over yonder? he said. - A Scotch mist?

He meant Saint Eugene's Cathedral. It was just across the road from us.

- But *you* cannay go in there, I said.

- Siz who?

I couldn't answer and we stood there looking at each other and then he said - Mawn.

We went in. I wanted us to stay at the back round about where his Uncle Gregory did the prowling two Hallowe'ens after but Stevie marched right up the middle aisle and stopped at the altar rails. I left the ball at the side of the bookstall and ran and caught up with him and told him he was supposed to take off his Derry City hat. So he took it off. He kept staring away at the tabernacle and I told him Jesus was in there. He didn't laugh or anything and he just started looking all round him, not saying a word. After a wee while I got this kind of a tingly feeling in my back that I could maybe capture a soul for Christ. Imagine saving a soul from hell, I thought. Or even Limbo. The feeling got really strong when he said to me - Whass all them stacchies fur?

I told him that we don't actually pray *to* statues or adore them like Prods say we do, we just *look at* them so's to make it easier for us to think of whoever it is we're praying to. He kept nodding away but it was very hard to tell what he was thinking, you know, with his googy eye and all. Most of the time I didn't know if he was even looking at me.

After I got to the end of the thing I was saying to him about the statues I genuflected and knelt down at the altar rails and bowed my head. He knelt down beside me. My heart was banging away like mad. I closed my eyes and tried to pray for him. I started a Hail Mary about five times into myself because I couldn't concentrate right. When I opened my eyes he wasn't there. I looked around and I couldn't see him anywhere. I froze a wee bit. You're not supposed to raise your voice in the chapel unless you're praying out loud or singing hymns so I started to walk around to see if I could see him. He was standing on a form over near Our Lady's altar squeezing his Derry City hat onto the top of the head of a bust of somebody important. He'd the red and white scarf round the man's neck already. I stood at the altar rails hissing away at him and then I heard the slow tlottily tlot of high heels and I turned around and there was this woman coming up the side aisle towards us. I froze a wee bit more because I knew the hat. I couldn't see the face but I knew the hat all right. It was Mrs Canavan from Marlborough Street. She's a teacher in the girls' school up the hill. She'd remember me, that was a cert. She caught me one time hiding in a garden after Charlie roared in her letter-box - What IS your name anyway, Missus? Is it Cannibal or Cannonball ?

She let me off that time. But that was that time. This was this time and this was the chapel. She'd tell Big Snuff if she found out it was me standing there. He was our headmaster and he was a giant and he scared the shit out of me. Nearly every time he came into our classroom he banged the cane on one of the front desks and let this roar out of him - Thatsnuff! Fingers to lips NOW!

I turned away and walked as quick as I could over to the other side aisle and I didn't even genuflect when I was passing the big altar. That saved vital moments. I hid behind a pillar. I heard Mrs Canavan's voice echoing away but I couldn't make out anything she was saying. I only heard Stevie's voice the once. Then there wasn't a sound out of them and I waited for ages. You should have seen the cut of him when he came. He was wearing the hat and scarf and he was slouching along with his hands dug away down in his trouser pockets.

He said - Thass a wile clivir wummin. Ye wanted tay hear what she towl may about the head.

I heard the tlot of her shoes fading out the front door. Probably she was on her way over to the parochial house. Maybe she'd meet Father McNally or Father Sheerin on her way over and she'd stand talking to them.

- Did she ask ye who I was? I said.

- She siz he was a vurry important bishop and none of the two of us had any respect, he said.

- Did ye tell her who I was ? I said.

- I think he musta bin a builder as well as bein a bishop. She siz he built this pliss an some other pliss as well, he said.

- What other pliss? I said. I caught on it was better to let him finish because he'd a real bad look in his eyes.

- Some other pliss. I cannay mine. D'ye wannay know how long it tuck im tay build this pliss here? he said.

- Naw. How long? I said.

- D'ye ivir luck at the size a this pliss? It'd mick ye dizzy luckin up, he said.

- Aye, I know, I said. - How long?

- Twenny-two years she siz. Or mibby it was twenny-thee. Or thirty-two. Sometimes I git mixed up in them two. Anyway, whativir it was, he musta bin some bricklayer. How d'ye go tay Confession?

- How d'ye what ?

- Go tay Confession. She towl may I'd hiftay go tay Confession after wha I did.

I was getting really mad. I forgot where I was for a minute and I grabbed him by the scarf and put my face right up against his.

- Right, Robinson, I said. - Did ye tell er who I was?

- Ye shouldn't do that, Conn. It micks ye go all googy. I towl er ye wur some Prod outa the Waterside, he said.

- Ye swear tay God that's what ye towl er? I said.

- Honest tay Jesus, Conn. Luck, thur's may right han, he

said.

And he put up his hand as if he was swearing in court. I let him go and stood back a bit. I wasn't feeling too good. I knew I'd committed sins right, left and centre. Violence in the chapel, running in the chapel, talking in the chapel, hiding in the chapel, not genuflecting in the chapel, taking a black Prod into the chapel *and* letting him make a laugh out of a dead bishop and tell lies for me as well.

Then he said - Naw, right enough, Spud. Gawn tell us.

- Tell ye what? I said.

- What d'ye think? he said - Tell us how tay go tay Confession. Whur d'ye go? What d'ye do?

I stared at him. I really liked him and I wanted him to turn. But he was mad. You wouldn't know what he would do. I got this flash of him sitting in the priest's place in the confession box and listening to somebody telling their sins and roaring in his wee man's voice - Ye WHAT! Ye did WHAT! Out tay fuck ye dirty bastard ye!

So I grabbed him by the arm and pulled him down the aisle and lifted the ball from beside the bookstall and got him out of the side door and back up to the park.

I made sure I didn't hear the things Sylvester was saying about hell. As soon as he started I put my hands up to the sides of my head as if I was really concentrating and I stuck my first fingers into my ears. I didn't want to listen to him going on seeing I think about it so much anyway. I think about it every time I commit a mortal sin and it doesn't go out of my head until I get to Confession. He went on about it for more than a quarter of an hour. I heard bits and pieces of it here and there, the times I took my fingers out to see if he was finished. Stuff about the unquenchable flames and the pain of loss and remember the pleasures of the world aren't worth it. I was watching him all the time so's he wouldn't jube on I wasn't listening and I swear to God he was lapping it up. You know, the big crowd taking in every word. All except me. But I started to listen again when I knew he'd gone on to something else. You could tell he'd moved away from hell from the way his face and hands were going. Here's what he was saying:

- But, my dear boys, God's faithful servants will enjoy the fruits of their service forever in heaven. For He will say to the sheep on his right - *Come, you blessed of My Father, into the kingdom prepared for you since the creation of the world.*

That was it about heaven. The end. Completo. Finis. Fin. The lot. Fifteen minutes about hell and fifteen seconds about heaven. Why do they tell you nearly everything about hell and nearly nothing about heaven? I mean, if you could only look forward to it the way you think of a fish supper or a football match or a big feed of chocolate or a half day or a great show you're going to or a girl. The thing is, all we know about heaven is, God's there and you'll meet all your dead relations. If they got there, that is. Not many people get there. Sheila said one of the children Our Lady appeared to at Fatima got a vision of hell and it was overflowing. But imagine if you could say to yourself when you're tempted - No, I'm not going to take any chances because I don't want to miss all the fantastic things that are waiting for me up in heaven, instead of saying to yourself - I'd better not do that because I might only end up in hell and I know about all the terrible sufferings that are waiting for me down there.

There's some things in my head about heaven. Nobody told me them. I just thought them up. Or maybe I dreamed them. A whole lot of them are a wee bit mad but I was nearly thinking I might write them down to see how they turned out. Maybe that's what I'll do, make them into a story. I haven't written a story since my last year in Rosebawn, that's the elementary school I was at. I tore it up after Bernard wrote A NUTTER LOAD OF TOSH, BOSH AND BUNKUM with his purple biro on every page. I thought the time I did it it was very good. I remember I got the idea when this brilliant substitute teacher, Mrs Quirke, told us that priests never lost their powers to hear confessions and all even if they were sacked. After that the plan of the story kept going on at me for about two days. I wrote the whole thing in less than an hour. Well, less than two hours. I called it *Father Cease Your Blessings*. It was about a priest called Father Conn Doherty who was sacked after being framed for stealing the Saint Vincent de Paul money by the sacrestan who hated him. So Father Conn joined the Yankee airforce and was shot down by the Korean commies and ended up in a prisoner-of-war camp. All the other prisoners were either Prods or pagans or atheists and of course the guards were all commies. After about two years of Father Conn getting tortured every day the part of Korea the prisoner-of-war camp was in was struck by an earthquake and buildings were tumbling down all over the place and the ground was opening up and people were falling in. Everybody in the camp was petrified except Father Conn. He started to tell the other prisoners how they could get to heaven and a guard heard him talking and before that day was out the whole camp turned to be Catholics, commies and all. The earthquake miraculously moved away to somewhere else and Father Conn was a hero. It ended up the pope hearing about it and making him a bishop and sacking the sacrestan.

The more I thought about that later on the more I realised how childish it was. I'll try and make this story about heaven like a real novel grown-ups would like. A fantasy novel, like *Alice in Wonderland*. I've a feeling it's going to take me a while.

PREFACE: Before I start there's something I have to tell you. I'll not be writing Monday or Tuesday or Day One or Day Two because the whole thing's just one long day. And there's no point writing stuff like - I had a chat with God this morning, when there is no morning. Or evening. Or night. (Anyway, nobody gets chatting with Him.) And there's another thing that's hard to get used to. You don't talk about the weather up here because it's perfect. The sun's shining all the time and the sky's completely blue so what can you say about it? Maybe somebody said away back in the beginning - It's keepin up rightly, but they never mention it now.

AGE ONE: This is heaven. There's golden walls all around you but they always seem to get further away any time you go near them. Another thing, there's no ground to walk on, just clouds. You know the brilliant kind of white bunchy clouds you were always mad to get bouncing on when you were wee? Well, that's them. But the only wains here are wee girls. There's about a thousand of them and the time I saw them they were all kneeling praying in dead straight lines. *So* holy looking. And not one of them doing any bouncing. As far as I could see the only part of them moving was their lips. I haven't seen God yet but just after I came this woman with a scarf on her told us we were to go to the orchard right away and take anything we wanted. There were stacks of fruit, every kind you could think of and every kind you couldn't think of. And talk about flavour. You know that lemony orangey ice pop that's very dear and you can only get it in Jack McDaid's shop? Well, it wasn't like that at all. But that's the nearest you could get to it. It was funny being *told* to take as much fruit as you wanted. You know, without being chased and all. I ended up not eating that much.

There's two things annoying me. First there's Dan McDonald. He's dead this good while. I've been avoiding him like the plague since I landed and I can see him looking at me sometimes, trying to place me. He's bound to remember soon because I'm one of the ones used to laugh at him and call him Desperate Dan and Mousey McDonald. He never lay out of the chapel and he was always first up to Holy Communion. You know the kind I'm on about. Him and these other three men always held the canopy over Wee Rosie's head on Corpus Christi. He went round the Stations of the Cross on his knees as well. I'm not saying there's anything wrong with *that*. I mean, I even felt like doing it myself sometimes to make up for the dirty things I was always thinking but I was afraid somebody would see me. The thing about Dan was, he *wanted* people to see him. But the thing that made him a desperate case was the way he took dog's abuse and never said a word. He worked in a Protestant shop down the town for about thirty years and then they brought in this wee Prod just out of school and gave Dan the boot. He did damn all about it. He didn't even complain. Mammy used to always say he was a living saint. - He nivir had a bad word tay say about anybody and he'd nivir turn a word in your mouth. That's what she always said. And I used to think - Well, I wouldn't want *him* for a daddy anyway.

The other thing's about Daddy. Oh, don't worry, he's here all right. Well, he's here in a kind of a way. I'd better tell you about it. I wasn't in that long before I saw him. It was the biggest thrill I ever got. He looked exactly the same as he is in the photo I have of him. You know, big and strong and good, like somebody you could really depend on. He was sitting on a puffy white armchair on this cloud near me. I shouted over to him. There were millions of things I wanted to tell him and I couldn't wait. But he didn't hear me with the noise of the waterfall. I forgot to tell you, there's this water runs very fast off the edge of our cloud and it would deave your ears it's that loud. It's the place I go a whole lot of times when the music gets a bit much. It's organ music and it just keeps on playing and playing. Don't get me wrong. I'm over the moon about being here. Do you see when I woke up and found out it wasn't hell I was in, I couldn't believe it so I couldn't. Honest to God, I never thought I'd make it, you know, with the way I died and all and with me thinking about *that stuff* day and night down there. But this music. It was dead on at the start when you didn't think it was going to go on and on forever. The two hymns they play are *Holy God* and *Sweet Heart of Jesus*. It's starting to get me down now and I can't hardly think straight sometimes. I mean, they've been playing the same ones since I came. I wouldn't mind getting on to God about it but I never saw Him yet. You keep expecting Him to appear any minute but He still hasn't come. Anyway, I was saying about Daddy. He'd his head leaning on his fist and he was looking around him as if he was waiting for somebody. He was so lonely looking I wanted to go over and hold him in my arms. I kept walking towards him and roaring out of me at the same time but he never even looked near me, So then I started jumping up and down and waving my arms like a madman and that soon did the trick. He waved back but it was a kind of a wave you'd give to a stranger. Then I remembered he hadn't seen me since I was a year and three months old. So I roared as loud as I could - Daddy! This is nineteen fifty-four and I'm Conn! But he just turned his head and looked behind him. Whoever it was he was waiting for, they still hadn't turned up. When I think of it now, he was probably saying to himself - This maniac'll probably get lost if I ignore him. I went right to the edge to see if I could maybe jump across. To tell you the God's honest truth, I was getting really angry. - This is all His fault, I thought. - Who does He think He is anyway? Then it happened. I slipped on my backside and the water started carrying me away. I thought I was a goner. I was right over the edge when something caught me round the neck and pulled me away far back. I stood up and lifted the thing away from my neck. It was a shepherd's crook and Desperate Dan was holding on to the other end of it.

- It's young Conn Murphy, isn't it? he said. - Are you all right ,son?

I didn't even say thanks I was that mad he knew me. I just walked away.

- You need to be careful round here, Conn, he shouted after me. - Did you not see the sign?

I turned round and looked. LUCIFER FALLS, it said.

I hightailed it but he kept following me and it took a quare while to shake him off. But do you know what was the most annoying thing about seeing Daddy? It wasn't him not knowing me. It wasn't even not being able to talk to him and hug him. It was this. After I got rid of Dan I didn't even feel bad about it. It was like the time I was told to count to ten before I got my appendix out. One minute I was all tensed up and the next minute I didn't give a hoot.

AGE TWO: No sign of God yet. I heard somebody saying He stays in His office all the time. Anyway, wait till you hear the crack. Tina's here! Yes, Tina Lyttle! I'm not sure how she died yet but she looks well. Very, very nice indeed. I'm wondering how she got in, with her being a Prod and all. She must have turned.

- What about ye? she said.

- Stickin out, I said. - Any bars?

- Nothin much, she said.

- I love yer hair, I said. - Whur d'ye git it done?

- God naw, it's a real sight so it is, she said. - I dunno the last time I put a brush tay it. D'ye know the new pliss down the Strand Road? Prime Cut? What am I talkin about? How cud ye? Sure it jist opened.

All the time she was talking she was taking a real good look at me.

- I'll tell ye somethin, Conn, she said. - Ye're not too bad luckin way yer close off.

- Not up tay yer standard yit, Tina, I said. - *You* luck dead on so ye do.

I touched her skin.

- D'ye know this? I said. - I nivir knew ye'd a birth mark there.

- Sure how cud ye? she said. - I always had may skert on whin *you* wur aroun. Naw, but I'm serious about ye, Conn. Ye're not near as skinny as I thought ye wur. I used tay always think, His legs is lick two sticks, his knees is all knobbly an he's got a wee chicken chest but thur's wan thing about im. He's got a nice fiss. As God's may witness, Conn, plenny a times I felt lick rippin the trousers offa ye but sure ye nivir lucked near may. All ye wanted tay know about was them bloody comics.

She put her hand up to her mouth.

- God forgimme. Are ye allowed tay say that here? she said.

- Bloody? I said. - I don't think they'd say a word about it. But I dunno tay tell ye the truth. I've hardly bin talkin tay a soul since I come here.

- How long are ye in fur? she said. - I mean, how long *hiv* ye been in fur?

- Thass a good question, I said. - I dunno fur sure. Ye sorta lose track a time in this pliss. Gawn *you* tell *me*. How long am I dead about?

She screwed up her face and thought hard.

- Right. I jist got here so this is still August, she said. - It must be aroun the two year mark. It was the end a the summer holidays, wasn't it? Ye see, I git mixed up, cause way wur back at school a good wee while before they fished ye out.

- TWO YEARS! I said. - Ye're not serious.

- Thur's may right han up tay God. I'm sixteen now and I was fourteen then. Ye know somethin I nivir foun out fur sure, Conn? Why d'ye do it?

- Why did I do it? I said. - I'll tell ye why I did it. I cudn't fiss goin back tay the College so I cudn't.

- So thass the reason, she said. - Tell may this much. Here's somethin I wannay ask ye. Did anywan else from Marlborough come in after *you*, not countin *me*?

- Naw.

She was very quiet all of a sudden.

- What are ye askin me that fur? I said.

- No reason, she said.

- Mawn, Tina, I said. - Tell us.

- Well, she said. - Fur wan thing, it means ye nivir heard about the fuss tay do way ye not gittin buried in holy groun.

- Ye're jokin, I said.

- Naw, straight up, she said. - May ma and da really lapped it up, especially when your ma went down wan night an dug up a whole lotta six-foot holes in the Cathedral lawns. The bishop sid she was off er head an he towl the priests not tay tick er on. She's runnin the Mormons in Derry now so she is.

- Now howl on a minute, Tina, I said.

- I swear tay God, she said. - She was dressed lick a million dollars the last time I seen er. Ye wannay luck at the style of er now. Iviry day whin she's ready tay come out the dour Mrs Wilson an the two Misses Dortys are out doin the brass at the wan time. They always done that anyway tay hear the bars from wan another but since yer ma joined up thur out tay see the litest fashion. Conn, ye wannay see them. Thur lettin on they're jist civil tay er whin she comes out way er leaflets an Bibles an all or whativir it is she has in that wee briefkiss of hers and thur shoutin, 'Ye're all away way yersel the day, Murray'. But thur brekkin thur necks tay tick it all in, so they are, an they've near got the knobs an knockers rubbed off thur dours, so they hiv.

I was finding it hard to take it all in. I was thinking all that diggin would have been bad for her varicose veins. And the Mormons thing was even worse than that. I started wondering if she'd ever get to heaven. She could end up down in hell because of me and here was me up in heaven after drowning myself. Then I put everything else out of my head and tried to imagine her all dressed up. But I could only see her with the apron on no matter how hard I tried. What's this it was she used to say? *A sight fur sore eyes.* That's what she'd be. A sight for sore eyes.

- Conn!

I wouldn't have minded seeing her all dolled up.

- Conn! D'ye hear what I'm saying? Wur ye not feared?

- Sorry, I was away up in the clouds there, I said.

- I'm askin ye wur ye not feared, she said.

- How d'ye mean, feared? I said.

- Ye know, feared a goin tay hell? she said.

- I was not. tay tell ye the truth, Tina, I jist didn't care. I didn't think it cud be any worse than Sint Paul's, I said.

- Geemidy! I nivir knew it was *that* bad, she said.

- I'll tell ye whass wrong, I said. - Most a the mas and das tick it fur granted ye git used tay it after ye've bin bate up a few times. Thass jist the way it is. The funny thing is, *my* ma hadn't a clue what it was really lick because none of us that wur at the College towl er. If she'd known she'd a tuck us away even though it wuda broke er heart. A lotta the boys in my class seemed tay bibble tay tick it but I jist cracked. Probbly I didn't hiv what it tuck.

- Thass terrible, Conn. Iss not lick that at Londondray High. Thur wur wan or two bitches in that pliss whin I was there but they'd nivir hiv made ye do away way yersel, she said.

- I was wantin tay ask ye, Tina, I said. - What happened ye died so young.

- I didn't die. I got kilt, she said and she put her hand up to her neck. - I was jist stupid so I was. I got may head tore off bay a branch of a tree up at Strabane.

- Gawn away tay hell, I said.

- Naw, honest tay God, she said. - Me an may boyfren wur comin back from a day out in Dublin and whin we wur comin intay Strabane I stuck may head outa the train winda tay git the thrill. Ye know, the rushin wind thrill.

- I know the wan, I said. - I done the same maysel a whole lot a times on the Buncrana train. But the worst *I* ivir got was a bitta smut in may eye. Tell us this. Whur exactly did it happen?

Now that was a really stupid question because I was never in the Dublin train in my life and I hadn't a clue where the railway station was in Strabane. But it was too late. I'd said it.

- Right, she said. - D'ye know the tree comin intay the station?

- I don't think so, I said.

- Ye *muss* know it, she said. - Iss about a hunnerd yards on the Dublin side a Strabane. Iss jist roun the ben comin intay the station.

- I cannay think of it now, I said.

My heart started sinking. I wanted her to finish telling it but a blind man could have seen things were getting a bit tense.

- I think iss a weepin willa, she said, and I didn't like the way she was looking at me. - I nivir got the time tay git a good luck at it but I cud nearly swear now it was a weepin willa.

I caught on then that if I didn't let on I knew where the tree was I'd never hear the end of it. So I said - Aw, the weepin willa! Sure I know the wan ye're on about now.

That satisfied her. I'm pretty sure she didn't believe me but I know it satisfied her anyway because she started getting all relaxed again.

- But wait d'ye hear the laugh, she said. - I did it all fur four pair a nylons. Thur was this half price sale on in Clery's up in Dublin an I hadday queue up fur bout an hour. I had the nylons stuffed down the front a may jeans in the train fur fear the customs man wud tick them off may. An d'ye wannay know the ridiculous part?

- I know what ye're goin tay say, I said.

- I nivir even got tay put them on. I wonder who's wearin them now, she said.

- Probbly yer ma, I said. - They won't go tay waste. She'll wait tay it's decent and then she'll wear them.

- I dunno about that, Tina said. - She doesn't go out since may da died.

- Yer da's not dead! I said.

I was in heaven.

- Aye, he died last year, she said. - He was cleanin his gun and it jist wint off.

Seventh heaven.

- He lived fur bout two weeks but he was in wile pain so he was , she said.

- Aw dear, I said.

Address: cloud nine.

- Thass the other thing I meant tay say tay ye, she said. - Ye didn't see im about, did ye?

- Naw, I did not, Tina, I said, looking very worried.

Lucifer will be giving him a good roasting, I thought. Well done, Luce.

When Tina was rattling on about her and her mother going down to the hospital to see the dying bollocks I started to think of some of the other pricks that will probably end up in hell. You know the ones that walk past you with their noses up as if you were a whirl of shite stuck to the pavement. The ones the Derry Journal tells you about:

> Saint Paul's College is in deep
> mourning after news of the sudden
> passing of Father Ride McBride, the
> brilliant and saintly Irish and
> Religious Knowledge teacher.

And

> A great sense of loss was felt in
> Derry when people learnt of the
> death of Mr The Pogue Mahoney, the
> great Gaelic speaker and teacher.

And

86

There were inspiring scenes at the
funeral mass of the respected priest
and teacher, Father Cain Couchman.
Mr Schuberts Hughes was at the organ
and his Lordship Bishop Rosie Healy presided.

And in the middle of the deep mourning and inspiring scenes and great sense of loss The Couch and The Pogue and McRide are getting the arses burnt off them. This place isn't so bad when you think about it. It'll not be that long before somebody arrives and tells me that those three really are dead. The Crackling Commandants. Anytime I get a bit bored I can get Dan to curl his crozier around my ankle and I'll hang out at Lucifer Falls for a while and see them screaming for mercy and old Luce going at them with his pitchfork. And I'll see them facing every boy they ever tortured and they'll have to look into our eyes and our minds and then go through exactly the same as we did. Forever.

AGE THREE: You want to know who I met just there now? Jo Stafford! I wouldn't have known it was her because I've never even seen a photo of her but Tina told me who she was and then she introduced us. She's nearly like the way I imagined. You know, from the sound of her voice. I think she is anyway. To tell you the truth I'm not exactly sure what I imagined. Anyway, I asked her to sing *You Belong to Me* but she just shook her beautiful head and said it wasn't quite suitable. So I said - Please Jo. Sing *something*. And she sang *The Bell of the Angelus*.

It lasted for about ten minutes but it sounded brilliant. Even with *Holy God* blaring away in the background it still sounded brilliant. It's great Jo's here. I'm glad she's dead. She's really nice. And interesting too.

AGE FOUR: The three of us love taking a dip in Lake Eden. We always sunbathe when we come out. But this thing came into my head the last time and I'm working out what to think about it. We lay on our bellies the way we always do and then we all turned over on our backs at the same time the way we always do. But then I got a wee bit fidgety and started scooting these ladybirds that were crawling up Jo's legs. I was sort of having a competition with myself to see which one I could scoot the farthest. Jo told me to stop it so I left the ladybirds alone and lay on my side and had a good look at the two of them. You wouldn't believe how perfect their skins were and they'd a brilliant tan all over them as well. But I was telling you about the thing that came into my head. I just started to feel dead unhappy and I knew I was remembering the day me and Charlie made a big rise on empty lemonade bottles and went to the Strand to see *Dial M for Murder*. That was some day. We got this new kind of ice cream with wee bits of chocolate in it. I nearly took sick when I went home because I must have eaten about half a pound of wine gums as well. But it was still great. It was the first day of the summer holidays and it was goodbye Saint Paul's for two months. I was nearly going to tell Jo and Tina about it. You know, how a day can be even *more* perfect when you know you're only out on parole. But I didn't bother because I'd a feeling they wouldn't have had the baldiest clue what I was on about.

AGE FIVE: Still no sign of God. Funny that. I was just thinking something. I was thinking I really like being with Tina and Jo. Especially Tina. I don't know why that is. Maybe it's because she's a sort of a connection. Anyway, I grabbed the chance to ask Tina something when Jo was away talking to the organist.

- Tell may this, Tina, I said, - if ye don't mind may askin. Did ye turn before ye got yer head tore off?

- Aw aye, she said. - Did I not tell ye? I got baptised down in the cathedral the Sunday after may faller died. Jesus, what a day. Thur was screamin wains an red-faced mollers an godmollers all roun may. That Faller Sheerin's a funny wee man, isn't he?

- How d'ye mean funny?

- Well, I towl im I wanted tay be christened Marilyn an he

88

stud howlin this jug a water an starin at me and then he siz, 'What?'

An *I* siz, 'Marilyn.'

An *he* siz, 'Don't gimme that. Murray'll do.'

So he christened may Murray after the moller a God.

- Thass a goodun, I said. - I nivir got on that well way im maysel. But ye didn't tell may *why* ye turned, Tina. Or shud I say Murray?

- Don't gimme that, she said. - Tina'll do. I was goin way Harry McCorkell an I was that mad about im I wuda stud on may hine legs tay git im.

- Harry McCorkell from Rosemount? I said.

- Aye, she said. - D'ye know im?

- I do surely, I said. - Great fella.

Harry's a real bad bastard. He treats girls like shite. He's always going on about them being beneath him, a different one beneath him every night, he says.

- May ma an da siz I was stupid, said Tina. - Ye know way me jist sixteen an oney left school an all. But the big thing was Harry bein a Taig. They didn't lick that wan wee bit. That was the day may da had the accident. In the middle a all the ructions about me an Harry he sid, 'I've had enough. I'm away up the stairs tay clean may gun.'

I wonder does that prove all the stuff about there being no salvation outside the Catholic Church. You know, Tina being in heaven as a *Catholic*. The reason I'm saying is, I haven't seen one Derry Prod in here yet. I'd have no bother spotting them, with their eyes close together and their wee tight mouths. Tina never actually looked like a Prod anyway. I mind Gander saying to me there were Catholics on her ma's side. But I suppose when you think of it there could be Prods from other places here for all I know. *They'd* probably have normal faces, just like us, so you wouldn't know.

AGE SIX: I wish someone would tell me why this is happening. I'm starting to get really pissed off. Everything I see annoys me. Like, for example, this past while every single person here's got the same shiny marble kind of face and the same wee watery smile. Even Tina. Forget about holy Jo. Ever since she got the organist to play *The Bell of the Angelus* instead of the other two hymns she's looking more and more like a gravestone. Her and that bloody choir she started. And now she's got Tina in it as well. They're like a singing cemetery the whole lot of them. I never thought I'd say this but I'm starting to miss *Sweet Heart of Jesus* and *Holy God*. Where the hell's God anyway? Wherever He is, He's got plenty of explaining to do. As far as I can see, the only good thing about heaven is, it's not hell. I mean, you'd think He could come up with something better than *this*. I know what *I'm* going to do. I'm going to go and talk to Him, even if I have to break down that office door.

AGE SEVEN: It took me a good while to work up the nerve but I did it. I'm not saying I broke down the door or anything. I'm not saying that. But I stood there banging away at it even though I was going like a leaf. There wasn't a mute coming from inside so I started roaring out of me - I need tay talk tay Ye, God, but He still never appeared so I got a brilliant idea. I started singing this dirty song that's called *Sweet Violets* as loud as I could.

> *There once was a farmer who took a young miss*
> *To the back of the barn where he gave her a--*
> *Lecture on horses and chickens and eggs*
> *And told her that she had such a beautiful--*
> *Manners that suited a girl of her charms,*
> *A girl that he'd li-ike to take in his--*
> *Washing and ironing and then sometime maybe*
> *They could get married and raise lots of--*
> *Sweet vi-olets,*
> *Sweeter than the roses,*
> *Covered all over from head to toe,*
> *Covered all over with sweet vi-olets.*

It doesn't look that bad when you write it down but I knew

God wouldn't like it because the first time we heard it Sheila nearly broke her neck trying to get over to turn off the wireless. A whole crowd of us learnt it up at Gallagher's wall and I got a wee thrill out of singing it to myself some days when I was going to the College.

Anyway, it did the trick. I didn't actually see Him but I heard Him all right. What a boom.

- Pack it in, He roared.

- Okay, okay, I said. - Tick it easy. I oney did that tay git talkin tay Ye. I'm really sorry so I am. Heartily sorry. Truly sorry if I offended Ye.

- Luck, mere a wee minute tay I tell ye somethin, He roared. - I've had a vurry bad week an I'm tryin tay git a rest in here. So I don't wanney know. Come back the marra.

But then suddenly He stopped talking and the next time He opened His mouth He sounded different. He was still scary but quieter scary.

- Howl on a second tay I think, He said. - Mibby I better listen tay ye now. I'm jist rememberin I've a big day the marra. Thur's an earthquake startin in the mornin an I'll be up tay May eyes all day sortin out the new wans that'll bay comin.

- Aw, I see, I said. - Thass okay. I'll come back some other time, sure.

- What are ye on about? He was roaring again. - Ye come in here shoutin yer head off, ye damn near brek the door down, ye sing dirty double-meanin songs and now ye tell May ye're goin tay come back another time. What the frig d'ye tick May fur anyway? Eh?

I stood there wondering what to say. I'd been waiting for ages to get talking to Him and now I was starting to chicken out. I thought I might try to put Him off by asking why He was going on about the week and the day and the morning and tomorrow and the minute and the second when there were no such things up here but I'd a feeling He'd know I was only trying to bluff Him.

- Luck. I hivn't all day, He thundered.

I was getting desperate. This picture came flashing into my head of the thing that probably happened the time Luce and the boys got the boot.

Lucifer: Lord, Almighty One, way wur jist wonderin if way cud hiv a wee word way Ye.

God: Gawn away.

Lucifer: Naw, tick it easy. Way jist wanted tay tell Ye, ussins here's a bit fed up. Ye see, iss the same thing roun this pliss all the time, if Ye know what I mean, lick. Way wur jist wonderin if Ye'd mine if way got a bitta crack goin. I mean, wur not exactly luckin fur Carlisle Road on a Saturday night or anythin but way jist thought–

God: Gawn away tay hell.

Lucifer: Naw, honest tay God, wur serious.

God: I don't think ye folly May meanin. What I'm sayin is, Gawn away down tay hell the whole damned lotta yeez.

Lucifer: Now, howl on You. Jist howl on there. Ye've got millions a marbleheads in here way gacka wacka smiles on thur fisses an Ye expect us tay tick it furever. Fur God's sake. I mean, that crowd's got about as much angelality as a busted jawbox.

God: I'm warnin yeez.

Lucifer: An thur's wan other thing. Before Ye made us tay start way, Ye knew me an this crew along way me here was goin tay act up sometime an Ye still went ahead way it. So don't be blamin us. Right?

God: Right. Thass it. Down yeez go.

- Right, He roared. - Mick it quick.
- What? I said.
O God.
- Did ye not hear May? Mick it snappy, He roared even louder.
- I was jist wonderin, Lord....
- Ye wur jist wonderin what? Out way it!
- ... if thur was any chance of a start.
- A start? A start? He roared. - What d'ye mean a start?
- ... any chance of a start in the choir.
- Aw, the *choir*. The *choir*, He said. - Aye, I'm sure that'd probbly bay awright. Hiv a word way Miss Stafford an she'll fix ye up. Ye'll find er over there at the organ.
- Oh, thank You, Lord. Thank You.

All right. I know heaven couldn't be like that. I suppose maybe I got a bit carried away. But do you see when I was writing the part about Him in His office and all, do you know what I was thinking? I was trying to work out if He was God the Father or God the Son. You see, I used to think the Father was the One came down on you like a ton of bricks and it was Jesus that was really gentle and kind. Do you remember that old picture *The Ten Commandments* I went to in the Midland? You know the one where the Father sends out the killer angel that rubs out all the biggest brothers in the land that He didn't tell to cut the lamb's throat and splatter its blood on the threshold. And later on He drowns millions of Egyptians because they're the other crowd and a good while after that He destroys a whole lot of His own crowd for going on like sex maniacs and adoring a golden calf as well. And then thousands of years after, Jesus came and did away with all that sort of stuff but they didn't show that because that had nothing to do with the ten commandments. But you know what I mean about Jesus. Always forgiving people and curing them and completely against violence and all. That's what *I* thought anyway. Until about a year ago when we got the retreat before the last one and the priest started talking about Jesus and the Judgement. He'd this big hairy face and he was dead crabbit. He wasn't like Sylvester at all. He was more like Lon Chaney, remember, in that werewolf show in the Fleapit where he tears into his best friend. He said - Then the Son of Man will say to the goats on His left, *Depart from Me, ye cursed, into the eternal fire prepared for the devil and his angels.*

Now we all know who the Son of man is. Gentle Jesus. I still say that prayer a whole lot of nights even though I'm not a little child any longer.

> Gentle Jesus, meek and mild,
> Look on me a little child.

Pity mine and pity me
And suffer me to come to Thee.

But the more I think of that prayer now, it's like a fairy tale. You know, a *good* fairy tale. Because when you get past a certain age you're ready for the fire and that's it. Do you see the big Sacred Heart picture in our kitchen, with Jesus' heart in the middle, all burning and bleeding? Now that's an ordinary picture that was bought in some shop. We got the frame changed there last year but the picture's still the same. I used to think it was supernatural because no matter what part of the kitchen you moved to, the eyes followed you. It was nearly like one of those portraits in murder shows where the eyes are cut out and the murderer's in the next room, watching everything. But our picture seemed to change expressions as well. The day I was eight I was sitting there on the sofa crying because Frankie called me a smelly wee skitter and dug his knuckles into the backs of my hands because I wouldn't let him read the Beano annual Auntie Maggie bought me. She's my godmother and she still always gets me something. My sister Frances said to me after Frankie ran out - Oh, Conn, Jesus gits so upset if a boy cries on his birthday. Luck at Him.

And, right enough, there He was and He seemed as sad as anything. But then if I did something bad, like shouting at Mammy or getting caught eating a handful of cocoa and sugar, the eyes would be sort of disappointed looking and a wee bit angry at the same time. Seemed to be, I should say. But it's funny. One morning last week there when I came down after committing mortal sin with myself before I went to sleep the night before that Mammy shouted in from the scullery - Gawn luck an see if the Sacred Heart lamp's lit, Conn.

I was taking my cornflakes and I looked up to see and He was glaring away at me. I wouldn't say that to anybody else. But do you see Gander and Charlie and Stoopy and them, you know, the ones that would laugh at me if they knew about the picture, they're all sitting in the chapel on Sundays watching the priest turning bread and wine into the Body and Blood of Christ and then they're going up to the altar rails and swallowing

Jesus. And they'd have the nerve to laugh at me.

I was just thinking last night about the time I ran away from home. It was really mad. I ran away because I wasn't allowed to go to Saint Paul's after me passing the Qualifying Exam. What do you think of that! *Now* I'd nearly *swim* away from home because I'm not allowed to *leave* the place. It turned out I was three days too young to go and I had to stay on at Rosebawn for an extra year. When the letter came in the door from the College I went flying up to the attic and hid in the black hole where the water tank is. Then after a wee while I said to myself, What's the sense of this? So I ran down to the stairs landing and I shouted - I got the exam the same as Stanley Strunks and *he's* gittin goin.

Mammy seemed to take that really serious about Stanley Strunks and she went up nearly right away to ask Big Snuff could he do anything about it and he told her he couldn't but I was a very lucky boy because he was putting me in sixth class again with the best teacher in the school, Mr Madden. Well, that nearly finished me. I started running from one end of the kitchen to the other roaring out of me and Mammy and Sheila had to grab a hold of me and pin me down on the sofa. You see, I knew all about Madden because I'd got him the two full years before that. Everybody calls him Mad Den because he goes out of his mind sometimes. He screams and tears his hair out and lifts boys up by the ears and bangs their heads against the blackboard to knock brains into them. He's a nervous wreck. Sometimes he can't hardly hold the chalk in his hands he's shaking that much. He's dead skinny and he's got black hair and a very pale face and he looks like a vampire. Everybody knows, whatever you do don't look at him unless he calls your name. Then you *better* look at him. The worst times I always remember were the Friday mornings once a month when he did this thing called parsing and analysis. That was the only time he did it, when we came back from confessions. Every first Friday all the ones above first class had to march four deep over to the

Cathedral. Then we sat down in lines outside the confession box. We were nearly afraid to breathe out because Mad Den was staring away at us with those dead man's eyes of his that never seemed to blink. He always made sure our class got to the cathedral before the other classes so's we could get back first and then he'd have plenty of time for parsing and analysis before the lunchhour. A whole lot of boys had nightmares about coming back from Confessions. I know they had because they told me. As soon as we got back into the classroom he made us open our English books very quickly. That was over four years ago and he did it two years running and I'm telling you now, anytime I ever see the word Parsing or the word Analysis written anywhere, I think right away of the terrible hammerings some boys got. I was okay. I was good at it. But I hated it because I couldn't stick seeing other boys getting beaten up and not being allowed to fight back. Stim McCullough made up a whole lot of extra sins one Friday so's he could stay in confession for longer so's Den wouldn't have as much time for hitting him. Gunga Doherty fainted one other Friday just as we were lining up to go back out of the cathedral. I think he was only putting it on. Dekky Crossan said he was definitely putting it on. But it didn't do him any good because Gunga was the first one Den asked when we got back up and then he gave him a really bad doing. Probably he *was* putting it on but do you see when he was lying on the floor of the cathedral, he was as white as a sheet. Honest to God.

But bad and all as Mad Den was, he was nowhere near as bad as the three commandants. Probably that was because he never actually slapped me or lifted me up by the ears. He nearly made me wet myself a whole lot of times and I hated him but he never actually *hit* me. But do you see those bastards in the College, they hit me nearly from the very start. It wasn't just me. They hit everybody except the geniuses. The first day I went I was up to high doh but dead happy at the same time. I'd got a bath and my hair was washed and I was wearing Frankie's old blazer and my own new grey flannel trousers. There seemed to be hundreds of us in the Main Study, all crammed in waiting for something to happen. The thing I remember most at the start was the smell of paint and sweat. There was a line of teachers along one wall and big rays of chalk dust coming in the windows. This boy standing next to me said to me - Was that you farted? and I didn't answer and McRide came down and grabbed him by the collar of his blazer and dragged him up to the front and gave him six with a big black strap. I didn't know who it was then but it was McRide all right. I nearly fainted when I saw it was a priest. I couldn't believe my eyes. Then he came down to me and started looking at me as if he was waiting for me to say something. It was scary. He's a big countryman and he's got these shoulders like the top of a barn door.

He said to me - What's your name?

That was the first time I stammered at the College but I got it out quick enough.

- Have you got a brother Frank? he said.

I wanted to say no because Frankie's a bit of a gangster sometimes but I had to say yes and then he said - Well, I'm telling you now so that you'll know in the future. You're going to have to watch yourself.

Then he went back up against the wall and folded his arms and said something to the priest beside him and the two of them started laughing away. You know the kind of laugh some big people do that's very loud and all but it's not a real laugh? That's the way they were laughing.

Those are the things I remember the most. I don't even remember anything about the English and Arithmetic tests we had to do right away. But it's funny. Even after what McRide did I was still happy. I knew the schoolbag I'd got from Frankie was soon going to be packed with books. Latin and French and Irish and Maths and Science and Religious Knowledge. And English. Novels and plays and poetry books. I'd close the buckles and fix the bag on my shoulders and clip the front part across my chest and walk down Marlborough Avenue to get the bus to the College every day. Mrs Wilson and the two Mrs Dohertys would probably be out doing the brass and saying things to each other.

- Who's that way the great big bag?

- That's Conn Murphy, Murray's youngest. He's supposed

to be a right clivir wee boy.

- He lucks well way the schoolbag on im, dozen he?

I didn't tell you before but Mammy bought Frankie a new bag as soon as I got the Qualifying and he passed his on to me right away. So the time they told me I was too young to go to Saint Paul's I'd this brilliant bag and I couldn't use it. It would have to lie in the attic for over a year. I mean, imagine going back to Rosebawn with this big brute of a schoolbag on your back and about three books in it. You'd never hear the end of it.

- Hi, Murphy. Whur ye goin way that? Are ye away on yer holidays or what?

That's where you'd have thought I was going if you'd seen inside it the day I ran away. Two T shirts, one pullover for the nights, two pairs of underpants and an extra pair of shoes wrapped up in an old Derry Journal. And still it wasn't even a quarter full. No socks. I forgot all about the socks. I got my savings, ten and sixpence, out of my dried milk tin and headed up Creggan Hill past the police barracks. I remember I looked over at it and I thought, It won't be that long before the cops are out hunting for me. Dragnet! I bought a sliced pan and a pint of milk in Paddy Sweeney's in Lewis Street and then I went on down Park Avenue. If they thought I was going to go back and sit in the same class as a whole lot of boys that were a year behind me they'd another think coming. And I'd be seeing all these new ones getting the tripe beaten out of them by Den. I wasn't sure where I was going but I was going all right. Not for good. Just long enough for them to know I was in earnest. When I went back Mammy would go up to see the president in Saint Paul's and I'd get in then.

By the time I got to the bottom of the Glen Road my feet were sore and I was sweating. I walked on out the Northland and then I stopped and leaned up against a gate pillar. The sun was scorching me so I went up this gravelly driveway till I got to a big oak tree. It was really massive. You couldn't see the top of it it was that high. The grass around it was like a big thick carpet. I knew this was going to be my first bed. It was lovely and cool. I sat down and looked over at a big grey mansion and then I let the tickly sweat trickle back into me. There's a poem called

The Vagabond in the reading book we did with Den and I started thinking of it when I was sitting there. He never did it with us but I learned a whole lot of it myself.

> Give to me the life I love
> Let the lave go by me.
> Give the jolly heaven above
> And byway nigh me.
>
> Bed in the bush with stars to see,
> Bread I dip in the river.
> There's the life for a man like me,
> There's the life forever.

There's two pictures beside it. In the first one the vagabond is walking dead happy along this country road with a bag at the end of a stick over his shoulder and in the second one he's lying down on his belly drinking water from a river.

I got a cramp in my leg so I stood up. I thought I'd better walk a bit. I hid the schoolbag behind the tree and went on up the road. That's how I got to Springtown Camp. The Yanks built Springtown when the war was on and then when the war was over they moved out and thousands of Catholics moved in. They'd no place to live because Creggan Estate wasn't even built yet. But the time I ran away Creggan was started about four years. Dermot Doherty out of my class in Rosebawn lived in Springtown and he told me his ma and da were going to get a house in Creggan. I don't know if they did or not. He'd a bed called a pallyfooky. That's a mattress that's filled with straw and you lie on it on the floor. I thought that was class. I still think it is. There was a top twenty song out when they were starting to build Creggan and people in Derry changed some of the words in it.

> - Abee, Abee, Abee my boy,
> What are you waiting for now?
> - A house in Creggan.
> - You promised to marry me

Some day in June.
It's never too late
And it's never too soon.
- This day, that day,
I dunno whadda say.
- Abee, Abee, Abee my boy,
What are you waiting for now?
- A house in Creggan.

Willie Cassidy was my desk partner the first year we had Den and it was dead funny because this day after school he brought me down to where he lived in East Wall beside Saint Columb's Hall and there seemed to be about a hundred other people living in his house. It looked like he'd forty or so brothers and sisters mostly near our age and tons of uncles and aunties. I didn't really think that but what I'm saying is, it looked like it. Then he told me him and his brothers and sisters and his ma and da lived in the one room and there were about ten other families in the house. But the really funny thing was, the next week he took me to his house again, only this time it was the new one in Creggan. The name of the street was Greenwalk. I loved that name and I still do. Not Something Street or Something Road or Something Avenue but Greenwalk. It must be called that because it's all green out in the front of the house, nearly like a field. The best thing was this secret space at the bay windows downstairs. It was the shape of a semi-circle because Willie's ma had a curtain going straight across from one wall to the other near the windows. The secret space was for Willie to do his homework in. He didn't need a desk or anything, he just lay on the carpet. I had to do mine on the kitchen table. There were brilliant echoes in the house and we roared up and down the stairs about fifty times. His ma didn't even scold us. She just kept smiling at us all the time. I wouldn't have minded going back but he never asked me.

Anyway, I was supposed to be telling you about me landing in Springtown. I was never in it before. There were all these huts the shape of tunnels and there was a fierce amount of boys and girls and about a hundred dogs at the very least. One of them was actually playing in a football match and when I was watching he jumped up and headed the ball. He was brilliant. Then the ball was hit past me for a throw in and I ran and got it and kicked it back. They stopped the game after a minute and one of them asked me if I wanted a side. So I said yes and he said - Right. Ye're fur us. Play up front. Ye're not allowed tay mooch.

Some boys on the other team started acting up and everybody gathered round and started shouting their heads off even though they were right beside each other but then our captain roared at the dog - Go home, Davy! Go! Go! and he kicked him up the arse and he went then.

Next thing was, the captain said - Okay, wur even now.

I was that tired with the walking and all I missed two sitters in a row. The second time one of the boys in my team shouted at me - Ye tube ye, ye kin play noan. The dog was bettern fucken *you*.

I shouted back at him - Who d'ye think ye're callin a tube? and that's when I remembered I was a yellabelly. But it was too late. I'd said it.

- I'll root yer hole! he roared and he came over and pushed his nose up against mine.

- You an whose army? I roared back but I felt like crying.

- I'll stick may fucken boot so far down your throat ye'll be shiteing leller fur forty days, he roared.

- Mick up yer mind, Brads, somebody shouted.

- Give over, Brads, somebody else shouted. - Wur sick a hearin that wan.

The whole two teams were crowded round us in a circle and I said to myself , This is me in here, this isn't some other boy. This is me.

I thought I was going to faint but I still kept my mitts up and my nose pressed against his.

- Who sid that? roared Brads and then everything happened dead fast. These two men came out of nowhere and pulled me and Brads apart and nearly right away two women with voices like foghorns started shouting.

- Yer dinners is ready!

- If yeez don't come now thur'll bay noan left fur yeez!

That was the match over. Most of the boys went right away and then after about a minute I was standing there on my own. I suddenly found this smell of fried onions. I started to think of the sliced pan. I hadn't any butter with me. A big brown dog came over and sniffed away at my bum. He was a bad-looking article so I didn't chase him or try to walk away or anything. I just stood there and let him smell me. After a wee while he got fed up and went over and did a pee against the side of one of the huts. I wondered if I should go home for my dinner and not say anything and then run away again the next morning.

I was nearly a complete wreck by the time I got back to the house. The smell of the Irish stew hit me as soon as I went in the door and Mammy showed me this parcel of Dell comics that came from our cousins in Chicago. Frankie had already opened it and he was up in the attic reading some of them. She seemed really pleased to see me and she didn't even ask me any questions. I took the milk and bread out of my schoolbag that I'd put behind the sofa in the front room and brought them in to her and said - I bought these fur ye, and she just said thanks and told me to go to the toilet and wash my hands and then she put out my dinner.

I'm finished with Sally. That's the reason I didn't write anything this good while, because I didn't feel like it. Charlie says how could I be finished with her when I wasn't even started with her? But he's wrong about that. We did start but I never let on to him. We started this day she came over to me when I was playing headie by myself at our gable wall and she asked me would I go to *Hamlet* with her that night. Well, honest to God, I never even knew it was the name of a picture and I said - Wh-wh-whur is it?

I meant Where's the hamlet? You know the way hamlet means small village. And she said - Iss on in the Midland. Sister Immaculata towl us way hadday go tay it seein wur doin it. Second house okay?

That's when the penny sort of dropped or maybe it was more like a halfpenny. So I said - Aw. Right.

And she said - Annemarie was tay go way may but she's got the flu an the night's the last night iss on.

I was that glad she never jubed on how stupid I was I didn't even understand right at the start that she was making a date with me. But after I got into the house I thought I was going to take the diarrhoea. I went up and locked myself in the bathroom and sat on the edge of the bath. I couldn't kept steady with the trembling. You know, thinking about *her* going to be sitting beside *me* in the dark and her leg about three inches away from mine. I let on to Mammy after dinner I was going to the shows with Charlie and I did it that well I nearly believed it myself. I'd money left from the Saturday before when I was going to see *The Secret Life of Walter Mitty* until Gander told me it was shite so there was no problem *there*. But before I went I must have peed about ten times inside of two hours. I changed my underpants just in case there'd be a smell off me and I washed my hair and cleaned my teeth and washed my face with Frances's soap. It was the only soap there was in the bathroom and it was inside this white plasticky shelly thing. I was that long in there Mammy probably thought I was sick.

- Are ye awright, son? she shouted.

- Aye, I'm awright, I shouted back.

My heart was going like drums along the Mohawk. Jesus my Saviour, I thought, what's it going to be like when I'm walking beside her, *sitting* beside her? What's she going to do? And why did she pick the last house when she must have known it would be really dark when we'd be coming back and for all she knew I might do *any*thing to her? Probably she couldn't get out of the house before that. Probably that was the reason.

I didn't call at her house. The way I worked it, we were to meet at the Waterside bus stop in the Guildhall Square at eight o'clock. We only live five doors from each other but I didn't want anybody to see us walking down Marlborough Avenue together. When I saw her coming towards me at the bus stop my thing shot up and it wouldn't come down. Debbie Reynolds. Her hair was, I don't know how to describe it, it was like an angel's, I suppose, and she'd on this wee short blue overcoat and you could see her legs a bit above the knees and they were sort of light brown. When she stood beside me I smelt the perfume and the powder right away. Jesus, Mary and Joseph, this is serious, I thought.

- Ye smell lick a girl, she said.

- Wh-wh-what d'ye mean? I said.

- Thur's some smell off ye lick a girl, she said.

- Ye're off yer head, I said. - Wa-wa-what are ye talkin about?

I didn't mean to say that but I hardly knew what I was saying.

When we got on the bus she told me Annemarie was a bitch because she wouldn't go to *Hamlet* with her.

- I thought ye towl may sssshe was ssssick, I said.

- Aw aye, she said. - She *is* sick. Aye, she's sick awright but she wussin goin tay go way may anyway. Two fur the Midland.

The conductor gave her the tickets and the change. I sat there really sore. It was still standing up and there was me letting on to be all casual as if it wasn't even there. All she had to do was look down once and it would be obvious. I kept staring straight ahead, thinking, Why are you such a disgusting brute, Murphy? Here she is right beside you and she's so beautiful and perfect and look at you, you dirty animal. Dear Jesus, what's it going to do if she kisses you or holds your hand or even presses against you?

- Hiv I got the plague or somethin? she said.

- Wa-wa-what d'ye mean? I said.

- Well, if ye wur any furler away from may ye'd bay sittin in the passageway, she said.

- Naw, I said. - I jist doh wa-wa-wannay be ssssssteppin on yer toes bay accident. I lick your shhhhhoes bay the wa-wa-way.

Jesus. I hadn't even *looked* at her shoes.

- No danger a that, anyway, she said.

- No danger a wa-wa-what?

- No danger a ye steppin on may toes, I'm sayin.

- I hadday do fffffifty lines fffffur Bonzo, I said.

- Ye did not.

- I did sssso. He was at the Brandywell on Ssssaturday an he ssssaw may usin may mirror tay ffffflash the sssssun in the Linfield players eyes. Ye know I do ballboy.

- Aw aye. Right.

- I waited tay the sssssecond half tay they wu-wu-wur playing way thur backs tay the sssssun an then I tried tay bline them.

- An what?

- The Derry Journal ph-ph-ph-ph - man come over n tuck the mirror offa may n towl may tay catch maysel on.

- How'd Bonzo come intay it?

- He wa-wa-was at the match n he sssssaw may. Then - wa-wa-wait tay ye hear - then the nixt day I was doin a bitta experimentin wa-wa-way another mirror in our ffffront room. I got the sssssun sh-sh-sh - reflectin in it n ffffflashed it ontay the big mirror in Bonzo's ffffront room jist across ffffrom our house. I was tryin tay git it tay come back at may if ye know wa-wa-what I mean.

- I folly ye.

- But then wa-wa-wait d'ye hear. I got a real sh-sh-shock cause I sssssaw his ffffiss appearin right in ffffront a *his* mirror. He sssssstared over at may n I jooked down as quick as I cud but he musta knew it was me awright cause there on Monday he towl may I hadday write *I must not refffflect the rays a the sssssun in the eyes a unsssusssspectin people* ffffifty times in Fffffrench. D'ye wannay hear may translatin it?

- Naw. Why wur ye tryin tay bline the Linfield players?

- Cause last week they wa-wa-wur playin Derry in the Irish Cup up in Wa-wa-windsor Park up in Belfast n a whole lotta thur sssssss - ffffans thew Derry su-su-su-supporters outa the big grandstand.

- Gawn away tay hell, she said.

- I sssssswear, I said. - D'ye not read about it? It wa-wa-was all over the Journal sssssso it wa-wa-was. But wait tay ye hear the laugh anyway. Two a the wa-wa-wans they thew out wa-wa-wur Protestant ministers sssssupportin Derry. They thew them out cause they thought they wur priests.

- But what had the Linfield players got tay do way that? she said.

- Eh?

- What had the Linfield players got tay do way that?

- Ye don't understand. Thur all the wan.

- I do unnerstand, Conn Murphy. Ye're oney a bigot, she said.

- I wa-wa-wa-wa-what!

- Ye heard may the first time. Ye're oney a bigot.

- I'm sssssayin nothin more, I said.

I was jumping mad with her. But there was one good thing about the blazing row. It got me all calm down there and I stayed that way for a good while. I was still so raging I didn't even realise she'd got the tickets to get in till I was standing there at the wee office paying for mine and she said - Mawn on. I got them.

I never even offered to give her the money for mine. We didn't say a word to each other for about an hour after that but it didn't matter much anyway because the Movietone news was on when we got in and then the trailer and then the picture.

Hamlet was useless. It was all about this gack called Hamlet that talked away to himself about getting revenge on his uncle for killing his da and stuff like that and he never did anything about it till it was too late. I didn't understand it that well but you knew to listen to him he'd half his slates missing. And there was this girl in it that wasn't the full shilling either. I don't remember what you called her but Hamlet was supposed to be going out with her and she was a real beaut and he never gave over slagging her and she ended up drowning herself. Do you see by the time it was over, there must have been nearly as many dead bodies as there were in *The Bodysnatcher* that was on in the Palace after Christmas. You know the one where the two heavies kept digging up graves for the doctor and then when they ran out of stiffs they started killing people. But you'd have thought that with all the different people getting revenge in it *Hamlet* would have been fantastic and it was actually one of the worst shows I ever saw in my life. The boy that did Hamlet was a puke anyway. You could see the whole time he was only acting. You know, shouting away when he didn't need to shout and things like that and going on dead dramatic and speaking this perfect English. I wonder if Arthur or Bernard ever saw it. They'd probably think it was brilliant.

I whispered to Sally in the middle of it - This is wa-wa-wile lick a play.

- It *is* a play. Are ye stupid or what? It *is* a play, she hissed back at me. - They made it intay a picture. Did ye not see at the start of it it was bay William Shakespeare?

I kept my mouth shut after that. We're doing *Julius Caesar* and Shakespeare wrote that and that's really good but *Hamlet* was desperate. But do you want to know the worst part of it? It was the filth that was in it. I don't know why it wasn't made an X picture. Near the end when Hamlet and this other boy started fighting each other with swords they'd on these funny sort of tights that made their tool boxes stick away out and swing about like moneybags. It was a disgrace so it was. I didn't know where to put myself. I knew Sally could see everything so she couldn't help knowing what *I* was like. I sat there wondering how could I ever look her in the face again or go on all nice to her when she knew what I was like underneath. Okay, I wasn't anywhere near as big as them yet but I might have been for all she knew. It's a mortal sin anyway to be showing that with girls watching. It was completely disgusting. There was Hamlet and the other boy prancing round showing off their big things and dirty bulging bollocks as if they were *muscles* or something. There was no need for it. All the *Robin Hood* and *Three Musketeers* shows I was at, you never saw anything. And then do you see the time Hamlet was lying dead and this other boy, not the boy he was fighting with because he was dead too by that time, but this other boy that liked Hamlet, *he* said - *Goodnight, sweet prince* to Hamlet, and as soon as he was finished saying it I felt Sally's head on my shoulder and she whispered - *Goodnight, sweet prince*. Isn't that wile sad, Conn? and all you could see was Hamlet and the other boy lying on their backs with the whole caboodle nearly busting out of their tights and there was Sally snuggling up to me. *Me, another man.* I felt her breath tickling my ear and my cheek and that was it. Up it went. I was afraid she was going to start reaching for one of my hands. I would have been in bother there because the two of them were sitting on my lap covering it up and I didn't want her poking around *there*. I sat looking at the screen and saying aspirations in my head she would leave them alone. She did but she wasn't finished with me yet. Coming out of the Midland she linked on to me and said - Mawn up Distillery Brae way.

I felt her right pap pushing against the outside of my arm and that's when I panicked a wee bit. I said - Sh-sh-sure thur's a bus ssssstop here right outside the picture house.

She said - Way kin git the other bus up in Spencer Road jist as quick. *I* feel lick walkin.

The Midland's just next to Duke Street and Duke Street's parallel to Spencer Road and Distillery Brae goes up in between the two of them. It's also the darkest street in Derry. Well, *I* think it is . It looked pitch black to me that night anyway.

- Mawn, she said.

- Naw, I said, - I think iss goin tay rain. Wa-wa-way'd git ssssssoaked before wa-wa-way got half wa-wa-way up.

- Sure we kin tick shelter at that git up there, she said.

There's this big gate part of the way up and it's like a really deep alcove and you could be in there doing *anything* and nobody passing by would even see you.

So I said - Luck, I think thass our bus comin now.

And she said - What the frig's wrong way ye anyway?

And I said - Wa-wa-wa-what are ye talkin about? Thur's nothin wrong wa-wa-way may. I doh wa-wa-wannay miss the bus. Luck, here it is now.

She never opened her mouth to me all the way back. But the time I was leaving her at the door I said - That lucks lick a great sh-sh-show thass on Thursday, Fffffriday and Sssssaturday.

- What show? she said.

- The wa-wa-wan thass on in the Midland. *Kansas Raiders*. Sh-sh-sure ye mine wa-wa-way ssssssaw the trailer the night jist after wa-wa-way come in. Audie Murphy's in it. He does Jesse James in it.

- What about it? she said.

- Wa-wa-wa-wa-wa-wa-wud ye go?

- What d'ye mean wud I go?

- I mean wa-wa-wa-wa-wud ye go tay it?

- Who way?

- Way me. Who d'ye think wa-wa-ay? I'll pay fffffur us this time.

She didn't say anything for a good while. Then she said - Awright.

- Sssssso. I'll sssssee ye at the Guildhall at eight on Sssssaturday? Okay?

- Okay.

- Sssssee ya, I said.

The next night I went to Father Friel in the Cathedral. He's new and I thought he might be all right. But he nearly ate the bake off me. I said to him - Ffffaller, isss fffffive days sssssince may last Confession. I've no sssssins tay confess. I jist wa-wa-wanted tay ast ye sssssomethin.

- Yes, child?

- Thur's this girl, Ffffaller....

- Yes?

- ... an she really licks may, Ffffaller , and I lick *her* too but I doh wa-wa-wannay commit a mortal sssssssssssssin.

- What age are you, may I ask?

- I'll bay fffffifteen June comin.

- You're still at school?

- Yes Ffffaller.

- What school would that be now?

- Sssssint Paul's, Ffffaller.

- Ah! Well now. You shouldn't be thinking about girls at your age and you studying. You'll be doing your Junior this year, will you?

- Yes Ffffaller.

- Well, concentrate on your studies. There's be time enough to think about girls when you're eighteen.

- But Ffffaller....

- Yes?

- ... Fffffaller, I really lick er an I wa-wa-wanny go wa-wa-way er but I think sh-sh-she's goin tay go wa-wa-way sssssomebody else if I don't do sssssomethin.

- What age is this girl?

- She wa-wa-wants may tay go up this alleyway–

- That's enough of that. There's only one reason a redblooded Irish boy would take a girl up an alleyway and you and I both know what that is, don't we?

- Yes Fffffaller. But Fffffaller.....

- Yes?

- Is it a sssssssssssin tay kiss a girl?

I heard the rustle and the swish of his soutane and he started to move his feet about on the floor.

- I suppose this is something you should know, he said. - If you kiss a girl you commit a venial sin and if you embrace her you commit a mortal sin. Are you clear about that now?

- Yes Fffffaller.

- I'm warning you now. Stay away from girls until you're eighteen.

- Yes Fffffaller.

- Now tell me a sin from your past life and I'll give you absolution.

Two days after that was Saturday. That's the day we get out early from the College. On my way home I went to Confession in the Long Tower chapel. I knew there was a young priest there called Father Duff so I went to him. When he opened the shutter I said - Fffffaller, iss oney two days fffffrom may last Confession but I've no ssssssins tay tell, I jist wa-wa-wannay ast ye about sssssomethin.

- Yes, my son. Calm yourself down. God is good, remember, God is good.

- Yes Fffffaller.

- Now, what is it?

- Fffffaller, is it a sssssssssssin tay kiss a girl or embrace er?

There was no answer.

- Fffffaller?

- Yes. Yes. What age are you?

- I'm nearly ffffffteen, Ffffaller.

- Hmmm. Kissing in itself is harmless. A mother kisses her child to express love. In many countries kissing is used as form of greeting. Did you know that?

- I think ssssso, Ffffaller.

- But the act of kissing can sometimes cause arousal and is therefore dangerous. Do you understand what I'm saying?

- Yes Ffffaller.

- As for embracing, that's another matter. The best rule to remember is this. If the top halves of your bodies touch, it's a venial sin. If the bottom half of your bodies touch, it's a mortal sin. Is that understood?

- Yes Ffffaller.

- Now just tell me any sin from your past life and I can give you absolution.

Kansas Raiders wasn't great. Jesse James shows aren't anywhere near as good as they used to be. Sally didn't enjoy it. I knew that for certain because she kept sighing and puffing out very hard sometimes as if she was blowing flies away. When it was over we got the Duke Street bus back to the Guildhall. On our way up to Marlborough I asked her if she would go to *Return of the Frontiersman* that was going to be on the Saturday after.

- Whur's it on? she asked me.

- The Ffffflaypit, I said.

- The Flaypit! she said. - Ye muss bay mad. I wudn't bay seen dead in that pliss.

- I'll tick ye tay the balcony, I said.

- Naw, she said. - Sure the flays in there kin climb.

- Thur's a good sh-sh-show on in the Palace, I said. - Wa-wa-way cud go tay that.

- What is it? she said.

- Iss a new wa-wa-wan. *Drumbeat*. I said. - I cannay mine who's in it but I hear iss a great sh-sh-show.

111

- I dunno, she said. - Way'll see.

- Wa-wa-wa-will ye let may know the marra? I asked her.

- I dunno, she said. - Don't you bay astin may agin. *I'll* let ye know if I'm goin.

I didn't like the sound of that. But I'll tell you the thing about it that makes me really sick. I've committed so many mortal sins since those two nights thinking about her sitting beside me and the smell of her and the tickle on my ear and my cheek and her hand on my arm outside the first night and imagining her thinking about Hamlet and the other boy's tool-boxes and what *could* have happened at the gate that I would probably have had less to tell the priest if I'd gone up Distillery Brae and got stuck into her.

The Saturday after that was hard to take. It was starting to get dark and a crowd of us were sitting on Gallagher's wall and four wee girls from Creggan Hill came over and we were all talking for a while and then Gander said - How about a game a Spin the Bottle?

Smith went into the house and brought out an empty wine bottle and I leaned back and got my ball out of Gallagher's garden and said - Anywan fffffur a game a bootie?

- Sure wur playing Spin the Bottle, Gander said.

Charlie and Stoopy were there but none of the two of them would come with me so I practised by myself using my left foot up against our gable wall. That meant there were the exact same number of boys and girls. The ones from the hill are wagons anyway. The whole four of them fancy Gander. Spin the Bottle's a dirty game. What happens is, everybody stands in a circle with the bottle in the middle. Somebody spins it and whoever the neck ends up pointing at goes up Cnoc lane and waits. If it's a boy, then it's only the girls that stand in the circle for the next spin. Whoever it points to has to go round the lane to the boy and they do whatever they want round there. Even thinking about it makes my bowels all watery. Anyway, whenever they're finished the boy comes back down and the girl stays up and then it's the boys' turn to stand in the circle. It means nearly everybody gets at least two gos in a row up the lane. So anyway, I was there booting the ball up against the gable with my

left for practice because I've got a very bad left and after a wee
while they stopped the game for a minute because Head the
Ball Boggs came. You'd nearly think he smelt the girls or something from away up Demesne and ran to get his tightest
trousers on because when he landed down he'd on these lime
green ones and you could see everything. He's only a gack but
gack or no gack they let him join in anyway and once he got
started he kept pulling away at his trousers as if they were loose
at the waist. He's an animal. Then the next thing that happened
nearly finished me because who came up the avenue but Sally
and you wanted to see her. She was wearing these bright yellow
shorts that were dead wide at the bottom. And she'd on a sort
of a mauve T shirt and I'm nearly sure I saw the track of her nipples. What a bitch. She went over and waited till they were
ready to spin the bottle again and then she asked if she could
join in. She was really beautiful. Jesus, you should have seen
her. I forgot all about my left and started to bang the ball as hard
as I could with my right and I was keeping turning round about
every three seconds. The first two times she was up the lane it
was Trevor Smith and Charlie and she was back down that
quick they would hardly have had the time to say hello to her.
But then the time Boggs was up waiting by himself the neck
pointed at her and she walked up towards the lane really slow.
She must have been up there ten minutes. Whatever it was, she
was that long I knew to listen to the rest of them they were
thinking of going home.

When Boggs came back down again he looked like one real
satisfied bastard. He'd his back to me but I could tell. Sally did-
n't wait for the next boy to come up. She came flying down right
behind Boggs and ran on home. She went racing past me and I
stopped kicking the ball and looked at her. I couldn't see her
face because she'd her hand up to it but I saw her shorts and
they weren't yellow anymore. Not at the back anyway. At the
back they were all green. It was pretty dark by this time but I
could see them and they were as green as grass.

The whole crowd of them started to go home. I could hear
people shouting Cheerio to each other, and I kept kicking as
hard as I could. My eyes were watering away and I didn't know

who to hate the most, Sally or Boggs or me. After a while I stopped and turned round and they were all away. The street was empty except for me. I went into the house and ran straight up to the attic and lay on the bed looking at the wall. I knew if I closed my eyes I would cry so I just lay staring at this stupid pattern on the wallpaper. I was glad when I heard Mammy's voice calling me to come down.

I know how I got the stammer. I remember. I was three or four at the time and I was out in the back yard hoking away at the ash pit with a wooden spoon Mammy always used for mixing the dough and I ended up with this Flag sauce bottle stuck right between my eyes like a big brown horn. I still have the scar and it's the shape of an X. Mammy says I got the stutter from copying Uncle Eddie but that's not true. I didn't. She calls it a stutter. Eddie's brilliant at the substitute word. If today is Tuesday and somebody asks him what day he's getting off work early, he starts saying Wednesday and then he realises in a split second that he won't be able to say it right so he says - The marra.

The substitute word got me into bother one time last year. Charlie said he was going to call for me and I told him I'd homeworks to do and he asked me what time I'd be finished them and I started saying Six but I couldn't say it so then I tried to say About six and I still couldn't say it so I said - In about an hour's time. Well. That meant I had to do them nearly twice as fast as usual and I ended up getting scalped the next day.

The funny thing about it was, it never actually affected me till I started going to the College. I had it but nobody knew except me. It's hard to explain. Anyway, once I got to the College I couldn't talk right. The Irish classes were the worst. It's bad enough if you've got a stammer in English but do you see if you've got it in Irish too, well , you may as well go and jump in the Foyle, especially if you've got The Pogue and McRide day about. It's hard enough to speak in Irish even if

114

you're normal. You want to hear the sneers of McRide at some of the boys trying to pronounce things. You're supposed to speak as if you're clearing your head to get rid of one of those big watery snotters that you can sniff from your nose sometimes down into your throat. I'm so scared of the two of them I haven't even one ordinary spittle left after I get the first word out. That's *if* I get it out. And if you don't have plenty of spare spittles you end up trying to talk Irish with a Derry accent. It's the stupidest language I ever heard. I hate the Pogue. His real name's Mahoney but we call him The Pogue because Pogue Ma Hone's the Irish for Kiss My Arse and we all know that's what he wants us to do to *his* arse. It's not written like that in Irish. That's just how it's pronounced. If you think I'm going to write it in Irish you can forget about it. He's a big filthy animal with a fat red face and gleamy glinty glasses and two rows of rotten teeth. He wears really loud clothes like mustard shirts and red ties with blue spots and he walks with his legs away out wide like a spider that hasn't changed its underpants for a month. He's the most disgusting looking brute I ever saw in my life. Some days he makes us come out one at a time and obey his orders in Irish. I'm going to write them down now in English.

Sit on the floor.
Put your foot on the chair.
Take your foot off the chair.
Put your other foot on the chair.

The whole lot of us still wear short trousers although I'll be getting long ones if I get into Senior. When you were sitting there doing what he wanted he always crouched away down looking at you, but he wasn't looking at your face. He was looking up your trousers. A whole lot of the time he was doing it the front of his tongue stuck out between his lips like somebody's wee thing and it jerked about for a while and then he told you to go back to your seat. Each time he finished with me I went back and I always sat looking at the wall. I'm not going in for the College sports next year. My first three years I was lined up with other boys for the start of each race and The Pogue was always sitting on a chair nearly beside us looking us up and down. It was because we were standing in our vests and shorts. He just sat there gawking with his big mouth lying half open and his tongue going round his lips. He doesn't even help the other teachers to organise things. He just sits there like a big spastic. I'm sick of it. The dean's always at the sports and he must see him and he still lets him do it. I don't know where the president bes. Probably in his office.

I never said to anybody about him. You never hear boys saying he's a dirty brute or anything. Nobody talks about him as far as I can see. Nobody tells either. I know that for sure because I would have heard if any ma or da came up to the President. Would *you* tell? *I* wouldn't. What would I say? She couldn't handle it. She's really embarrassed since she got the false teeth in and anyway the president would only make her feel stupid. She never went past the sixth book. That's what fourth class is called down in the Hillside. Sometimes I think what it would be like if she did go up to see him. I know she wouldn't sleep right the night before and then the day she was going she'd take about an hour to fix her hair and get on the right clothes when she should be doing other things. She'd have to go down the breakneck steps and walk over half a mile to get the bus and another quarter of a mile nearly after she got off the bus. That part would be bad. I mean the part where she'd be going up the walks. I know she'd be thinking people were looking at her out the windows and they probably would be and some of them would be laughing too because she's only a wee woman and that's the way boys at the College go on. After that she'd have to go up those six steep steps that have no railings on them and then two big flights of stairs before she got to the president's office. By that time she'd be ready for the hills.

Anyway, it would only do *me* harm as well. The president might get on to The Pogue but he wouldn't sack him. The other commandants wouldn't be long hearing about it and they'd give me a bad time. A thing happened the year before I left Rosebawn. Frankie came home from the College this day and one of his ears was all big and purple. It turned out some teacher banged his head up and down on the desk. Mammy was sick in bed with blood pressure but Sheila was ready to go up and tear the teacher's hair out. That's what she said she was going to do. She would have done it too only Arthur and Bernard, who were left the College long before that, said she was to leave it to them. And do you know what they did? I was there. I heard them. They told Frankie to keep his head down or he'd only get into more bother. Frankie said back to them -How far down? On the floor so they can kick it?

The Pogue's not the only dirty brute. McRide's nearly as bad. And he's the biggest savage of the whole lot too. One day we had him he kept slapping Martin Ward on the same hand even after Martin told him it was cut. And one other day he hit Sticky McEldowney on the side of the head with his fist and knocked him out. Sticky's a boarder. Boarders get it harder. I never told you that. Boarders get it really hard. McRide just said - Wheel him out, and then when the two boys were carrying Sticky out, the bastard just went on calling out sentences and swaggering back and forward with this fancy walk he has. A while before we got the summer holidays he got us to translate this sentence into Irish:

There is a protuberance on every boy's body.

He kept smiling away to himself at the start when boys were telling him they didn't know the Irish for protuberance. Then he told us to try and think of a word in English that meant the same as protuberance. I was one of the first ones he asked and when he asked me I felt all tight and annoyed. His big red ploughman's face was staring down at me and he kept shouting - Well? Well? and I said Bulge before I knew what I was saying. I shouldn't have said anything. I should have let on to stammer. But, anyhow, I said it. Somebody else said Extension and then Toads Walker, who's a bit of a genius, said Projection and McRide said Very Good and then he wrote the Irish on the board.

He's a dirty cunt. He's from a place called Slievefada that's up the arse of Donegal. He talks with this put on posh accent but that's where he's from. I know because my Aunt Biddy

117

works in the parochial house there and she's friendly with him. She wouldn't believe what I said the time she was down in Aunt Stella's house last Christmas. I told her everybody hated him at the College and she couldn't take it in. She said he was very well thought of in Slievefada. Charlie was there with me and he backed me up. He said to Biddy - Does he hiv a different name up there or what? Day the wans up there call him Faller Jekyll?

Biddy said that was a very unchristian thing to say about a priest and me and Charlie laughed. But we never told her about him being a dirty brute. We were going out when she called after us - I'll tell yeez wan thing I'll bate ye yeez don't know. He's an exorcist so he is. The Bishop appointed him an exorcist. So what day yeez think about that? Eh?

We said nothing back and, to tell you the truth, we didn't know what to think about it. We told Gander the next day and all *he* said was - An exorcist. Fuck me. A fucken exorcist. That's the best wan I ivir heard.

The Junior results came out last Thursday. I got three distinctions and two credits and I passed everything except Science. I even passed Irish. So it just shows. There's one Irish genius that's not a wanker. I'm not talking about me. I *am* a wanker. I'm talking about whoever it was marked my paper.

Mammy got a letter yesterday saying I'm allowed into Senior. That means I'll be getting long trousers. Charlie said that'll make the hairs grow all around my tool-box. I didn't tell *him* but they're growing there already this long time.

We're back over a month. You want to see the amount of work they give us to do. And I've got The Couch for History and The Pogue and McRide again for Irish. I need a good puke. (And what I've got are three bad ones!). I know what you're probably wondering. You're probably wondering why I haven't left this dump. Well, I'll tell you why. Mammy. I tried to get her to let me leave last July and this July too but by the time she'd finished with me I was sorry I ever opened my mouth. The same thing the two times. Well, nearly. Last year I told her I'd work really hard if I got changing to the Strand Tech and this year I told her I wasn't smart enough for the College anymore. I said I'd take care of her and get the messages and do the dishes and keep the house clean and give her nearly all my dole money and look for a job as well. You think that's sissy, me saying I'd do all those things? Wait till I tell you this then. I'd put an *apron* on me to get out of this place. I'd nearly wear a skirt so I would. But she was fit for me anyway. Each time she went on about the College helping me to get a job with a pension. That got me all excited, I *don't* think. But then she came out with this stuff about her and Daddy being worried about money from the day and hour they got married and the two of them knowing nobody'd ever get anywhere if they hadn't an education and then this year she told me about him asking her to promise the time he was dying that she'd put all the younger ones through Saint Paul's. What could I do? *I* was the one getting the shite knocked out of me ten months a year and each of the two times *I* ended up feeling sorry for *her*. Last year I walked away in a sort of a huff but this year I told her I'd try and stick it out.

There was one day there I really thought she was going to die. It was last Saturday ,the day the choir boys' excursion to Portrush was on, and the doctor and the priest landed in one after the other. Nobody told me they were coming. I was on my way out of the toilet and I saw the back of Doctor O'Sullivan's head going down the stairs. I waited for him and Sheila to finish talking in the porch and as soon as I heard the click of the front door I went down and asked her what was wrong and before she could answer the knocker went and nearly made me jump out of my skin. It was Father McNally. When he was up the stairs I asked Sheila again and she said Mammy's blood pressure was up a bit and all she needed was some rest. She must have thought I was really stupid. You don't get a doctor *and* a priest for somebody if they just need a wee rest. I told Sheila I wasn't going to go on the excursion. She said not to be acting like a big wain because she'd enough bother without that and it would only put Mammy's blood pressure up even more if I stayed. After Father McNally left I went up to see her. She was lying flat on her back, not on her side the way she usually lies. She was all flushed and she looked very old and she had her teeth out. I wished she'd put them back in because it's terrible to say this but I stood there looking at her thinking I was too young to have a mammy that age. She'd the beads in her hands and her eyes were half way up to heaven, the same way they always are when she's praying. I wanted to put one of my hands on top of one of her hands or hug her or do something like that but I didn't because if I had she might have thought she was going to die and anyway I'd only have ended up crying probably. She told me to make sure and enjoy Barry's Amusements so I knew then I was going. I told her I'd see her when I got back and she said to tell Sheila to give me five bob and that made me feel good and bad at the same time because I was only supposed to get half a crown.

For the most of the first half of the day anytime I forgot about her and then remembered I felt like a real prick. Each time that happened I prayed hard for her into myself because I knew if I didn't and she got worse and died I'd be partly to blame. So after a good while I decided the best thing to do was to be really sad and not to go on any more of the amusements or buy ice-cream or anything like that. But then Gander got me standing at a wall outside Barry's and he said he'd pay for me on the ghost train so I went. I don't know why. I didn't really want to go. It turned out not much good anyway. It was changed from last year. It wasn't very scary at all. I couldn't believe the way Gander was going on, shouting out of him. You know, things like - Jesus! What about that, Spud! Did ye see that? I thought to myself, He's nearly the same age as me. It's about time he grew up.

When it stopped these two girls got off in front of us. One of them had blonde hair and the other one had black hair. They'd spent the whole five minutes or whatever it was we were on the ghost train screaming their heads off and I just thought, Girls! and I hardly even looked near them even after I nearly tripped over the wee dark one when she was bending down to pick up a hanky she dropped. But whenever they moved on Gander started his big man stuff.

- Je SUS! he whispered at me. - Wud ye luck at the tits them two has on them!

Well, the thing that happened next changed the day. He got me to follow them with him. The only reason I went was to make him think girls were no bother to me.

- Don't worry, Spud, he said. - Ye're safe enough. Wur not goin tay chat them up or try an git off or anything lick that. Ye'll be awright way me.

They'd these ponytails like some of the girls in Derry have now. They're sexy things all right, ponytails. I don't know what it is but there's something very sexy about them. I think maybe it's the way they bounce about. As well as that these two had tight jeans on them and they'd scarves round their chests. I'm telling you. They'd scarves covering their paps and they'd got them tied in big bows at the back. Blackie's was pink with green spots and Blondie's was brown. Brown or red. I'm not sure. I was walking along thinking, All you need to do to strip them right down to the waist is loosen the bows. Just one pull for each of them. I could hardly believe what was going through my mind and Mammy lying sick in Derry, maybe even dying. I said the Memorare into myself but the whole time I was saying it my belly was swinging back and forward like a cement mixer. *Remember, O most gracious Virgin Mary, it has never been known that anyone who fled onto thy protection, implored thy aid or sought thy intercession was left unaided by thee.* I couldn't remember what came next. I knew it off by heart but I forgot it. I tried to keep my eyes on the backs of their heads so's I wouldn't be looking at their bows or their bare shoulders or their blue jean bums but it didn't work. The backs of their heads had ponytails and you know what *they're* like. Everything about them was sexy and I

121

hadn't even seen their faces yet. Just when I was going to say to Gander that we were getting too close to them what do you think happened? The fair haired one turned round and looked straight at us and then she dunted the other one with her shoulder and *she* turned round too and she was the dead spit of Natalie Wood out of *Rebel Without A Cause*, only a bit younger. But they didn't stop. They just kept on walking, only now they were starting to slow down a bit. The blonde one had freckles and she was about half as good-looking as Natalie, which was still pretty good-looking. And they were so smooth the way they walked and the way they talked to each other and they weren't in the least hurry about anything. I don't know why it is but classy-looking girls always seem to be thinking really deep thoughts that you couldn't think yourself in a hundred years and there's always something mysterious and dead special about them and you can never think of what to say to them except maybe something stupid. I know ordinary-looking girls could have brilliant minds like Agatha Christie or Richmal Crompton but you never think that when you look at them.

All of a sudden the two of them turned round together and we nearly banged right up against them. Jesus. Imagine if we had. You know what I'm talking about? Jesus.

- Are yous lookin for somebody? the blonde one said. She sounded like a real hard ticket but she'd these amazing blue eyes like you'd see on a Crolly doll.

- I'm waitin, she said. - What's your game?

- Ah, I said.

Gander said damn all.

What I was trying to do was not look at their chests but that was a total impossibility. And I'm not even going to tell you about the part of their jeans below their stomachs. I'm not even going to think about that now.

- Well? I'm waitin.

That was still the doll talking. I was just going to open my mouth to say something else. It might have been Ah again for all I know, but whatever it was going to be I didn't get saying it because Gander started at last.

- Whur yeez from? Derry? he said. He didn't sound like

himself at all. I don't know what he sounded like but he didn't sound like himself.

- Naw, we're not from Derry, but *yous* are, aren't yous?

That was Natalie talking.

- I know yous are from the sound of yous, she said.

How could she have known that about me? All I said was Ah and you can't say Ah with a Derry accent. But I started nodding away at my head anyway, dead civil and all, to let her know she was right about us being from Derry. I wanted her to see I wasn't arguing or anything. You know, that I was really mature. The only thing was, I kept nodding for ages. She was a real beaut. I tried to stop the head going but I couldn't. Do you believe that? I couldn't stop nodding the head. She was the most beautiful person I ever saw in my life except maybe the real Natalie Wood or Marilyn Monroe. And the amazing part of it was, she was looking at *me* all the time. She never even took Gander under her notice and *he's* really good looking. I couldn't even think right then but you know what I think now? Do you see girls? They're just completely different from us. How did God do it? No, what I mean to say is, *why* did he do it? Okay, I know all that about procreation and God's plan for mankind. But he didn't have to go *that* far. You know what I mean? The shape of them and the way they talk to you and look straight into you and the way they move their whole bodies, even if all they're doing is bending down to scratch their knee or something, *every*thing about them, but mostly the way you feel as weak as water when you're standing there looking at them. They're like some sort of creatures from another planet. They really are.

- What's wrong with your head? said Natalie. - Have ye got the shakes or somethin?

I don't like saying it but she talked like a bit of a slag, even slaggier than the Crolly doll. You know, like one of these hard licks that go round bumping into people looking for a row. I got the nodding stopped and sort of half looked at her eyes. They were green and they were shining away and I'd this feeling they were going to redd me out any minute.

- You know what I think, Sylvia? she said and she never

took her eyes off me. - I think them two shouldn't be out on their ownio. Sure they're nothin but wains.

- What are ye on about? said Gander. - I'm fifteen an a half an *he's* - what age are *you*, Spud?

- Ah, I said.

I wasn't afraid of stammering. I definitely wasn't. That didn't even come into my head. The reason I only said the one thing was, I could hardly open my mouth. To tell you the truth, I really thought I was going to conk out right there in front of everybody. I knew Blackie and Blondie were probably wondering if I was a bit simple or what and mostly I didn't give two hoots about that. All I wanted was to get away. But then I started doing this stuff before I even knew I was doing it. I started going on all weird like James Dean that acted along with Natalie Wood in *Rebel Without A Cause*. You know, mumbling away and rubbing my nose and scratching my head. I saw Gander out of the side of one of my eyes and he was staring at me as if I was mad. I'm not sure about Natalie or the other one because I was sort of looking half way between them most of the time without seeing any of the two of them right and the rest of the time I'd my eyes nearly closed.

- What are you sayin anyway? Natalie said and I was nearly sure there was a bit of respect in her voice. I started pulling one of my cheeks out of my face and I'm pretty sure what I was going to do next. I was going to come out with the biggest load of balls you ever heard. Only it didn't happen because wee Natalie said something that shut me up before I even got started.

- Right, she said. - Do yous two wannay come for a walk with us? What about *you*, Spud? Are *you* comin with *me*? Why are you called Spud anyway?

That was three questions or maybe four and I couldn't even answer one of them with the shock I got. She was staring at me, dead cheeky. Her scarf was moving up and down fast on her chest and her jeans must have slipped down a wee bit because I could see her belly button. I wasn't looking at it but I could see it all right.

Jesus, I thought. What am I going to do? I've never kissed

124

a girl or even held her hand and this one will probably want to do everything. Whatever that is.

You know why I was thinking that? Sylvia. The other one was called Sylvia and that's a Protestant name. So Natalie must be a Protestant too. And everybody knows what Prods are like.

- Are you deaf or what? she said. - You. Spud. D'you wannay go for a walk or d'you not?

She said that last bit in a singsongy voice as if I was some sort of a nincompoop.

- Wa-wa-whur? I said.

- Wherever you like, she said back. - That's unless your mammy'll be lookin for you.

- *My* ma's in Derry, said Gander. - I kin do whativir I wannay.

- Right. Let's go, said Natalie. - Let's go down tay the beach. Okay, Sylvia? Are you and him comin?

That's when I walked away. When I think of it now, James Dean would probably have done the exact same thing if he'd been in the spot I was in. I just walked away. It was simple. I went outside and round to the helter-skelter. I paid the big boy and he handed me a mat. As I was going up the steps I heard Gander roaring behind me like some sort of a madman.

- I shuda fucken knew. What the fuck got intay ye? Jesus, them two wur two cert rides. Wan mat please.

- Fffffffuck off, I said.

- Fuck *you* off, he shouted. - Ye're fucken chicken as per usual. Ye cudn't ride a brush, so ye cudn't, if it was fucken handed tay ye on a plit.

- Wa-wa-what are ye talkin about? I shouted back. - Ye towl may ye wu-wu-wurn't goin tay chat them up.

- Thass right, he shouted. - I *did* tell ye that, didn't I? An I *didn't* chat them up, did I? It was *them* that chatted *me* up. Ye're wan fucken disaster, Murphy. Thass all ye are, a fucken disaster. Yon wee dark wan wuda let ye do anythin ye wanted so she wud. Ye know what *I* think? *I* think ye're a fucken queer boy. Thass what *I* think. A real fucken homo.

- Lave may alone, I shouted and got on my mat and went down the helter-skelter. Then I headed straight for the toilets

125

but he was right behind me, still shouting.

- Ye ruined may chances way wee Sylvia, ye stupid wanker ye.

- Wa-wa-wise up, I roared. - Sh-sh-sure wa-wa-what wa-wa-was ssssssstoppin ye? Ye don't need me tay howl yer han.

- Holy fuck, sure didn't the wee wan that fancied *you* git all huffy an say tay Sylvia, 'Mawn on now. Mawn away.' An whinivir *I* kep asting Sylvia tay tick a dander she kep sayin back tay may, 'Whass may fren goin tay do on er ownio whin I'm away?' An then she siz tay the wee dark wan, 'Will ye bay awright on your ownio fur a wee while? I'll not be long.' An the stupid wee bitch siz, 'Naw, I will *not* be awright. Ye'll stay right here way me.' She was fucken ragin way *you* so she was. Dead hurt. Ye know what *you* are, Murphy ? I'll tell ye what ye are now. Ye're nothin but a fucken fruit.

I locked myself in one of the privates.

- Listen tay who's talkin, I shouted out.

- What d'ye mean bay that? he said and he wasn't shouting anymore. I didn't like the sound of him. - Mawn outa there an say that tay may fiss.

- Fffffucken fffffruit! I shouted.

- I'll brek down that fucken dour so I will, he said and he gave it a bang with his boot. My heart was going like the hammers of hell.

- Ffffffuck away off, I shouted. - Sssssstanislaus!

- I'll fucken Stanislaus *you*, fucken Pius, he said. - Wee Pius. Yer ma picked the right name so she did. Pius the fucken thirteenth.

- Gawn away now an lave may alone, I shouted. - It's all yer own ffffault anyway. Jist lave may alone, wu-wu-wud ye.

There was silence for a few seconds and then I heard him walking away. But he came back just to shout the one thing.

- Fucken fruitcase!

That was it. He went away then. At least he seemed to be away. But I wasn't for taking any chances. I sat down on the toilet seat to wait. When I was sitting there I started thinking about Jackie McHugh from Beechwood Avenue. Just out of the blue I started thinking about him. I was saying to myself he'd none of this bother. He's going to Kilkenny soon to start training for the foreign missions. He's walking on air at the minute. I can see it. Then, in the middle of all that going on in my head, I saw this thing written beside the bolt on the door and it nearly made me sick.

I had a boy of thirteen in here last night and he was sensational.

Sure I should have known. Portrush is where all the Prods come for their days out. And there was me sitting on the same seat as some dirty animal that did things to boys. He should get his two legs broken. I jumped up and that's when I felt my trousers all wet at the back. I knew right away what it was. Somebody must have pished all over the seat. I pulled big wadges of toilet paper off a roll that was on the back of the door and tried to dry my trousers with them. When I was chucking one of the wadges down the toilet a long pancake of shite fell off it. I nearly puked. I'd be stinking for the rest of the day and nobody would believe me if I told them why. So I wouldn't bother saying anything. Maybe I'd get a seat on my own on the way home. What a filthy dump. Charlie told me a couple of years ago it was Protestant but I never cared then as long as I got going to Barry's. I stood there thinking wasn't it a good job I was in the state of grace coming to Portrush. You never know what I would have done if I hadn't been. Those two were nothing but tramps. Anyone would have known that a mile away. Imagine trying to tap us up and them never even saw us before. That's the way dogs do, sniffing away at other ones they've met for the first time. And then after all the bum smelling's finished the she just stands there dead casual with the he up on her as if he's got convulsions or something. The time I was standing there in the toilet this thought came rushing into my head of me doing it to Natalie on a big flat rock in a cave next to the beach and her looking all round the place completely bored. Not shocked. Prods don't be shocked. They know all about boys. They're at it every chance they get.

Anyway, I got rid of that thought right and quick by pulling over the bolt very fast. I nearly cut the hand off myself doing it but it did the trick all right. That was the end of the impure thoughts. Well, for a wee while anyway. I opened the door and looked outside. Gander wasn't there. I walked out of Barry's sucking away at the fingers and went over and sat down on a summer seat across the road. I asked a man the time and he said half four. That meant an hour to go till the bus left. Then I got this really funny feeling. There was something about all the things in front of me, the buildings and Barry's and all. Not just the things but the *positions* they were in. Then after a minute I knew what it was. I'd sat in the exact same place with Frankie years and years before. I was eight or maybe nine at the time. I'm not sure which but it was the day me and Frankie were in Portrush with Mairead on the Derry Journal office excursion. That's where she works, the Derry Journal office. The two of us came out of Barry's because we hadn't a bean left between us and we sat on the very same seat and I asked some man the time and after the man walked on Frankie told me I was a cheeky wee so and so for asking the time. That was the day he let me drive the bumper car even though he was nearly two years older than me and he was beside me and he told me I was brilliant driver because I never let one car touch ours. I *was* brilliant. He wasn't just saying it. I really *was* brilliant. I think that must have been nearly the best day of my life.

There was a big sign in black writing outside this Protestant church that was over to the side a bit. It said THE WAGES OF SIN IS DEATH. It's typical. And it's disgusting too. They put that sort of stuff up on a board and then they let the ones that come to church do whatever they want and they don't say a word to them. You want to hear Trevor Smith. He says everybody should get in as much riding as they can because nobody knows for sure when the world's going to end. They've no religion at all. Do you see the whole time I was sitting there on that summer seat, there must have been fifty couples or more passed me and they were nearly all doing the same thing. They had their arms around one another's waists and their hips were rubbing against each other. Some of them were even touching each other's bums. This one couple nearly sent me mad. They were about three feet in front of me. The girl had on some kind of a white blouse with no sleeves and a red pleated skirt and you could see the hairs under her oxters. They stopped right beside me and started kissing. Then she put her arms round the boy's neck and leaned the top half of her body back and pushed away into him. I'm not exaggerating. He had her tight round the waist and he was pushing even harder into her. Jesus.

- Gawn away a that, she said to him. - Ye're not from Bally....what d'ye call it again?

- Ballywildrick, he said.

- Ballywildrick? she said. - I don't believe there's any such a place.

I closed my eyes and prayed into myself. *He* was the one was at her and *I* was the one was going out of my mind. What do you think of that? He was standing up against her that way and it wasn't taking a fizz out of him. How did he do it? How *could* he do it? You know what I think? It was because he was a Prod. If you're at it nearly all the time it's probably something the same as going to the toilet. He was a Prod all right. For a start his eyes were dead close together and you could hardly see his mouth it was that small. He'd bright blond hair too and it was permed. That's right. Permed. It looked like a corrugated iron roof. He was definitely a Prod. I don't remember now which prayer it was I said. Probably it was the Prayer to Saint Joseph. The reason I'm saying is, I nearly always whisper that one if I think it's going to be a long temptation. Joseph spent years and years with Mary and he never went near her so that's why I usually pray to him those kind of times. And, as well as that, it takes you ages to say it so your mind's off the dirt for a good while. Anyway, at the end of it I opened my eyes and the two of them were still at it, only worse. She was a real hoor if you ask me. She had a white face and red lipstick and this long black hair and it looked *really* long the way she was leaning back. I'm telling you, she was that far back it was nearly touching the footpath. And people were having to walk round them and they didn't even care. I felt it coming. I closed my eyes tight but I couldn't stop it starting. I tried to think of Mammy sick but I couldn't see her. The badness was coming out of me.

I knew I should have been keeping it in because even worse badness was going to take its place inside of me. But I was too weak. I put my two fists on top of myself and I pushed down as hard as I could but all that did was make it jump through me even more so I stopped. It was like someone putting a hose inside of you and the water rushing out of it at sixty miles an hour and it hitting everywhere from the inside of the top of your head to the inside of the soles of your feet. I was nearly ready to cry it was that good. In the middle of it I heard this voice.

- Are you all right, son?

I opened my eyes. It was Mister Nugent, the choirmaster. He didn't know my name. He never knows my name. He calls me son.

- Sssssssir yes.

- Are you sure? You look to me as if you might have a sore tummy.

- I'll bay awright in a wa-wa-wee minute, sssssir.

- Do you think you might have eaten too much?

- I dunno.

Jesus make him go away, I thought.

- Probably too many sweets, son.

- Aye, probbly.

He sat down beside me. It was still going on. It wasn't like other times. This time it seemed as if it was going to go on for-ever nearly. The boy and the girl weren't there anymore. They were probably away somewhere eating ice cream or something like that and it was still happening to me.

- Do you think you're going to be sick?

- Naw, I'm awright. Honest.

Please. PLEASE.

- You know we're leaving in about half an hour, don't you?

- Sssssssir yes.

- Did you enjoy the meal?

- Sssssssir yes.

- I hope you didn't eat too much. Did you eat too much, do you think?

- Sssss–

130

- Or maybe it was the lemonade? I think I saw you drinking lemonade on the bus. I always tell the boys they shouldn't drink lemonade on a long bus journey.

He got up and looked at the wall behind me.

- I've just been noticing, he said. - Those toilets don't smell so good. Maybe you're better not sitting there. It's not healthy. Why don't you get one of your friends to go for a walk with you on the beach? The fresh air would do you good. Don't be too long though.

- Ssssssir yes.

He looked at his watch.

- The bus will be going in just....

And he stopped for a good while. It seemed a good while to me anyway.

- ...just over twenty-five minutes.

- Ssssssir yes.

He went away then. I waited for the beating to slow down and stop and when it did I told God I was sorry. I said the words in my head but I knew He wasn't listening. I got up and started walking. I didn't know where I was going. I remember standing at the bumper cars for a minute and not really looking at them, thinking away to myself. I was thinking maybe Mammy was dying when all that was happening to me. If she was dead now it would be the punishment of God on me. And then I'd have to kill those three. I tried to put it out of my mind, standing there listening to the cars banging into each other, but it kept coming back again. Somebody had to see about scum like that. *Somebody* had to do it. I never wrote about it this good while, as you know rightly, but I never forgot about it either. I just had too many other things to write down about. I remember I walked away from the bumpers thinking, I still have the three of them. None of them touched me in Senior yet except McRide. (I got mad when Tommy Wright said to me on the way home that day the two of us got six - Furgit about him, Conn. Sure what d'ye expect from a cow only a kick.) The Couch *seems* changed. History's easier now and he doesn't treat us like wains anymore. The Pogue's raging because I've got the long grey flannels and he keeps looking away at them. I know he's still at it with the first and second and third years. I know that without asking. And I know the whole three of them are beating the crap out of the Juniors every day and I'll tell you this for certain. Nobody's going to do a thing. It'll just go on and on. Unless. Please God let her not be dead.

Your prayers don't count when you're in the state of mortal sin but I prayed anyway. That's what I was doing when Charlie Murphy gave me a bang on the back with his hand.

- Hi, Conn, mawn quick, he shouted. - The bus is ready tay go. Nugent's rippin mad, ye know. He's got half the choir down at the beach luckin fur ye. What are ye doin standin here anyway?

That's when I knew I was right in front of the merry-go-round and there was all this music and singing going on through some loudspeaker. It only seemed to start when Charlie arrived. But the horses weren't moving. They were just stuck there in mid air. If you'd been really small you'd have thought somebody had put a spell on them. There was this big white one right above me and it was holding one of its front hoofs away up high. There were no children about and the wee office in the middle was empty. It was a funny place to be standing all right. When I think about it now I must have been there a good while because I'm nearly sure I only stayed at the bumpers for a minute or so.

- D'ye hear may? shouted Charlie over the noise. - What are ye standin here fur?

I let on to him I lost a tanner somewhere and I was standing there trying to remember the last place I was.

- Wise up, he said. - Ye'll not git it now. Let's go. Nugent's gittin ready tay skin ye so he is.

We started to walk to where the bus was. Suddenly Charlie stopped.

- Whass that smell? he said. - Is that you?

- Naw, I said.

- Howl on a minute, he said.

I half stopped. He sniffed at me. I started to quicken up but he kept sniffing away at me.

- It *is* you, ye liar ye, he said. - What the frig's wrong way

132

ye anyway? Hiv ye the runs or what?

- Naw, sssssnot me, I said and I started sprinting.

He tried to sniff at me again but he must have looked really ridiculous the way he was running behind me, all bent over.

- It *is* you. Iss you awright, he shouted. - Jesus, Conn, ye smell lick a travellin shit house. They'll nivir let ye on the bus so they won't.

They did let me on the bus. They were hardly going to leave me in Portrush. I got a seat on my own because Gander was sitting beside somebody else on the way back. Some of the boys behind me started whispering away at me - Hi! Murphy Manure! and - Ye know what *you* are, don't ye, Spud? Ye're nothin but a load a shite.

But then Gander came down to them and he said - Hi, c'mere a wee minute. Thur's no call fur that. Day yeez hear may? Jist lave im alone. Right? RIGHT?

The way he said it they knew to keep quiet. There's nobody in the choir fit for him.

When the bus was moving off Nugent got people to open all the windows. Then for the next half hour or so I sat with my eyes closed and I said a fifteen decade rosary into myself without taking out the beads. I meditated on all the Mysteries, the way Father Bosco told us to do, instead of thinking on the meaning of the prayers. He's the priest we had in the College retreat last June. It's funny. The more I meditated on the third Sorrowful Mystery the more I knew the way Jesus must have felt the time the Roman soldiers crowned Him with thorns. Remember they stripped Him and blindfolded Him and hit Him on the head with big sticks and said to Him - Tell us now which one of us was it that hit You last.

After I finished the rosary I just stared at things rushing past me outside. When we were going through Coleraine some of the boys got Gander to sing *Rosemarie*. He's got a trembly sort of a voice but he's a brilliant singer. Everybody was dead quiet till he was finished it. But then in the middle of all the cheering and clapping, this happened. The tingles started going all through me. First the tingles and then the rest. You know what I'm talking about. I couldn't believe it. I really thought on the summer seat that was me finished for the day. When it was all over I sat there wondering if it was me made it happen or if it just happened by itself the way it does sometimes when you're sleeping. And then I thought, Who do you think you're fooling? You weren't exactly sleeping, were you?

I felt that sort of a way as if I was going to vomit but I didn't want to ask for the bus to stop because I didn't want anybody to notice me. So I kept swallowing to keep it down and that wasn't easy. I mean, this was somebody else's shite and somebody else's pish and God knows how long ago it was they did them. And the next thing was, in the middle of all the swallowing I found this other smell coming from up the inside of my shirt. It was that sweet sort of a smell you get off yourself in the morning sometimes when it's happened to you the night before. You know, like fish that's turned rotten. And I thought to myself, What a hypocrite. Imagine sitting there saying fifteen decades of the rosary one minute and the next minute letting *that* happen.

Somebody started singing *We're gonna Rock around the Clock* and everybody joined in. Everybody except me and Nugent. Nugent put his hands over his ears but he was smiling at the same time. I just sat looking out the window working something out. The lights were on inside the bus now and it had got very dark looking outside. All I could see was the sky and hedges and fields bouncing along with the reflections of boys going mad. The whole bus seemed to be jumping up and down on the road. And it's amazing but I was able to think better with all the noise. I was wondering if I'd get back in time for Confession in the cathedral. They only hear till eight at night this time of year and I knew I'd have to go to the house first because I couldn't kneel in a confession box the state I was in. After they finished the Bill Haley song they clapped and cheered themselves for ages and then I asked one of the boys in front of me the time and he said - Iss time ye tuck a bath, but then he said - Bout a half six, I think, and then I asked him what time did he think we'd get back to Derry and he said - Search me.

I knew there'd be no Confessions until the Friday after and

that was six days away. That would be too long a time to be in the state of mortal sin. I'd only go mad thinking I might die. I'd have to ask for one of the priests to hear my confession down in the parochial house the next day. But then he'd definitely see who I was and every time he saw me after that he'd think back on what I'd told him. It's not fair. You shouldn't have to tell those sort of sins except you're in the dark. I was glad when Shaker McGeehan started singing something because they all joined in so they were too busy to catch me thinking. What I was thinking was, if I missed Confession that night God would know I was going to tell my sins the next day. Then if I died in my sleep or was killed before I got forgiveness I wouldn't go to hell because I had the *intention* of going to Confession. So that was how I worked it out. I knew then I was okay. I didn't have to do any more swallowing after that. My stomach got a good lot better and I started to feel happy as well.

As soon as I got home I went straight up to the bathroom and washed my trousers and underpants and the bottom half of me and then I dried myself and flew up the attic stairs on tiptoes with the towel round me and got changed into clean clothes. I was nearly wrecked by the time I was finished. Then I went down and hung the wet things out on the line and when I was doing that I saw Sheila jooking out the kitchen window. She waved for me to come in. I looked but I couldn't see the time in through the window because there was a shine on the mantelpiece clock but I saw it when I went in. It was a quarter to eight.

- Is that clock right? I asked her.

She looked up at it. I don't know why she had to look up at it to know if it was right or not because she'd no watch.

- Naw, iss two minutes slow, she said.

She didn't sound in a good mood to me. She was ironing and the kitchen was dead stuffy and she'd a scone doing on the range as well and you could smell the heat off it.

- What wur ye doin out at the line? she asked.

I told her about sitting on the dirty toilet seat in Barry's. She said - That was a terrible thing tay happen. Did ye enjoy the day apart from that?

I let on to her I did. She sounded as if she couldn't have cared less.

- Wur ye up way Mammy yit? she asked.

- Naw, I said. - Sh-sh-sure I wa-wa-wanted tay git cleaned up fffffirst. How is sh-sh-she ssssssince?

- I think she's a wee bit better than she was, she said. - She was asting a while ago if ye wur back yit.

It was two minutes after a quarter to eight on the clock. That meant it was really eleven minutes to. They'd probably be stopping hearing confessions nearly anytime.

- I hiftay go sssssssomewhur, I said.

- What! she said, dead sharp.

She put the iron down. She was very red in the face. I think she was just looking for an excuse.

- Ye're not goin tay Charlie Murphy's an you oney in the dour an Mammy lyin sick in bed? she said.

- Naw, I wa-wa-wasn't goin tay Charlie's, I said. - I jist hiftay…..

- Ye jist hiftay what? she said. - She's bin asting about ye, ye know. Sure did ye not hear may sayin?

- Aye, I did, I said. - I'll not bother then. I wa-wa-was oney goin tay go out a minute anyway.

- Gawn on out if ye wannay go, she said. - If thass what ye wannay do, gawn ahead.

- Naw, I'll not bother, I said.

I went up to see Mammy. She was still lying the same way, flat on her back. It was hard for me to tell if she was flushed the same as she was before because the kind of bulb that was in, even her hands seemed red. She'd the beads in them and I could hear the whistling and the wee hissing noises coming out of her mouth. That's the way she prays. Her right hand was jerking a bit but it nearly always does that. It's got some sort of a nerve in it.

- How ye doin? I said.

- Aw, it's Conn, she said. She'd the teeth back in. - Are ye awright, son? Tell may, did ye enjoy yourself?

- Aye, dead on, I said.

- And did ye go on all the musements? Did ye go on the

dive bomber?

- Naw, I towl ye before, Mammy. Thur's no dive bomber in Portrush. Thur wa-wa-was a dive bomber up in Brooke Park that time they'd the fffffunfffffair there but thass the oney pliss thur wa-wa-was ivir a dive bomber. It wa-wa-was useless anyway.

- Well, did ye go on the rest a the things? she said.

- Aye, most a them, I said. - Nearly them all ccccccep fffffur the wa-wa-wans they hiv fffffur wa-wa-wains.

- I was jist thinkin when ye wur away, she said. - Ye missed doin your exers the day. Ye'll hiftay do them the marra now.

- Naw, iss always a Sssssunday I do them anyway, I said. So it is. Dreadoomday.

- Aw, I thought it was on a Saturday ye did them.

- Naw, I always lave a Sssssaturday fffffree, I said. - I always do them on Sssssundays. How ye fffffeelin anyway?

- Aw, I'm grand. Grand, she said.

She flashed the false teeth at me. I always used to laugh at her before and tell her they were too big for her mouth. So they are too. But I didn't say anything this time because I didn't want her to take them out.

- There's nothin wrong way me that a good lick a paint wouldn't cure. I'll be outa this bed in a couple a days. Doctor O'Sullivan's comin back up tay see may on Monday an we'll see what he says then. I'll be grand.

I took a half crown out of my pocket and put it on the dressing-table.

- Here's a half a crown back, I said.

- God, ye musta spent harley anythin, she said.

- I didn't need tay, I said. - A whole lot a boys paid fffffur may tay go on things.

- That was very good a them, she said. - Ye must be very well licked. Naw, Conn, keep that fur yourself. Gawn, keep it. Sure it'll do ye fur the picture house nixt Saturday and ye'll hiv plenty left over tay buy sweets fur yourself.

Jackie McHugh told me when I was going down to twelve mass the next day that Derry drew one all away to Portadown the day before. I nearly forgot they were playing. After mass I got my breakfast and then I went up to Tessie's field with Charlie and Smith and Stoopy and this boy Charlie knows from Creggan called Tucker Wade. We played two-a-side long shootie and it was me and Charlie against Smith and Wade. Stoopy got left out because he's useless but we told him he'd get on the next game. We had to stop for a minute when we were three none up for Smith to tie his lace and Charlie said to me - Who ye bangin?

I said - Wa-wa-what?

And he said - Who ye bangin?

And I said - Wa-wa-what ur ye on about?

- Ye know rightly, he said. - Ye didn't go up tay Communion this mornin. Ye muss bay bangin somebody.

Sometimes Charlie comes out with stuff like that to try and act the slick man and I usually laugh to please him but this time I didn't feel like laughing.

- Wa-wa-wise up, I said. - Wa-wa-wise up and catch yersel on.

- Oh. OH! he said, going on all shocked.

Then Stoopy started.

- Are ye joking or what? he said. - Conn bangin somebody? Conn'd hiv bother bangin a drum so he wud.

The big cunt was right behind us all the time and I didn't know. He was standing there like the hunchback of Notre Dame trying to look like a teddy boy with the shoulders stuck away out on each side of him.

- Wa-wa-watch! I said to Charlie. - Sssssmith's ffffinished tyin his liss.

They're a good laugh, the two of them, Charlie going on like that as if sex was the most natural thing in the world and Stoopy trying to talk big as well. If they ever got off with two bits of stuff they wouldn't know what to do with them unless some-body told them and then they still wouldn't be able to do it.

We won twelve one and I said I was going. Stoopy got tak-

ing my place. I went home and fixed myself up a bit and headed down to the parochial house. I know the priests would all
have their breakfasts over them by that time. I rang the bell. I'd
always wanted to ring it because it's the kind of a one you pull
out from the wall but I'd never done it before because there was
always somebody with me any time I was ever sent there and I
always let them ring it because I didn't want to look childish.
The dong came from away at the back of the house somewhere.
That's something I never tried to work out. This big one Nellie
came to the door and opened it about two inches. She's from up
the country somewhere, a real cuiltie. I don't know if her real
name's Nellie or not but everybody calls her Nellie the nag
because she's got a face on her like a horse and she's always giving out as well.

- Yis? she said.

- Ssssscuse may, I said. - Cud I sssssee wa-wa-wan a the
priests, please?

- Whass it about? she said.

- Ah...., I said.

- Stitt yer business, she said. - What d'ye want a priest fur?
Who sent ye?

- Nowan, I said.

- Well then, what d'ye want? she said.

- I jist wa-wa-wannay ssssee wa-wa-wan a the priests, I
said. - Iss private.

- Which priest ye wannay see? she said.

- Doesn't matter wa-wa-which, I said. - Any wa-wa-wan a
them'll do.

- Who's callin? she said.

- Wa-wa-what? I said.

- Who shall I say's callin? she said.

- Iss awright, I said. - I'll tell the priest may name wa-wa-
whin I sssssee im.

- Wait here in the porch, she said. - Sit there on that sit there.

Her eye and her nose went away and the door closed. I sat
down on the hardest seat I ever sat on. It was a tiny wee pew
that would have held about three people. It was like a rock and
it was as cold as ice as well.

After a couple of minutes she opened the door, wide this time. She jerked her head for me to come and I came. She pointed to another door that was in the hallway.

- Wait in there, she said. - Father Sheerin'll be down tay see ye in a minert.

I went in. The room had a big high ceiling and there was this massive marble fireplace up along the side. I thought it would be cheeky to sit down so I stood exactly where I was standing when Nellie closed the door, just alongside a big long table I could see myself in. There were a whole lot of chairs up against the walls all round the place. It was freezing in there and the shivers were going through me. I was just starting to look up at a picture of some very strict looking bishop, or arch-bishop maybe, that was above the fireplace when the door opened and Father Sheerin came in. He was rubbing his hands round and round together as if he was in good form.

- How are you? he said. - What can I do for you?
- Fffffaller, I wa-wa-wanted tay git tay Confession, I said.
- Oh, I see, he said. There were big bushes of hair coming out of his nose. - Do you not know the times?
- Ah…Ah…, I said.
- The times for Confession? he said.
- Yes, I do, Ffffaller, but, but….
- I see. All right. All right.

He smiled. This was the first time I ever really looked at him. He was small and fat and he'd a very red face.

- I'll hear your confession right away, if you like, he said.
- Thanks, Ffffaller.
- Now, would you like to sit here?

He lifted one of the chairs over to the table and I sat down on it. The big glassy chandelier was nearly straight above us. I didn't have to look up. I could see it right there in the table beside me. He pulled over another chair and fixed it a certain way so's when he sat down he nearly had his back to me. He smelt soapy.

- Now, he said. - What's your name?
- Conn Murphy, I said.

I think he was just trying to be friendly to calm me down

and all but that was one question I didn't want him to ask because my name would stick in his head after the filth I was going to tell him and, as well as that, he might start remembering the time I asked him about my balls. I told him my name then too. But that part seemed all right because he was going on as if he didn't know me from Adam. He'd know me after this all right. He'd know I was a disgrace. He'd know every time he saw me.

- Now, Conn, he said.

And he waited.

I took about half a minute to get started. I made the Sign of the Cross and said - Bless may Fffffaller fffffur I hiv sssssinned. Fffffaller, iss two days sssssince may last confession.

- How long did you say? he said.

- Two days, Fffffaller.

- Two days, he said. - Right. That's all right. Continue.

- Fffffaller, I said. - I committed two sssssins of impurity sssssince may last confession.

There was silence for a good wee while and then he said - Yes? Anything else?

- No, Fffffaller. Thass all, Fffffaller.

- Nothing else?

- No, Fffffaller, nothin else.

There was another silence, only a longer one. This wasn't good. I knew it wasn't good.

- Tell me, he said. - Were you alone or with another person when you committed these sins?

- Fffffaller.....

- Yes?

- Fffffaller, I ....

- Yes!

- Fffffaller, I cannay mine. I mean, it doesn't matter.

- Who are *you* to say it doesn't matter? It *does* matter. I'm asking you to explain the circumstances.

- Fffffaller, I'm sssssorry fffffur may sssssins. Cud I not jist go now?

- Now, listen here to me, young man, he said. - You don't want to be hiding anything from God. Nothing. You hear? You must remember that it's not really me you're confessing to. It's God. I'm here simply as a channel, nothing more. Do you understand that?

- Yes, Fffffaller.

- Now, tell me. Were you alone or with someone else when you committed these sins.

- Fffffaller, the choir wa-wa-was there wa-wa-wan a the times–

- Choir? What choir was that?

- The Cathedral choir, Fffff–

- Where did this happen? Did this happen in the Cathedral? Was it in the gallery?

- Naw, naw, Fffffaller, it wa-wa-was on the bus.

- The bus. The bus. I see. And tell me, how many people were involved?

- I dunno, Fffffaller. I think thur must a bin round fffforty.

- Forty. Forty, you say.

- Yes, Fffffaller. The whole choir wa-wa-was away.

- Away. Away where?

- Away on the excursion, Fffffaller.

- This is yesterday's bus run to Portrush you're talking about.

- Yes Fffffaller, cccccept it wa-wa-was on the wa-wa-way back.

- What was on the way back? Tell me what happened.

- Fffffaller, I wa-wa-was sssssittin on may own wa-wa-whin it happened may. Nowan come near may.

- When what happened?

- Fffffaller, this boy wa-wa-was ssssssingin this ssssssong an he wa-wa-was yodellin. Mibby it wa-wa-wasn't the yodellin. Mibby it wa-wa-was jist the song.

- The song, he said. - The song. I see. The song excited you?

- Yes, Fffffaller. Mibby, Fffffaller. I dunno, Fffffaller.

- Right. We'll come back to that. Now, tell me about the other time. Were you alone or with another person the other time? You know what I'm talking about when I say that, don't you?

142

I didn't answer.

- You understand your sins can't be forgiven unless you confess them fully?

- Yes, Ffffaller. No, Ffffaller.

- Now, I'm asking you about the other sin of impurity. Were you alone or was there someone with you?

I didn't answer.

- Remember, Conn, he said. - This is the Sacrament of Confession. God is listening.

- Yes, Ffffaller. Mister Nugent wa-wa-was there ffffur part of it but he'd nothin tay do wa-wa-way it.

- Who did you say?

- Mister Nugent.

- Mister Nugent the choirmaster?

- Yes Ffffaller. He ssssat down beside may in the middle of it. I wa-wa-was ssssittin bay maysel on this ssssummer sssseat up in Portrush, ye sssssee, an these two in ffffront a may ssssstarted doin dirty things an Mister Nugent come over after a wa-wa-wee wa-wa-while cause he thought thur wa-wa-was sssssomethin wrong wa-wa-way may or I mean tay sssssay he *knew* thur wa-wa-was sssssomethin wrong wa-wa-way may.

- *What* two in front of you?

- This boy an this girl. Mister Nugent jist thought I lucked sssssick. He'd nothin tay do wa-wa-way it.

- Of course he didn't, said Father Sheerin.

He waited a minute and then he said - So you passed seed? That's what happened?

- Ffffaller.....

- You passed seed. You ejaculated.

- I'm sssssorry, Ffffaller. I dunno wa-wa-what that means. It jist happened tay may. It come out. I wa-wa-was prayin an all an it sssssstill come out.

After that he didn't speak for a wee while. In the middle of not speaking he let this long sigh out of his nose and *that* brought back memories. But then when he spoke he sounded really friendly and I started to feel better.

- Tell me, Conn. What age are you? he said.

- Fffffifteen, Ffffaller.

- And have you been out with any girls yet?

- Wa-wa-well, not really, Fffffaller, cccccept fffffur–

- It seems to me, Conn, that you're too excitable for your own good. Perhaps on these two occasions you only *thought* you were committing mortal sin. Perhaps you couldn't help these things happening. Do you know what's needed before you can call a sin mortal?

- Yes. Fffffaller. Grave matter, fffffull knowledge an fffffull consent.

- Very good, Conn. Good boy. Now. Perhaps you're being too hard on yourself. You seem like a very sensitive person to me. Perhaps these things weren't intentional.

- Fffffaller, I didn't *wa-wa-want* them tay happen but I *knew* they wa-wa-wur happenin an I enjoyed them awright wa-wa-wa-wa-wa–

- I see.

Then there was more silence. I wanted absolution and I wanted out but *he* didn't seem to be in any hurry.

- Tell me, Conn, he said. - Are you still at school?

- Yes, Fffffaller.

- What school would that be now?

- Ssssssint Paul's.

- I see. And have you ever thought of what you would like to do whenever you leave Saint Paul's? You'd be in your Senior first year now, wouldn't you?

- Yes, Fffffaller. I wa-wa-wannay bay a ssssschoolteacher.

- A what? he said.

- A ssssschoolteacher, Fffffaller.

- A schoolteacher. I see. That's what you really want to do, is it?

- Yes, Fffffaller. I'm goin tay apply fffffur the Queeng's Sssssscholarsh-sh-ship tay git goin tay Ssssint Joseph's Trainin College.

- Yes. You think that would be a suitable job for you? You hadn't thought of doing anything else?

- Naw, Fffffaller. I always wa-wa-wanted tay bay a ssssschoolteacher ssssso I did.

- I see, he said.

144

He seemed stuck for a minute but then he started up again.

- Teaching is a calling of a sort, he said. - But, you know, Conn, it just may be that it's not the job for you. It just may be that God wants you to do something else. Did you ever think of that?

- Naw, Fffffaller.

- It may be that this strong sensitivity that you have is God's way of calling you. Tell me, did you ever think of the priesthood?

- I dunno wa-wa-what ye mean, Fffffaller.

- I mean, did you ever think you'd like to be a priest someday?

- Naw, Fffffaller.

- Never?

- Naw, Fffffaller.

- You know, Conn, someone once said that too many young people live their lives in a state of noisy desperation–

- I wa-wa-wannay git married sssssomeday, Ffffffaller.

- Indeed? Why's that now?

- Wa-wa-wa....

- Why do you want to get married someday?

I said nothing. I wasn't going to tell a lie in Confession.

- Certainly there's no doubt that many people are called to the holy state of matrimony, he said. - But this noisy desperation I'm talking about. There are many , many boys and girls of your age, Conn, who think that they must have a good time at all costs. They feel it's what other young people expect of them. It's possible that you're not suited to this kind of rough and tumble, Conn. The priestly life is one of great serenity, you know. It's a life of dedication to God and it involves a lot of sacrifice but it has its own rewards. It's just possible that it's the life for you. Will you promise me something now, Conn?

- Yes, Fffffaller.

- Will you promise me that you'll pray that God will open your mind to His call if it comes?

- Yes, Fffffaller.

- Because that's what a vocation is, you know. A call from God. I'm sure you do Latin, don't you?

- Yes, I do, Fffffaller.

- Good. Well, as you know, *vocare* in Latin means to call. And that may be just what God is doing. Calling you.

- Yes, Fffffffaller.

- Good man. Now, tell God that you're sorry and for your penance say one Hail Mary.

As I was saying the Act of Contrition and listening to him giving me absolution I was thinking, He's not too bad. He's okay. Imagine only giving me one Hail Mary after me doing *that*.

In the middle of my home exers that day I started thinking maybe it would be all right being a priest. If girls knew I was going to be going away to be a priest they wouldn't look at me the way some of them do. And also I wouldn't be looking at *them* the way *I* do and thinking and wishing away about them because there'd be no point in it. I'd be giving myself to God and there was nothing better anybody could do than that. Then after I was ordained I wouldn't be giving in to bad thoughts or letting it happen because I'd have extra graces from God with all the masses I'd be saying and all the other good acts I'd be doing. It must be nearly impossible to commit mortal sins if you're holding the Body and Blood of Jesus Christ every day and sending people to heaven with the Sacrament of Extreme Unction. But then I started thinking maybe the bishop would send me to Saint Paul's. And I thought, If I had to teach in Saint Paul's I'd leave the priesthood. Maybe I could train down in Kilkenny like Jackie McHugh. I could write to him after he was there awhile and if it turned out to be a dead on place, then I'd go maybe. When they're ordained in Kilkenny they're sent to the foreign missions. Father Michael Mulvenna was out in Burma years and years ago and he baptised a terrible lot of people. Imagine bringing souls to Christ. Daddy gave him a gold watch and chain when he was ordained and he always wore it but then he was captured by the rebels and they took it off him.

Jackie's a chancer. I think he's only going because he knew all along he wasn't going to get the marks to do anything else. Gander says it's ridiculous. But God moves in mysterious ways. It could be this is all part of His plan to make Jackie a priest. Sure the Curé of Ars was supposed to have been stupid too and he kept failing his exams but then they let him finish his training anyway. And when he was made a priest God gave him the power to read people's minds and now he's a great saint. I heard a whole lot of boys go to Maynooth just so's they can get their degrees and then they leave and start teaching. But I'll bet you there's some of them discover they've got a vocation when they're there a while and then they stay and maybe turn out to be great priests. Sure look at the apostles. They were all disasters except for John and they all ended up doing brilliant, giving their lives for Jesus and all. Well, Judas didn't but that's because he gave up hope. That's what happened to him. If he'd told God he was sorry he'd have ended up another martyr. If I go to Kilkenny to get away from temptation it doesn't necessarily mean I couldn't still be a great priest. Maybe this *is* God's way of calling me. Father Sheerin's right. If I keep praying I'll know when the time comes.

It's hard to believe some of the crap they tell you to read in this place. Honest to God. We're doing *Emma* by this one Jane Austen and we're supposed to know the first twenty chapters of it for the Christmas exam. I bought it second-hand off Molly of the Moor and I don't know who had it before me but, whoever it was, it smelt as if they'd vomited all over it and then tried to wash it with Lifebuoy soap. I knew as soon as I took it out of the shop because I opened it and the smell hit me. But I didn't take it back in seeing I only paid a deuce for it. After I got home I rubbed some of Mairead's perfume on it with cotton wool that she had in one of her drawers but then the whole thing nearly turned my stomach. So I sat it open out on the window-sill one day it wasn't raining and now its not too bad. That's until you start reading it. It's nothing but a load of hoity toity pish. I mean, I haven't read that much of it yet but so far all it's about is this stupid interfering bitch called Emma Woodhouse that lived about a hundred and fifty years ago and goes round trying to get people fixed up with each other or else she's trying to get them to give the one they're going with the shove. And talk about a snob! She says you're for nothing if you're not a lady or a gentleman and she's always watching away at people and listening to every word they're saying to find out what they are and who they are. If your da's a tradesman you're bad news but if he owns about fifty thousand acres then you're the bee's knees. She's a bit of a wanker all right. It's ridiculous anyway us having to read stuff like that for exams. What do they think we are? Except for Brendan Burns we're all less than sixteen and most of the boys I know, if their da was a tradesman they'd be shitting all over you from a great height. It really is a farce. This one Emma's only supposed to be twenty but the way she goes on you'd think she was about ninety. And you want to see the amount of brock she comes out with. Brendan Burns says half the book's her talking. The part I was reading yesterday, she was going on to some boy for a page and three quarters and he just kept standing there taking it. Brendan's good crack. He told me a couple of days after we got it that he read it before, the time he was in hospital, and he said it was absolutely filthy. I told him to wise up and he opened his eyes dead wide and said - Honest to God, but you have to be able to read between the lines, he said, and then the next day he brought in his one with bits of paper sticking out all over the place. He showed me the word *intercourse* seven different places in it and it seemed to be nearly all between Emma and this other girl and there was stuff too about her admiring the other one's soft blue eyes and the last part he showed me was about their satisfaction in each other increasing. I never thought girls could be that way but I didn't let on about that to him. I just said to him - That sssssounds interesting. I must hiv a luck at it.

- Stay with it, he said. - It gets pretty hot around about the last thirty pages.

My brain didn't believe him but the rest of me wasn't a hundred percent sure. I kept saying to myself on the way home that they'd never have a book like that on for the Senior exam but all I could see in front of me when I was sitting on the bus was Emma on top of this other one. Read between the lines, he said. The way I looked at it, the thing was on for the Senior and I wasn't just *allowed* to study it, I was *supposed* to study it. I worked out walking up Marlborough Avenue that if I read the last thirty pages when I got home the book would mean more to me and then I'd be able to follow the story better. I headed straight up the stairs and lay down on the attic bed and started at page two hundred and ninety. I was that excited I didn't even feel nervous about committing mortal sin. But it turned out, the only part that was worth reading was about Emma getting married to this old boy and stuff about the perfect happiness of their union. I knew what *that* meant all right but it didn't tell you any more about it. I'd the numbers of the pages *intercourse* was on but I didn't bother reading them because I was thinking then it probably had some other meaning so I looked it up. I had to laugh. I never let on to Brendan he'd caught me but I think he probably knew even though he didn't say.

He's a slick character. He's really smooth and sophisticated and, as well as that, he makes you feel good and sort of grown-up whenever you're along with him. He's very aristocratic looking, with floppy shiny fair hair, and he's got this accent that's half Derry and half proper but he's not a snob or anything. I told him one time he looked like the son of an earl and he said back dead quick - Not a word to the oul man about it now.

The two of us sit together at the back of Mc Ride's and The Duck's classes. One day before we went home he told me he'd this dirty picture with him. He wouldn't show me it because he said I was a prude and it would only scandalise me. But these three boys must have heard him because they came over and kept on at him to let them see it. So they went into the jacks with him and when they came out they looked around them and then they were saying stuff like - Jasus, Burns, where'd ye git that? and - Ye're wan dirty brute so ye are, and - That's fucken brilliant, and - Hiv ye any more?

I was waiting outside and the two of us headed down the

walks and half way down he exploded laughing.

- The stupid shits, he said.

- Wa-wa-what d'ye mean? I said.

- D'you want tay know what they were luckin at? he said.

- Wa-wa-what? I said, trying to act normal.

- An ear, he said. - A flippin ear.

He took the picture out of his pocket and showed it to me. It was an ear all right but it was really close up and pink and pale red and colours like that and you had to hold it sort of sideways diagonally a bit away from you to see it right.

- Ye're a wa-wa-wile man, I said.

- You know what would've been good? he said. - It would've been good O'Donnell Duck or somebody lick that comin in and catchin us and thinkin he'd got us and bringin us and the picture up tay Meehan and us standin in a line waitin tay get hammered for luckin at an ear.

- Ye wa-wa-wudna let that happen, wa-wa-wud ye? I said.

- Course I wouldn't, he said. - I'd have towl Meehan before he got a chance tay do it just tay see the luck on their oul faces.

- Sh-sh-sure they cudn't doke you, anyway, cud they?

- They couldn't doke me for showin a picture of an ear anyway, he said.

They're not allowed to go near him. He told me that the time McRide gave me and Tommy Wright six each and left him alone and none of the three of us knew the irregular futures. I don't think he likes talking about it but he was sort of embarrassed that day when we came out of the Irish class and that's probably why he told me. He was nearly dead last year. Meehan came round all the classes for once in his life and he asked us all to pray for this boy Brendan Burns that was gravely ill. It was really strange hearing the president asking you to do something instead of telling you.

- I'm appealing to you, boys. Storm heaven with your prayers. Thank you.

Something like that. I don't even know what was wrong with him. I think it was his blood vessels but I never asked him. I don't like to. He missed nearly a full year so he's a good lot older than me. But I don't think he's mature and all because of his *age*. That's just the way he is. There's plenty of boys older than him that I know and none of them's anywhere near *his* class.

The only good thing we ever did in English was *Julius Caesar*. One of the reasons I thought it was great was, when we were about half way through it, it was made into a film. Marlon Brando was in it and you wanted to see him. He was doing Mark Antony and he was brilliant. But the best about it was, you could really understand how these boys were right to kill Caesar. You know, the conspirators. And you were hoping all the time they'd get away with it. Everybody in the Strand picture house was hoping the same. That's what *I* thought anyway, the night *I* was at it. Now wouldn't you think even a newrp like The Duck would have been pleased when he knew a whole lot of the class were at the film but naw, he just ignored us when we put our hands up and tried to tell him about it.

- Sir, iss on the Strand.
- Sir, thur's some great actors in it.
- Sir, iss a good show so it is.
- Quoiet! says The Duck. - Naow, con anyone tell me anything abeout the Feast of Lupercal which Antony refeahs to in his funeral speech?

He's a born prick. He goes on like an actor and he's got this big deep voice but anybody would know a mile away he's just putting it on.

One of the best parts in it I remember really well is where the soothsayer's trying to warn Caesar he's going to be killed on this certain day in March. He keeps shouting - *Beware the Ides of March* and Caesar calls him a dreamer and walks away. And then Caesar comes along later on and says to whoever's with him - *The Ides of March are come* and the soothsayer shouts out - *Aye Caesar, but not gone*.

And of course Caesar gets killed before the day's out. It's a brilliant play.

I'll never forget the time Arthur did this completely stupid thing. He took me to see *The Winslow Boy* in the Guildhall when I was only very small. I didn't even know what a play was. That shows you how young I was. All I'd ever seen on the stage was *The Babes in the Wood* in Saint Columb's Hall. On the way down he said to me - Now, Conn, I'm taking you to a play and I wawnt you to be very good and very quiet. Listen to whawt the people aw saying. Theah's a boy in it thawt's a bit oldah thawn you. You'll really like it.

I asked him what a play was but he never answered because he met this big baldy boy and the two of them stood talking for ages and I was getting fed up and I wouldn't have minded pee-ing. When we went into the Guildhall I knew right away I did-n't like it. There were all these archways and statues and stained glass windows and big high ceilings and echoes everywhere and dark pictures on the walls a bit like the Stations of the Cross. I'd a feeling in my stomach we were going to be there for *hours* so I asked Arthur would he buy me a packet of Rowntree's wine gums because they always last great. But he told me unfawtunately there was no shop in the Guildhall. Unfawtunately. He really loves saying that. We had to go up two massive flights of stairs and I was nearly ready to go home by the time we got to the top. I noticed all these men and women going past us and every single one of them was dressed to the nines and the accents would have sickened you. Then we went into this place that was nearly as big as Saint Columb's Hall and there was a stage at one end of it and a balcony at the back nearly like the gallery in the Cathedral. I knew for sure then there was going to be some kind of a show but at the same time there was something funny about the stage. It hadn't got a curtain like there was for *The Babes in the Wood* and there was no thing round it like the frame on a picture.

We sat down anyway and Arthur handed me a programme but I didn't know what it was at the time. He'd one himself and he told me to read mine but all I got reading before the lights went out were advertisements for Mundie's wine and Austins and Co. of the Diamond. I couldn't believe how dark it was. The whole place was pitch black. I whispered to Arthur I had to do a number one and he shooshed me and said - *Now* you tell me, and I said it again and he shooshed me again and then he gave me a wee slap on the knee and you would have heard it all over the place. Of course he didn't say a word to this crowd of women with big hats that were blethering away right in front of us. Just when I was about to tell him I couldn't keep it in any longer the stage appeared like magic and the play started. I was completely bored inside of about two minutes. There were these ones going about shouting at each other as if they were all deaf. I thought the whole thing was stupid but how was I to know they *had* to shout for us to hear them? Did you ever say to yourself a time somebody took you someplace when you were wee, What am I doing here? I mean, what am I *doing* here? Well, that's what I was saying to myself sitting on that hard chair and my bum getting scratchier every minute. The actors were going on even swankier than the ones on the stairs and the clothes they'd on them were stupid looking. They were like the kind of get up your ancestors would have had on them about a hundred years ago.

Early on the wee boy in it went out into the garden through the French windows because his ma and da were coming and he was scared they'd see him. It turned out then he had to stay where he was even when it started pouring the rain because the ma and da stayed put after they came on to the stage. Of course there was no garden at all and it wasn't raining either because all this was going on inside the Guildhall but the actors kept looking through these fake windows and saying - Gosh, isn't that rain terrible! or something like that and you were supposed to be feeling sorry for the wee boy outside. I could swear now that not one person in that hall really believed the boy was get-ting soaked but you were supposed to pretend to believe it. The thing was, the more they went on about the rain and the wet the more I needed a pee. But then something happened. I heard somebody saying the wee boy got expelled from the school he was at because he was supposed to have stolen a five shilling postal order when he didn't do it at all and that's when everything changed. I started to get really interested, especially when I found out there might be a chance of him getting off, and I forgot all about the lavatory. I'm not even sure now if I *thought* I had to pee at the start when I didn't really have to go or if I *forgot* I had to pee later on when I did really have to go. All I know is, this thing about the wee boy getting expelled really annoyed me. But nobody near me could have cared less. I knew. I just knew the way they were sitting there like statues that they weren't even *pretending* to be annoyed. After a while this big tall skinny lawyer that looked like a bit of a nance to me came in to see if he could get the boy off and before you knew what was happening he was giving him a desperate slagging and calling him a liar and a thief and I don't know what else. And him supposed to be standing up for him. But the thing that sickened me most of all was, the wee boy was crying his eyes out and every time his da and his big sister got up out of their seats to tell the skinny boy to lay off a bit, he told them to shut their mouths and they never told him to get lost once. And all the snobs watching it just sat there like dressed-up dummies out of Austin's window. *I* wasn't going to take it anymore. Just when the big nancy boy was in the middle of saying for the ninth time that the wee boy stole the postal order I stood up and roared out of me - Aw naw he didn't! and before he could get a chance to shout back - Oh yes he did! or something like that I roared on - Lave im alone! Lave im alone wud ye! Are ye stupid or what? Sure ye *know* he didn't do it!

Arthur had about seven kittens of course. He slammed his hand on top of my mouth and the smell of the fags off it nearly killed me. Even though it was pretty dark I could still see some of the creeps with the hats in front of us and they were turning round all dramatic and exaggerated and one of them said - Would you be *quiet*! and another one said - Get that child *out* of here!

I couldn't believe it. I really couldn't. They were sitting there and not a word out of them the whole time Skinnymalinkylonglegs was going on like a mad bull and the very second I opened my mouth they were nearly looking for the cops. But when I think back on it all now, the ones up on the stage must have been really good actors because they just went on as if nothing had happened. I actually thought at the time that the wee boy might give me the thumb but all he did was keep on crying. And then my heart gave a big jump because this amazing thing happened. The lawyer turned round and said all dramatic - It's obvious the boy is innocent! and then three other things happened in a row. The stage went black, all the lights came on and suddenly the actors had disappeared.

Arthur got me out of the hall in no time before anybody else could get on to me. I was scared to look near him but then I heard him laughing away through his nose. It sounded nearly like he was trying to clear it but when I looked up at him he was smiling away to himself with his mouth tight shut. He took me down the stairs by the hand and when we were about half way down he started grunting and gasping and laughing so hard I thought he was going to take a fit. He tried to say something three or four times but each time he couldn't say it because he kept doubling up. Then when we got to the bottom he made me sit on a seat with him and he took out a hanky and wiped away at his eyes.

- Is it over? I asked him.

He didn't say anything. He just shook his head very hard.

- Are way not goin back in? I asked.

- Neo, he said and he was breathing very heavy but he was coming round a bit.

- Wull he git off awright? I asked. - Ye know, the wee boy?

- Eoh yes, said Arthur. - I think he's got every chawnce of getting off *now*.

His shoulders started going again and I could feel the bench we were on shaking. Then after a minute he said - You kneow whawt I think, Conn?

- What? I said.

- I think you'ah right to stawnd up aginest injustice.

I didn't know what he meant so I said nothing.

- I'll tell you anothah thing, he said. - Thawt wouldn't be the first injustice thawt evah took place in this building.

155

And the bench started shaking again. He was in good form all right. I still didn't know what he was on about but I was getting a strong feeling there might be sweets coming so I thought it was better to say something to keep him happy.

- In the big hall, ye mean? I asked.

- Aws faw aws I kneow, he said. - Ceahtainly in the building. Tell me, Conn, do you kneow whawt a cawporation meeting is?

Then he said right away - Neo, of course, how could you? He got up.

- Would you like a knickahbockah glory? he said.

Would *I* like a knickerbocker glory! Imagine asking *me* a question like that!

We missed French on Wednesday because Bonzo was off and The Duck took us instead. He spent the whole class asking us all to name our three favourite books. Brendan says that's the sign of a waffler. We all had to write down the books and the authors and then tell him when it came our turn. Brendan showed me what he'd got down. *Duel in the Sun* by A.N. Animal, *Lolita* by Somesky Dirtsky Oldsky Russky and *Anything* by Mickey Spillane. But the ones he called out were *Emma* by Jane Austen, *Wuthering Heights* by Charlotte Brontë and *Martin Chuzzlewit* by Charles Dickens. The Duck said - Excellent choice, Beuns, and Brendan winked at me.

I was stupid, of course. I said - *The Black Cat* bay Edgar Allan Poe, *Return of the Sssssint* bay Leslie Charteris and *Treasure Island* bay Robert Louis Sssssstevenson. The Duck looked at me the way you'd look at a slug and he said - Oi think the feust two speak volumes faw youah mind, Meuphy. In any caise, *The Block Cot* is not a book, it's a shawt story, and *The Reteun of the Saint* is not literatuah, it's gawbage. As faw the theud. Tell me, whot aige aw you?

- Sssssir, fffffifteen, I said.

- Well, he said. - If you weah eleven aw twelve Oi moight

156

undahstawnd youah theud choice. Howevah, you should by naow be long pawst the staige of buccaneahs awnd buried treasuah. It seems to me, Meuphy, thot you aw retawded in the literary sense. Do you kneow the meaning of the weud retawded?

I knew *tard* meant late in French and *tardus* meant slow in Latin so I'd a good idea what the fat cunt was on about, but I wasn't sure of the exact meaning in English so I wasn't taking any chances.

- Sssssir no.

- Thawt's because you aw retawded in the literal sense alseo. Next mon.

It doesn't matter what he says. He's wrong about *Treasure Island*. That really *is* a classic. I don't care what age you are. Do you see if there was some way they could show the first twenty pages or so as a trailer, the book would be sold out in no time. But that reminds me of this amazing thing about it. I think it must be the only story I ever read that doesn't even *need* illustrations. And that's counting *The Black Cat*. Because you can see everything in your head. You know, like Billy Bones arriving at the Admiral Benbow Inn, all brown and filthy and really dangerous and him singing

> *Fifteen men on a dead man's chest–*
> *Yo-ho-ho, and a bottle of rum.*

And do you see at this very moment, I can picture the road and the inn and the sea near it and the sign that says Admiral Benbow swinging and it all gashes with Billy Bones's cutlass when he hit it by mistake trying to split Black Dog right down the middle. And then Pew the blind beggar (only he wasn't really a beggar) coming to the inn and scaring Billy Bones nearly to death with the Black Spot. But what about Long John Silver that sometimes you like and mostly you hate and still you always want him to be on your side? I can see him hopping along on his peg leg and under his oxter he's got the crutch that he also uses as a club to kill people with and up on his shoulder is Cap'n Flint the parrot that's called after the evillest pirate in

157

the history of the seven seas. But the thing I like most of all is the way the squire and the doctor never talk down to Jim and he's only a boy, remember. I'd give any money to be him. And to have his name. Jim Hawkins. All Murphy makes you think of is spuds or some Irishman they tell jokes about on the wireless but Hawkins is like, I don't know what it's like. It's like wild birds and big wide prairies and danger. The time I was reading *Treasure Island* I even pretended to be Jim. I remember it was the winter time and I was nearly ready to go to sleep when I heard this tap-tapping right outside the house. I started imagining it was the evil hunchback Pew out there on the half-frozen road, wearing the big green shade on his forehead and below it the two dirty black holes that used to have eyes in them. What happened to them? Did Captain Flint tie him to the mast and let the birds peck them out of him? And what was he doing outside our house? He was coming to put *my* eyes out if I didn't give him the map. His henchmen were with him, Johnny and Dirk, and the three of them were coming for me. I was a wreck by the time I got to sleep that night and I'd nothing but nightmares till the morning. Imagine being able to write the way Robert Louis Stevenson does. I never had an adventure in my life, except once, but it would be fantastic to sit in a room by myself working out the greatest adventures of all time, thinking them up as I'm writing them down. Maybe some day I'll do it. The once I'm telling you about was the time of me and Charlie and Barney and Deery's horse and cart. It happened in the dead end Lucky Lane when I was nine. I'm nearly sure it was the first real thing I ever wrote about. It was dead strange, actually, because about a week before it happened there was all this stuff in the front of the Derry Journal about another horse and cart belonging to Deery. It said the horse ran down the breakneck steps with the cart behind him when the milkman was in a house getting paid. The breakneck steps are those ones between Marlborough Street and the bottom of Beechwood Avenue and there's twenty-six of them and they're very steep. The reason it got on the front page with the big headline MIRACLE HORSE BOLTS above it was, the horse stopped right away when it got to the bottom and the milkman told the reporter that not one crate fell off and not one bottle was broken. Shite, of course. The bottom of the bottles would need to have been cemented to the crates and the bottom of the crates would need to have been cemented to the cart. Complete shite. But it looked good in the newspaper and probably a whole lot of people believed it. The thing that happened me was far more exciting than even the pack of lies the milkman told. I actually escaped death by *inches*. But the funny thing was, I couldn't describe it right when I was writing about it that night. No matter how hard I tried I couldn't make it as dramatic and scary as it really was.

What happened was, me and Charlie were down in the dead end Lucky Lane with Barney McKenna. There's actually three Lucky Lanes. The top two meet each other like the lines of a capital L back to front and the dead end one's at the foot of a big drop below the bottom part of the L. The two of us were trying to get Barney to climb up the drop. It was really stupid because it's about nine foot up but we were only wains at the time. We really thought we could do it seeing he's so clever and it was obvious he knew what we meant when we told him we were going to give him a hand. We had him about half way up when we heard this fierce thundering noise coming closer and closer and louder and louder till it was nearly like it was inside our heads, my head anyway, and we didn't know where it was coming from but you'd have thought an earthquake hit Derry. Then, before we knew it, a horse and cart came flying out of the top Lucky Lane and went right over the edge at the corner of the L into the dead end where we were. The horse landed on its back on bits of bricks and broken glass that are always lying there and the cart and crates and bottles and everything shot over the wall of a Marlborough Street back yard just as if they were fired out of a catapult. This was only ten yards at the most from us. The horse started trying to get up and Charlie climbed the wall into the bottom Lucky Lane in record time. He was safe there but he still vamoosed. I saw his face looking down for about a second and then he was away. He told me the next day he was expecting another horse and cart to come any minute and that was why he cleared. I stayed there trying to save Barney. I tried to push him up the wall again and get him to climb the last bit but he was going all panicky and he wouldn't do it for me. Then the horse stood up and started coming towards us slowly like a drunk man. Me and Barney were trapped because the dead end bit was right behind us and the two garden walls nearest us had glass sticking out of the top of them to stop boys climbing over and the two doors were bolted on the inside the way they always were. The horse stopped for a moment and then it's whole body shook as if it was drying itself after a dip. Barney nearly went hysterical and that made the horse worse and he started running at us all staggery. I was too scared even to pray because there were these big long foamy slabbers hanging down from his mouth. Just as he came to us he reared away up on his hind legs and his hooves were right above me. I ducked and ran for my life until I got to the Creggan Hill end of the lane. Then I looked back and he was lying on his back with his front legs jerking up and down just as if he was shadow-boxing. I couldn't see Barney so I thought he must be squashed under the horse. I ran up the hill and the tears blinding me. I flew round the corner of Marlborough Road and into the house. I went straight up to the attic and lay on the bed. I didn't cry anymore. I was trying to think what I'd say to Mrs McKenna about Barney but my mind went blank for a while. Then I got up and knelt at the side of the bed with my head under the clothes. After I don't know how long I went down the stairs and over and rang McKenna's doorbell. I knew it wasn't my fault but I knew at the same time it would seem like my fault. Mrs McKenna opened the door about one inch and before she even looked at me she turned her head right round and said - Barney! Stay! Stay!

Then she said - Hello, Conn.

And I said - I ….

And she said - Yes?

And I said - I was wonderin, kin Barney come out tay play?

And she said - Not just now, Conn. I have to give him a wash. He's been a bad boy.

(Don't ask me. *I* don't know.)

I didn't open my mouth about it in the house. The next day at school Charlie told me he knew all the time I wasn't dead or

160

anything because he'd have heard. On the way home he said to me - How's about goin down tay see the dead horse?

We went but there was no horse. Or blood or cart or anything. I looked at the next four Derry Journals and it wasn't in any of them. I don't know about Charlie because I never asked him but *I* didn't tell any grown-ups about what happened.

I'm getting a play on the wireless! It's going to be on Children's Hour in two weeks time. It's called *The Hermit*. The only reason I didn't tell you before about writing it and sending it away and all was, I didn't want to think about it in case they wouldn't take it. There was a cheque for a fiver in the envelope and the letter was signed at the bottom by Cecily Matthews, Co-ordinator and Presenter, Northern Ireland Children's Hour. I heard her on the wireless a whole lot of times so it was funny seeing her handwriting in a letter to me. I got the word about it this morning and I can still hardly believe it. I wouldn't even have written it if it hadn't been for a boy called Brian Harley from Creggan. He'd a play called *The Light at the End of the Mountain* on the Home Service last year and I listened to it and I thought, *I* could do that. I didn't mean I could have done Brian Harley's play if I'd thought of it first. I meant I could write one just like he did. It turned out I was right. It was dead easy. It's actually far easier than writing a story. The only part I didn't like was doing the corrections. Arthur told me a real writer has somebody to do the corrections for him. He said W.B. Yeats the famous poet and playwright couldn't spell right and he needed some man to check every word he ever wrote.

The hermit's an actual person. He lives near Granny and Granda up in Cloghan. Years ago I used to hear them and Auntie Cassie and Auntie Nellie talking away about this oul boy that lived by himself near the bottom of the lane. So I started asking about him and they told me he lived in a hut the size of nothing and I wasn't to go near it. I looked for it the first chance I got. It isn't even as big as our coalhouse and it's a bit like a workman's hut you'd see on a building site except this is built with stones and sods and there's no glass in the window. There's no chimney either but it has a hole in the roof because I saw smoke coming out of it the day I found it. The roof is just bits of corrugated iron with big flat stones holding it down. He was never there any time I stopped although one day on my way back from Marley's shop I thought I saw a black face looking out of the dark at me and I ran like hell. I know now I was probably only imagining it but I was sure it was him at the time. In the play I wrote I made up a whole lot of things about him and I had a boy and a girl in it and a happy ending just like Brian Harley had. It's actually sort of embarrassing because when I read the copy I have of it after I got the letter from the BBC it seemed really childish. I was just over fourteen when I wrote it and by the time I got round to asking Mairead to type it and she got round to getting permission to do it in the Derry Journal office where she works I was fifteen. And by the time it's broadcast on the twentieth of March I'll be sixteen all but three months. You know what I mean? I made it simple, for children of nine of ten to listen to, because that's the kind of plays that are on Children's Hour. But I think now there's plenty of ones going to say it's completely corny and what was I doing writing a thing like that? But just because the boy and girl in it are only wains, that doesn't mean I'm like them. It's a cert nobody ever tells Richmal Crompton she's stupid writing about William and Ginger and the rest of the gang and her a grown woman. I'm wondering if I should say to people that Frank Richards is probably a very intelligent man who thinks like an adult except when he's writing the Billy Bunter books. But there's no point in it because I know some tube would only turn round and say - Hah! Did yeez hear that? Murphy thinks he's another Frank Richards.

Maybe I'll just tell ones I know not to bother listening to it because it's only for wains. But how can you get round everybody?

I told Mammy I'd a sore throat yesterday and I stayed off. I didn't want people saying to me about the play after the thing being in the Journal. There was this bit on the front page about it that Mairead got put in. But then as soon as I landed in the College gate this morning the president was waiting for me at the bottom of the walks. He was ripping. You always know to look at him if he's ripping. That's if you can recognise him. He only comes out of the office about four times a year. He'd these dark glasses on I saw him wearing a couple of times before and you couldn't see his eyes at all. But you didn't have to see them to know he was on the tear. He said - I want to see you right away, Murphy. Come with me.

Then he turned round and started moving as if he was in a walking race. He's a bit of a tub but he was really travelling. I had to run half the time to keep up with him. I knew boys were staring at us and I wasn't even looking at them. I didn't care, to tell you the truth. All I was thinking of was what I was going to say when I got to the office. The only thing I couldn't work out was how he'd heard the play already when it wasn't even on yet but he seemed to know. Okay, I'm going to tell you now and I should have told you before. I cogged some parts out of *Silas Marner*. Well, I didn't exactly cog them but I might as well have. I didn't even want to say to *you* but I have to now seeing I'm going to be telling you about what happened in Meehan's office. I don't know why I put down all that stuff about not wanting people to hear it because it was childish. Remember I said the hermit came from me hearing about the oul man that lived by himself up in Cloghan? Well, he did, but he came from *Silas Marner* too. There was a part of it in our reading book in sixth class at Rosebawn and when I was thinking up the play I couldn't get *Silas Marner* out of my head. I really thought it was just a wee story in a reading book. But then one day about three months ago I was over at the library in Brooke Park looking for this book *Rebecca* by a writer called Daphne du Maurier Brendan told me about. I couldn't find it and as I was standing there half dreaming my eyes wandered to the Es and I saw the name *Silas Marner* by George Eliot and I nearly fainted. My play was sent in already and I was waiting for an answer from the BBC. I took the book off the shelf and looked through it without taking anything in. Then after a minute I started to think clearly. I found a part near the front about the author. It turned out it was a woman even though she was called George but the really important thing it said was that she was a renowned writer of classic novels and it gave a whole list of them. She was famous! She wasn't just somebody anonymous that did wee stories for school reading books. I didn't panic but I wasn't far off it. It took me a while to get a hold of myself but then I checked to see were there many Brooke Park Library stamps on it. There were two. That meant only two people had read this copy. I looked and there were no more copies of it. There are no other libraries in Derry. I don't think there are, anyway. I took it home with me. I never read it but I kept renewing it every time the two weeks were up. Then they started fining me so I told them I lost it. But last week this big wagon behind the counter got on to me. You want to have a look at her. She's like one you'd see running a girls' reform school. And the voice!

- You hawve two options, young mawn, she said to me. - Eithah you paiy the vawlue of it aw you replaice it with a new aw almost new book of equal vawlue. Othahwise you'ah no longah a membah.

I'm going to bring over *Children of the New Forest*. It's been sitting on the floor in the alcove in the front room for over a year and nobody's gone near it except for me. I read the first fifteen pages and then chucked it. I wouldn't even have gone that far only Arthur bought it for me and I wanted to be able to tell him something about it if he asked. But he never said a word about it and it's been there since the Christmas before last. I know what's going to happen. The day after I bring it over to the library he's going to say to me - Eo, by the way, Conn, hawve you finished thawt Cawptain Marryawt novel? I'd like to read it if you deon't mind.

When I was going up the steps behind the president I'd it worked out that he was probably going to take his own copy of *Silas Marner* out of a bookcase or something and slam it down

on his desk as soon as he got me in the room with him. Either
that or he'd say he read it years ago and he remembered it all
and he'd tell me I'd disgraced the College. I wasn't feeling too
good by the time we got to his room. When he was closing the
door he pointed for me to go over to his desk. Then he came
and sat down behind it and started puffing away and the colour
of him would have scared you. That'll teach him not to walk so
fast, I thought. Maybe he'll die now.

- Are ye awright, Ffffaller? I asked.

He just kept on puffing.

- I wa-wa-was ssssick yistirday, Ffffaller. I've got this note.

I took it out of my pocket and put it on the desk. He didn't
even reach for it.

- Are ye sh-sh-sh-sure ye're awright, Ffffaller?

He spoke and I nearly jumped out of my skin.

- No, I am NOT all right, he gasped. - How DARE you ask
me if I'm all right! And stand up! Who told you you could sit
down?

I dived out of the chair and stood there shaking. I didn't
even remember sitting down.

- Who? WHO told you?

- Nobody, Ffffaller.

- Well, then, stand. STAND. And stay standing until I tell
you otherwise.

- Yes, Ffffaller.

- Now, Murphy, I want you to explain the meaning of this.

Oh Jesus, I thought.

And Jesus answered. Well, maybe not, but something came
into my head just when I was nearly sure I was finished. I'd tell
him I never heard of *Silas Marner* OR George Eliot and it must
have just happened that me and her had some of the same
ideas. No, make that me and him, I thought. Or me and he. Or
I and he. Oh fuck.

- Do you understand what I'm saying? he roared.

- Yes, Ffffaller.

- You submit a play to the BBC without asking my permission. And then, to compound matters, you neglect to inform me
even after the play is accepted.

165

I couldn't speak.

- Well? Do you hear me?

Hey nonny no, I thought. Hey nonny *nonny* no. And hey ring-a-ding-ding as well.

- I'm sssssorry, Ffffaller.

- It's much too late to be sorry, Murphy! he thundered. - This was a gross dereliction of responsibility on your part. Have you no sense at all?

- Ffffffff–

- Yes? YES?

- Ffffaller, I didn't know I wa-wa-was sssssupposed tay.

- I'm giving you a warning now, Murphy. If you ever submit anything, ANYTHING, to the BBC or any organ of ANY description, without first seeking my permission, I'll, I'll, I'll, I'll take a very dim view of it. Do you hear me?

- Yes, Ffffaller.

He picked up a pen and put it down again. Then he leaned to the side and opened a drawer. He's taking out the strap, I thought. But he wasn't. He was bringing out a glasses case and taking his glasses off and putting them in it. Then he moved his fingers along the big blotting paper in front of him about twenty times as if he was cleaning dust off it.

- When is the broadcast? he asked. - Next week, isn't it?

- Yes, Ffffaller.

His eyes looked funny. Sort of sunk away in, nearly as if they were hiding.

- Mmmmm. Tell me, is this the first play you've ever written?

- Yes, Ffffaller. I used tay write wa-wa-wee sssssstories but I nivir sssssent them anywhur.

- Mmmmm. What are you hoping to do with yourself when you leave Saint Paul's?

- Teachin, Ffffaller. I'd like tay do teachin.

- Teaching. I see. You know - Cornelius, isn't it? - you know, Cornelius, while teaching may not exactly be a vocation, it does require certain gifts and one gift in particular. To be a successful teacher you must never lose sight of what it is to be young. Because, above all, you must hold on to the youthful

166

enthusiasm which most people tend to shed when they leave their teens. Do you understand what I'm saying?

- Yes, Ffffaller.

He got up and stared at me for ages. Then he said - Sit down. Yes, it's all right. Sit down.

I sat down.

- You know, Cornelius, he said, - if your mind is set on teaching, you're really going to have to do something about your stoppage.

He started walking up and down the room. It was massive. It was nearly as long as a street. On the side opposite the windows there were bookcases and there must have been thousands of books in them. I could see a whole lines of Shakespeare ones and I don't know what else. Up above the fireplace right behind his desk was a picture of Wee Rosie inside a big fancy frame and there was another one of some cardinal with a red hat on him facing me on the desk, only it was small. I sat there waiting for Meehan to start again and wondering about the smell. I'm still not sure but I think it was a mixture of leather and pipe tobacco and some kind of really sweet perfume. The bell for first class started ringing. I'd missed mass.

- You couldn't teach with a stoppage like that, he said, standing right behind me.

- Yes, Ffffaller.

- Oh, you think you could then?

- No, Ffffaller.

- No, of course you couldn't. There is one person who might help, however. I'm sure you know that Mister O'Donnell is very much involved in the theatre. I imagine he would be excellent as a speech therapist. If I were you I would ask him. What do you think?

- Yes, Ffffaller.

- You'll ask him then?

- Yes, Ffffaller.

No fucken chance.

- Good.

He sat down at his desk and started at the footering again. The pen, the blotting paper, the glasses case. The bell stopped.

I looked down at the carpet and waited. I heard his chair sliding back and looked up. He was wearing the dark glasses again.

- Well, Murphy, he said. - You'd better go on to class. What teacher do you have now?

- Mister O'Donnell, Fffffaller.

- Mister O'Donnell. Indeed. Yes. Tell him I detained you. You needn't tell him why.

I got up to go. He stood behind me when I was opening the door. As I went out he said - Remember what I told you, Murphy. Look for my permission if you plan to submit anything in future. You hear?

- Yes, Fffffaller. Thank you, Fffffaller.

The Duck didn't take me under his notice when I came in the door. He was talking away to the class and I went over towards him but then just as I got to him he held up the palm of his hand without looking at me and said - Stop theah! Stop roight wheah you aw. Do you heah me?

Before I could say a word he went on talking as if I wasn't there and started poncing back and forward. He'd make you sick the way he walks. You want to see the springs of him, as if he's going along on a horse or something. And the big hair bouncing up and down back into the same place every time. Brendan says he gets it permed but Gander says he keeps it in place with wank oil. I stood in front of the class feeling a bit stupid. I could see this mouthful of stuff written on the blackboard: Audience participation in Elizabethan Drama. And underneath it he'd : At least three pages by Monday.

After a couple of minutes he waved me to my seat, flicking the back of his hand at me as if he was chasing away a bad smell. Then he said - Naow. Maiy we hawve awn explawnaition from the laite Mistah Meuphy? I stood up and said - The president had me in his office, sir.

So it works, I thought. If you say sir at the end you don't

168

stammer on it.

- Nothing serious, Oi heope?

- No, sir.

- Well, thot's a relief. Naow, Meuphy, you maiy as well kneow thot you hawve an essay to do faw Mondaiy of next week. *Next* week, moind, not the week awftah. Beuns will neo doubt supploy you with neotes you missed whoile you weah in consultaition with Fawthah Meehan. Cleah?

- Yes, sir.

- Then Oi'll proceed.

I sat down. Brendan whispered to me - What's the crack?

I whispered back - I'll tell ye later.

When I told him outside he laughed and said - That'll larn you tay be writin plays. Just get the work done, boy.

The stuff The Duck was talking to us about wasn't that bad, believe it or not. When he's on about plays and all he can be interesting sometimes. He was telling us about this theatre called The Globe that some of Shakespeare's plays were in. A whole lot of the muckers that came to watch had rotten tomatoes and cabbage and things hidden under their coats and if they didn't like the play or the actors they'd plaster them with this stuff. They nearly always sat in these cheap seats that were called the gods because they were so high up and whenever they felt like it they started slagging away at the actors and pegging rotten fruit and vegetables at them. I don't know why but Harry Harkin started laughing away in the middle of that part and The Duck lit on him.

- Whot's seo funny, Brothah Balloon? he said.

- Nothing, sir. Sorry, said Harry.

Harry's a big fat lump that wouldn't annoy a fly. He only came to the College last August. He wants to go away to be a priest. That's why he left the Christian Brothers' Tech. Wee Rosie doesn't let them teach Latin there so Harry had to leave. Rory Doherty and somebody else started hissing from behind their hands and The Duck slammed his cane up against the blackboard.

- One moah animal noise from one moah snaike ond everyone will do this essay three toimes. Is thot cleah?

There wasn't a sound.

- Oi taike it thot it's cleah then. Naow, wheah was Oi?

Toads Walker put his hand up.

- Sir, you were telling us about the plebs abusing the actors.

- Yes, good. Good lod, Cecil. Plebs abusing the actaws. Oi loike thot. Well done, Cecil. Oi con think of cehtain plebs among theose present who would hawve been quoite at heome in the gods. Aw pehawps not. Pehawps they wouldn't hawve gined admission even to thawt pawt of the theatah.

He stopped for a few seconds and pressed his fingers against his forehead.

- Theah was something else, he said, and he gave Harry a dirty look. - Eo yes. Oi was geoing to mention a maikeshift Elizabethan theatah which was once a tawvern called The Red Bull. The Red Bull was used faw some toime but it eventually becaime notorious because of young apprentices rioting during pehfawmances. Aws a result, every theatah in London was shut daown faw a yeah. Seo, aws you will readily undahstawnd, it wasn't quoite enough faw actaws to be tawlented in theose daiys. They hawd to be strong-moinded aws well. Naow, whoile one con eonly condemn the appalling behaviah thot the-atah-geoing thugs got up to in Elizabethan toimes, theah weah many exawmples of propah audience engaigement. Sometoimes a gentlemon would stawm up to the staige in the middle of a plaiy and complain to the actaws about theah pehfawmances aw even abaout the plaiywroight. Awnd we hod numerous othah exawmples in theose daiys of membahs of the audience jeering the villain ond cheering the hero. In con-trawst, audiences naowadaiys aw much too pawssive, much too removed from the auction. In this regawd, theah is neo doubt thot the proscenium awch ond the ceutains aw barriahs to genuine audience pawticipation. Naow, con anyone tell me whot a proscenium awch is?

One hand went up.

- Yes, Cecil?

- Sir, it's a frame-like structure around the outside of the stage.

- Well said, Cecil. Awnd, of cawss, thot structah hos been a retreograide step in drawma. We sit watching actaws encleosed in this unreal fraime awnd we aw expected to suspend aw disbelief.

He stopped and swept one of his hands through his lovely hair.

- Suspend aw disbelief? he said. - Anybody?

- Send it home fur two weeks tay teach it a lesson, came the whisper from Sparrow Scanlon.

- Oi head thot, Scanlon. We'll hawve neo moah of youah thoughtful contributions, thonk you. You will wroite out the Seven Aiges of Mon speech from *Aws You Loike It* three toimes faw tomorreow. Dawty, perhawps *you* would tell us, if you'ah finished exawmining the contents of youah neose. Yes, thot Dawty. YOU. *Rory* Dawty.

- Sir what? said Rory.

- Sir, awnsaw the question, said The Duck.

- Sir, I don't mine the question, said Rory.

- You *do* moind the question, Dawty. You moind it because you deon't *remembah* it.

Rory said nothing.

- Dawty, said The Duck. - Oi'm not awsking faw youah involvement in great drawma. Oi'm meahly requesting thot you do me the ceutesy of listening to whot Oi'm saiying and not sit theah loike some rotting cawbage. Do you heah me?

No answer.

- Oi said do you heah me!

- Yes.

- SIR yes!

- Sir yes.

That's when the bell went.

Outside I started telling Brendan about being up with the President but after he came out with the crack about getting the work done he was only half listening. He didn't even let me finish. When I was at the part about Meehan taking off the dark glasses and all Brendan said - Tell me later about that. I must go now. Listen, are you goin tay *Julius Caesar* the night?

- Wa-wa-what d'ye mean? I said.

- Jesus Christ, it's on in the open air down the Guildhall Square. What's wrong with your head? Did you forget or what?

- Aw aye, I said.

I *had* forgotten. And The Duck's been on to us for weeks about it too. He's producing it and everything and he's these notices up all over the College saying about the modern dress production on the fifteenth of March for one night only. That's the exact day Caesar was assassinated. It was called the Ides of March in Roman times. But, anyway, I told Brendan I wasn't going because I really liked doing it in Junior and I didn't want it ruined.

- Stop talkin shite, he said. - The crack's bound tay be nine-ty. You know who's actin Brando in it?

- Who? I said.

- The Duck, he said.

- Ye're jokin, I said. - Sh-sh-sure how can he be doin Mark Antony wa-wa-when he's the wa-wa-wan's producin it.

- Well, he is. It was in yesterday's Journal. I swear. It did-n't get tay the front lick *The Hermit* but it was in it all right.

- I'm not goin, I said. - I hear enough a The Duck in the College. I hope it pisses on yeez.

- Come on, said Brendan. - Have you no adventure in you at all? Wait tay you hear who's goin to it.

- Who?

- Rory Doherty and Tubes O'Driscoll.

- Rory? How's *he* getting tay it? I said. - Sure he's ground-ed.

Rory's da barred him from going down the town in the dark since the night he fired the sky rockets at ones going into Saint Paul's past pupils' do in the Guildhall. The College never got to hear who did it but the da found out all right. I don't know how but he found out anyway and he nearly lost the bap complete-ly. I heard there was going to be murder till the ma came up with this idea about a curfew. The whole thing started when

Rory kept a clatter of sky rockets from Hallowe'en and then on the night of the do he fitted two on to each of the cannons up on Derry's walls right opposite the Guildhall. But he must have got the angle wrong or maybe they slipped or something because none of them got anybody. Some woman that was passing fainted but she didn't get hit. Rory says it was The Duck's wife and he got her up the arse when she was walking into the Guildhall. None of us ever argues with him about it but I heard it was a maid coming out of work in the City Hotel and the reason she fainted was, it was the shock of one of the rockets hitting the wall just beside her. Rory was okay till after his big brother Frankie went to England. It was him that had the row with McRide about the black babies and that was the reason he left the College. Anyway, Rory's off his head a bit now.

Brendan said - He towl his da *Julius Caesar* was on for the Senior and we all had tay go down or else we'd get intay bother.

- Sh-sh-sure his da knows he did it in Junior, I said.

- You must be jokin, said Brendan. - His da hasn't a baldy clue. Rory says he thinks Shakespeare's an English brewery.

- Naw, I'm not goin, I said.

- For God's sake! said Brendan. - Sure it'll be great steam. You know who O'Driscoll's goin tay get tay go?

- Who? I asked.

- Sparrow Scanlon and Shaker Doherty, he said.

This was different. If those two came The Duck was in for it. Shaker's not the full shilling and Sparrow's a bit of a headcase as well and when those two and Rory get together the three of them are wired up to the eyeballs. The SAS left last June but this crowd's nearly as mad.

- Ye're sssssserious about Sssssparra an Sh-sh-shaker? I said.

- Honest tay God, said Brendan. - Tubes towl me he'll have them there even if he has tay drag them down bay the teeth.

I met Brendan at the bottom of William Street at a quarter to eight and we headed straight for the Guildhall Square. There was a good crowd and I'd say at least half of them were College boys. We stood near the back looking round us. Tubes and some other boy were over at Shipquay Gate chatting up these two Thornhill girls. Suddenly Brendan said - They're here. They're all here.

- *I* don't sssssee them, I said. - The only wa-wa-wan *I* kin sssssee is Tubes an I don't think any a the others are wa-wa-way him.

- Naw, that's cause he's got them nicely scattered. Look. There's Rory takin up position over at the side of the stage. Naw, on over towards the City Hotel. And turn round tay you see who's behind us.

I turned round.

- Yes, Burns. How's the Spud? said Sparrow.

- How's about ye, Ssssssparra? I said. - Tell us this. Is Sh-sh-shaker here?

- Is Shaker here! he said. - *He's* the wan in charge. He fuck-en *betther* bay here.

- Sure I thought it was Tubes that got *yous* tay come, said Brendan.

- Aye, but then Shaker tuck over, said Sparrow. - Jesus, I can-nay wait. This is wan great fucken play.

And he rubbed his hands together.

When The Duck opened his mouth to speak for the first time I heard the shout Wanker O'Donnell! from over the City Hotel direction. It was Rory all right and you'd have known it was him a mile away.

- Speak up! he roared. - Yer cousin Donald cud do betther!

Then Sparrow started.

- Button yer fly, ye animal ye! Ye wudn't see Brando goin on lick that!

- Lave im alone! came the shout from Shipquay Gate. - Thur's fuck all in there tay see anyway.

I stood shaking. I wasn't doing a thing wrong and O'Donnell couldn't see me anyway with the lights shining on him from all around the stage and from Derry's walls too but I was still on the nerves. For all we knew, there could have been teachers in the crowd. I was afraid to even laugh. The Duck couldn't open his mouth without somebody shouting up at him or coughing or sneezing or doing that kind of a fake nose blow where you put a hanky up to your face and make the farting noise with your lips and tongue. The more the play went on the worse the language got. The time Antony begged the conspirators to kill him too after they'd assassinated Caesar Brutus said no and that's when Shaker joined in.

- Fur Christ's sake, Brutus, finish the bastard aff. Putt im tay the fucken sword, or whativir way ye say it. I'm supposed tay hiv im fur a double the marra an I hivn't a fucken tap done.

There he was, over to our left, lying up against the Northern Bank, dead cool, with his hands in his trousers' pockets.

Everybody in the play got peace to speak except The Duck. The time he was making his big funeral speech he was trying to use the audience in the Guildhall Square as if they were the real mourners and in the middle of it he shouted - *For Brutus is an honorable man*, dead sarcastic and all, and a whole crowd of College boys started hissing. Sparrow shouted up at him - Give over, ye schemin cunt ye. Sure a bline man kin see yer oney tryin tay git im intay bother. Well, let may tell ye now, Duck, wur all behine Brute an Cass an the boys so ye kin furgit about it.

O'Donnell ignored him. You had to hand it to him. He was really professional. He just went on as if Sparrow was part of the play. Then, a couple of minutes after that, when he pretended to be all emotional, trying to get the mourners on his side, he put his hand up to his chest and said:

> *My heart is in the coffin there with Caesar*
> *And I must pause till it come back to me.*

He put his other hand on top of the coffin and there was dead silence for about two seconds and then there was this screech from the direction of the city hotel.

- Aw, fur *Jesus* sake, give us a rest, ye fucken phoney.

O'Donnell came to the front of the stage. He tried to shade his eyes from the lights and looked slowly around the whole

Guildhall Square as if he was taking in everything. My legs went all numb. Brendan had his hand up to his mouth and started sinking down on his hunkers. Then the Duck walked backwards to exactly the place he'd been standing and went on as if nothing had happened. He started tempting the crowd about Caesar's will. He was going to tell them what was in it to show them what a great man Caesar had been and what he'd done for the Romans and all but he was trying to keep them waiting for a while before he read it so as to put them into a state that they'd end up wanting to tear the conspirators to pieces. I really thought all the interruptions were over because the only ones shouting now were these people that were acting the mourners. They were standing right at the front of the audience, dressed in ordinary clothes just like the rest of us.

- Read the will, came one voice.

- We'll hear it, Antony, came another.

- Read the will. Read the will, they started chanting, and Antony kept holding on because he wanted them up to high doh before he'd read it. But the suspense must have been too much for Shaker.

- Fur fuck sake. Read the bastardin will an git it over way! he roared and suddenly the whole Guildhall Square seemed to be jeering.

That's what did it. The Duck forgot his next lines and you could see him moving away over to the side and putting his hand up to his ear so that he could hear the prompter. But before he opened his mouth again some boys standing up on Derry's walls started giving him dogs' abuse. That was the first time I knew there was anybody up there.

- Wanker Antony!

- Stuff the Duck!

- Quack quack!

- No surrender!

- That'll do! screamed Sparrow from right behind us. He turned round and looked up at the walls and put his two hands in the air as if he was in charge of a choir. - Give the man a chance, wud yeez!

They stopped but The Duck didn't seem to be ready to go

on. After a minute he started to speak but he only said a couple of words I couldn't hear and then he just stood like a statue. Sparrow lost his patience.

- Thass it, he shouted. - I've heard enough fur wan day. How many times day I hiftay tell ye, O'Donnell? Thur's no fucken point comin on tay the stage wayout knowin yer lines. Right, fur the marra then, ye'll write out the funeral speech three toimes. Three toimes, d'ye hear?

The Duck went over and spoke to somebody standing at the side of the proscenium arch. The next we knew, two of the spotlights at the front of the stage were pointing out instead of in. I was blinded for a few seconds and then when the lights moved on Brendan grabbed me by the arm.

- Quick, he said. - Run for it now.

We ran.

Round in William Street we met Tubes and Rory outside Greasy Barney's and in no time we were all doubled up laughing. But I was only laughing with the nerves and I kept looking behind us in case there was a teacher coming. Then Tubes said - Luck. I think thass the boys inside. Are yeez goin in fur chips? Mawn.

We went in. Sparrow and Shaker were up at the counter puffing away at two wee Woodbines.

- Here come the culture vultures, said Shaker.

- Aw *I* admit it, said Rory. - Ye cannay bate a good Shakespeare play.

- Naw, not even way a big stick, said Tubes.

- It must bay the only Julius Caesar play Antony ivir died in, said Sparrow.

- Whur wur yeez, lads? said Barney.

- Down the Guildhall Square at an open air play, said Shaker.

- Was thur a fair crowd at it? said Barney.

- Well, I dunno about that, said Rory. - I don't think the Duck wud a thought they wur vurry fair. They wur lick some a them rowdies outa *Blackboard Jungle* so they wur.

- Listen, lads, said Barney. - Thur's other people in front of yeez and yeez are blockin the counter. Day yeez wannay sit down or are yeez tickin out way yeez?

- Way'll stay in. Right boys? said Sparrow.

We sat down and ordered three plates of chips between us.

- Hi, said Tubes, - how day yeez think Brando wuda done up there the night?

- Brando? said Sparrow. - I dunno but I'll tell ye wan thing. He wudna stud fur yon abuse.

- Naw, ye're right there, said Shaker. - He'd a come down an redd up.

- So he wud, said Rory. - He'd a fucken cleared the square in nixt tay no time. He's a tough nut, that boy.

- Watch your language, lads, shouted over Barney.

- Sorry, Barney, said Rory. - I was gittin sorta carried away there.

- That's all right, said Barney. - Just keep it pure.

- Day yous think The Duck saw any of us? said Brendan.

- *Nat* at all, said Sparrow.

- He cudna, said Tubes. - Wur any a yeez ivir up on the stage? I mean actin?

- *I* wa-wa-was, I said.

- So was *I*, said Rory. - Ye see damn all out in front a ye cep fur light an black.

- That's a fact, said Tubes. - He saw fu– He saw damn all.

- Naw, said Brendan, - but you know the time he got that boy tay shine the spotlights out? Day yous think he saw us leavin?

- He didn't see *me*, anyway, said Tubes. - *I* slipped roun behine the walls.

- An *I* went roun the back a the Guildhall, said Rory.

- Hi, I'd say the oney wans he saw wur Burns an Murphy, said Shaker. - I'd say the two a yeez ur fur it the marra, boys.

- Tell us this much, Spud, said Tubes. - *You* live near O'Donnell. Whur'd he git that accent anyway?

- I dunno, I said. - But iviry time I'm in Brooke Park library he's in there chattin away tay this hoity toity wa-wa-wan behine the counter that talks lick the Queeng. Ye know the wa-wa-wan lucks lick Khrushchev.

- It was probably him taught *her* tay speak lick that, said

178

Brendan. - Sure he's a freak.

- Somebody towl *me* he's a Docthor a Letthers, said Tubes.

- Docthor a Letthers may hole, said Shaker. - He's a fucken quack, that's what he is.

- Right, lads, that's it, said Barney from behind the counter. - I warned yeez about yer language. Out yeez go. These chips'll do somebody else.

- Aw Barney, said Rory. - *Be* reasonable.

Barney came over to us.

- I'll be reasonable awright. Now, out yeez git.

We all got up.

- Kin way nat even tick the chips out way us, then? said Sparrow.

- The oney thing yeez kin tick is yersels, said Barney. - Out tay fuck.

After we went Sparrow poked his head in the door again and shouted - I wannay tell ye somethin now, Grazy. That's the last time wur ivir comin in here. *Ivir!*

- Ye kin say that agin, Barney shouted back.

On the way up William street Brendan said - What do yous think'll happen the marra with O'Donnell?

- Fuck all, said Rory. - What the fuck kin he do? Sure he cannay prove fuck all. He's a stupid cunt.

- I'll tell yeez wan thing, said Sparrow. - He won't furgit *that* night in a hurry.

- Iss lick the man siz, said Tubes. - Ye mine the wee man near the start. The truthsayer or whativir ye call im. He shuda listened tay im.

- Aw, aye, I mine now, said Sparrow. - Whass this it was he siz?

- Ye not mine? said Tubes. - He siz *Beware the Ides a March*.

Shaker and Rory and Sparrow got a rough time the next day. They were hardly in the door of first class when The Duck arrived and marched them up to Meehan and they weren't back

179

down till near lunchtime. Boys were saying at the break that Tubes wasn't sent for. That's probably because he's not in our English class. Anyway, where was a big crowd round the three of them down near the handball alley after we got out at half twelve. I heard when I was taking my lunch that none of them owned up and nobody stooled on them either. Brendan said there should be a monument put up.

We were supposed to have The Duck second in the afternoon but he didn't show up. Meehan took us instead. He came in a bit late puffing like mad and he nearly went through us because of the noise we were making. He called out Shaker and Rory and Sparrow and told them they were to spend the rest of the class in the chapel.

- Father McBride is hearing confessions there at this moment, he said. - You may avail of the sacrament if you feel the need. Do you hear?

After they went out he didn't speak for about two minutes. He just kept walking back and forward like somebody demented . He hadn't the dark glasses on but he was cleaning away at these ordinary ones with a hanky and putting them on and taking them off about every ten seconds. He's got this funny way of moving when he's wearing his soutane. It's a bit long on him and you can't see any of his legs or his feet and you'd think he was going along on roller skates. That's the way he was walking now. But then he stopped and put on the glasses again and stuffed the hanky inside his soutane and started straightaway about Shaker and them being a bad influence. He tore them to shreds for a while and then suddenly he changed his tune for a bit.

- It is possible, of course, he said - that there are certain people here who are friendly with these three...fellows. Some of you may even look up to them. Indeed, I have no doubt they have their good points. But if they were responsible for some or all of the abominable behaviour of last evening then it would be misguided for any of you to shield them. Saint Paul's has a deserved reputation for high standards, moral as *well* as academic. We have been educating the Catholic cream of this city for almost seventy years and it is deplorable that our name should be dragged through the mire by...by...by a bunch of... of... louts. I have it on good authority that students from Foyle College and Londonderry Girls' High School were present in Guildhall Square. What sort of message do you think last evening's ... shenanigans send out to them? What sort of reports do you think they have brought back to their places of education? I say this to you now, boys. The culprits should not be protected, not even for their own sakes, *especially* not for their own sakes. Their behaviour was dishonourable and shameful and they must be made be understand that.

Then he gave us this spiel about what a great teacher The Duck was and the brilliant results he got for boys in the Senior and how he *lived* for teaching.

- I should tell you, he said, - that Mister O'Donnell was most distressed at the intolerable treatment he was made to endure in Guildhall Square at the hands of...of boors. He spent literally months, MONTHS, preparing this production only to have it sabotaged by...by...by philistines. He did not feel able to take classes today although he came in this morning fully intending to do so. He knows he has so much to offer you and he did not want you boys, or any of his other students for that matter, to miss out on even one period. He told me so himself. His dedication to teaching is second to none. But, of course, you all know that already.

His voice was changing. It was softer now, friendly nearly.

- I find myself in a peculiar situation here, boys. I remember when I was a young student like yourselves that it was looked on as unacceptable for one to tell tales on one's school-mates. I understand those sentiments completely but in this particular case there are certain malevolent people who trespassed on the rights of our Junior Final students attending last evening's performance. These young boys will be required to answer difficult questions in their Ministry of Education examination in less than three month's time. The understanding and appreciation of *Julius Caesar* which they should have experienced were trifled with, *trampled* upon, by Seniors who should have known better. How would *you* have felt if it had been, say... What Shakespearean play are you studying this year?

- *As Ye Lick It*, Faller, said Staunch Stevens.

- Ah, yes, one of Shakespeare's better plays. Indeed. Now, if it had been *As You Like It* and Mister O'Donnell had been playing Bottom, say, and…and - yes? What is it?

Toad's hand was up.

- Father, Bottom was in *A Midsummer Night's Dream*.

The president stared at him.

- And what? he demanded.

- Father, he wasn't in *As You Like It*.

- Is THAT so?

- Yes, Father.

He walked down to Toads.

- Stand up when you're speaking to me, sonny, he barked.

- Father…

- STAND UP!

- Father, I *am* standing up.

The president went closer.

- Well, stand up *straight* then! Do you understand what I'm saying?

- Yes, Father, said Toads. He was really pale.

- Now, sonny, as you're such a Shakespeare enthusiast, I take it you were in Guildhall Square last evening?

- Yes, Father.

- And what did you see?

- The play, Father.

- Don't get impertinent with me, sonny! I KNOW YOU SAW THE PLAY! What *else* did you see?

- Nothing, Father.

- Nothing? NOTHING? The play was disrupted by a gang of hoodlums and you saw NOTHING?

You could nearly smell the shite off poor Toads.

- Well? WELL? roared Meehan.

- I couldn't see who did it, Father. It was too dark.

Meehan stood there like a beetroot. There was dead silence for about a minute and then he said - Mmmm. Sit down. What's your name, sonny?

- Cecil Walker, Father.

- Hmmm. Yes. Right. I see. So.

He walked back up to the front of the class.

- Now, he said, - as I was trying to say before I was interrupted, if it had been *As You Like It* that was being performed last evening and you boys were required to answer questions on it in three months time in your Senior examination and some...some *thugs* had arrived on the scene and...and interrupted by howling disgusting obscenities up at the stage, how would you have felt? Well? Well?

There was no answer.

- I'm asking you how you would have felt!

There was still no answer.

- Have you all been struck dumb or what? he roared.

- Outraged, Father, said Toads, shooting up like a jack out of the box.

- What? snapped Meehan.

He stamped down towards Toads with the eyes standing in his head.

-What did you just say sonny? he demanded.

- Outraged, Father, croaked Toads. - We'd have felt outraged.

Meehan stopped and stared.

- Oh yes indeed, he said. - Outraged. Exactly. Outraged. What's your name, sonny?

- Cecil Walker, Father.

- Walker. Yes. Good lad, Walker. Outraged. You'd all have felt outraged. And you'd want to know who was responsible, wouldn't you?

- Yes, Father, said Toads.

Meehan stood there brushing away at the front of his soutane with the palms of his hands. Then his voice got all soft again.

- I want to ask something of you now, boys. If you know the identities of any of the culprits, come and tell me in my office or, if you'd prefer, write the names on a page, sign it and post it to me. I can give you a guarantee that your privacy, your anonymity, will be respected. I would not allow any intimidator to...to...to intimidate you for doing what you are morally bound to do. I have already spoken to the Junior boys who were there last evening and I know from their reaction that information will soon be forthcoming. Be assured, whichever Seniors give me the names will be merely corroborating facts I will already have in my possession.

He turned round every quickly, knelt on the platform, looked up at the crucifix above the blackboard and gave out the Hail Mary. After we'd said the Holy Mary part he turned round to get up and the bell went. He said - Thank you, boys. Out nice and quietly now.

I looked up and he'd this big smile on him. There was something scary looking about it. It was like a trap door lying open waiting for somebody to fall in.

The Hermit wasn't up to much. They'd great music on at the start and the end and those were the two best parts of it. The actors were no good. They were very confident and all but they didn't talk like real people. They'd these voices and you wouldn't have known where they came from. They weren't Derry and they weren't Donegal. I don't think they were Belfast either. I don't know what they were. The thing was, you knew they were acting the whole time. That's what really sickened me. Mairead and Frances taped it. I'm going to wait a few days and then I'm going to accidentally wipe it out.

Kathleen Murphy's in Gransha. I only heard on Saturday. It was Mammy told me. She said to me - Your Aunt Stella was luckin fur ye tay go out way er tay see Kathleen.

And I said - Out where? Where's Kathleen?

And she said - She hadday go intay Gransha fur a wee while way er nerves. Gawn out way er, Conn, would ye? I don't lick askin ye but she's got nowan else. She asked may tay ask ye seein ye git on so well way Kathleen.

It was a quare gunk I got. The last time I saw her was a good while ago. I think it was about three weeks. Mammy sent me down to Stella with the Journal for her to see who all was dead. Kathleen was sitting at the fire just staring into it and she never even lifted her head to look at me. I didn't put much pass on it at the time but then Stella told me when we were going to Gransha on the bus that she wasn't out the door for two months.

- Ye heard about er brekkin it off way Dwayne, she said.

- Aye, ssssomebody wa-wa-was tellin may, I said.

- She hasn't bin out since, she said. - She handed in er notice tay the factory, ye know.

- I nivir knew that, I said.

- Aw, she's bin in a wile state altaygeller, Conn, said Stella. - She wasn't sleepin or anythin. I dunno what come over er so I don't. Dwayne was at the dour a ho lot a times but she sid he wasn't tay git in. She wudn't even go out tay talk tay im. It got she was goin about the house all hours a the night talkin tay ersel an prayin away out loud.

- God. Did sh-sh-she not ssssleep at all? I asked.

- She slep a wee bit on an off but she wud nivir a slep oney fur the tablets the docthor give er.

I know now I shouldn't have gone with her even though it seemed all right at the start. Gransha looked okay from the outside. It's a modern sort of a place and you'd never know from looking at it that it's an asylum. There's gardens and lawns and nice trees and flowers but once you get inside and see the patients you just want to get out. We were put in this big room and there was a woman near us rocking back and forward very fast in an armchair and another one with her hair sticking out everywhere and she was making noises like a donkey. There were people in visiting them trying to go on as if there was nothing wrong.

Stella said - Thur not all lick that, Conn. Some a them's as normal as you or me.

She started on about mental illness being different from madness and in the middle of it a boy about my age walked in the door and came over to us and said - I'm all finished now. When are yeez takin me home?

I didn't know what to say and then I didn't have to say anything because this big man dressed like a butcher came out of nowhere and caught him by the arm and said to me and Stella - Excuse us, and the next thing was, the two of them were away.

Stella started talking a mile a minute then and I sat looking at her but I wasn't half listening. I was thinking I could end up in here. I didn't want to write about it but it's got worse since January. Don't ask me why but it got desperate from then on. If I'm standing with Brendan or Charlie or somebody and they're talking to girls it starts going mad on me. I knew people probably noticed my lips moving with me saying the aspirations so I found this other thing to do. I close my hands and dig my fingers into the palms of them. People never look down at your hands and you don't get cut if you keep your nails really short. I made up my mind about something. I'm not going to wear bathing togs anymore. Last summer we were down at Greencastle for two weeks and I saw ones looking at me on the beach and that made it stand up more. I know it probably gave some people bad thoughts but other people were disgusted because no matter what your brains or your personality are like, once they've seen you down there they know the kind of you. One time in my second year at the College Sheila asked me to go to Carrie McKinney's with her. Carrie's her best friend in Richie's factory. She'd a wee girl about seven and I was hardly in the door till she got up on my lap. That was bad enough but then she started moving about as if she was trying to scratch herself on me. Carrie laughed away and said - Wud ye luck at that, Sheila. Luck. She's mad about im so she is.

I tried to smile but I was getting bigger and harder and I was dead scared the wee bitch was going to jump off me and point and shout - Thur's somethin stickin intay may, Mammy.

I wanted her away from me because I'd a feeling it was going to start happening to me all of a sudden but I didn't want her away from me at the same time because as soon as she got up they'd all see the shape of me. So I let on to have a sore stomach. When I said that Carrie pulled the wee one off me that hard she nearly took thing and all with her. She said - Ye shouldn't bay bouncin up and down on Conn lick that, Suzanne. Wee boys are funny down there, ye know.

I didn't look near any of them. I walked all stooped to the bathroom and after I locked the door I stood against the wall till I came back to normal and then I pulled the chain so they'd think I'd gone to the toilet.

You'd nearly have thought Kathleen was sleepwalking the way she came in. She was staring straight ahead of her and not even blinking. Stella went over to kiss her but she wouldn't let her. She sat facing us but she didn't seem to be looking at us. Her face was like a sheet and there were brown bags under her eyes like you see on old people. She spoke after a minute.

- Hello, Conn, she said and she sort of smiled. Sort of.

- How ye doin, Kathleen? I said.

- Aye, how are ye since, love? said Stella.

- What about the College, Conn? said Kathleen. Her voice was funny. It was nearly as if her tongue was stopping the words from getting out right.

- An the football? How's ivirythin goin?

- Not too bad, I said.

She leaned away forward towards me.

- Don't ivir let anywan putt ye in this pliss, she said. - Don't ivir let them do that, whativir ye do. Ye're too good a fella.

- Och, Kacchleen, said Stella. - Sure iss oney tay ye settle a bit. Sure ye know yersel ye wurn't gittin any betther in the house.

- This crowd in here's got may drugged tay the eyeballs, Conn. I kin harley see straight so I cannay.

She closed her eyes and put the fingers of her two hands on her temples and pressed hard. Then she took them away and looked at me. Her eyes were always blue before but now they were black. And I don't know why it was but she only looked about fifteen. I think she's nineteen or twenty but she didn't look any more than fifteen. Maybe she hadn't any make up on her face or maybe it was the thing she was wearing. It was like a school uniform without the blazer.

- They didn't say, she said, - but I think thur goin tay putt an electric current through may brain. Mibby the marra. ECT. That's what they call it. ECT.

- Who towl ye that? said Stella. - Sure they'd nivir do that.

- Ye think they wudn't!

The words came hissing out of her.

- Luck roun ye, wud ye. Luck at the zombies. Gawn. Luck. Or are ye too scarred tay luck?

- Och naw, pet, whispered Stella. - Themins yer talkin about are probbly in this long time. Thur what ye call long-term patients. Sure ye're only goin tay be in a ween a days.

- What scent is that ye've on ye? said Kathleen.

- Aw, that? said Stella. She giggled. - That's the perfume I got fur Christmas from yer Auntie Minnie. D'ye lick it?

- It wud knock ye down, the smell of it, said Kathleen. - How many times day I hiftay tell ye? Ye dab it on, ye don't tick a bath in it. Jesus.

Stella laughed very loud.

- Aye, she said. - I suppose mibby I overdid it a wee bit. *By* the way, I furgot tay tell ye. Dwayne was at the dour agin yistirday. He was astin away about ye an he wants tay know is it awright if he comes out tay see ye. An here.

She opened her handbag and took out a wee plastic bag. She reached it over to Kathleen.

- He ast may tay give ye this. Iss a relic a the true cross.

- Don't talk tay may about *him*, said Kathleen. - He's lick all the rest a them.

She took the relic out of the bag and held it against her lips.

- Och now, Kacchleen, said Stella. - He's a vurry good livin fella. Sure he's at mass near iviry day.

- Don't mick me sick, said Kathleen. - Thur's oney wan thing *he's* interested in an, believe you me, iss got nothin tay do way the mass.

- Kacchleen!

- Don't Kacchleen me. Ye're not the wan histay stan way im in the front porch at half wan in the mornin tryin tay git im tay keep his hands tay imsel.

- Sacred Heart a God, whispered Stella.

Kathleen put the relic back in the plastic bag and held it

between her finger and thumb. Her hands were trembling.

- Ye wannay know what he'll bay doin the night? she said.
- What night's the night?

- Sathurday, said Stella.

- Right, she said. - I'll tell ye what he'll be doin the night then. He'll bay goin roun all the stickin plasters he kin find in the Corinthian an tryin them out an whin he gits the wan he wants he'll buy er a mineral an–

- Dear God, Kacchleen, said Stella. - Don't bay sayin things lick that in front a Conn.

She turned to me.

- Gawn on outside fur a wee minute, Conn, an wait fur may. Wud ye do that, lick a good fella?

I got up to go. Kathleen started crying.

- I'm sorry, Conn, she said. - I shudna bin givin scandal lick that. I'm wile sorry. Don't bay thinkin about what I was sayin, won't ye not.

- Naw, I wa-wa-won't, I said.

- Ye promise? she said.

- I promise, I said.

- Gawn gimme yer hand, she said.

I leaned down and she took my hand in hers. My stomach jumped.

- Ye're a good fella, Conn, she said. - Gawn now. Mammy shudna tuck ye out here at all but I'm still glad ye come. I'll bay seein ye. Ye'll say a prayer fur may, won't ye?

She tried to smile. I nodded my head and pulled my hand away and went outside.

We must have been nearly half way back before Stella stopped the crying. I kept saying things like It's awright, she'll be out soon, but I was cheesed off. The only thing that stopped her crying was when I said I would sleep in her house that night but that was after she asked me three times. When I told Mammy she pointed her eyes to heaven but she didn't argue. At about ten o'clock I brought my pyjamas and *Hatter's Castle* down to Stella's. She was all over me. She gave me two packets of crisps and so much lemonade it was coming out my nose. The two of us sat listening to some useless murder play and we hardly talked to each other. After the eleven o'clock news she brought me up the stairs.

- I hope ye don't mind sleepin in Kacchleen's room, she said. - I hadn't time tay git the other wan ready.

- Naw, thass awright, I said.

Hatter's Castle is really sexy. The only reason I started it was because Bernard told me not to. He saw it lying on the sideboard beside some of my College books and he must have thought I got it out of the library. I never saw it before in my life.

- I wouldn't read thawt if I weah you, he said. - A.J. Creonin was suffering from a mental breakdown the time he wreote it awnd he haws some crude pawts in it thawt he would nevah nawmally hawve written. It's not a suitable book to be reading.

I soon got to some of the stuff Bernard was on about. I knew it was coming from two nights before and I kept it for the Saturday. I knew because when I left off on Thursday Denis and Mary were walking away from the fairground full of longing for each other. Now it was Saturday and they were lying in each other's arms in the dark rushes and he was doing it to her. But it's funny. The way it was told it didn't seem dirty. It's hard to explain right. I was all going from head to toe but it wasn't from bad desires, not even earlier on when he knelt down and pressed his face against the front of her dress and wrapped his arms around her and felt her legs trembling or when his fingers followed the vein from her neck down to her lovely breasts. Then at the part where their two souls rose up from the rushes and met and the last lights twinkled out away back at the misty fairground I left down the book a bit out of breath and lay on my back. The tingles went away after a minute or two and Bernard came into my head. Imagine him saying that was crude, I thought. But he was older than me and he was more mature, of course. I started to wonder if he could be right. I wondered about it for a while and then I said to myself, He *must* be right. Sure the two of them weren't even married and there was this boy pressing away into the girl and her lying there with her legs open wide like a real bloan. If they'd really loved each other they'd have used self control and had respect for each other's bodies instead of using each other for pleasure. The priest that came looking for vocations warned us about dirty books. *Literature that goes by the name of art but only snares the soul.* That's what he said. He told us about people becoming slaves to sex and the diseases they get. I never heard the College chapel as quiet.

I turned back over on my side and read on a bit.

> *With the falling mist all sound was*
> *blotted out and the stillness became*
> *absolute until after a long time a*
> *trout jumped upstream and splashed*
> *heavily in its pool. At the sound,*
> *Mary stirred slowly and, conscious-*
> *ness of the world half returning, she*
> *whispered softly: "Denis I love you.*
> *Dear, dear Denis."*

I couldn't work it out. The way A.J. Cronin wrote it, it was as if there was nothing else they could do at the time, they needed each other that much. When they walked away from the rushes you knew Denis wasn't saying to himself, I got her right and good there. What a ride! You knew he loved her and it was the two of them that did it to each other. There was nothing else they could do but what they did.

I read about thirty pages more to where Mary told him that her father had forbidden them to meet and then my eyes started to close. But I didn't go to sleep because I remembered I'd forgotten to tell Stella to let me lie on till twelve mass. I went down the stairs and was just about to open the kitchen door when I stopped. Mammy was in there and she sounded annoyed.

- Stella, would ye listen tay may. Close the bottle now and I'll tick it up tay the house way may.

- I'll jist tick another wee sope, Murray, came Stella's voice.

- Ye won't, Stella. I'll hide it away somewhur and I'll give it back tay ye when this is all over. Way God's help Kathleen'll be home soon. Keep the rest of it fur a wee celebration then. Now wouldn't that be a good idea?

- I know iss not good fur may, Murray, but sure I harley slep since she wint in. Them tablets Docthur McArdle give may aren't much good. An then I'm walkin about all day lick a–

- I hope ye're not tickin *them* on top a the drink.

- Aw naw, Murray. Aw naw, sure that wud kill ye. Naw, I wudn't do the lick a that.

- Would ye not just close the bottle now, Stella? Sure ye've mass tay go tay in the mornin.

- I wull, Murray, I'll putt it away now in a minute.

Then I heard her crying.

- I blame maysel, Murray, so I do. I brung er up too strict. But sure she was a bad age whin Gerry died. Just startin tay luck at the boys. Ye mine, Murray? Ye mine how good luckin she was?

- And still is, said Mammy.

- But God, Murray, ye shuda seen er the day. She's far shuck, Murray, even since *you* seen er last. Whin I think a them boys roun er lick dogs roun a bitch. May oney child. It was disgustin so it was. I hadday keep er in. Sure ye *know* I hadday.

- I do Stella, said Mammy. - I know rightly.

- See, Murray, I'd a bad time maysel. Didn't I tell ye the way it was in the convent? Sure I towl ye before. The time I worked in the convent the nuns made me an the other girls wear this thing roun ur busts, ye know, lick a big thick bandage, so's nobody'd see nothin. Sure I grew up thinkin thur was somethin wrong way hivin a figure.

- Sure I know, Stella.

- The figure God gimme, Murray. The figure God gimme. An then, ye see whin I got married, sure I didn't know a dang thing. I knew nothin, Murray. Nothin. Sure I near died a shock the first time. Them nuns has a lot tay answer fur. I'm tellin ye. They've a lot tay answer fur so they hiv.

- Sacred Heart, said Mammy.

- Sure I wasn't fit tay bay bringin up a child an me wayout

a man. Day ye know this, Murray, an I nivir towl this tay a sowl
before. Nivir onced did I ivir see Gerry wayout his close on, nor
him me. Nivir onced, tay I washed his body.

I heard Mammy on her feet.

- Tick it easy now, Stella. It's not right fur ye tay be–

- Winter an Summer way tuck ur close off in the dark an he
jist lifted may nightdress under the bedclose an then I pulled it
back down whin he was finished.

- God bliss us and save us, Stella, said Mammy. - Ye should-
n't be sayin things lick that. Here's this hanky. Gawn, tick it. It's
clean.

- Aw dear God. Tick the bottle way ye, Murray. Wud ye do
that fur me? Wud ye? God furgimme fur goin on lick that an me
oney at Confession the night. Ye're right, Murray. I shudna bin
sayin them sorta things.

- I hiftay go, Stella, said Mammy. - I'll tell ye the reason I
came over. I wanted tay ask ye would ye let Conn lie on a bit in
the mornin. Would ye let im lie tay half eleven? He's in the choir
and he sings at twelve Mass, ye see. And don't bother givin im
any breakfast. He always goes tay the altar.

- He's a lovely fella, Murray. Kacchleen's wile fond of im so
she is. I mine er sayin wan day he's jist the sort a fella she'd lick
to end up marryin.

- Aw now, Stella.

- Naw, naw, Murray, she didn't mean him *imsel*. She meant
somebody *lick* Conn. Sure thur cousins, Murray, an anyway,
he's too young fur er.

- I'm away, Stella, said Mammy. - Git tay bed now, would
ye?

- I wull, Murray, and thanks.

I was half way up the stairs by this time and I got to the
landing before the kitchen door opened. When the front door
slammed I was back in bed. I lay there shivering. After a minute
I put my head under the clothes and gathered myself up into a
ball to try and warm up. That's when I smelt the perfume. It
was coming off the sheet under me. It was just there and no
more. I had to press my nose hard into the sheet to really get the
smell of her. I moved my head down and then further down.

She *fancied* me. She fancied *me.* Maybe she lay here sometimes, thinking what it would be like to have me lying beside her. I straightened up and slid the flat of my hand from the pillow to the very bottom of the bed. There was one time we were nearly ready to leave Battisti's ice cream parlour. Dwayne sat on at the table for a minute telling me and Charlie something and Kathleen was standing waiting for us at the door. She was getting really impatient, folding away at her arms and stamping her foot and the light from outside was shining through her skirt the whole time. Dwayne had his back to her and Charlie couldn't see her either because of the place he was sitting but I could see her right up to where she'd the wee short knickers on. She would have died if she'd known. Sometimes after that I thought about her but not for long because she's my cousin and it would have been unnatural as well as being a mortal sin. Anyway, Dwayne was built like a tank so that was the kind of man she liked. I *thought.* But I was wrong. I was wrong all the time. When I thought about it, she hardly ever talked to him when we were walking along the street. And she nearly always seemed to be facing me in Bap's and Fiorentini's and there was always a good gap between her and him. *I* was the one she talked to most of the time. Dwayne never seemed to mind. What did we talk about? I closed my eyes. Me. It was me we talked about. She was always asking about the College and films I saw and books I read and she laughed at a whole lot of the things I said. She hated him trying to get fresh with her. She said that in Gransha. Maybe the two of us were made for each other. She was different, just like me. You know what other girls call boys that treat them with respect? Martyrs. Gander told me . They call the clean ones martyrs and laugh at them behind their backs and they throw themselves at the slags that are only out for the one thing. I could ask her to meet me up Sheriff's Mountain. There's places there nobody ever goes near. I'd get her to close her eyes and then I'd kiss her very softly and caress her white neck and maybe her shoulders later on if she'd let me. Once I knew she was going away with me I'd apply for a teachers' training college somewhere in England. She'd come over the week after me and we'd get married right away. I'd have the flat ready and all. Then we'd write a long letter each to Mammy and Stella. The babies could be deformed or backward or maybe both. But not necessarily. Trevor Smith's going on to be a doctor and he told me those kind of babies are sometimes completely normal. Maybe God would reward us for being pure. *He* would understand how we kept each other in the state of grace by not going with anybody else, each of the two of us ready for heaven no matter when He called us.

Were you ever sorry *before* you did it? That's the way I was but I knew I couldn't stop myself. I turned over onto my stomach till I was right on top of where she lay. My head was even on her pillow. I kept my pyjamas on and when I was finished I cleaned my hands and around my front with the tail of my shirt and hung it over the chair away from my other clothes. I looked at the undersheet. There wasn't a spot on it. I lay down again and said the Act of Contrition. I couldn't go to the altar in the morning but I still said it because even in the middle of doing it with myself I made a firm purpose of amendment. I knew I was finished with her, you see. I'd never touch her. The whole thing was stupid. Imagine thinking of getting married to your first cousin and you a Catholic. I was finished with the book too. I was only at page seventy-four and there were nearly four hundred pages to go but I'd leave it back on the sideboard where I found it. Or where Bernard found it, I *should* say. Then I started wondering if it was better to dump it in the bin under a pile of ashes so that nobody else would get corrupted by it. I could tell Khrushchev it was lost and give her the Hilaire Belloc book of funny rhymes that Arthur bought me for getting the play on the wireless. But it wasn't out in my name so there'd probably be a whole handling. Let whoever's reading it read it, I thought. It's their lookout.

I got out of bed and went to the toilet. There wasn't a sound but as soon as I put on the bathroom light Coulson's stupid setter started going mad out their back as if I was going to attack it. It kept running about, barking like a maniac even after I switched off the light and went back into the bedroom. But it didn't stop me from sleeping because the next thing I remember was Stella calling me in the morning.

Gander's left the college. He told me the day we got our Easter holidays. He's supposed to be getting a job with his da over in England. I wish I was him. Well, in a way I do, but in another way I want to be a teacher and if I'm going to do that I have to stick it out in this hole. His ma's going to be staying in Derry. I didn't ask him why but it seems funny, her staying.

I wrote a letter to Jackie McHugh on Sunday after mass before Charlie and me went down to the Sinn Fein thing. I was asking him what he thought of Kilkenny. I just wanted to know what it was like, what subjects they had to do and if they were hard and if they played soccer as well as gaelic. Things like that. I hardly saw him at Christmas and I want to make sure I'm not trying to find out about it at the last minute if I decide to apply for there instead of doing teaching.

I posted the letter on the way down. There was a big crowd in Meenan Park for the speeches. That was because it was the fortieth anniversary of The Rising. It's Charlie gets me to go every year. He's mad about Irish history and it's really annoying sometimes because he gets on to me for not knowing things. Like De Valera getting the ports back from England and the Free State becoming a republic and all. He never gives over about this boy Dan Breen the great rebel that gave the English a bad time and he knows the names of all the ones that signed the 1916 proclamation. I only know two of them, Patrick Pearse and James Connolly. They had a thing in the Derry Journal about James Connolly last week. The English executed him sitting in a chair because he was that badly injured from the fighting he couldn't stand. This is the third Easter I was down and, to tell you the truth, the first two times the boys making the speeches were a bunch of weirdos. I don't know what it was but they were just weird. Maybe it was them all having the same kind of hat on, you know that stupid soft hat some people wear, and every one of them having these fierce-looking eyes. And they kept coming out with all this stuff about birthright and Ireland unfree never being at peace. They're the only ones I ever heard going on and on about birthright and *I* never saw any sign of Derry not being at peace. It's so peaceful it's half dead if you ask me. But it's funny because the people on Sunday seemed to be a completely different crowd. I actually knew one of them, Sparker Kelly, and there's nothing weird about *him*. I waved up to him and all but I soon stopped because people were looking at me and, anyway, he never noticed me. Sparker does work in our house sometimes and he's always good crack. He was a scream the day he was putting in a new switch in the kitchen. I was the only one there and he was telling me about how Scraggy McCallion from down Creggan Hill keeps a living fly in her tea caddy so she'll know if anybody's been at her tea when she's out. The way she knows is, she opens it when she comes back in and if the fly's not inside she starts asking questions. She knows it's never her husband Sucker because he can't make tea. Sparker had just finished telling me that one when who walked in the door but Scraggy herself.

- How ur ye, Sarah, may love? he said, dead cool. - Way were jist talkin about ye there.

Her face lit up.

- Aw Johnny, she said, - I'm all lured away. What wur ye sayin? Gawn tell may.

- I was jist tellin Conn here about the grand cup a tea ye make.

She was as pleased as a peacock. Then he started her about the time Tessie McGillicuddy did her number two up in Cloghan. Anybody would have known to listen to him he'd heard the whole thing before but he kept going on at her to tell it. Cloghan's the place Uncle Eddie and Daddy and them used to live and, the thing is, there's no toilet there. You have to go up the hill. So Scraggy told us about Tessie going round the side of the house to do the number two because she couldn't have been bothered going up the hill and then when she was finished she

197

couldn't find anything to wipe herself with.

- Aw, ye shuda heared er tellin it, Johnny. 'Thur wasn't even a bucken blade a grass, Surrah', she siz. 'So what did ye do anyway, Tessie?' I siz. Siz she, 'I siz a prayer an this wee white goslin come roun the corner from behine the house. So I let on I'd somehin in may han an I coo-cooed it an it come over tay may an I used *it*.' *I* siz tay ur, 'Ye didn't do that, Tessie. Did ye?' An she siz, 'I did so. Sure what else wud ye expeck may tay do?'

Sparker gave a big laugh and said - Ah, she's a star turn, that wan Tessie. A real star turn, Sarah.

It was Sparker that gave the best speech of the whole lot. There was one part where he said - Just because people have powers to do whatever they want, it still doesn't give them the right to do wrong.

I thought that was brilliant. He was talking about the Unionists on Derry Corporation and Basil Brooke and all that crowd up in Stormont and it just seemed exactly right the way he said it. I was standing there saying to myself, That's class, and then I started thinking you could say the same thing about the College, and that's when my mind started to wander. I was staring up at Sparker but I wasn't listening to a word he was saying. Some of the nights I don't sleep right these things come into my head about wee boys being pushed into the gas chambers by the Germans and the mas and das standing over at the side saying, 'Stop your gurnin. Yeez wouldn't be getting this if yeez didn't deserve it'. But the wee boys have College blazers on and when I look at the Germans' faces they're really the commandants, of course, and the one in charge of them is the president, only *he's* in the office. Sparker shook his fist in the air and we all clapped. Sure they can do whatever they want, I thought, and nobody's ever going to make a speech against *them* and there's never going to be a protest march either. People are just going to keep saying - That place turns out some great students. Look at the exam results. Wasn't it four Exhibitions they got last year?

- Up the Republic! somebody in the crowd shouted and Charlie whispered to me - I hope thur's no cops about. Ye're not allowed tay shout that.

I looked all round Meenan Park. I couldn't see one anywhere. But there were two of them standing at the top of the
New Road when we were going back home. We walked right
past them and the two of us completely ignored them. I'm not
sure if they were looking at us or not but we ignored them anyway.

The Saturday before Gander left we went up to see Derry
against Linfield in Windsor Park. Uncle Eddie hardly ever goes
to soccer matches because it's a foreign game but he had to be
in Belfast that day to get a part for his van and Charlie got
round him to take me and Gander and him up and then Stevie
Robinson came at the last minute. Talk about a bumpy journey.
We were hardly out of Derry till I was sorry I went. We sat two
on each side at the back and I was beside Gander. Charlie and
Stevie were talking away to each other but us two didn't say
anything for a good while. Then I said to him - Ye cud ssssstill
ssssstay, ye know.
    - What are ye talkin about? he said.
    - The College. I'm talkin about the College. Wa-wa-why ye
leavin anyway?
    - Jesus. Wull ye give over about that.
    - Naw, but I'm sssssserious.
    - An so am *I*. So am *I* serious. I wudn't go back tay that pliss
if ye paid may. Fucken Belsen isn't in it.
    - Wa-wa-wud ye not sssssstick it out fffffur another year an a
bit? Thass all iss goin tay tick. Sh-sh-sure ye'd fffffly through the
Sssssenior sssssso ye wa-wa-wud.
    - Naw, I'm cheesed off way it. Thass it. I'm goin tay bay
earnin a packet over there, ye know. May da's got a job fur may
an all. I towl ye that, didn't I?
    - Aye. Bricklayin, isn't it?
    - He writ an towl may thur's fuck all in Derry. He's fucken
right too.
    - Wa-wa-what about yer ma?

- What *about* may ma?

- Wa-wa-what does sh-sh-*she* think?

- May ma says she wants may tay stay but she's oney sayin that. She's sick tay the teeth listenin tay these wans goin on about exams. I don't mean *your* ma. Ye know the wans I'm on about.

- Aye.

- May Aunt Susie's the worst a the whole fucken lot. Ye see yon wan? She's bin tormentin may ma about results since the time a the Qualifyin Exam. Ye know er, don't ye?

- I don't think ssssso.

- May Aunt Susie? Ye know er rightly. She's may ma's sister an she's got exams on the brain. Fucken wanker. Did ye nivir see er daughter? Pauline McDermott? She runs roun way Caroline McCusker.

- Naw, I dunno er.

- Thur from down Pennyburn. This wan Pauline's a fucken brainbox. She lucks lick fuck all but she's a fucken brainbox. Ye must know er. She's the same age as me an er marks wur always bettern myins. Ye wannay see the reports she gits. Er ma always ticks them up tay our house the day she gits them. Imagine comin up from Pennyburn tay Marlborough tay show off a report. Fucken tube. Ye know what she got in the Junior? Pauline, I'm talkin about.

- Wa-wa-what?

- Ten fucken distinctions an a fucken credit in Geometry. I says tay her after, 'What happened ye? Ye must a bin out huntin the night before the Geometry.' She's nivir out the fucken dour. Fucken stew so she is.

- Hi, said Stevie. - How day yeez think way'll do the day?

- Wur goin tay git fucken stuffed, said Gander. - An I'll tell ye somehin else. Ye better keep that Derry scarf well hid ur ye'll git *it* stuffed up yer arse the pliss *wur* goin.

The match didn't really matter because Linfield have the league won and Derry are fourth from the bottom so there's no danger of us having to apply for re-election. But you should have seen Stevie. The way he was going on you'd have thought it was a cup final we were going to.

- Wait tay yeez see, he said. - I bate yeez Tommy Houston'll score the winner fur Derry in the last minute.

He's mad. Tommy Houston plays left back and he's never scored for Derry in his puff. But it's funny all the same. The nearer we got to Belfast the more I started to feel the wee butterflies. Even if we weren't going to win I'd a feeling it was going to be exciting. Something dramatic nearly always seems to happen against Linfield.

After Eddie got the thing he was looking for out of this garage he drove to near Windsor and parked up a side street. We had to walk a good bit and the more we walked the scareder I got because there were things like TAIGS OUT and FUCK THE POPE written in big letters on some of the footpaths and gable walls and a whole lot of the kerbstones were painted red, white and blue. I left Gander and Stevie ran and caught up with Eddie and Charlie.

- Wa-wa-wur not goin tay the sssssstand, are way, Eddie? I said.

- Are ye jo-jo-jo- are ye tryin tay cod may? he said. - Sure the sss- the grandstand wa-wa-wud rob ye. Iviry penny ye pay here goes intay the pockets of the fffffreemasons, ye na-na-know. Na-na-na-naw, wa-wa-wur goin tay the unreserved sssssside, ssss-son.

- Thass okay, I said. - I wa-wa-was jist thinkin about wa-wa-what happened tay the Derry sssssupporters last year. Remember at the cup match?

- Aw aye, said Eddie and he laughed. - That's the time the two Protestant ministers fffffrom Derry wa-wa-wur thew outa the grandstand.

He stopped suddenly and put his hand up to his mouth.

- Ssssorry, Sssssstevie ssssson, he said. - I ffffff– I didn't remember about ye bein there.

He was right alongside us all the time probably, and I didn't know either.

- They wurn't Protestant, Stevie said and he didn't sound too pleased. - Themins wur Presbyterians.

- Aw aye. Right, said Eddie. - I thought they wa-wa-wur Ch-ch-ch- Anglians.

- They wur Presbyterians, said Stevie. - May da towl may.

- I cuda ssssswore it ssssssid Anglians in the Ji-ji-ji-journal at the time, said Eddie.

- Naw, they wur fucken Presbyterians awright, said Stevie. - I'm fucken tellin ye now. Sure the wan that got his arm broke's may da's second cousin so he is an all may da's crowd's Presbyterians.

- I didn't na-na-know that, Sssssstevie, said Eddie. - I'm ssss-sorry tay hear that na-na-now.

He put his hand on Stevie's shoulder.

- But ye na-na-know this, sssssson, he said. - Ye'd na-na-need tay wa-wa- be careful about the language ye use wa-wa-whin ye git intay this pliss. An ye're better not tay let anywan na-na-know ye're ssssssupportin Derry. This crew inside here kin git very thick, ye na-na-know.

- An button yer coat over that fucken scarf, shouted Gander. - They'll hang ye way it if they see it so they will.

It was a desperate match. Derry played like a crowd of tubes. We were hardly in the gate till Linfield scored and they'd have been about ten up by half time if Charlie Heffron hadn't saved a bagful. Eddie turned to me when it was two none and whispered - Na-na-nivir agin! Imagine payin tay sssssee *this* load a brock!

The worst part of the whole thing was, we had to clap like mad every time Linfield scored in case people would know we were Derry. But not Stevie. Stevie didn't clap. Stevie just stood there and he seemed to be getting smaller and smaller as the match went on. After Linfield got the third with about five min-utes to go he put his hands on his head and you'd have thought he was going to cry. He never even argued when Eddie said - Mawn. That's enough. Let's go, boys.

Then out of nothing Eddie Nash scored a beaut from about thirty yards. There was complete silence in Windsor Park. Except for Stevie, that is. He started jumping up and down like a madman. He pulled open his coat and took the Derry City scarf out and waved it in the air.

- Brilliant goal, Eddie! he screamed. - Brilliant! Keep goin, Derry! Thur's still time!

The rest of us kept going all right - towards the exit - and I said to Eddie - How long's left? and Eddie said - Ji-ji-ji-ji-jist long enough fffffur us tay git out alive, if wa-wa-wur lucky.

But then three big brutes came from behind us and one of them ran and grabbed the scarf out of Stevie's hands.

- Hi! Gimme that! shouted Stevie. - That's fucken myins.

- It's mine na, Croppy. That's for lightin the farr when I get home.

Eddie was about ten yards away and me and Gander and Charlie were half way between him and Stevie.

- Mawn, Sssssstevie, shouted Eddie. - Fffffurgit about the sssssscarf, ssssson. The fffffinal wa-wa-whistle's goin na-na-now any minute. Derry's wa-wa-well bate. Mawn.

There was no chance. Stevie wasn't for budging. And you'd have known to look at him he was getting ready to come out with a whole mouthful. It wasn't wee butterflies now I'd got. It felt more like big half-dead moths bumping into each other inside of me. You wanted to see the breadth of these boys. And the big red faces of them and the eyes dead close together. They stood looking down at Stevie.

- Who the fuck day yeez think *yous* are, callin *me* a croppy! he roared.

He was standing with his hands out in front of him, and his legs wide apart as if he was going to do the jujitsu. One of them started mocking him.

- Who the fuck day yeez think *yous* are! he chanted. - Who the fuck day yeez think *yous* are!

One of the others pointed at Stevie and shouted - Right, get outa here na before way quarter ye. Gawn and join your brave Papish friends away over thur. They might be cawrds but thur not stupid.

I was never as scared in my life. We couldn't leave Stevie but if we didn't run we were going to be for it.

- Listen tay me, ye stupid big cunt, roared Stevie. - *My* Uncle Gregory's a B man. I'll bate ye none a *yous* are B men. Are yeez? Well, *are* yeez?

The three of them stared at him. You could see them looking away at his face trying to work out if he was telling the truth.

- What's his name? Your uncle. What's his name? said the one with the scarf in his hand.

- Christ! said Stevie. - Are ye fucken deaf as well as stupid are ye? I towl ye his name. Gregory Robinson. An I'll tell ye somehin else fur nothin. His forefallers fought in the Siege so they did. An wan a them died a hunger an all. So that micks them *my* forefallers too. An that micks *me* a loyal son a Ulster. What are *you* a loyal son a? Lundy? Or the James gang outside a the fucken walls.

The boy with the scarf made a mad dive at him and he would have got him too only for the other two standing in front of him and holding him. - Get away tay fuck na! one of them shouted.

- Go, or you're fucken dead. I'm tellin you. Go!

- Whur's may scarf?

- Go!

- I'm not goin wayout may scarf.

- Go!

- Bastards! screamed Stevie as he ran towards us. - Stupid big cunts. Yeez dizn't even know a Caccholic from a Prod. Yeez thew may third cousin outa the stan last year. The Reverend Stanley Milton Robinson. Bline bastards!

The boy the other two were holding back slipped out of their grip.

- Christ Almighty, whispered Eddie. - The big fffffella's goin tay destroy him.

He ran back and pulled Stevie along by the arm. The final whistle went and inside of about five seconds we were all sort of swallowed by the crowd leaving. We couldn't see the big Linfield boy with the scarf anywhere. Well, I suppose we weren't exactly looking for him. When we got out of the ground the rest of us had to run like hell to keep up with Eddie and Stevie they were going that fast. Eddie never spoke till he started up the engine and then he shouted into the back of the van - Na-na-na-na-nivir agin! Na-na-na-na-nivir agin!

Gander's ma had a party two nights before he went. You wouldn't have known from him he was going but you'd have known from her all right. The time I went into the kitchen she was sitting sniffing away and these ones around her all sympathising.

- Sure he'll harley bay away tay he's back, I heard one of them saying to her. - Believe you me, he'll soon find thur's no cookin lick home cookin.

There was a picture up on the kitchen wall of me and Gander the time we made our Confirmation. It wasn't there this long time and it wasn't there when we came back from the Linfield match on Saturday so she must have just put it up for the party. Gander was out in the scullery with this crowd when I came in. Trevor and Stoopy and the two eejits from Bishop Street I haven't seen for donkeys and this boy I didn't know called Gerry something. They were going on very loud about Stanley Matthews being a brilliant winger and being from Stoke. When they were finished talking about that I said - Has yer da a house of his own over ler?

- Naw, said Gander. - He's in digs. I'll bay stayin way im. He says iss a great house. Fantastic food an all. They've got a television set, ye know.

- Ye're jokin, I said.

- Aw aye, he said. - He writ in a letter tay me about the class programmes bes on. He says the futball's great on it.

- I bate ye thur's some sexy shows on as well, said one of the Bishop Street mutts. - Weemin ticken aff thur close an all.

- I'd say ye'll hiv no bother way the birds over there, Gander, said the other mutt.

- Ye're right there, said Gerry. - Sure they believe in fuck all over in England.

- I wonder whass the talent lick in Stoke, said Stoopy. - Iss Stoke ye're goin tay, isn't it?

- Same as nearly anywhere, probably, said Trevor. - Only difference is, it's mostly Prods and pagans over there and anythin goes. Right, Gander? Sure you can do whatever you want with Prods and pagans. Isn't that right, Gander?

- Fucken right ye can, said Gander. - Ye're fucken right there, boy.

- I must sssssee who's in the front room, I said.

As I was going through the kitchen Gander's ma said to me - Be a good fella, Cornelius, an tell Stanislaus an them tay come in outa there, wud ye? Me an Susan has tay go out now tay git some more sandwiches done.

- *I'll* do it, said this one that was probably Susan. - Sure me and Bernie'll do it. You sit there, Molly, an talk tay Nellie an them. Sure ye're done out gittin the house ready.

I went back and told Gander and them and then I went on into the front room. As soon as I opened the door this mingin smell hit me in the face and I heard a voice saying - Is that Conn Murphy? *I* hink thass Conn Murphy. Mawn in son a minute.

It was perfume and sweat and farts, but mostly farts, I think. I'm not even sure who it was that spoke, the place was that stuffed with women. It was the oldest crowd of people I ever saw in the one place. I swear. The youngest one was at least seventy-five.

I said - I'm sssssorry, and I made to go but this big he-woman took the knob out of my hand and closed the door on me before I could get out. It was Tessie McGillicuddy the gosling woman from the foot of Rosemount Hill.

- Aye, ye're right, she said. - Thass Conn awright. Mere a wee minute tay I ast ye this, son. How's yer moller anyway?

She turned to the whole room and said - Thass Murray Murphy's wee boy, ye know.

- Sh-sh-she's gran, I said.

- God, said another one, - I nivir knew Murray'd wan *that* young.

- Aye, that's Murray's wee boy, said this woman sitting beside Tessie I never saw before in my life. She'd a voice like a cement mixer and she didn't look like a woman at all. I'll tell you now who she was nearly the exact same as. Edward G. Robinson.

- Tell us this, son, she said. - What about Kacchleen? Any word about Kacchleen?

- Sure Kacchleen's out, came a voice from the far corner.

- Aye, sh-sh-she got out the other day, I said.

They started rattling on to each other about Kathleen and I looked around the room. They were a fierce sight, the whole lot of them. There was one over to my left that had a moustache like Zorro and you should have seen the shoulders she had on her. I thought of something very quickly and I don't know why it came into my head. It was this. They couldn't *all* have been wagons when they were young. Probably some of them were really glamorous. It would scare you thinking about it. It really would.

- God luck tay the poor wain, said somebody.

- Poor wain may fut, some other one said. - Sure thon wan's spoiled rotten so she is. Sure iviry time ye see er she's a fiss on er as long as the day an the marra. Yer woman Stella has er ruined so she has.

- Ye're right ler, said Zorro. - Ruined. She's always knyamnin about somehin. Ivirythin has tay bay *jist* right fur *her*.

- Wait tay yeez hear this, said Tessie. - *I* seen Stella sittin in the middle of er dinner an her havin tay git up tay mick a cup a tay fur yer ladyship.

- Ye don't say! came a voice from over at the window.

- Ler's may right han up tay God, said Tessie.

- The wan *I* feel sorry fur is Stella.

I recognised *that* voice. It was Scraggy. She was round the far side of the piano with a glass of Guinness in her hand and three empty bottles sitting beside her on the lid.

- Thon woman's far shuck. Sure ler's harley a pick on er, said Scraggy.

She caught me looking at her and she said - Yer mother's keepin awright then, son?

- Aye, sh-sh-she's dead on, I said.

- What d'ye say? said Scraggy. - What's he sayin? I cannay hear ye, son. I've this wax in may ears this two days.

- Somebody wiz tellin may yay've a sister gittin married, Conn, said Zorro.

Who is this one anyway? I thought. How do they all know

207

me?

- Which wan is it, Conn? said Edward G.

- Sh-sh-sheila, I said.

- Sure she might as well, said Zorro. - As long as she picks the right man. I'll tell yeez this now about that wee girl Kacchleen. Lady Muck or no Lady Muck, God wiz luckin afther er whin she broke it aff way thon Yank.

- How day ye mean? said Tessie.

- That boy wiz on reefers so he wiz, said Zorro.

- Reefers? said Tessie. - What's them? I nivir heared a them.

- Did ye nivir hear a reefers? said Zorro. - Ye're hivin may on.

- Nivir in may life, said Tessie. - What are they?

- Reefers is dope. Dope that ye smoke, said Zorro.

- Aw aye. Reefers, said this dying-looking wee woman with a big head of red hair on her. - Sure Guy Mitchell was caught way them.

- Thass newins tay *me*, said Edward G.

- Who's she talkin about? shouted Scraggy to a woman beside that looked about ninety. -Who's Guy Mitchell?

- I cannay hear what ye're sayin, shouted the oul one.

The wee redhead let out a screech of a laugh that went right through me.

- Ma God, she said. - Ye musta heared a Guy Mitchell, Surrah. He's a great singer.

Then she started.

> *Ler's a pawnshop on the corner*
> *In Pittsburg, Pennsylvania,*
> *An I jist gotta git five ur ten*

And nearly everybody joined in singing *Five or ten* after her like an echo.

She was going on by herself when Zorro stopped her.

- Howl on, howl on, howl on, she roared. - Let may tell *you* somehin *now* dear. Guy Mitchell did *nat* tick reefers. I kin tell ye now fur a *fact* he didn't. Don't you *ivir* bay sayin that about Guy

208

Mitchell.

- Whur'd ye hear that about Guy Mitchell? said Tessie.

- Aye, who towl ye that? said Zorro. Her big shoulders were going with rage.

- I dunno, said the wee redhead. - I thought I read it some-whur.

Her eyes were full of tears. She was a beaten docket.

- Whass the world comin tay, anyway? said Edward G. - Sure ler's that fella over in the Stits they say's in league way the divil.

- Who's that? Who's she talkin about? said Scraggy.

- I cannay mine his name, said Edward G. - He wears these tight trousers an he sings. They say he's not daysant.

- I hink I know who ye're talkin about, said Zorro. - Elvis Preston is it?

- That's the wan, said Edward G. - Elvis Preston. The girls bes all screamin at im. Iss not right the way he goes on.

- Iss wile hard fur the young wans now, the temptations ler is, said Tessie. - Sure luck at that poor young fella, Molly's wee boy, what d'ye call im. Sure he shudn't bay goin away at all. Imagine the age of im goin oer tay England.

- Thass right, Tessie, said Scraggy. - Ye're right ler. Sure ler's no morals over ler at all. Sure ye oney hiftay listen tay the filth they hiv on the wireless.

- *Life Way The Lyons* is a nice programme, said the wee red-haired one, dead nervous.

- *Mrs Dale's Diary's* good, said Zorro. - I lick *Mrs Dale's Diary.*

- Aw aye, said Edward G. - *That's* good.

- Molly shudn't bay lettin im go at all, said Tessie. - Yeez know whur he's goin tay be livin, don't yeez?

- Whur? said somebody. - Stoke, isn't it?

- Way the faller, said Tessie and she closed her lips tight.

- An what? said somebody else.

- An ye know who *he's* livin way, don't ye? said Tessie.

- Naw. Who? said Zorro.

- His fancy woman. His lanlady, said Tessie.

And then she mouthed the words *He's livin in sin.*

- What's she sayin? shouted Scraggy to the one beside her.
- Why's she whisperin?

- I'm not goin tay say, the oul one answered. - Ye betther ast er yersel.

- Is that true, Tessie? said Edward G.

- Ler's may han up tay God now, said Tessie.

- Jesus, Murray an Sint Joseph, said Zorro.

- Whass she talkin about? shouted Scraggy. - What ur ye talkin about, Tessie?

- Thass the kinda house that poor young fella's goin intay, said Tessie.

- He nivir come back afther the wee boy died, ye know, said Edward G.

- Who? Who's she talkin about? said Scraggy.

- She's talkin about Jeremiah, shouted Zorro.

- Jeremiah who? shouted Scraggy.

- Jeremiah McLaughlin. Molly's man, shouted Zorro. - Day ye not know Jeremiah?

- Aw aye, shouted Scraggy. - I know *now* who ye mean.

- He blamed *her* an sure nobody cuda done more, said Edward G.

- Isn't that a nice young fella, that Trevor Smith, shouted the oul one next to Scraggy.

- He is, said Tessie. - Ye wudn't know he was a Protestant at all, so ye wudn't.

- Aye, he's vurry ordinary, isn't he? shouted the oul one. - Naw, the reason I'm sayin, Molly was tellin may he offered tay keep Stanislaus in his house the marra night.

- Aye, she towl *me* that too, said Zorro.

- What day ye mean? shouted Scraggy.

- Stanislaus has tay git the Liverpool boat vurry early on Tuesday mornin, shouted Zorro, - an Trevor Smith has a flat up in Belfast an he's lettin Stanislaus sleep ler the marra night an then he's lavin im tay the boat in the mornin.

- God, isn't that vurry obligin of im, said Tessie.

- He's goin on tay bay a docthor, ye know, said the redhead. - He's vurry clivir they say.

- Wait ler a minute, son, Tessie said to me when she saw me

going for the door. - What ur *you* goin tay do?

- I'm goin out tay the kitchen, I said.

- Naw, I mean, whin ye lave Sint Paul's? said Tessie.

- *I* hink he'd mick a lovely priest, d'*you* not, Tessie? said Edward G. - Wud ye not hink a goin on tay bay a priest, son?

- I dunno yit, I said.

It's funny they started talking about that because I got a letter back from Jackie McHugh last Saturday just before we went up to the Linfield match. He told me Kilkenny's brilliant and he's the vice-captain of the soccer team and they play friendlies against other seminaries sometimes.

The course is very interesting, he said, *especially Theology and Philosophy. But the best thing of all as far as I'm concerned is that I know now for sure that God has called me. It's the most amazing feeling, Conn. It's like being on a different plane. The only way to find out if it's the life for you is to enrol in the ranks and give it a go. You're very welcome to come down here any weekend you want (before our summer holidays - they start 3rd July) and see the place for yourself. I think you'd like it. You're really away from things here and all the lads are completely sound. If you let me know when you're coming I can tell Father Dunne and he'll arrange to have a room ready for you for two nights. Father Dunne's the president. He's sound too. It's a million miles away from Saint Paul's here. You know, Conn, I was just thinking a funny thing the other day. Don't be shocked at what I'm going to write. It's about my penis. I was thinking to myself when I was in the showers that for the rest of my life I'll only be using it as a water spout. That doesn't annoy me one bit because, as you know, self-control is a part of the religious life.*

I'll pray for you.
Yours in Christ,
Jackie.

- I hear ler's a big crowd goin away this year, said Zorro. -

211

Celestine Strunks is goin tay Dalgan, Fanny siz. Isn't he, Fanny? An Willie McShane an Danny Doherty outa Rosemount.

- So I heared, said Fanny. - I'm tryin tay hink who it was towl may.

- What McShane's that? asked Edward G.

- Ye know Lizzie Bradley from the Creggan? said Zorro.

- Aye?

- Wan a her's.

- Noan a your brothers wint away, didn't they not? Tessie said to me. - Ler's a wile big crowd a them, ye know, she said to the one beside her.

- Naw, I said, with my hand on the knob.

- Here, if ye're goin out tay the kitchen, son, tick this tray out way ye, said Fanny. - Wait tay I pit some a these dirty dishes on it. Surrah'll give ye that stuff, over ler.

- Lave them empies, said Scraggy. - I'll tick them way may whin I'm goin.

Tessie opened the door for me and, as I was about to go out, Zorro said - Howl on. Ler's somebody singin out in the kitchen. Lave that dour open, Tessie, wud ye.

- That's Molly, said the wee redhaired one. - I know er voice.

- Whisht a minute tay way hear er, said Zorro. - Here, son. Don't bay goin out ler way that tray tay she's finished. Here, put it down on the tibble quick.

I put it down and stood at the open door. There was a big crowd of boys standing very quiet in the hall. Gander's ma was singing a bit out of tune and her voice was really trembly.

The summer's gone and all the flowers are dying.
Tis you, tis you must go and I must bide.
But come ye back when summer's in the meadow.
Or when the valley's hushed and white with snow.
Tis I'll be here in sunshine or in shadow.
O Danny boy, O Danny boy I love you so.

And if you come when all the flowers are dying
And I am dead, as dead I well may be,

You'll come and find the place where I am lying
And kneel and say an Ave there for me.
And I shall hear, though soft you treads above me
And on my grave will warmer, sweeter be,
And you will bend and tell me that you love me
And I shall sleep in peace until you come to me.

The clapping went on for a good while. Then Fanny said -
Hasn't she the lovely voice.

- She always *had* a lovely voice, said the wee redhead. - Sure
I mine the time–

- What about yous young wans out ler in the hall, shouted
Zorro. - Kin noan a *yous* sing at all?

She hardly had the words out of her mouth till Gander
started.

Well, since ma baby left me
I've found a noo place to dwell,
It's down at the end of Lonely Street,
It's Heartbreak Hotel
Where I'm a - so lonely, baby,
Where I'm a - so lonely, baby,
Where I'm a - so lonely I could die.

Where bell hop tears keep flowin,
The desk clerk's dressed in black,
He's been so long down Lonely Street
That he never will come back
And he's a - so lonely, baby,
And he's a - so lonely, baby,
And he's a - so lonely he could die.

So if your baby leaves you
And you got no place to dwell,
Just take a walk down Lonely Street
To Heartbreak Hotel
Where you'll be so lonely, baby,
Where you'll be so lonely, baby,

Where you'll be so lonely you could die.

There was a whole lot of roaring and people stamping their feet out in the hall. When it died down a bit Zorro said - What kine of a song is that, anyway?

- Sure that's not singin at all, said Fanny.

- Who wiz it doin the singin, Conn? said Zorro. - Day ye know who it wiz?

- Gander, I said and went on out.

Gerry was standing just outside the room door and he said to me - What time's it about?

- Iss jist after twelve on the clock in there, I said. - *I* hiftay go.

- Same here, said Gerry.

There must have been about ten people between us and the porch. We got out past them and just as Gerry was about to open the front door we heard the voice behind us.

- Whass wrong way yeez? Yeez aren't goin already?

We turned round. It was Gander's ma. She was all red around the eyes and there was a sort of a black smudge down one side of her nose.

- Aye, wa-wa-we hiftay go, I said. - *I* hiftay be in early in ssssschool in the mornin.

- Same here, said Gerry.

- Gawn stay another wee while, wud yeez? she said. - I'm jist goin in here a minute tay git a tray. Gawn on out tay the scullery, wud yeez. I'll bay straight out. I nivir got a chance tay git talkin tay yeez.

She was looking at me. I knew it was me she meant.

- Gawn now, she said. - Ler's lemonade an chocolate bis-cuits out ler. Ye mine whin yeez wur wee and yeez wud be playin in the room and I used tay.....

She stopped. I didn't like the look of her. I thought she was going to start crying again. But she didn't.

- Tick as much as yeez want, she said. - I'll be out in a minute.

- Naw, really, I said. - I really hiftay go.

- Me too, said Gerry. - Thanks vurry much anyway.

- Stanislaus! she shouted through the crowd. - Cornelius is

goin now! Are ye not goin tay say Cheerio tay im?

She suddenly leaned over and gave me a kiss on the cheek. Her lips were dead soft.

- I know ye wur his best friend, she said. - Sure I mine the great times yeez had.

She's beautiful, I thought. Gander's da's a stupid bastard.

- I don't think he heard may, she said. - He's sittin over there on the stairs, him an Trevor. Gawn over now an say Cheerio tay im, son, if ye kin git thew that crowd. He'll bay away the marra before you git back from the College, ye know. Him an Trevor's gittin the wan o'clock train.

- Naw, iss awright, I said. - I ssssid Cheerio tay im already.

- So did I, said Gerry.

She mustn't have heard us because she started shouting again.

- Stanislaus! Stanislaus! Cornelius is goin now! Mawn an say Cheerio tay im!

- Thass awright, ma, he shouted back. - I heard ye the first time. I'll bay over in a minute.

- He won't git up off his backside, she said. - He heard may rightly.

- Right, sssssee ye sssssoon, Mrs McLaughlin, I said. - Wa-wa-wur away this time.

I closed the porch door behind us and went on out with Gerry.

Brendan's always on to me to buy *Reveille* and *Tit Bits*. They're the magazines with all the pictures of half-naked girls in them. The only time I ever saw the inside of any of them was the first day of the summer holidays when he got me to go into this second hand shop beside Castle Gate with him. He just handed over the money and took the two magazines as if he was buying the Catholic Herald or something and then slid them inside his coat.

We went down Magazine Street and up the steps leading to

the Walls and sat on the ground with our backs to one of the cannons.

- You get a bit of privacy here, he said.

He gave me *Tit Bits* and he read *Reveille.*

- You know why they call it *Tit Bits*, don't you? he said.

- Wa-wa-why? I said.

- Cause you can only see bits of tits. It's against the law for them tay show the full set.

To tell you the truth I'd my eyes half closed and my brain screwed up tight most of the time I was turning over the pages. But I dropped the guard one time when he held *Reveille* right in front of my face and I got the full blast of a girl standing with wee short pink shorts on her with enough space at the bottom of them for you to put your hand up and as well as that her nipples were nearly bursting out through this white curtainy blouse she was wearing.

- Have a gander at that, he said to me. - What do you think? How would you like tay be tickin your breakfast with that?

- Sh-sh-she's really sssssomethin, I said.

- The top thing she's wearin's Chantilly lace.

- Wa-wa-whass Sh-sh-chantilly lace?

- I don't know a fuck. It says it underneath. But I'll tell you somethin now. The girl *I* marry's goin tay be wearin that the first night.

He started singing *The Girl that I Marry* and we sat there with the magazines propped up against our legs. Time seemed to be crawling and then, just as he was about to switch with me, the rain started. He kept singing away.

- Come on, I said. - Wa-wa-wur goin tay git sssssoaked.

I got up.

- What's your hurry? he said. - We'll be alright. Here, give me yours now.

But then it came on heavy and he *had* to shift. As we were going down the steps I said to him - Wa-wa-whur's the magazines?

- I left them up there, he said.

- Ye did not! After payin fffffur them?

- Do you really think I'm goin tay tick that stuff home with

216

me? he said.

He's hard to work out. He goes on like a dirty brute sometimes but do you see if the two of us are ever standing talking to girls, he's all shy and dead nice and he never says anything dirty about them whenever we walk on. One day he told me about this one he's mad about. He wouldn't tell me her name but I think she's from Creggan Estate. He fell for her down in Malin Head last year the time he was on his holidays. She fancied some boy called Gabriel that comes there every summer from Belfast and when Brendan tried to chat her up she asked him to bring a note to this boy Gabriel and he ended up a message boy between the two of them. It was funny listening to him telling about it because you'd never have thought he could be like that. He always seems to be in *control*, if you know what I mean. I started feeling sort of guilty after he told me because, even though I definitely felt bad for him, I felt good for myself at the same time.

- Wa-wa-why did ye keep bringing the notes? I asked him.

- I don't know, he said. - I suppose it was the only way I had of gettin close tay her.

One other day before McRide came in he grabbed me by the arm.

- Hey, listen, he said. - Do you know who's gettin married the day over in Monaco?

- Who?

- Grace Kelly.

- Aw aye. Right, I said.

- Good Christ of Almighty! he said. - Are you livin on the same planet? Do you hear what I'm tellin you? Sure it's enough to drive you mad.

- Sh-sh-she's ssssome looker awright.

- Did you see her in *Rear Window* with James Stewart? Remember the big long snoggin session they had early on? How can you sit there lookin so calm, you puritanical prick?

He was starting to bubble at the mouth a bit and he didn't even realise. It's desperate, I thought, how thinking about sex can nearly turn you into a slabbery dog.

Jackie McHugh called for me yesterday to go away a run in his da's car. He got a loan of it for the day and two other boys that are at Kilkenny with him came as well. Liam Doherty and Manus Kelly from the Waterside.

We stopped in Buncrana for a while and had a feed of fish and chips. Then we headed on to Dunree beach. Manus didn't say that much but every now and then he shouted Faugh! and clapped his hands on his knees. It was dead funny the way he did it. Liam told a whole lot of jokes. They were mostly dirty but they weren't too bad at the start. The best one was about the pope being nearly ready to die and the Vatican was giving out bulletins all the time and one day there were these two head-lines on boards leaning up against the wall outside Melican's newspaper shop down Creggan Hill. The first one said GINA LOLLOBRIGIDA IN ROME and the second one said POPE HAS GOOD NIGHT. The three of them roared at that one. They were in great form and they didn't seem to have a care in the world. I was sitting there thinking it might be all right being away with them in Kilkenny. You should see the way people go on with Jackie. I saw our Bernard talking to him up Marlborough Road last Sunday and it was like two grown-ups standing there. You could see the respect from Bernard. I mean, Jackie's a bit stupid. He's okay but he's a bit stupid. Now *I'm* not stupid and still most people treat me like shite. And here's another thing. Jackie and them seem to be going a run somewhere nearly every day during the holidays. If it's not the bus it's Willie McHugh's car. I can just see Bernard lending me *his* car. If I could drive, that is.

I'd a feeling when I came out of the house first and saw the other two sitting there that they were all going to try and get me to go to Kilkenny next year but they didn't say a word about it and Jackie never mentioned either about me not coming down for that weekend. We stayed on Dunree beach for ages and we played a two-a-side long shootie, me and Jackie against Liam and Manus. Liam turned out to be a bit of a dirty brute, actual-ly. When we were driving out of Buncrana he started the real filth. It didn't seem right, him dressed like a priest and all. On our way up the Gap of Mamore it got worse. Every time he finished telling a joke Jackie and Manus roared laughing and Jackie banged his hands up and down on the steering wheel. I laughed too so that they wouldn't think I was odd but I was getting a bit cheesed off, to tell you the truth. When we came to the top of the gap Jackie stopped the car and we all sat quiet for a while looking down at the scenery. Then Manus said - Isn't that magnificent? and Jackie said - God's own country and Liam said - Did yous hear the one about the two away on their honeymoon?

- What was that one? said Jackie, starting to laugh already.

So Liam told this really disgusting joke and the three of them went into hysterics for about two minutes and when they calmed down Jackie said - Wait tay I tell you this one. Yous know may Uncle Mick the schoolmaster. Well, he used tay teach in a country school out past Dungiven for a while and there was a wee boy came in late every mornin and he'd always have some excuse ready. You know, lick - May mother was sick and I hadday feed the hens for her or - The cow fell intay the sheugh and I hadday lend a hand tay get her out. But this particular mornin anyway he arrives in about half ten and Mick says - Well, what happened ye the day? And wee Paddy says - Sir, I'm very sorry, sir, but I hadday bring the bull tay the neighbour's heifer. And Mick, bein from the town and not understandin these things very well, says - And what had ye tay to do that for, if ye don't mind me askin? And wee Paddy says - Sir, well, sir, I hadday tick it for tay service the heifer, ye see. And Mick says - This is intolerable. Ye've been late every day this week. What was the matter with your father? Could *he* not have done it? And wee Paddy says back tay him - No, sir. I'm sorry, sir. It hadday be the bull, sir.

You'd have thought they were going to take convulsions the way they went on. In the middle of them laughing I just sort of snapped and before I knew it I was out of the car and walking away. It wasn't the dirty jokes so much. I minded *them* all right but it was more the people that were telling them. I was sick to the teeth of the whole lot of them. Jackie came out after me and started slabbering all over me, apologising like mad. Anyway, he got me to come back in. He started up the car right away and Liam said - Sorry, Conn. I think maybe we were getting a bit out of order there. No more smut. Right?

I looked at him as if he was mad. I didn't say anything. I just looked at him. What was he asking *me* for? *He* was the one was coming out with most of the smut.

Jackie started driving down the other side of the gap and there wasn't a word out of any of us. I was just thinking I might tell the one about the pope to Brendan when there was a terrible screech of brakes and a big bang and we stopped dead. We were all thrown away forward. After that we seemed to be sitting there about five minutes before anybody spoke. Then Jackie said - Are yous all all right?

We all said we were and Manus said - What happened? What did you hit?

- I hit that boulder that's right in front of us, said Jackie and he put his head down on the steering wheel and said - O dear Jesus. O my sweet Jesus.

- They shouldn't have those big brutes at the side of the road anyway, said Manus.

- I think it saved us, said Jackie. - If it hadn't been for that big brute we'd have been over the edge. O sweet Jesus. O sweet Jesus. God forgive us.

We all got out and went round to the front of the car. There was a drop of about forty or fifty feet on the other side of the boulder and all you could see when you looked down were these sharp rocks like big grey teeth. It was scary all right.

- God forgive us, said Liam and he put his two hands over his eyes. - That's what we get for goin on lick that. Conn was right. You were right, Conn.

- What's may da goin tay say? said Jackie. He was nearly crying . - Look at the bonnet and the radiator. Look, d'yous see the bumper? The whole lot's caved in. Look.

We all looked. It was bad. Manus went to the other side of the road and sat down on a stone. His lips were moving away. He was definitely praying. Then he got up nearly right away and came over to me and held me tight by the arm.

- Conn, could I talk tay you a minute? he said.

He walked me down the road holding my arm and I kept looking back. It didn't feel right. Jackie was standing staring at the front of the car as white as a sheet. I couldn't see Liam anywhere.

Manus said - Conn, I've somethin tay tell you. I did somethin wrong.

- Wa-wa-what d'ye mean? I said.

- You remember the play you had on the wireless?

- Aye?

- Well, I wrote it out again and got paid for it.

- How day ye mean?

- Plagiarism. It's called plagiarism, he said. - I wrote it out as a short story and got it published in Ireland's Own.

- Plagiarism? I said. - I nivir heard a that.

- I called it *The Outcast*, he said. - Plagiarism's what you do when you copy what somebody else writes and pass it off as your own.

- God, sh-sh-sure that's awright, I said. - How much did ye git fffffur it?

- Ten quid, he said. - I'm really sorry so I am. I'll give it tay you in instalments.

- Ten quid, I said. - That's brilliant. *I* oney got fffffive. *You* must hiv talent.

- What are you talkin about, Conn?

He started shouting.

- D'you not hear me? *I cogged your play*. I *cheated*. I committed a mortal sin. *Two* mortal sins. Stealin and lyin.

- Naw, thass awright, Manus, I said. - Don't bay givin me anythin. I don't wa-wa-want anythin. Honest.

- You see, Conn, I've been tryin tay write stuff this years. I fancied myself as a bit of a writer and all. I really thought it was an easy thing tay do, writin. But I found out after a while I hadn't got it. I wasn't *creative*, you see. But I still thought I must have *somethin*. So last summer I worked on this poem of John Hewitt's and sent it away tay an English newspaper and got three quid for it. Then around Hallowe'en I used a story of O. Henry's that I read and changed it around a bit and I got a ten-

221

ner for that. And then in March I heard *The Hermit* on the wireless down in Kilkenny and I decided tay have a go at it.

I felt really good listening to him. You don't know how good I felt.

- Listen, Manus, I said. - I'm not goin tay tick a penny off ye. If ye wa-wa-wannay putt money intay the Sssssint Vincent de Paul box at the door a the chapel then that's up tay *you*. But I'm not tickin any. I don't wa-wa-want any.

We heard Jackie calling us.

- Hi, c'mawn. C'mawn up. The car's workin. I want tay get back. C'mawn. Hurry.

We ran up the road. He'd the car facing back towards Buncrana and the engine was going. It sounded loud to me. We got in. Liam was sitting in the passenger seat and he didn't turn round to us or say anything. None of us spoke on the way up to Derry except for Jackie. I think he must have said the same thing about nine times.

- That's it. I'm hammered. I'll never get the car again.

I won't forget that day in a hurry.

I got back from the Hillside on Monday. I was down with Bernard. His appendix burst near the end of July and he was a bit slow coming round so Mammy wrote to Auntie Maureen to see if it would be all right for him to go down to convalesce and then at the last minute she asked me to go with him for company. The way it worked out I hardly saw him the whole time I was down because I spent most of the week with Josephine and Mickey. They're my cousins. Hillside's where Mammy's from and I used to always love going down there. Years ago Uncle Eamon put up two swings in the shed with the open front on it and Josephine and me used to be on them every time I was down. She'd some nerve. She went up that high you'd have thought sometimes she was going to go right round in a circle nearly and get wrecked on the corrugated iron roof. She used to shout down to me that she could see over the hills to the

Atlantic only *she* always called it *they Aglantic*. But that was years ago. The swings were tied up the summer before last because Paddy got the shed filled with turf and then they were never loosened. Paddy's my eldest cousin. One day I remember Josephine telling me there were kittens born and the two of us went into the wee barn that's inside the front field and we saw them. Mixed in with our sweat was some other kind of a smell that made me go all quivery just below my heart. When we were kneeling down my shoulder went against hers. I thought about that a good lot. I never told her, of course. I couldn't have told her a thing like that. Hillside was always great. Sometimes at night in the attic after I got back to Derry I'd be lying nearly ready to go to sleep and thinking back on the two weeks or the three weeks down there and I'd get a good feeling inside of me, a really good feeling, but sad at the same time. Josephine's face was in my head but there were plenty of other things too, like haystacks tumbled from me and Mickey being on them and hundreds of corn stooks all in lines and the stepping stones on the river over near the forest and the bends on the road from the house down to the shore and then from the shore back up to the house and the smell of cow clap and turf smoke mixed togeth-er. And I always remembered the first time Paddy lifted me up on the horse and me nearly falling off it when I looked down at how far away the ground was. And Auntie Maureen after the breakfast going Chooka chooka chooka chooka to the hens in the front street and her with the bottom half of her apron held away in front of her like a tablecloth before she emptied the crumbs and scraps out for them to eat and them running to her all lopsided as if they were going to topple over any minute. And wait till you hear this for a laugh. I used to always think the red combs on their foreheads and chins and ears were the best bits of the bacon. I really did. The ducks were a scream. They'd get all excited if you went anywhere near them and start that stupid laugh as if they were taunting you. Me and Josephine used to laugh back at them and they they'd come paddling over to us honking away, the same every time, and never once did we give them a thing to eat. And I used to won-der if she ever did those things when I wasn't there but I'd say

223

she didn't. One of the best parts was sitting down at the big kitchen table for the poundies and scallions and mince. Up here in bed in the attic when I got back to Derry I thought about the nights in the Hillside bed and wee bits of the straw mattress sticking into me. And the rain slapping away sometimes at the water in the water barrel right below my window and bouncing like mad off the top of the shed. And it's funny, every time I came back home it was the same and it's the same now. For two or three days or more every smell off me is the Hillside.

I'm just thinking when I'm writing this. It might be years before I see Josephine and Mickey again. They're going to England with Uncle Eamon in September. I think he'll be getting them work. He's away most of the time in a place called Ilkeston in Derbyshire. I'm not sure what it is he does. Frankie says there's a big coalfield in Derbyshire and Eamon works in it. But Josephine told me one time he did bricklaying.

He's a wile man. You never know the next thing he's going to come out with. One day I was helping him to gather spuds and I brought this one over to him that looked like Charles Laughton in *The Hunchback of Notre Dame*.

I said - Luck, Eamon. Quasimodo.

And he said - What in hell's name are ye taakeen about?

And I said - Quasimodo. It lucks lick Quasimodo the hunchback. D'ye sssssee the nose an the mouth? An luck. There's the hump.

- Damned apt, he said. - Damn a hell use this bloody land is. *Damn* a hell use.

And he took the spud out of my hand and threw it in the air and kicked it about twenty yards down the field. Then he started to shake with laughter but it was a while before you heard it. His big shoulders were going for about a minute and he'd the mouth tight shut the whole time. Then he exploded with this big hoarse laugh.

I'm going to tell you about Sunday before I finish. Sunday was the start of a heat wave and it was that hot in the chapel they had to open all the doors at mass. After the breakfast Maureen handed me and Josephine a pillowcase between us and got us to go to the shore to get some carragheen moss for

Bernard. It's supposed to be full of goodness but you could break your neck on the rocks trying to find it. I was in a bad mood at the start because I was looking for Mickey to come too and he was away up the hill with Paddy for something. As well as that I didn't like being sent a message with my wee cousin.

- Run down tay the shore lick good wains and see if yeez kin pull a bit a carragheen moss for Bernard.

Wains! She's good crack, Maureen. I was thinking going down the road too that there wasn't any fuss about me after *I* got my appendix out. If somebody had walked two miles to the shore to get carragheen moss for *me* the whole connection would have heard and they'd have been nodding their heads for years about me being spoiled.

- What age are ye now, Conn? said Josephine, whacking away at the stone ditch with this big brute of a stick she got out of somewhere.

I didn't answer. She knows rightly what age I am. A year and two days older than her. I sort of half looked over at her on the other side of the road from me. It was funny to see her marching along in her yellow flowery Sunday frock and her trying to go on like a wee ploughman. She used to wear a thing that was like a spud sack and when she hadn't that on it always seemed to be some other kind of a wagony looking catastrophe. Then last July when I was down she'd on this tartan skirt for the first three days but I hardly saw her because I spent nearly the whole time with Mickey.

- Wa-wa-when are yeez goin? I asked.

- The fifth a September, I think, she said.

- D'ye know wa-wa-what ye're goin tay wa-wa-work at yit?

- I do not. I think maybe I might thrain tay bay a nurse. I dunno yit. D'ye wanna dhrink?

She got down on her knees at Suzie Hirrel's spring well and got up in slow motion with her hands cupped together.

- Here, she said. - Tick some now before it goes.

- It's awright, I said. - I'll git may own.

- Why? D'ye think may hands are dirty or what? she said and then dropped the whole lot on top of my shoes.

- Luck wa-wa-what ye did, I shouted. - Wa-wa-what did ye

do that fffffur?

She laughed and ran down the road in front of me.

- Gawn away an wa-wa-wise up, I shouted and I went down on my hunkers to drink out of the well. When I stood up she was at the bend waiting for me. I felt the sun starting to burn me already and I wanted to take off my shirt and fit it over my head and shoulders but I knew if I did she'd see how skinny I was so I got a whole pile of docken leaves from over at the side of the road and held them on my head as I walked towards her.

- Julius Caesar, she said.

- Wa-wa-what are ye talkin about?

- Ye're lick Julius Caesar or somebody lick that with them leaves.

I said nothing and neither did she till we got to the cut. Then she ran up the grassy lane and shouted back at me - I'll bate ye a race tay the beach.

I knew to look at the way she was moving she was going to try and vault the stile but then she must have remembered the frock because she screeched to a halt just in time. She went through it the right way like a rocket and started running again. I walked the whole time. I wanted to run all right because I was starting to feel this excitement with the kind of a day it was and everything. But I still walked. You can't see the water until you get to the far end of the lane but I knew the tide was out because I could smell the wrack already.

Dunree beach is brilliant. The sand is pure white except where it's harder near the water and when you go over to the rocks at the far end the massive fort is nearly right above your head. There's Irish soldiers in it now since the English left and I think it must be hundreds of years old. The sea was giving out big sighs the day we were there and it was the bluest blue you ever saw. There are two caves near the point. I was in one of them with Mickey last year and I was in the other one with Frankie when we were small. They don't go in very far but it's supposed to be that pirates used to hide their booty in them. I remember Mairead told me that one time. I suppose it could be true.

We couldn't find any carragheen moss so we pulled dulse instead. It was dead easy as long as you watched your step because the tide was well out and the rocks were thick with it.

- Dulse has oils and minerals in it too, ye know, said Josephine after we'd the pillowcase full.

- Sh-sh-sure I know *that*, I said. - But I don't like the ssssstring dulse ye git down here. Ye git ssssshell dulse in Greencastle. That's not half as sssssalty an it's not as hard tay sssssswally either.

- It's not hard tay swally if ye dhry it right, she said. - Ye have tay dhry it right first.

- Of *course* ye hiftay dry it right, I said. - Day ye think I'm ssssstupid or wa-wa-what?

- Aye.

- An it's *ssssstill* harder tay chew than the ssssshell dulse no matter *how* wa-wa-well ye dry it.

- How is it? she said.

I threw the pillowful down on the rocks and she picked it up.

- Did ye ivir taste the sh-sh-shell dulse? I said.

- Naw, I did not, she said, dead cheeky.

- Wa-wa-well then, ye don't know wa-wa-what ye're talkin about.

That's when the row really started and it kept going till we got to the stile again. We never spoke after that the rest of the way up.

There's a girl that lives over in Oakfield Drive and I can hardly stop thinking about her. I never saw her in my life before last Friday and I don't even know her name. We nearly walked into each other when I was coming out of Jack McDaid's shop and she was coming in and she said - Sorry, I beg your pardon, and she smiled. She's nearly exactly like the sister of the girl Robert Wagner murdered in *A Kiss Before Dying*. She has straight black hair nearly down to her shoulders and beautiful blue eyes just the same as her. I know she's from Oakfield because Charlie told me. Last night I imagined for about half a split second that she got into bed beside me and my heart was thumping for the next ten minutes at least. I don't know what I'm going to do if I ever get married. I'm serious. I'll probably die of a heart attack the first night or go raving mad. I can't imagine doing it. I can't even imagine being *allowed* to do it.

I found out. She's called Jenny McCallion and she's at Thornhill. What a fantastic name! Jenny McCallion! I saw her twice since and she never said hello to me yet but I know she noticed me. I'd say she's shy. I was sitting thinking about her after my tea today when this amazing song came on the wireless as if it was reading my thoughts. It's called *Only You* and I think it's ones called The Platters that sing it. It's a funny name for a band because I'm almost sure a platter's a plate. The only time I ever saw the word was in The New Bible History, the part where Salome asked Herod for John the Baptist's head on a platter. I think that was the word anyway.

> *Only you can make this change in me*
> *Yes, it's true, you are my destiny.*
> *When you hold my hand I understand*
> *The magic that you do.*
> *You're my dream come true*
> *My one and only you.*

Maybe I *will* be holding her hand soon. The exact words she said to me were - Sorry, I beg your pardon, and the smile wasn't just good-mannered. I'm not saying it was love at first sight but I think she likes the look of me all right.

I can't stand Trevor Smith. We were coming back from Derry City match on Saturday and he started this filthy talk about a boy that's up at Queen's with him.

- Honest to God, Conn, he said. - You want to see the balls he's got on him. I was standin next to him in the showers two or three times and I couldn't help noticing them. They're like *tits*. I'm tellin you. You know the way yours and mine come down from the back of the penis like a chicken's neck. I mean, that's *normal*. But his stand out like two massive diddies. He's *magnificent*, so he is. And you know the thing about it? He's only about four and half a foot tall. I never saw anythin like it. It's unbelievable so it is.

I didn't like the remark about yours and mine. He'd probably like to see mine all right. What's he doing standing next to the same boy in the showers two or three times anyway? Sure you should have seen the way he used to look at Gander. And I don't think he was ever out with a girl in his life. He's definitely a queer. Normal people don't come out with that sort of talk. And he's going to be a doctor too. Imagine a boy like that examining you. You know what I mean? It's disgusting.

I was down in Charlie's today and we heard on the wireless about six Customs huts getting blown up last night. They didn't say who it was did it but Uncle Eddie said it had to be the IRA.

- Who else cud it bay? he said. - I wa-wa-was ji-ji-just thinkin sssssomethin wa-wa-wud happen fffffore the year wa-wa-was out wa-wa-way it bein the fffffffortieth anniversary a the Risin an all. Ye mine may sssssayin, Bridie?

- I thought that crowd packed it in ages ago, said Patricia.

- Wa-wa-well, they've unpacked it out agin now, may dear, said Eddie, - sssssso wa-wa-what d'ye think a that? Shhhhhhh. Listen tay ye hear.

The newsman was saying there was no security because the B men all got the day off to go to the war memorials for

Remembrance Day.

- Ha, said Eddie, rubbing his hands together. - Wa-wa-what about that fffffur a sssstroke a genius, sssssstartin a na-na-new push ji-ji-just wa-wa-whin the other crowd's rememberin the big wa- wa- war endin? Wa-wa-what d'ye think a that, eh?

- Ye shudn't bay goin on lick that, Eddie, said Bridie. - They cuda kilt somebody.

- Na-na-not at all, he said. - Sure them posts are na-na-nivir manned at na-na- after a sssssartin time a the evenin.

- I don't care, said Bridie. - Iss wrong. Somebody's bound tay git hurt if they're goin tay start the bombin agin. Nothin's worth that.

Eddie stood up.

- They're na-na-not *goin* tay sssssstart it, Bridie. Did ye na-na-not hear the man talkin? They *have* sssssstarted it.

His eyes were really shining.

- Tell may this, he said, pointing away at her. - D'ye really think Basil Brooke's goin tay give us our rights outa the goodness of his heart? *Day* ye?

- Naw, I know all about that, but iss not worth anywan gittin kilt over. Ye know rightly what happened before.

Eddie walked out to the scullery shaking his head.

- Ye hivn't a clue, Mammy, said Charlie. - Sure thur hasn't bin trouble fur donkey's years and thur still walkin all over us. What about the Special Powers Act?

- Ah, don't *you* start, said Bridie. - Wan a yeez is bad enough. Fur God's sake wud ye give over now before yer daddy comes back in.

- What d'ye mean, give over? said Charlie. - Ye really hivn't a clue. I bate ye ye don't even know what they kin do way the Special Powers Act.

- Aye, said Patricia. - They kin stuff it an *you* kin stuff it too.

- Thur'll bay none a that sorta talk in this house, said Bridie. - D'yeez hear may?

- They kin put ye in jail as long as they lick, said Charlie, - an they kin flog ye whin ye're in an thur's damn all anywan kin do about it.

- Flog ye! said Patricia. - *Flog* ye! Don't bay stupid. Who day ye think they are? Captain Bligh or somebody?

- Wise up, said Charlie.

- Captain Bligh wa-wa-wudna got away wa-wa-way *a half* a wa-wa-what *they* git away wa-wa-way, said Eddie from the scullery door. - I'll tell ye na-na-now wa-wa-what that crowd kin do. They kin keep ye locked up the rest a yer life wa-wa-wayout fffffindin ye guilty a anythin.

Patricia looked completely disgusted. She got up and Eddie went and stood with his back to the fire.

- D'ye sssssee if they wa-wa-wanted, he said, - a whole crowd a B Sssssspecials cud come in here an tick over our back yard out there an build a biss in it fffffur themsels.

- A WHAT? said Patricia.

- A biss, said Eddie. - D'ye na-na-not na-na-know wa-wa-what a biss is? God help us! She doesn't na-na-know wa-wa-what a biss is.

She walked over towards the door.

- I'm away out, she said. - Talk about fanatics!

- Who's the fffffanatics? shouted Eddie. - *Who's* the fffffanatics ye're talkin about? Listen, may dear, tay I tell ye sssssomethin na-na-now.

He took a step forward.

- An don't wa-wa-walk away wa-wa-whin I'm talkin tay ye! he shouted.

She stopped at the door and turned. She was nearly ready to cry.

- Lave it, Eddie, wud ye, said Bridie. - Gawn lave it. Thur's no sense arguing way yer own daughter.

- In the Sssssspecial Powers Act, said Eddie, and his voice was trembling, - thur's a bit na-na-near the end that sssssays : If thur's any other powers wa-wa-way fffffurgot tay include in, bay the wa-wa-way, yeez kin all ji-ji-just tick it na-na-now that thur included in anyway.

He stopped and stared at Patricia and then sat down in the armchair.

- Sssssomethin lick that, he said.

- Gawn on, love, if ye're goin, said Bridie.

Patricia opened the door and went out to the hall.

- Wear yer scarf! screeched Bridie. - Iss cowl out there!
She turned to Charlie.

- Gawn out an tell er tay put er scarf on, son, wud ye.

Charlie looked out into the hall and said - She's away.

- God, she'll git foundered, said Bridie.- That wind out there wud cut ye.

We all sat quiet for a minute and then Charlie said to me - How about a game a headie out the back? Mawn. I got a new ball.

- Right, I said - Let's go.

Brendan put on that look and said - Remember last April I was tellin you about Grace Kelly gettin married?

- Aye? I said.

- She'd a wain last night, he said.

- Right enough? I said.

- Aye. She was married on exactly the nineteenth of April. You know how long ago that was?

- How long?

- Nine months and four days. How about that?

- Phew, I said.

- Phew's right, he said. - You're comin on, Murphy. There's hope for you yet. Hey, did you hear about Frankie Flaherty?

- Naw. Wa-wa-what about him?

- He was arrested for givin his name tay the cops in Irish.

- God. Ye're not ssssserious? I said.

- I swear tay God. They stopped him on the Lone Moor Road when he was comin home from the College yesterday and they asked him his name and he said Proinsias O'Flatharta.

- Wa-wa-why'd he sssssay that?

- Because that's his name in Irish, you fucking ignoramus.

- Naw, but I mean Princess, I said. - How's Princess the same as Frankie?

- Not Princess. *Proinsias.* That's the Irish for Francis, you stupid gulpen.

- Wa-wa-wise up, Burns. Tell us wa-wa-what all happened, I said.

- They tuck him down tay Victoria Barracks and kept him in a while.

- Is he goin tay be up in court? I said.

- I couldn't tell you. Would *you* do it?

- Do wa-wa-what?

- Give your name to the cops in Irish?

- Naw.

- You're not an Irishman then, he said.

- Wa-wa-what are ye talkin about? I said. - Sh-sh-sure I don't even *know* may name in Irish.

- My God, he said. - You're *definitely* not an Irishman then. What a wanker!

Probably he's right. Probably I should know it in Irish

Sheila had a baby boy about three weeks ago and some of the hardest looking wagons you ever saw start going all gooey when they see it. Sometimes you see a whole crowd of them standing round Cornelius's pram looking in at him (That's right. Cornelius. I don't want to talk about it. Okay?) and they're saying things to Sheila like - Och, isn't he the wee dote! and making these stupid noises at him that would make you want to puke all over them. I called up at her house in Beechwood one day there and she was just coming out to wheel him round Demesne Gardens and Broadway so I went with her. We were only away about half an hour and we had to stop at least ten times with these ones appearing out of nowhere. It was all Coochy Coochy and Och, he's a wee doll so he is and Who does he luck lick, day ye think? and Is he good? and Are ye up much way im at night? and stuff like that. Disastrous. Absolutely disastrous. And do you know the best part of it? They're all admiring away at him now and do you see inside of about three years, he'll be running round clattered with snotters and him dirt to the eyeballs and they'll be calling him a filthy wee pig and Sheila will probably be roaring at him - Now, git outa may sight, ye cheeky tinker ye.

They're good crack the whole lot of them.

I was reading in the Derry Journal about sixteen IRA men getting a hundred and four years in the court up in Bishop Street and Mammy came into the kitchen and stood behind me.

- Are ye readin the thing about them IRA men? she said.

- Aye, I said. - A hundred and fffffour years. Imagine.

- That's *between* them, ye know, she said.

- I know *that*, I said. - But did ye sssssee wa-wa-what the judge ssssssid? Wa-wa-wait tay ye hear. He ssssssid - wa-wa-wait tay I fffffind it - he sssssid, 'I'm ssssssorry to sssssee men as respectable as you in the dock. I know you're not members of the criminal class in the ordinary sense.' Did ye sssssee that?

- Aye, I saw that, she said.

- And *they'd* no respect fffffur *him*, I said. - They wa-wa-wudn't even ssssstand up and they wa- wa- wudn't recognise the court either.

- They're no good, ye know, she said.

- Wa-wa-what are ye talkin about?

- The IRA. They're no good.

- Wa-wa-what d'ye mean?

- Your daddy left it, she said. - Your daddy was in it and he left it.

I was going to say I never knew that but I couldn't get it out.

- He left it the time they started robbin post offices, she said. - He sid they wur a bad lot. When they started tickin ordinary people's money he left.

I started to say something else and it wouldn't come out either. I think I was going to say that Charlie told me you're not allowed to leave the IRA so how come Daddy was able to leave it?

Mammy said - He asked me tay promise before he died that none a yeez would ever join a political party. He never wanted

234

any a yeez tay git involved way politics. He sid politicians wur no good.

She started footering about the range and she didn't say any more. I turned to the back of the Journal to read about the football but I couldn't concentrate on it. I kept my head down as if I was dead interested in it and then after a few minutes I got up and went into the front room to get my homeworks done.

I found out my name in Irish. It's Conn Ó Murchú. Do you know that I'm doing my Senior exams in four weeks' time and I can't even speak Irish right? The English have been trying to destroy our language for hundreds of years because they know if we don't have our native language we don't have a real culture either. It makes me feel ashamed. I learnt *A Soldier's Song* in Irish off Charlie. I don't even know it right in English and I can sing it in Irish! I never applied once to do the oral they have in the College for getting to the Gaeltacht. It's too late now. I never bothered because I'd never have passed it with the stammer I have. And anyway, even though you get staying up in Ranafast for two weeks for next to nothing, The Pogue's one of the supervisors and he looks in peoples' bedrooms windows at night. You know, as if he's checking the lights are out. And I heard as well that if you're caught speaking English you get sent home. I never went to the craobh in Derry either because it's supposed to be full of freaks that just want to be talking Irish all the time. I was coming home one day and two of them started walking along with me, don't ask me why, and after a wee while we met these two other freaks and the whole four of them stood spouting Irish to one another for the next five minutes. Talk about feeling stupid. They were probably talking shite but it was shite *in Irish* and you were standing there with an expression on you like a busted tube and cover.

I've actually been stewing the written work like mad since after Christmas, since Frankie told me it's easy to get a good mark in. He says none of the Prods in the Ministry of Education know any Irish and all the Catholics up there want you to do well because Catholics are discriminated against and they're trying to balance things out a bit. I know the verbs pretty well and I've over a hundred idioms written on cards which I read every time I go for a sit down on the toilet. If I can get about eighty per cent that'll lift my average and maybe get me into teaching. Then once I'm in Belfast I can start learning to speak it properly.

I met Jenny McCallion and I was talking to her! It was near-ly six months ago that she spoke to me in Jack McDaid's shop and I never had the nerve to speak to her once. I was afraid even to look at her right any time I met her in the street. But today Brendan and me were coming up the Strand Road and she stopped to talk to him. She has a lovely soft voice. Not broad Derry. Just right. They went on for about five minutes about this film *Tea and Sympathy* that's on. Brendan kept saying Deborah Kerr was an aunt of John Kerr's and Jenny said - Were you at it? and Brendan said - Naw, and she said - Well, if you saw the two of them taygether in it you'd soon know from the way they go on they weren't related.

I couldn't take my eyes off her during all this but then Brendan said - You know Conn Murphy, don't you? This is Jenny McCallion, and she said - *I* know *him* all right but I don't think *he* wants tay know *me*.

Brendan said the next thing nearly at the same time she was talking so I'm nearly sure he didn't hear her right. What he said was - He's applied for teaching too. Right, Conn?

Too. *Too*.

I nodded. She stood looking at me, waiting for me to say something. Her eyes had little cloudy bits sort of floating in the blue and her hair seemed longer than it was the last time I passed her four days ago.

- Maybe I'll see you up there, she said.

- Wa-wa-where? I said. - Aw, aye. Right. I might sssssee ye.

I might see you! I've no idea. I'm a disaster. She lives round the corner from me and I tell her I might see her in Belfast! We walked on and Brendan said - Nice girl.

He said it the way you'd say Nice car. I thought he'd know class when he saw it but it just shows you. He's not as sophisticated as I thought. She's incredible. She's even better looking than the girl in *A Kiss Before Dying*. I'd never need to do anything to her. All I'd ever want is to be with her.

We'd our last class ever with McRide today and wait till you hear what the cunt did. Just before the bell at a quarter past three he came down and started asking me and Brendan and Tommy Wright questions in Irish. None of the three of us had a monkey's what he was saying and we just sat staring up at him. I was trying to recognise even one word that might help me to give some sort of an answer but before I could do that he gave me six. Then he asked Tommy and Brendan the same questions over again and when they couldn't answer he gave them six each. When Brendan put his hand out the pain just left me. I only looked for about a second and he was sitting there very pale and it was obvious he didn't know the right way to put his hand. I was nearly going to stand up and say he wasn't allowed to be doked but I'm a coward and, anyway, I knew McRide must have known because he never touched him once the whole two years he had him. But I'm still a coward. I didn't look and all I could hear in between the dokes was Brendan taking short breaths. The bell went after he gave him the first one but the bastard kept on till he finished giving him the whole six. Then he went straight out the door swaggering away at the arse as if to say Fuck yous and the rest of the class scattered and the three of us sat there for a minute not talking. Then Tommy said - Are ye okay, Brendan?

Brendan said - Aye, I'm alright, and started gathering his books up. I didn't look at him.

Tommy said - Don't mind McBride. McBride's just McBride.

Sure what d'ye expect from a cow only a kick?

Tommy's that gentle he'd make you sick sometimes. One other time he said that I said back to him - I'd expect it tay git sssssslaughtered wa-wa-when its time comes, but he only laughed and said - God forgive ye. Murphy.

None of the three of us spoke going down the walks but when we got to the gate Brendan
said - Hey, have any of yous heard Little Richard?

- Aye, the wee black singer, said Tommy.

- He does this one *Tutti Frutti* and it's class, said Brendan and he started singing it. I'd heard it a couple of times on Radio Luxemburg but it was so weird I didn't bother trying to remember it. It was funny watching him going *A-wop-bom-aloo-mop* and him so aristocratic looking and all. He told us he actually saw Little Richard doing it one night when somebody from his street brought him into their house to see this American variety show on their new television set.

- Yous ought to have seen him, he said. - He was jumpin up and down at the piano when he was singin it. Jumpin up and down and him playin the piano! I never saw anything lick it in may life.

That's it for now. We've only the one more day of classes and then the Senior exams start next Friday. I'll be stewing so I won't have time to write any more till we get our holidays.

Brendan died this morning. He died in the History class. He came in and sat down and right away he put his head in his hands and roared out of him. I wasn't there. I was down at the Art room handing in my course work. Sticky McEldowney told me what happened. Somebody said - What's the matter with you, Burns? and pushed him on the shoulder and he shoved them away and shouted - Leave me alone, and then he started roaring out of him again even worse and Shaker Doherty ran and got The Couch. I think he died when The Couch was with him but I'm not sure. Four boys carried him over to the porch of

Junior House and put him lying on the tiles and somebody got a pillow for under his head and then the ambulance came. He was away to hospital by the time I got to the History class. Word went round we were to go to the chapel. Father O'Donoghue took us. He made the Sign of the Cross and then asked us to say a prayer for Brendan and his family. I couldn't pray. I couldn't even try. I still can't. But I can write okay. I think I could sit here and write all night. What's wrong with me? I'm writing this now and I'm looking for wrong spellings as I go along. What's wrong with me?

The results came out last Thursday. I got an average of 71.4 per cent. I didn't write till now because I was waiting for the Call from Saint Joseph's Training College. It came this morning and I have to go up for an interview on Friday. If I pass that I'm in. I know I won't stammer even if they ask me to read something out. I'm free. I'm so full of confidence I really think I could do anything. I can't wait for my first teaching practice. I'll be like all the best teachers I ever had rolled into one. But why is it that something always ruins it when you're happy? Yesterday it was on the news that an RUC man was killed by a booby trap bomb. Also, Jackie McHugh isn't going back to Kilkenny. I haven't seen him out of the door for over a week. His ma took it very bad. Trevor Smith says he was passing the house yesterday and he heard her screeching away at Jackie to get out and find a job and make something of himself.

I did the interview and it went great. Every word right, even the esses and the effs. But that's nothing compared to the other thing. I've got a date with Jenny! This is what happened. She was in the same carriage as me going up to Belfast but there were two other girls with her and they were about three seats behind me so all that happened then was that we said hello to each other twice, once on my way past them going to the toilet and once on my way back. I knew they must have been going up for their interviews too. On the way down to Derry they weren't in my carriage and I was wondering if I should walk through the train all casual to see if I could see her. You know, just to look at her and get her to look at me. I was sitting there trying to make up my mind when she came down the passageway on her own towards me. She'd on a light blue two-piece suit and the skirt of it must have been tight because she was taking wee short steps nearly as if she was afraid of slipping. Her hair was up some way and she looked like a queen. That's what she looked like, a queen. She sat down opposite me and started going on dead friendly as if we knew each other really well. She asked me how I'd got on in the interview and I asked her about hers. After a minute she started laughing away about one of the girls with her, Ann I think it was, calling the Reverend Mother Miss because she was so nervous. I don't remember what all I said at the start but I know after a while I was babbling away about being a Derry City supporter. I hardly knew what I was saying. I was scared she was going to get up and leave me, you see, and I thought as long as I went on talking she'd stay. I think I was in the middle of telling her about the new goalkeeper when she asked me about Brendan.

- You knew him, didn't you? she said.

I nodded.

- It was terrible, she said. - He was such a lovely fella.

She talked about him for a minute or so. I was listening to every word she was saying but I couldn't take my eyes off her freckles. I never noticed them before. They're all over her face, especially around her nose and under her eyes, and they're so perfect I wished I could kiss every one of them. But I never will, I thought.

- Did you know him well, Conn? she said.

- He was one of my best friends, I said.

- Oh, I'm so sorry, she said. - I jist thought you knew him. I didn't realise.

There were tears in the inside corners of her eyes and I think that's what got me going. Did you ever start saying something and it seemed to come out of your mouth even before it came into your head? Inside about five minutes I was telling her things I didn't even know I knew. Like how you had to put down your anger at the College because, if you didn't, it would only get you into bother and maybe even expelled. So you had to just be afraid of the real bad ones and try not to let on even to yourself how much you hated them.

She was nodding away at her head the whole time I was talking and when I was finished she said - You're a very interestin person, you know.

My stomach did about three somersaults and that was *before* she said the next two things.

- Helen Doherty thinks *I* fancy you but I don't really.

I didn't say anything. What could you say?

- I towl her I didn't *fancy* you but I wouldn't mind goin *out* with you.

- *Wud* ye go out with me? I said.

- Aye, I suppose so, she said.

It was as simple as that!

- What about the shows? I said. - Are there any good shows on, d'ye know?

- I couldn't be bothered goin tay the pictures, she said. - I'd rather go out a walk.

- A walk. Right, I said. - I'll call fur ye the marra. Okay? What time d'ye want me tay call?

- What time suits you? she said.

- Naw, what time suits *you*? I said.

- Three o'clock, she said.

- Are ye sure? I said.

- Aye, I'm sure, she said. She looked as if she was getting a bit fidgety so I decided to be really decisive.

- Right. Three it is, I said. - I'll call fur ye at three. Right?

- Right, she said.

We didn't say anything for a while after that. It probably wasn't for very long but it seemed like ages. Then, just as I was going to ask her what her favourite subject was, the other two girls arrived and squeezed into the empty seat beside her. She

241

introduced us.

- This is Conn Murphy. Conn, this is Helen Doherty and Ann Johnston.

The two of them started talking at the one time about this sugar daddy in the other carriage that kept looking at them like a dirty oul man but it sounded exaggerated to me. Helen's a wee speccy one with crooked teeth and Ann's the shape of a rugby ball. When they finished about the man they tried to find out how me and Jenny were getting on and they kept nudging away at each other. But then they really showed themselves up when the four of us were standing at the bus stop outside the Midland picture-house after we got off the train. The bus didn't come for about ten minutes and right from the start these two dogs were going at it out on the road in front of us and all Helen and Ann did was snigger. I just can't believe they're going to be teachers. Jenny and me kept talking to one another nearly the whole time but it was still dead embarrassing, I know I was talking at a wile rate but I couldn't stop myself. The big one on top went on and on and on and every time the wee one tried to get away he just stayed put, even going round in circles with it and the big floppy tongue out and the clingy slabbers dripping off it. It was so disgusting I was hoping a car would come and run over the two of them. Then just as the bus arrived he finally got off and all you could see was the long red shiny thing hanging down and it nearly trailing along the ground. I was never as glad to see a bus coming.

I didn't remember till I was taking my tea after I got home that Derry were playing Crusaders in the Brandywell this week, kick off time three o'clock! But I didn't care. I knew I'd hear all about it when I got back from the date. We went out Sheriff's Mountain. On the way up past the bywash she said to me - Did you ever go for a dip in there?

I said Naw. I'd a feeling about why she was asking. I'd a feeling she was trying to embarrass me. The water runs under the bridge from the waterfall into a kind of a small lake that's in a valley down behind Rosemount factory and in the summer a whole crowd of boys used to go in there sometimes in their pelt. I always thought they were real slags letting other boys and big people passing see them like that. One of the times me and Frankie and Charlie were walking to Grianan fort there were two girls sitting up on the banking watching them with their hands over their mouths and it was obvious they were even worse slags.

I wanted to tell her something funny so I said - Did ye ever notice how people that don't know ye never say hello tay ye in the town but they always talk tay ye if they meet ye out Sheriff's Mountain?

She nodded and let out a wee giggle.

- So they do, she said.

- Well, wait tay ye see this, I said. - D'ye see once we start movin away from Derry, I'm goin tay nod tay ones we meet and I bet ye they nod back. Then further out we'll all be smilin and noddin at the same time and d'ye see when we get tay the real cuiltieland, they'll all be nearly wantin tay stop for a chat.

She laughed and I felt as if she was touching me already.

- And these are all Derry people, she said, and she could hardly get it out with the laughing, - that wouldn't take you under their notice in the town.

- Aw aye, I said. - That's because they know they'd be certified if they were caught goin on lick that in the town.

- I've a cousin from out bay Dungiven, she said, - and she was hardly ever in Derry till she was about sixteen and this time she was in for the day and she said hello all friendly tay some man down the Strand Road and he went for her.

- How d'ye mean he went for her? I said.

- He went for her, she said. - You know. He'd his hands all over her and he was tryin tay kiss her.

- God, I said. I was picturing it.

There were plenty of Rosemount ones out, seeing it was a Saturday, and we'd great crack nodding and smiling and saying hello to them. When we got to the black hut where the Free State starts she stopped and went over to the side of the road.

- Here's what we used tay do when we were wee, she said and she stood with her legs wide apart. - Did yous ever do that? We used tay always say our left half was in Donegal and our right half was in Derry, she said.

She'd light blue jeans on and I was trying not to look down at them but I could still see every wrinkle and bend in the front of them. I'm losing my breath now even writing about it. I was just standing there working out that it was actually me and only me and nobody else she was with when she said - God, would you luck at that.

- What? I said, turning round and looking at this lane she was pointing at.

- The Scotch corn, she said. - The Scotch corn's out. Isn't it lovely! Mawn down tay see it.

She took me by the hand and we walked along the lane. I don't know how to describe it. It was the first time I ever held a girl's hand. The needles were shooting through me and my inside was trembling away. It sounds ridiculous but the ground didn't seem to be there. I can't describe it right. Her hand was soft and warm and sweaty and she'd no idea what was happening. I remember these big stalky things with orange flowers on them growing at the side of the lane and she was nearly fainting looking at them.

- I used tay nearly cry when I saw the Scotch corn down at Dunree, she said, - because it was so beautiful and it comin out was a sign the summer holidays were nearly over.

- Dunree? I said. - Did you stay down at Dunree?

- I've an aunt down there, she said. - I've been goin down there every year since I was no height.

- Does your aunt live near the fort? I said.

- I'll tell you were the house is now, she said. - D'you know Dunree any way well?

- Do I know Dunree! I said. - My mother's from the Hillside, a couple of mile up from Dunree.

- Is that right? she said. - Well, did she ever tell you about the bridge where the boys and girls used tay meet and dance on a Sunday away back.

- Aye, I heard her sayin about that a couple a times.

So I did too.

- Well, may aunt's is just about fifty yards on the Buncrana side of the bridge.

- *I* used tay spend nearly the whole a the summer holidays down there when I was small, I said - and I never remember seein ye.

- I'm glad, she said. - I was a real ugly wee duck. That's what everybody used tay say. Well, may sisters anyway.

She swung our joined hands forwards and backwards and then looked me full in the face and laughed.

- It's great to be out of Derry, isn't it? she said.

- Brilliant, I said.

- Isn't that a fantastic tree there? she said.

- Where? I said.

- There, on down a bit, she said. - The one with the berries.

- That's nice all right, I said. - I wonder what kinda tree it is.

- It's a rowan, she said. - Look. Those berries aren't red. They're scarlet.

So they were. They were the brightest berries I ever saw.

- Are you goin tay kiss me? she said.

We were standing looking up at the tree and she turned to face me and took my other hand so that she was holding the two of them. I leaned towards her and kissed her.

- Watch may nose, she said and she let out a wee laugh. She sounded different. - I hope you're not goin tay break may nose now.

I put my head to the side and kissed her again and then she let go my hands and put her arms round my neck and pressed the rest of herself in against me. I felt the different parts of her moving up my front and I knew she must be going on her tiptoes. I don't know where my arms were at the start but after a minute they were round her back and the heat of her skin through the blouse was nearly burning them. I was trying to keep the bottom half of me away from her but every time I moved it a bit she was in again. I thought, This is fantastic. This is terrible. This is a mortal sin. Jesus mercy, Mary help. This is a mortal sin already so what am I praying for? Dear Jesus, it's going to happen me anytime and I'll stain her good jeans.

I pulled back and took her hand again and said - Let's go. I think maybe it's going tay rain.

- What are you talkin about? she said. - Sure luck at the sky.

The two of us stood looking up at the sky. It was pure blue and there wasn't a cloud to be seen.

- Ye know somethin? I said. - I don't think this lane leads anywhere. I think it's a dead end.

Right enough, on down a bit the hedges on each side seemed to be nearly meeting in the middle.

- Ye could tear your clothes, I said.

- All right then, we'll go back, she said.

She didn't sound annoyed. I looked sideways at her as we changed the hands we were holding and she didn't look annoyed either. But she was pale. I really think she got a bit of a shock when she felt the hardness of me the time she'd her arms around my neck. Maybe she'll not be so quick to try and embrace me that way the next time, I thought.

We kept holding hands till we got in as far as Rosemount Hill and then I let go as casually as I could. When we were going up Marlborough Road Frankie and Charlie and Stoopy and Stevie were playing long shootie. I asked them how Derry did and Stoopy shouted - Nivir mine Derry. How'd *you* do?

- They won two wan, said Frankie. - Ye missed nothin.

We walked on. I was so proud to have her with me.

- What's that you're singin? she asked.

- It's just a song I'm trying tay remember, I said.

- Naw, gawn sing it tay I hear it, she said. - You've a nice voice.

- It's one of Little Richard's, I said. - I'm not sure if I know it all.

- Gawn sing it anyway, she said.

- *A-wop-bom-aloo-mop-a-lop-bam-boom*

- That's *Tutti Frutti,* isn't it? That's brilliant. Sing that bit again tay I try it, she said.

- *A-wop-bom-aloo-mop-a-lop-bam-boom*, I sang.

She tried it a couple of times and then she got it. Standing outside her house I taught her the whole song.

I wanted to get one thing straight once and for all so after I told my sins I said - Father, there's somethin I wanted tay ask ye about.

- Yes?

His name's Father McGonagle and he's only out of Maynooth last year. I thought he'd be okay because one day I saw him standing at the door of the parochial house talking to this crowd of boys and girls around my age and they were all laughing at whatever it was he was saying.

- That sin I told about givin intay pleasure, I said.

- Yes?

- I don't want tay commit mortal sin but how can I avoid takin pleasure if *she* wants tay embrace *me*?

- And why does she want to embrace you?

- Sorry, Father, I'm not sure what–

- I'm asking you a simple question. Why does she want to embrace you?

- Because she likes me.

- That could be true, he said. - But it could also be true that this girl is leading you into mortal sin and doesn't care. I'm sure you must realise that boys are much more quickly and easily aroused than girls.

- I know that, Father

- A girl can embrace a boy and have nothing more than a feeling of well-being whereas the boy has quite simply committed serious sin.

- But this girl *does* care, Father. I *know* she cares. I don't want to lose her, Father, and I know I'm goin tay if I don't take a chance.

- I see. You're prepared to take a chance with your immortal soul. I'm not sure that I can give absolution to someone as cavalier as that.

- But I'm not doin it tay get impure pleasure, Father. That's not why I'm doin it.

- You must be a very unusual young man, then. You

embrace a girl intimately and you're telling me you're not looking to be aroused.

- I *want* it, Father. I *want* it but I'm not *lookin* for it.

- I fail to see the distinction. Tell me, what age are you?

- Seventeen, Father.

- I don't imagine, then, that you'll be thinking of getting
married to this girl in the near future?

- Father, that's not–

- Look. Let me tell you something now. You say you don't
want to lose her. But there'll be plenty of other girls like this
one. Take it from me. I know. And, in spite of what you think
is expected of you, you must learn to treat every single one of
them with respect, even if they haven't the sense to respect
themselves. Purity is a very precious thing, you know.

- But, Father, even if she *is* a wee bit forward and even if I
do accidentally commit mortal sin, that doesn't mean she's not a
brilliant girl. For all *you* know, she could turn out tay be a great
wife. And how do ye know I won't keep goin with her for years
tay we get married?

I saw this white glow appearing and I heard him blowing
his nose. He was a bit long at it so I knew he was probably
thinking of what he was going to say. Then I saw the glow
going up and down fast and it disappeared and I heard him
sniffing away and shifting in his seat.

- Let me give it to you straight, he said. - There shouldn't be
the slightest intimacy between you and this young girl until you
get to know her much better and until you are committed to her.
How long do you say you've been going out with her?

- Today was the first date, Father.

He was quiet for a few seconds. Then he said - There are a
lot of other people out there waiting to get to Confession and
they've been very patient. Now, any other sins?

- No, Father.

- Well, let me make it clear that the absolution I am about to
give you is conditional on your making a firm purpose of
amendment. Do you follow me?

- Yes, Father.

- If you wish to continue keeping company with this young

girl you should avoid being alone with her for any length of time. Understood?

- Yes, Father.
- Good lad. Now, say the Act of Contrition.

The Ranch is class. That's what they call the Training College. They call it that because it's mostly wooden huts scattered about in big wide open spaces. There's an old-fashioned mansion too that we had four lectures in so far and it's where Doctor Rodgers lives. He's the president and we all call him the Doc but not to his face, of course. He's great crack the way he goes on. He gives us a sermon every Wednesday afternoon at Benediction in Saint Agnes's chapel on the Andersonstown Road and last week he'd the whole place in silent stitches. He was going on about students throwing money away on the horses and dogs and he said, dead serious and all - It would be a gross dereliction of duty if I neglected to caution you on the pitfalls and perils of placing wagers on the relative velocities of equine and canine quadrupeds.

I can see it's going to be brilliant.

I'm in digs in the Glen Road with Tommy Wright and this slabber from Armagh that thinks he's a real Romeo. Gary Houston you call him. He's okay some of the time but he'd sicken you when he starts the boasting. He told me the first day I met him that he was running out of girls in Armagh and Belfast came just in time. He's got this sun ray lamp that he uses on himself upstairs. He says it protects his skin against the sun and the cold as well. I went into his bedroom last Friday to get a loan of a book off him and he was lying completely naked on the floor with the lamp pointing at his stomach. He's got no shame.

The work's dead on so far. I applied to do an extra year in English with Special Emphasis on Speech and Drama. I wanted to specialise in English and when I heard you had to do Speech and Drama with it I hesitated for about one second. If I have to speak in debates and go up on the stage I'm bound to bury the stammer completely. English is dead on. We're doing this writer called Graham Greene that's obsessed with good and evil. The English lecturer, Mr Breslin, told us about him. He said Greene was a bit of a freak when he was young and he actually played Russian roulette with himself one time. He was a Protestant but then he turned to be a Catholic later. We have to do an answer on one of this novels for Hallowe'en. *The Heart of the Matter*. I never read anything like it. It's really good but I have to put it down sometimes because I can picture the sex in it. I don't think it's pornographic or anything like that but he can really make you see things happening. It's about this cop in Africa called Henry Scobie that's married but he's having an affair with a young girl called Helen. He's a Catholic and he has a conscience, of course, but he can't help what he's doing. I'm not going to say in my answer but he doesn't seem to me to have enough will power. He just lets things happen instead of controlling them *or* himself. I'm getting to the part now where I think he might be going to commit suicide because he loves Helen *and* his wife and all he's doing is betraying the two of them. His wife comes back from being on a cruise and when she finds out from him that he's stopped going to Sunday mass she gets him to go to Holy Communion with her. The thing is, it's a trick. He doesn't know it but *she* knows all about his affair and she's really trying to make him go to Confession so that then he'll start being faithful to her again. But it doesn't work because Scobie can't confess what he's not sorry for. Greene's a great writer. He makes the scene at mass really dramatic, with Scobie waiting for Holy Communion like a condemned man watching his last meal being got ready by the priest up at the altar. I'll tell you this. It might be a bit dirty here and there but it's still a million times better than *Emma* or *Martin Chuzzlewit*.

Jenny has to live in the girls' training college down the Falls Road. It's run by nuns and they don't seem in the least like any of the nuns you see in Derry. Most of them go round smiling, anytime I've been down anyway, and they're really sugary to the male students. She can go out in the evening but she has to be back by eleven. I've been out with her three times a week since we started in Belfast. Last Saturday night somebody painted VIRGINS on the front wall of the girls' place. It was rubbed out by the time I went down to meet her on the Sunday but you could still see the track of it. Helen Doherty was standing outside the gate with her and the three of us went to the other side of the road and stood for a minute looking across. Jenny laughed and said - I'll bet you any money the fella that did it's a virgin himself.

Helen sniggered and I said - Probably.

I didn't know boys could be called virgins too.

Helen went back into the college and we walked up to Falls Park. We sat on the grass talking for a while. Jenny had an amazing white frock on that I saw her wearing one time a good while before I got off with her. I leaned over and took her by the hand and told her I dreamed of her twice since the last time I saw her.

- But sure you were out with me yesterday, she said.

- That's what I'm sayin, I said. - I dreamed of ye twice last night.

- What were you doin tay me? she said.

- Wise up, I said.

- Naw, tell me, she said. - What were you doin tay me?

- Kissin ye, I said.

- Is that all? she said. - *That's* not very excitin. Gawn tell me. What else were you doin?

- Nothin, I said.

I stood and pulled her up by the hand.

- Mawn, I said - Let's go a walk. I want tay tell ye the crack about the Doc.

I thumbed it to Derry today. I was on my own and I got one lift after another till I was left off at Dungiven. But then when I was walking down the main street the heavens opened and I had to stand in a doorway for shelter. About ten minutes later it was still bucketing down so I went into Dan's Café and got fish and chips and a lemonade. The Irish News was sitting on the table and I was there that long I was starting to read through it for the second time when I caught myself on. Then the rain seemed to be going off a bit so I got up to go. The woman behind the counter asked me if I wanted to take the paper with me. I took it because there was nearly a full page in it about the Russians sending Sputnik up into space and I wouldn't mind reading it again. I'm not good at taking stuff like that in but there's something dead exciting about it. You know, the start of a new age and all. I headed off down the street and kept walking till I got to the bridge outside the town. It was getting dark now but the rain had stopped. I looked up at the sky and saw a light moving between two clouds. I stood there wondering if it could be Sputnik. I thought, Wouldn't it be really strange if that was it after me just finishing reading about it? The paper said Sputnik meant fellow traveller in Russian. That was a good name to call it because we're all travelling through space together, the whole lot of us, even the ones that think they're standing still. A shiver went through me but it wasn't the cold. It was just that I felt so happy. I loved being at the Ranch in Belfast, doing what I'd always hoped to do. And now I had Jenny too. Everything was so different from the way it used to be. It's funny. Waiting there at the bridge outside Dungiven I felt as if I could achieve nearly anything I wanted.

Spits of rain started to fall again and I said a wee prayer I'd get a lift soon. The second car that came stopped. I told the driver I was going to Derry and he said he would leave me off at the Waterside. A few miles out the road the B men stopped us. They asked us our names and where we were going and all and then they made us stand out in the rain for over five minutes so that they could search the car. I didn't like the way they were going on. They were a bit sarcastic and the boy in charge had this put on accent but he was a cuiltie all right. He asked me why I hadn't any luggage and was I really a student going home for the weekend and I said I didn't need any luggage for two days and I had a sheet in my pocket to do with subject choices if they wanted to see it. He didn't seem to hear me. He just said - In future, if ye're ever stopped by the special constabulary, tell them ye're goin to *London*derry, not Derry. Ye mightn't find the nixt crowd as understandin as us. Now, back in the car and on yer way.

On down the road the driver suddenly came out with this wee rhyme.

> *Ireland was truly a nation*
> *When England was only a pup.*
> *Ireland will still be a nation*
> *When England is buggered up.*

I laughed.

He said - That's a goodun, isn't it?

- Where'd ye hear that one? I asked him.

- Aw, God knows, he said and then his voice changed to a different kind of friendliness.

- Tell may this, he said. - Ye wudn't bay wan a the Murphys, wud ye?

- May name's Murphy all right, I said.

He gave the steering wheel a big slap.

- I knew it, he said - I *knew* it. I was just luckin at you when them boys wur searchin the car. Which wan's *your* father?

- May father's dead, I said. - His name was Jim.

- Ye don't say, he said and he looked at me that long I was getting scared he was going to crash.

- Ye're his image, he said. - His *image*.

And he started looking at the road again.

- Did ye know him? I asked.

- Aye, he said. - I knew im all right.

He pushed his peaked cap away back on his head. He was as bald as a billiard ball from what I could see but he had these massive grey eyebrows that didn't seem to go with the rest of him. He was very quiet for a while and then he said - Yer father was a great man. D'ye know that? I'm sure ye know that. The best man I ivir met. That's a fact. Tell may, what d'ye think a all this stuff's goin on now?

- What stuff? I asked.

- The bombin an all. Ye know.

- I'm not sure what tay think, tay tell ye the truth, I said.

- I'd say mibby ye are now, he said. - Is it Queen's ye're at?

- Saint Joseph's .The teachers' trainin college.

- Well, thur ye are. Ye're an educated man. What d'ye think a it all then?

- I think if they want a united Ireland they're goin the wrong way about it, I said.

- What wrong way's that? he said.

- The policeman they blew up last August there, I said. - That's not right.

- I see. An how day ye suggest they shud free Ireland, then?

- I think they should just wait, I said. - I think it's bound tay happen sometime anyway.

- An what's goin tay mick it happen, then?

- I dunno, I said. - People'll start tay understand better. It's *bound* tay change.

- An in the meantime way shud jist lie down an tick it?

- Well, the kind of things they're doin now aren't goin tay solve it, I said.

- D'ye not think way shud bay *helpin* things tay change? he said. - Tell may this. Ye wudn't know a milkman the name a Bill Ferry, wud ye?

- I think I might have heard of him.

- Well, Bill Ferry towl me wan time that he cuda spent the whole a iviry day deliverin tay about fifty houses in William Street an Great James' Street.

- How's that?

- Because thur's so many families livin in each house it wud tick the whole day jist tay git roun thim. *Now* d'ye git may?

- Not enough houses, I said.

- Not enough houses fur *Caccholics*, he said, - Plenny a hous-es fur the other boys all right. Not enough houses and not enough jobs and thur tryin tay redd the pliss a Caccholics.

- There must be some other way, I said.

- What other way wud that bay, then? he said.

- I dunno, I said. - I'm not a politician.

- I'll lave ye on over, he said. - Day ye still live in

Marlborough?

- Aye, I said.

- I'll lave ye tay the dour, he said.

He didn't say any more till we got to the house. I was just about to get out of the car after thanking him when he said - Ye wur sayin thur about not bein a politician. Thur's somebody lives not very far from here an he might bay very interested in talkin tay ye.

- What d'ye mean? I said.

- Well, he's not exactly a politician but he's very knowledgeable an I've a feelin he might bay very interested in talkin tay a man lick yersel.

He gave me the name and address of this person I'd never heard of. I took it in all right but all I could really think of was that he'd called me a man, twice.

I'm sitting here now in the attic and I'm thinking of Jenny. She's probably in bed. I wonder if she's thinking of me. I'm so happy. Sunday night can't come soon enough. The closest I ever got to this was the two weeks I was waiting to start at Saint Paul's (the second time). Nearly everybody else was at school and every day my heart was running around mad and I couldn't wait to get up in the mornings. Charlie called for me at about ten and then the two of us called over for Gander. It was so hot you could smell the tar. I remember it sticking to our shoes. I think we must have played cricket in Tillie's Field right next to Rosebawn school the whole fourteen days. It was great on the weekdays to hear the bell ringing and the teachers booming away in the big rooms and then the boys out in the playground having to go back in after lunchtime.

I'm getting the train back up on Sunday and I have to meet her outside Fusco's fish and chip shop at nine o'clock. We'll probably just go to a café and play some records on the juke box. I love her.

I didn't tell you. I'm in the Legion of Mary. I joined the students' praesidium at Clonard the first week I was in Belfast and we meet in the Redemptorist monastery every Tuesday night. I really like it. Father Roberts is in charge and he's got a great sense of humour. I'm training to give instruction to Protestant converts and I'm on the book barrow at Smithfield market nearly every Saturday morning. It's like the book stall at the back of the Cathedral in Derry except you can wheel this one along. The idea is, people come along and start looking at books and if they're still there after a few minutes you move over and start chatting to them. As Father Roberts says, they could be Protestants or they could be Catholics that are struggling with their faith and you could make all the difference just by talking to them.

There's this old boy Ben that was there two of the times I was down. He looks at the books and laughs away to himself. He's a Jew and he's nearly the dead spit of Alec Guinness the time he did Fagin in *Oliver Twist*. He's got big piercing eyes and a long nose and a straggly sort of beard down to his chest and he always has this wee tiny skull cap on. He's a real eccentric. Father Roberts laughs about him when the brothers report back at meetings. That's what you call other people in your praesidium. Brothers. Brother Parkes or Brother Doherty or Brother Murphy or whatever their name is. Father Roberts says Ben's got his own version of history. He's right there. The first Saturday, when me and Tony Parkes were on book barrow duty, the old boy cornered me and told me Jesus was illegitimate, only *he* used the word bastard, and then he came out with all these quotations that were supposed to prove it. I couldn't argue because I didn't know if the quotations were made up or if he changed them a bit to suit himself. Then he started about the Catholic Church being racialist.

- I'll bet you they didn't teach you about how the Spanish Inquisition was used against Jews that converted to Roman Catholicism, he said. - The excuse they made for murdering them was that they were still practising Jews in secret. But they'd no proof, you see. So they tortured them to try and find out. And wait till you hear what I'm going to tell you now. Listen to me. If they didn't confess they were burnt alive and if they did confess they got off easy. You know what happened if they confessed?

- What? I asked.

- They were strangled to death and *then* they were burnt.

- That's not true, I said.

- You wanna bet, young man? he said. - I'll tell you something else now. I'll tell you what they did after they murdered them. They confiscated their money and their property. *That's* what they did. Now, does *that* remind you of anything?

- What? I said.

- What? he says! What? he says!

He lifted his wee skull cap for a minute and scratched away at his baldy head.

- You don't know your modern history, young man, he said. - The Germans were doing the very same thing to Jews during the last war. They even took the gold fillings out of their teeth. Well? Well?

- Well what? I said.

- I'll tell you well what, he said. - Do you want to know what your precious Pius was doing while all this was going on?

- You mean the pope? I said.

- Well now, he said. - I don't mean Pius Hannah that cleans the jacks over in the City Hall there.

- I don't know what he was doing, I said.

- *I'll* tell you now what he was doing, said Ben. - He was being carried about on his big bejewelled throne over in Rome doing sweet damn all. Because Hitler was doing his dirty work *for* him.

Then he went very quiet all of a sudden and after a minute he said - Excuse me. If you don't mind my asking, what age are you?

- Seventeen, I said.

- Seventeen, he said. - Aye, that would be about right. I'll tell you now exactly what was happening the times you were being brought in and out of the chapel in your wee pram. Hundreds of thousands of Jewish children were being wheeled in and out of the gas chambers. In alive, out dead.

He turned round and stamped off as soon as he said that

257

and Tony came over to me and smiled.

- I see Ben was giving you a rough time, he said.
- He's mad, I said.
- Don't mind him, said Tony. - He gives all the new ones the same treatment. He'll not come near you again.

I'd a desperate experience last Wednesday. I've been going out to a flat on the Albertbridge Road once a week to instruct a Protestant that's going to be getting married to a Catholic soon. I haven't even passed my catechist test yet but Father Roberts was stuck and he asked me to take Dave. Dave's engaged to this Catholic girl called Teresa and he really wants to turn. The wedding's in February and he says he can't wait to become a Catholic. Anyway, at the praesidium meeting on Tuesday night, Father Roberts told me he'd got a phone call from Teresa to ask could I come two hours early to instruct Dave the next day. So I arrived at his flat at about half six and Teresa let me in. She said something must have kept him because he wasn't back yet. She took my overcoat off me from behind and pointed to the sofa for me to sit down. Then she put on an apron and went out to the scullery and called in - I'm out here gettin Dave's dinner ready for him. Ye don't mind waitin on yer own there, do ye? He should be here any minute. I think there might be some sort of a magazine on the sofa tay keep ye goin.

- That's all right. Thanks, I said.

I sat there waiting. She's a cheap-looking sort of a one. I met her twice before. She was just getting ready to go out the two times when I arrived at the flat and I thought she'd too much make-up on and her skirt came up a bit high above the knees and that's not the style. There's something about the way she looks at you as well. After about five minutes there was no sign of Dave so I leaned over and picked up the magazine. Talk about a shock! It was lying open at this page with a really filthy picture on it. It showed a girl from the back and all she'd on was this wee short shift that came down to just below her waist and she was bending down pulling at panties that seemed to be caught on one of her toes. There was a big red headline below it saying THE SECRET? GIVE HIM WHAT HE WANTS and then an article on down the page.

- D'ye like Frank Sinatra?

I nearly jumped out of my skin when I heard the voice from the scullery door. I looked up. She was standing there with a different apron on her but the thing about this one was, she didn't seem to have anything on under it.

- Who? I said and I closed the magazine very fast.

- Sinatra, she said. - Frank Sinatra.

- Yeah, yeah, I do, I said.

- I'll just put on one of his records tay while away the time, she said.

Then she put her hand up to her mouth and said - Oh dear, I'm just rememberin now. Dave towl may when he was goin out this mornin he wouldn't be back till late. Nine o'clock, he sid. He sid he didn't wannay miss the overtime when he'd the chance. I'm sorry, it just went outa may head.

She went over to the gramophone in the corner and bent down to pick a record up off the floor. She was completely naked at the back except for the strings going down from her shoulders and round her waist.

- That's may favourite Sinatra, she said, going on dead normal. - *Fly may tay the Moon.* Wait till ye hear it. He leaves Elvis standin so he does.

- I must go, I said. - Tell Dave I had tay go.

- Howl on, she said, coming over towards me. - What's yer hurry? It's Conn, isn't it? Here, Conn, help may off with this apron, would ye. It's killin may it's that tight.

She turned her back on me again and I headed for the door. I knocked down the coatstand pulling my coat off it and turned the Yale knob. But the door wouldn't open. I heard her behind me shouting - What's wrong with ye? Are ye tryin tay wreck the place or what? and Sinatra singing away behind her, dead smooth. I panicked and pushed and pulled at the snib and then turned the knob again. The door opened this time and I went down those stairs like a Russian rocket. I must have left the door open because I could still hear her shouting even when I was nearly out in the street but I couldn't make out what she was saying with the thumping in my ears.

I let it all come that night thinking back on what happened so I went to Confession the next day in Saint Mary's church round from Smithfield market. They hear confessions there every day of the week and they don't know you either, which is dead on. I only told about the masturbation. I didn't say why, of course. Afterwards I wandered up and down Royal Avenue trying to think. I knew I had to ring Father Roberts to tell him I wasn't going back to that flat. When you think of it, she wasn't even good-looking. I knew she reminded me of somebody and I was trying not to think of who it was but this face kept coming into my head. After about half an hour I knew I'd better clear it up or I'd never be able to make the phone call. So I went to the Central Library in York Street and sat there with some book about gardening in front of me. I got it nearly right away. The one with the glasses out of *Strangers on a Train*. Not Farley Granger's wife. The other one.

There's a phone box near the library and I rang Father Roberts from there. I told him I didn't feel ready to go through with instructing Dave.

- I'm hopin ye can find somebody else before next Wednesday, Father, I said. I told him that seeing I wouldn't be back at Clonard till the next praesidium meeting on Tuesday I thought it was better to tell him now so that Dave wouldn't miss any instruction.

- Will ye tell whoever takes over, Father, that I've done all the sacraments with him except Matrimony?

- That's fine, Conn, he said. - I understand. It's maybe too much of a responsibility for you this early. Don't worry. I'll get somebody else. Would you ring him and let him know? I've a number here for contacting him at certain times. Hold on.

- Who? Dave? I said and I knew I was just about to start stammering.

- No, on second thoughts, said Father Roberts, - maybe it's better *I* ring him.

- Thanks, Father. Sssssorry.

- Not at all, he said. - You did the right thing. Don't worry about it.

I don't even feel like writing. When I went down to meet Jenny today Helen Doherty was at the gate of Saint Mary's waiting for me. She told me Jenny was sick and I said - What's wrong with her? and she said - *You* wouldn't understand.

I gave her a look and she said - No, really, ye *wouldn't*, Conn. And there's somethin else she asked me tay tell ye.

- What? I said.

- She says she's not goin out with ye again.

- What d'ye mean?

- She says she can't stand it.

I felt as if the pavement was starting to move under the two of us.

- What are ye talkin about? I said.

- Look, Conn. She towl me she spoke to ye about it a whole lot of times. She says she knows ye don't care enough about her so it's better to finish.

- But she's wrong. I *do* care, I said and then I thought, Why am I appealing to this speccy bitch? And why did Jenny tell her our secrets when it's none of her business? And what all did she tell her?

- If ye don't mind me sayin, Conn, there's carin and there's carin. If ye don't *show* her ye care, then what else can she think? She towl me, ye know.

She told her what? What did she tell her?

- I *have* tay see her, I said. I could nearly swear now that this ugly wee crooked-toothed sniggerer swimming in front of me was smirking. - Tell her I'll call down tomorrow at half four tay see her if she's better.

- Look, Conn, she said. - Did ye not hear me? She doesn't want to see ye again. She's had enough. Right?

She turned with her nose in the air and walked back into Saint Mary's.

261

I didn't sleep at all last night and I took today off. I've been up here in the bedroom since Tommy and Gary left for the Ranch this morning. They don't come back for lunch and Mrs Hall goes out to work so I'll be okay till about four.

The time I remember most was when we went back to Derry on the train, just the two of us in one of the small carriages. She'd wanted to thumb it down with me when we were going home for the weekend but I didn't like the idea of a girl hitch-hiking so we went on the train. We'd the carriage to ourselves the whole way down. She told me I was the most special person she'd ever met.

- One of the best things is, you don't even know it, she said.
- Do you realise that every other fella that goes out with a girl does it just to see what he can get out of her. You're different. You're a dote, you know that?

I didn't answer her. I was just so full of happiness. I was sitting there holding her hand and thinking, I'm very lucky. The first girl I ever really went with and she understands what's important.

I'd like to know what's wrong now. Does she want me to go on like a dirty brute? Do you know what's ridiculous? I want to hold her so tight I want to be coming out the other side of her. She doesn't know what it does to me not to do that. And she hasn't even *got* those kinds of desires. Don't try and tell me I'm wrong. I know. I've read about it. I've read the problem pages. She doesn't have those kinds of desires but she's brainwashed. She thinks every date should end up with a pressing and feeling session. She thinks it's okay for us to be sitting talking really intelligent and civilised one minute and the next minute to be going on like two animals. She wants me to be the very thing she hates in other boys. How can you love someone if you use them to give you thrills or if you use them to have power over them? I'm not stupid. She's so good and beautiful and so clever too so why does she think she has to go on the

262

way others go on? What is it anyway? What's the big deal about behaving like a beast? We're supposed to have developed from the apes and have will power and intellect and holiness and concern for other people so why do we take them down back lanes and do them up against walls? Not we. They. And they boast about it. And the girls are disgusted but *they* still snigger about it and they think deep down that if a boy doesn't try it on he's not a proper man. He's *different*. He confuses them. So they let the dirties do whatever they want to their most precious parts. I don't get it. We're supposed to be controlling the animals or steering clear of them if they're dangerous. We don't *belong* with them. Why can't she just let me love her till the time's right?

One night in her house at Hallowe'en she wanted us to lie down on the floor. So I lay down sideways, facing her. Then she got me to come on top of her and said - This is how Mammy and Daddy do it.

She didn't know it had happened me already from the time she sat on my lap and kissed me and put her hand inside my shirt so she couldn't understand why I was keeping most of my weight off her. She didn't know I was thick with it and I was scared of it going through to her. My elbows were nearly wrecked with supporting my weight but I still made sure to kiss her. I kissed her all over the face and on the neck and in the middle of it she pushed me away and started to cry. She said it was obvious I didn't want her.

- Is there something wrong with me? she said.

I felt like saying - You're dead right there is, but I didn't want to talk. I was afraid she'd notice my trousers so I told her I was feeling sick and I had to go. All this on top of mortal sin, I was thinking.

It started to fall through after that. The next night I was holding her was in the outside passageway beside the students' entrance at Saint Mary's and she said - If it takes that much out of you, you shouldn't bother at all.

From then on, every time I tried to kiss her she pulled back. After that I just kept hoping. I tried to be really interesting, and give her news and all. Yesterday when I went down to Saint

Mary's I was busting to tell her about your woman the sex maniac from out the Albertbridge Road. She'd have laughed but she'd probably have started to appreciate me again too.

I'm doing teaching practice in Saint Matthews out in Willowfield and I've got a Primary Six. I feel pretty confident and I'm not really stammering. But I'm going through it all like a machine. I just feel empty. I keep wondering what school she's in and how she's getting on. I went down to the girls' training college last night to try and see her but I never made it inside. I was going along the outside passageway to the side door and in the dark some boy had a girl half up on the windowsill. I could see one of her legs sticking away out towards me and him jerking like mad. He was grunting really loud as if it was nearly killing him and there wasn't a sound out of her. I made it back out of the passageway before they could see me. I don't know why but I felt as if *I* was the one doing wrong and I didn't want them to catch me at it. I walked back up the Falls Road and no matter how much I tried I couldn't get the girl out of my mind. Whoever she was, she'd been teaching children in some Catholic school today. Probably if I saw her clip clopping along on her high heels during the day sometime I wouldn't be able to believe she could go on like that. Why do they do it anyway?

I used the cane on a boy and I'm praying his mother and father don't come up to the school. I didn't even check if his hand was okay before I hit him. It was stupid. Big Snuff used to always say in Rosebawn before he slapped anybody - Show me your hand. Is it cut?

What happened was, Mr Carruthers was called out of the classroom and before he went he handed me the cane and said very loudly - If there's a cheep out of any of them you know what to do, Mr Murphy.

As soon as he went the place erupted. About ten arguments started at the one time and there was this wee bastard near the back that nearly had the life strangled out of the boy beside him. I went down and shouted - Leave him alone and stand out at the front of the class.

- *You* leave *me* alone, he shouted back at me and him still strangling the other boy. - *You* cannay hit *me*. Now gawn away.

There was complete silence in the room. I could hear the teacher next door writing on the blackboard. I grabbed the strangler by the arm and pulled him out of his seat. His eyes were blazing so I pretended I was losing control of myself.

- Put out your hand! I roared.

He put it out right away. That took me by surprise. He was looking up at me all meek, like a different person. I held him by the left wrist and flattened his hand out with the cane and that's when I got the shock. I felt this excitement coming up in me. I gave him a slap and took a quick look at him. His big brown eyes were staring up at me, waiting, scared. His face was dirty over on one side of his mouth and there was water running down from his nose and you could see the freckles everywhere. I felt the erection and I hit him again. I knew from his eyes that he was expecting more. He was used to getting more than two slaps. A heat went through me. I let his hand drop and shouted - Now stand out at the front and wait for the master to come back in.

The class was quiet then except for a few of them that started telling on other boys, trying to get them into bother. I went and stood up on the platform just behind the boy I'd slapped. He was standing there dead still. I lifted the chalk and said - One mute out of any of you from now on and I'll write your names on the board.

As I was saying that the teacher came back in. The thing was, I didn't want to do it. We're not supposed to. The dean warned us that slapping could end our career before we even got started because we're not covered by insurance.

Donnelly the Education lecturer was in to see me. I took a lesson on the months of the year for him and I know it was a good one because it involved the integrated curriculum. That's the thing we learnt about combining different subjects into the same lesson. I used a hula hoop and a football and a tennis ball to illustrate the earth going round the sun. It was all to do with there being three hundred and sixty-five and a quarter days in each year but for handiness we just call it three hundred and sixty-five and then every fourth year we put the four quarters together to make the extra day. In the middle of it this boy started asking me about Sputnik and did I think any of us would ever go to the moon. I was just finished answering that when another hand went up and somebody said - Sir, do ye think a space ship could ever get near heaven?

I handled those two questions well and got back to the calendar pretty quickly. Donnelly had a chat with me at the end of it. He told me I was a promising student and he was signing my lesson notes when the bell went for the children's midmorning break. Carruthers took the boys out and came back in nearly right away with a cup of tea and a biscuit for Donnelly. He said after a minute - The headmaster is going to keep them in the playground until you're ready to go.

I'd a feeling Donnelly wanted to leave right away but Carruthers was all set for a chat.

- I couldn't help being struck by something when Mr Murphy was taking the lesson, he said. - Did you know that Sputnik is actually an artificial moon revolving round Earth?

- Oh yes, said Donnelly, - and do you see with all this hoo-ha about interplanetary travel being just round the corner, people simply haven't realised that the main purpose of the whole exercise is probably to develop a way of building better communication.

I got really sickened after that because Carruthers kept trying to impress Donnelly with his brilliant scientific knowledge. So I switched away from them. I was looking at the two of them as if I was listening but I was thinking back on what I'd said to the boy that asked me about heaven. I'd told him heaven wasn't a place but I was wondering now if I was wrong saying that. The Derry Catechism we learnt in Rosebawn said *Purgatory is a place or state where some souls suffer for a time after death on account of their sins.* So if Purgatory can be a place then the same goes for heaven. After the General Judgement at the end of the world the bodies of the just will rise to join their souls so heaven will definitely be a place *then*. So why not now?

I stopped thinking about that when I saw Donnelly backing away to the door. Carruthers was going on now about weightlessness in space. I thought, This teacher's one real bore.

Gary Houston said to me - Hey, I hear you're finished with Jenny McCallion. Is that true?

I said it was.

- You don't mind me steppin into the breach then, do you? I wouldn't want to–

I didn't wait for the rest. I got up and went into the sitting room and sat looking out the window. Stepping into the breach! Who does he think he is? Shakespeare? After a while I heard the television set going on and I went back into the kitchen. Tommy was just coming in the back door. He sat down with us and we watched The Dave King Show. In the middle of it Gary said - Hey, wait till you hear this. You know the debate about Windscale that was on in Saint Mary's last week? Well, I was down at it and I got talkin to this bird from Cookstown. One of these real serious ones but two of the best tits you ever saw. She was goin on all intense about them makin plutonium and radioactivity leakin into the Irish Sea and d'you know all I could think about? I was lookin away at her and agreein with every word and all I could think about was the fantastic arse she'd on her and the quickest way of gettin to it.

He laughed away to himself and Tommy said - Tone it down, wud ye, Gary, and I could see him out of the side of my eye looking at Gary and giving a nod in my direction.

- Aw aye. Right, said Gary.

He toned it down all right but not much.

- Hey, did you hear the one about Father Lynch? You know the priest in Saint Agnes' that's supposed to be really broad-minded. Well, this guy comes into him in Confession and says, 'Father, I rode a girl from Lisburn', and Father Lynch says back , 'Well, my son, it beats comin by bike anyday'.

He laughed his head off at that, sitting there like a piece of half roasted meat. It's ridiculous. It's December and it would skin you and he's going round with this tropical tan on him and he doesn't care what anybody thinks. And he knows it all too. Oh, he really knows it all. Tommy told him last week that sun ray lamps can give you skin cancer and he just laughed and said - Not if you use them the right way.

He's a slag. I saw him in McCloskey's shop up beside the Ranch one day and he'd this lovely wee Saint Dominic's girl of about fifteen over the counter and he was pressing away at her, in and out, in and out, as if he was really doing it. Her two friends were standing over at the side with their hands up to their mouths trying to look shocked but they were lapping it up. He's got his hair like Tony Curtis now, dead slick and all, and the extra shirt button loose so that people can see the hairs on his chest. I'll kill him if he goes off with Jenny. No I won't. I'll go mad. Oh Jesus, I love her so much. Please help her to come to me.

The priest Gary Houston told the joke about. Father Lynch. I'm down with him twice a week now in the parochial house on the Andersonstown Road. It started with me going back into Confession to him just after I'd finished telling him my sins. I went out of the chapel and I saw this girl going in and I just went weak. I thought of Teresa and the girl in the dark outside Saint Mary's and the girl on the counter in McCloskey's and I knew what I wanted to be doing to this one. I was nearly doing it looking at her. That's lust. I went straight back in to Father Lynch. As soon as I told him it was five minutes since my last confession he said - It's Conn, isn't it? and he asked me if I'd like to come to talk to him in the parochial house at five o'clock the next day. He said - We're goin to have to get you sorted out, Conn. You can't be destroyin yourself with these scruples.

He's great. He's small and fat but he told me he used to win medals for shot putting. He tries to get you to relax by telling you funny stories. On Monday he told me about the time him and the other priest in Saint Agnes' went for a holiday to Spain.

- Were you ever at Confession with Father Broderick, Conn? No? Well, it's mostly only wee wains and old women and unwary strangers that go to him now. I'll put it like this. He makes blood and thunder seem like the gentle rain from heaven. A tough man on sex. Anyway, I was tellin you about us in Spain. This place called Tossa de Mar. We were lyin sunbathin in our swimmin togs and these big lumps of fellas and beautiful Spanish girls were messin about with a beach ball. The boys were doin their best to get squeezin the girls of course and Father Broderick was tut-tuttin away to me. Then suddenly the ball lands plop right in my lap and this brown Spanish goddess comes and stands over me with her hands held out. It's obvious she doesn't want to pick the ball up out of such a delicate place so she just stands there above me, waitin. Without sittin up I lift the ball and before I throw it to her I say, 'You wouldn't care for another two, dear, would you?' And she answers in perfect English, 'No thanks. You're not my type'.

Father Lynch laughed. I think I tried to smile. I could hardly believe what he'd just said.

- The best part of it was, Conn, there was me blushin like a nun caught with her habit down and Father Broderick snortin and sniggerin like a sailor on shore leave. I'm talking about the great avenger here. Bulldozer Broderick himself. Can you imagine it?

He's getting to know what a disaster I am. I told him the first day I was down with him that I still felt guilty for never telling in Confession about getting an erection nearly every time The Pogue looked up between my legs. He didn't even bat an eye. He said - You shouldn't feel guilty about that. Your erection was just a spontaneous reaction to bein interfered with. Look, Conn. God gave you that organ to further your happiness *and* the happiness of your future wife. Do you know that?

- And to procreate, I said.

- *And* to procreate, he said. - You're right. But you're too serious about it all. Loosen up. No girl would want to spend time with somebody that sounds like a Catholic Truth Society marriage manual.

He laughed.

- No, really, Conn, he said. - You know what's going to happen to you if you don't shake yourself? You're going to waken some morning and you'll be fifty and it'll all have passed you by.

He stood up.

- Now, just sit where you are and say the Act of Contrition. I'm going to give you absolution and I don't want to hear one word about these terrible sins you've committed.

- Can you do that, Fffffather?

- Of course I can. I can do a lot of things you don't know about. Sure did you never hear about the power of the clergy in Ireland?

I think the two of us laughed that time.

Yesterday I walked past Saint Mary's but I couldn't see her anywhere. I didn't want to be hanging around so I went on down to Fusco's fish and chip shop and stood outside it drinking a bottle of Coca Cola. We bought a fish supper between us there one night and walked up to Saint Mary's eating it. That was only three weeks ago. I was standing at Fusco's for about five minutes when I saw her coming up the Grosvenor Road. She had a ponytail. Probably she has it to please Gary Houston. I think she saw me but if she did she didn't let on. She started running as she came round the corner into the Falls Road and as she ran up alongside the big red-bricked wall outside the Royal hospital her ponytail was bouncing up and down and her maroon raincoat was lifting up to above the back of her knees and I could see the white of her skin. I thought of her lying on the floor that night in the front room in Oakfield and I thought of Gary and I never felt as lonely in my whole life. I was all right till she came. *She's* the one that got off with *me* and now look. If Gary gets her pregnant and then doesn't want to know, I'll marry her if she'll let me and I'll take care of her and the baby. I won't touch her or anything if she doesn't want me to. Why can she not see what he is, dressed to perfection and putting on the civil act every time until he gets her alone? Can she not understand what real love is? I thought girls were supposed to know.

What am I anyway? Last night I woke up and I was on top of Tommy and the pyjama bottoms and underpants were off the two of us and my stuff was everywhere. I rolled back off him and pretended I was asleep all the time. I lay there wet the rest of the night because if I'd dried myself he'd have known I was awake. He didn't say anything at the time and he didn't mention it today either. What am I? Remember Gander and the things I wanted to do to *him*? And look what happened me when I was slapping the wee boy. How could I be a teacher and me like that? I'm not going to mention any of it to Father Lynch because he'd probably only tell me to go and get help. And there's me every night on my knees for about twenty minutes before I get into bed and Tommy's lying trying to sleep. I'm a real hypocrite. And I know I'm whispering my prayers too loud but I can't help it. And then every morning I lie waiting for him to get up and put his clothes on and get out of the room before I move because every single time I waken up I've got this terrible hard and I know he'd only notice it when I take off my pyjamas to put my trousers on. He calls me a lazy bastard but he laughs when he's saying it. He doesn't know it's a freak I am.

Father Lynch asked me today if I'd ever been to Barry's amusements in Portrush. I said I had and he asked me when was the last time.

- Wa-wa-when I wa-wa-was about fffffifteen, I said.

- And do you remember looking in the magic mirrors there? he said.

- I remember doin it wa-wa-when I wa-wa-was sssssmaller, I said.

- Now Conn, you know how you saw yourself and everything else distorted when you looked in those mirrors?

- Yes.

- Well, that's the way your conscience is now. It's been giving you a distorted image of reality. Do you know what I mean?

- Yes.

- Anyway, I've been thinking about this and I'll tell you what I'm going to do now. That confused conscience of yours needs a break so I'm going to take its place till it comes round a bit.

- I don't know wh-wa-what ye mean, Fffffather.

- This is what I mean. Until I say otherwise you're not to go to Confession and you're to feel completely free to go to Holy Communion every day if you want.

- But I can't do that, Fffffather.

- Yes you can, Conn. Because I'm takin on the guilt of all the imaginary sins you commit.

- But they're not imaginary.

- Yes they are. You're no more capable of committing sins of impurity than I am of running up and down Divis Mountain before breakfast. Or after breakfast, for that matter.

- But you don't know, Fffffather.

- Yes I do, Conn.

He got up out of his armchair and came over to me and put his hand on top of my head.

- Trust in me, Conn, he said. - I can guarantee you now that *you*'ll never go to hell because of impurity.

- But wa-wa-what if I wa-wa-went out tonight and....

- ...and worked out your frustrations on some wee unfortunate girl from up the Glen Road. *I* would carry the sin. I give you my word. My responsibility to God and to you is to bring you out of this and that's what I'm going to do.

This might sound funny but sitting there on the edge of the big deep armchair my shoulders started to prickle with a feeling like from years ago. Like the nights I used to sit in front of the warm range before I went up to bed and everything was nearly right.

- But it's too easy, Fffffather, I said. - It doesn't ssssseem to make sssssense.

- Does God make sense to *you*, Conn?

- Ah .... yes and no, I said.

- Mostly no at the moment, I'd say, said Father Lynch. - Right?

I didn't answer.

- Am I right? he asked again, very gently.

I nodded.

- Well, he said. - Put your trust in me now, because I'm doin God's biddin. You're a daily communicant, aren't you?

- I missed sssssome days because of–

- I know, I know, he said. - Well, from now on, go to mass and Holy Communion every day and let the joy of Christ sweep over you. And make sure and have a ball to yourself when you're home at Christmas. Right? And don't be coming back to me till - let me see now - don't come back here till the second Friday in January. You hear me? The Catholic faith is a marvellous thing, you know. God's not a policeman, Conn. He loves you more than I could ever describe. And remember what He said to the apostles. *Don't be afraid.* Well, He's saying it you now.

Before I knew it I was on my knees. I don't remember how it happened but I was kneeling down on the carpet and Father Lynch was standing right in front of me with his two hands on my head. I felt a peace and I took deep breaths and I cried. It was as if the air of heaven was right there in that room with us.

I've been cheating God. It wasn't too bad for the first two days even though I was feeling guilty about not feeling guilty but then last night I went to Romano's. I came in late and I was standing on the step above the dance floor just after the start of a ladies' choice and this couple right in front of me were out dancing, if you could call it that. They were so tight together the bottom half of him was nearly completely buried in her frock. It was a white frock, a billowy sort of one, and there were parts of it coming through between his legs at the back, all the way up. She was holding his face and kissing away at him and his hands were resting on top of her bum as if they'd just slipped down accidentally from her waist. I was trying not to look but I couldn't stop myself and then I heard this voice from behind me.

- Dance?

I turned round and this ugly skinny-looking one was standing there with a wee short skirt on her and the thing I noticed nearly right away was the knobbly knees. I went out on the floor with her and started doing the slow fox-trot the way Mairead taught me, with my left hand holding her right hand and my right hand around the back of her waist. But it was a bit embarrassing because the people round us were all doing close dancing and the one I was out with didn't know the steps. At the end of the first song we stood looking up at the band and then when they started the second one she put her arms around my neck and moved in. I won't forget that song in a hurry. *Unchained Melody.* She'd her stomach pressed in hard against me and it was cheek to cheek. I remembered Father Lynch and I didn't back off. I prayed but I didn't back off. The worst part was when we were standing like Siamese twins joined down there waiting for the last song to start and she leaned back from the waist as if she was taking a better look at me but all she was really doing was pushing further into me.

- Whur ye frum? she said.

- Derry, I said.

- Derry? she said.

274

She moved her stomach around a bit till she got it comfortable and then she said - *I* used tay know a girl frum Derry.

I looked at her and tried to say Is that right? but it got caught somewhere inside my throat. She had green eyes and there were little golden flecks around the green. I was thinking. How can a face like that have eyes like those? and then she moved again and one of her thighs was between my legs.

- She'd red hair, she said.

- Wa-wa-what? I said.

- She'd red hair so she had. Are ye nat dancin?

- Oh sssssorry, I said and we started shuffling around slowly and the moving made it worse. The singer was doing an imitation of Elvis singing *Love me Tender* and in the middle of that it started.

- I'm tryin tay remember er name, she said. - I'm near sure she wiz frum the Waterside. Is thur a place in Derry called the Waterside?

We were hardly moving at all now, nearly standing still to the slowest song I ever heard. She had a sequinny lilac top on her and I needed it against me really hard so I pulled her closer till I was nearly crushing her and she came easy. I held her as tight as I could and the pleasure was pumping out of me just the way I wanted.

- Are *you* frum the Waterside?

I heard her but I didn't answer. I was concentrating on what was happening to me and hoping the song wouldn't finish too soon. And then I saw this boy standing at the side watching us. He was staring and his fists were tight down by his sides. I tried to manoeuvre the girl so that I wouldn't be able to see him but I didn't seem to have the energy. His eyes hadn't just lit on us for a second or two. They were staying on us. He looked as if he couldn't take them off us.

- Thank you, ladies and gentlemen, the singer said. - Next dance *please*.

She stepped back from me and stood where she was for a few moments. Then she gave a nod of the head and turned and walked away. The tugging came slower and slower until it stopped and I realised there was nobody else out on the floor. I went over to the mineral bar.

- Yis?

The woman behind the counter was waiting for me to order. I said - No, nothing, it's all right, and I walked away and out of Romano's. As I was going up the Falls Road I started thinking of this comedian Max Wall. He just came into my head. He's supposed to be a bit of a dirty brute and one time I was sitting half listening to him doing a double-meaning skit on *Little Red Riding Hood* and Frankie was with me and he was holding in the laughing. Sheila came into the kitchen in the middle of it and after a minute she went over and switched the wireless off.

- That man has no respect fur wimmin, she said and then she started to tell us what Mammy told her once about when her and Daddy would be going a walk out in the country before they got married and sometimes they'd see a couple lying in a field together and they'd feel sorry for them because they knew what they were doing was only going to lead to unhappiness.

- I hope yous two remember that whin *your* time comes, she said. - Ye shud treat iviry girl ye go out way as if she was Our Blessed Lady an nivir do anythin that ye wudn't do in front a yer own mother.

She was wrong. I knew that when I was walking back up to the digs. Girls are like the vegetables and the animals. They're put here for man's use. If that's not true then why are they there for the taking? Even the ones you think are decent make it easy after a while if you go about it the right way. That's what Houston says and he's the boy that knows.

I came home on Monday. I hadn't slept since Thursday and I knew I had to do something. Houston's out with Jenny nearly every night of the week. Before he leaves the house he's up and down the stairs about a hundred times singing at the top of his voice and the smell of Old Spice is still about the place for hours after. He didn't come home at all on Friday and Saturday night. He landed in about ten o'clock each of the next two mornings and slept half the day. Mrs Hall told me and Tommy on Sunday that she's getting rid of him. I don't know how long I'm going to stay in Derry. I haven't even told the dean why I'm off. They all know about it in the house and Sheila got a loan of a Blessed Martin de Porres relic for me to touch and Mammy told me to write to Father Mullan. He's a priest from Altinure out near Claudy that's got a gift. He's a cripple and he's supposed to have a great influence on God. So I asked him in the letter to intercede for me. Arthur's trying his best. He got me to go a walk with him and when we were out he told me Ireland is a priestridden country and it would be a mistake to take what the clergy say too seriously.

- Priests aw all very fallible, you kneow, he said, - but the way some of them geo on you'd think they hawd the powah of God Himself.

Bernard took me to the Midland to see *Double Indemnity*. It was brilliant but the time Barbara Stanwyck put her hands round inside the back of Fred MacMurray's shirt I had to close my eyes and pray. What's going to happen to me? I missed the Christmas exams and all. Mammy says she's going to get Arthur to write to the dean and explain. I know they're all hoping I'll come out of myself the day of the wedding. I'm not sure if I told you. Patricia Murphy's getting married to Harry McCorkell after Christmas. She's stupid. McCorkell's a shit-ball. God forgive me but I can't forget the way he went on that time last summer I was standing with him outside Patricia's house. It was just me and him or he wouldn't have said it. There was a girl going up the other side of the street and he said - Jesus, look at yon, would you.

She was nice looking all right.

I said - Sh-sh-she's got a quare fffffigure.

He said - She wouldn't have much of a figure left nine months after *I* got at her. She'd be about fourteen stone so she would.

He must have seen the look on my face because he said then - You're a prude. You know that, Conn? You're a prude. You've a lot to learn, son. First thing you've got to learn is how to take care of Percy.

He tapped the front of his trousers.

- *Your* Percy, not *my* Percy. I'm tellin you, son. You see him right and he'll see you right.

I remember thinking to myself, Patricia's got no chance with a boy like that. She's so fragile and he's nothing but a big bull. He'll be doing the filthiest things to her you could ever imagine. He'll turn her stomach forever.

That's what I thought then. But I don't think it now. I know now. She'll take it all and she'll still tell him she loves him. Whatever she gets she deserves it for marrying him.

The mass was okay at the start. Mr Nugent playing *Ave Maria* on the organ made everything seem calm and quiet. And the wee barrel of a priest that was here from America with Bridie's cousin Eamon had this great way of talking and he made the words seem different. *Introibo ad altare Dei ... I will go in onto the altar of God: to God Who giveth joy to my youth.* I closed my sins out and thought back to what Father Lynch had said to me: *Don't be afraid.* I closed my mind to lying in the middle of last night picturing Patricia and Harry in some hotel and him getting her ready for bed. And here they were in front of me now, the black suit and the long white dress together, kneeling on the deep red carpet on the bottom step below the altar. And as the mass went on the sweat was pricking more and more at me and I thought, How can one human being give another human being *carte blanche* from God? Because that's what it was, *carte blanche.* Even a priest can't have that power, it's not in the laws of the Church. Father Lynch thought butter wouldn't melt in my mouth but he didn't know what I was capable of. He didn't know that the first opportunity I got I would take advantage and defile my temple *and* someone else's and the mind of the boy watching and God knows who else. How can you uncorrupt someone you've corrupted, I thought, even if you *were* able to meet them again? It's not like giving them back money you've stolen from them or even confessing in public

278

that you took away their good name. When it came to near Holy Communion and the priest said the Latin for *May the receiving of Thy Body, O Lord Jesus Christ, which I unworthy presume to take, turn not to my judgement and condemnation* I knew what I was going to do. I sat sick and shamed as the pews emptied and everybody else went up to meet Jesus and take Him down to their places with them. That was bad enough but then on the way from the cathedral to the Melville Hotel me and Charlie were sitting in the back of Harry's car and I heard Patricia and Harry talking to each other about the completeness of the nuptial mass if all the wedding guests receive Holy Communion and I knew what was coming. Would you believe that? I knew what was coming next. Harry said - That's fifty-two, and then he sort of half turned round and said - Did *you* receive, Charlie? and Charlie said he did and then he asked me and I said I didn't. I wouldn't put it past him going through all that just to embarrass me because he's only a dirty badhearted hypocritical bastard anyway. But it doesn't matter. Everybody knew. They saw me sitting there. And what did they know? They knew I didn't go to Communion because I was in the state of mortal sin. And that's giving scandal. That's another mortal sin. I've read up on all this and there's no magic mirrors about it. Giving scandal is mortally sinful. It's not as serious as sacrilege but it's still a serious sin.

I was really cheesed off with the dootery oul songs people were singing when the wedding breakfast and speeches were finished and after a good while of tholing this I followed Charlie out when he gave me the nod. I lost him for a couple of minutes but then I found him in the bar. He was sitting on a stool near Uncle Eddie and a crowd of men that were drinking round a wee table. Charlie whispered to me - Hi, wait tay ye hear what thur sayin.

I sat down beside him.

- *I* nivir heard no bell, one of the men said, - and I lived in Derry all may life.

- Aw, it rung awright, said Eddie. - An ssssstill does. Twiced a day.

Charlie whispered to me - Thur talkin about the curfew bell

that rings in the big Protestant cathedral at seven in the mornin an nine at night.

- And wa-wa-what? I said.

- Shhh, he whispered. - Years an years ago it used tay bay tay warn Caccholics tay git outa the part a Derry that's inside the walls from nine at night tay seven in the mornin.

- And wa-wa-why are they sssssstill ringin it? I said.

- Keep your voice down, he whispered. - I wannay hear what thur sayin. Listen tay ye hear.

- Iss newins tay *me*, one of the men said.

- Ye ssssssee, said Eddie, - ye wa-wa-wudn't na-na-notice the wa-wa-wan that rings at na-na-nine iviry na-na-night because, ye ssseee, that wa-wa-wan wa-wa-wud be drownded out bay the Angelus bells fffffrom Ssssssint Eugene's. An ye wa-wa-wudn't hear the early wa-wa-wan because ye're probbly in yer bed ssssssleepin at that time.

- *I* heard it, said somebody.

- Did ye na-na-now, Wa-wa-willie? said Eddie. - Thur yeez are. Wa-wa-willie heard it.

- Aw aye, said Willie. - *I* used tay hear it iviry mornin the time I worked in the bakery. But, tay tell ye the truth, I didn't know what it was fur.

- I na-na-nivir na-na-knew ye wa-wa-worked in a bakery. Wa-wa-when wa-wa-was that? said Eddie.

- Aw, away back, said Willie. - It was Stevenson's I worked in but I didn't lick the hours an I chucked it.

- Stevenson's micks powerful white bread, said somebody. - Did any a yeez ivir tist thur white bread?

- They do not, said Willie. - Thur white bread's shite. Sure all the goodness is ticken outa the flour they use tay bake the white. Did ye nivir know that?

- Naw, I nivir knew that now, said somebody else.

- Sure thur's nothin lick good wheaten bread, said Willie. - Roughage, ye see. An goodness. I wudn't touch the white. I'm tellin ye.

- God, said Eddie, - ye wa-wa-wannay tist the wa-wa-wheaten ssssscones Bridie micks. She does them on the range.

He turned round towards me then and said - Conn's mother there micks the Injun sssssscones. Isn't that right, Conn?

- That's right, I said.

- Aye, Murray's a grand baker, he said.

I sat there thinking. I used to always laugh at Mammy because after she mixed the Indian meal and all in the big delph bowl she stopped and looked out the kitchen window and tried to remember if she'd put the baking soda in. Every time it was the same. I think she must have had so many things in her head that she could never remember whether she'd put it in or not. So, just to be sure, she took a wee tiny bit of the wet dough on her thumb and flicked it on to the top of the hot range beside where the big black pan was sitting waiting with the shiny melted margarine in it and if the flick rose she knew she'd the baking soda in.

In the middle of all the chat about bread Patricia and Harry came in to say Cheerio. Patricia was wearing a cream coloured two piece suit and you could see the lovely wee shape of her. She was very nervous looking but Harry was going on dead cocky as usual.

- That was a fine piece a singin in there, Harry, said one of the men. - Yon foreign song ye sung.

- Latin, said Harry.

- I nivir knew ye'd a voice lick that, said Willie.

- Why? said Harry. - Did you never see me in the pantomimes?

- Aw aye, said Eddie. - Sure Harry's got medals fffffur the Fffffeis an all. He's in the men's choir. The Columbians, isn't it ye call them?

He got up out of his seat.

- Wa-wa-well, he said. - I ji-ji-jist wa-wa-wannay wa-wa-wish the two a yeez all the very best.

He shook hands with Harry.

- Ffffffur na-na-now, he went on, - and ffffffur many happy years in the ffffffuture. I know ye'll mick er a fffffine husband, sssssson.

- Thanks very much, Eddie, said Harry.

Eddie turned to Patricia and put his arms around her. She was shaking. Her whole body was shaking.

281

- Ye're awright, love, Eddie said. - Ye've a fffffine man there ssssso ye hiv.

He kept on holding her a good while. Too long, I thought, and too tight as well.

After they left Charlie said to me - He's a quare singer, isn't he?

- Aye, I sssssuppose he is, I said. - But d'ye not think he's a bit pretentious?

- How day ye mean? said Charlie.

- That classical sssssong he sssssang, I said. - I bet ye he doesn't even know wa-wa-what it means.

- Why, day *you*? said Charlie.

- *I* do, I said, - but I'll bet ye *Harry* doesn't.

- I'll bet ye he does, said Charlie. - I'll bet ye he picks up the Latin, him bein in the Feis choir an all. Anyway, that's not a classical song. That's from *The Student Prince* and *that's* not an opera. Did ye not see it in the Stran? Edmund Purdom was in it.

- I did sssssee it, I said. - He mimed tay Mario Lanza's voice.

- Okay, said Charlie. - *You* tell may now what it means. *Gaudeamus igitur* - what does that mean?

- Therefore let us rejoice, I said.

- *Iuvenes dum sumus*?

- Wa-wa-while wa-wa-we are sssssstill young, I said. - Sh-sh-sure *you* did Latin yourself.

- Jist checkin, said Charlie and he laughed. - Hi, wasn't that a goodun may da was sayin?

- Wa-wa-what?

I suddenly felt as if something flat and hard was pressing down on my head.

- Ye know, about them not lettin Caccholics intay the town at night, he said.

- Sh-sh-sure that wa-wa-was probably hundreds of years ago, I said.

- But imagine the Prods still ringin the bell, he said. - An from thur *cathedral* too.

- I don't know wa-wa-what the big deal is, I said. - Did that bell ever sssssstop you or me fffffrom goin up the town?

He gave me a look.

- Tell us this, he said. - Day *you* think ye *are* somebody now or what, seein ye're sposed tay bay goin tay bay a teacher?

- Naw, I said.

- Well, ye wudn't think tay listen tay ye ye wur a Caccholic, he said. - *Or* Irish.

- Wise up, I said.

He went on talking but I don't know what he said because the next thing I remember was standing shivering at the top of the steps outside the Melville. It was pouring sleet. I slipped twice when I was running along Foyle Street and the second time I slipped I fell and got my trousers soaked. The whole time I was running I kept saying to myself, I'll be okay when I get home. I'll change my trousers and dry myself at the kitchen fire and then I'll go on to bed.

Mairead was the only one in.

- Whur's yer overcoat? she said when she saw the state of me.

- I must have left it in the hotel, I said.

- God Almighty. If I didn't know better I'd think ye wur drunk, she said. - Ye'd need tay go upstairs an git them wet close off ye now.

I went up and changed and then came down and sat at the range. She started to ask me about the wedding but she stopped when I shouted at her and told her to leave me alone. She went out to the scullery and she was still there when I went to bed.

So that's it. It's all clear now. Imagine me ending up an instrument of the devil. Some people would have a good laugh about that if they knew. I thought first I was damning a saint to hell but that part's going to be all right. He convinced himself he was going to be carrying my sins but he was wrong. *I* know. I know because I'm training myself to be a catechist. It's amazing the things you come across when you're reading about sin and sacrifice. It used to be that on the Day of Atonement each year after the time of Exodus the priest laid the sins of the people on the goat and then they let it escape into the wilderness and they called it the scapegoat. But there was another goat that I'll bet you Father Lynch doesn't know about, or maybe he did one time and now he's forgotten. It was the one they cut open and sacrificed but before that was done the priest placed his hands on its head to transfer *his* sins to it. Isn't that the strangest thing? He did it without realising what he was doing. In trying to comfort me he was letting me damn myself and setting *himself* free.

People don't understand the sin of Judas. I don't mean betraying Christ, That's *easy* to understand. Sure they're all doing it. Oh, they were good at the start. At the start they learnt the sixth and ninth Commandments and they didn't even know what they meant. *Thou shalt not commit adultery* and *Thou shalt not covet thy neighbour's wife.* But they soon found out in the chapel and the house that God didn't write down all the other sins that were contained in those two because even a *hundred* tablets of stone couldn't have held them. And so they learnt them. Lewd looks and smutty kisses and immodest dress and impure touches. And dirty talk. And bad thoughts. And all the many filthy ways you can bring others to hell with you.

But of course the one they'll never understand is the other sin of Judas. Despair. It's waiting for them all and it scares them nearly to death but that's because they don't know to reach out for it. And if only they knew, it's the light that leaves no shadows, no worries, no doubts. Lucifer's light. You're shocked? Well, I'm not surprised. Lately I've been noticing how strange you've been, how distant you've got. You're my altered ego, that's what you are. I like that. My altered ego. Did you hear me? I don't think he heard. Probably he wasn't even listening.

There's no one left to talk to now. Definitely not the doctor anyway. I tried but it was no good. It's obvious he doesn't like me anyway. I can see it in his face. It's okay with me actually because I don't like him either. The day before yesterday he started asking me about dreams and I told him the truth. I told him I was having nightmares about this man called Ian Paisley going to take over the Six Counties and he said - What would be so terrible about that? Mister Paisley is a very good man and he has the interests of the Province at heart.

So I said - Are you another Prod then?

He didn't like that. He didn't like it one bit. He gave me this look and I think I know what it meant *You're for the ECT, boy.* Well, he's not going to get another word out of me from now on. Not after that. And I'm ready for the whole lot of the rest of them too. I'm staying alert. They think I'm taking their drugs but I'm not. I keep them away over at the side of my gum and then when I'm on my own I make them disappear down the wash-hand basin. I've my own room. That's the way I wanted it. I can bang away at myself and nobody knows. Well, nobody except the wee woman that changes the sheets. And Father O'Driscoll. He's the chaplain. I rhymed off my confession to keep him happy and he told me I must stop abusing myself. I didn't let on to him it's the only way I can get to sleep. If I told him that he'd end up telling the doctors in a crafty sort of a way and then they'd hold me down and *inject* the drugs into me. He went on and on about my body being a temple of the Holy Ghost and the sacredness of our private parts and stuff like that. Then he gave me absolution even though he knows I'm going to keep at it. He's not supposed to do that. But maybe I'm wrong there. Maybe there's a special dispensation for Gransha cases.

I got really annoyed with him the last day he came in. I was sitting on the bed and he saw me reading in the Irish News about Sputnik breaking up when it was coming back into the earth's atmosphere and he said - Now, if only Communism would fall apart the same way, and he laughed. I gave him a dirty look but he didn't see it. Next thing was, he started getting all serious, walking up and down right in front of me with his hands behind his back and nodding away to himself.

- They were going to spy on the free world, he said. - That's why they'd that thing up there. That's the real reason. Watching us. Trying to control us. Did you know that?

I didn't say anything. I wanted shot of him. He sat beside me on the bed and joined his hands into a big fist. His knuckles were nearly coming out of his skin. He took out his Confession gear and put round his neck.

- Would you like me to hear your confession, Conn? he said.

I just ignored him. I sat turning over the pages of the paper and didn't look near him. You're nothing but a prick, I thought. When I got to the back of the paper I went to the front again. He took the hint after that and left.

Nobody cares except Mammy and I can't even talk to *her* anymore. I can't talk to any of them. I say hello when they come in and cheerio when they're going and then when I'm on my own I don't remember anything they were saying. Sheila was here by herself this morning and after she went I found this wee leaflet crumpled up in my hand. I smoothed it out. *A Prayer for Purity*, it said. I know she pities me and she wants me to get better but that's only because she's embarrassed. They're all embarrassed. I suppose, when you think about it, it's no joke having a brother that's cracked and half of Derry knowing about it. It must be nearly as bad as having a spoiled priest in the family. Poor Jackie. Stupid cunt. But I feel sorry for Mammy. I really do. Her heart must be nearly broken with all the running back and forth. And to see her youngest in this sort of a state too. I wonder does she want to put her arms around me. She never touches me now but she used to. She did the first day she took me up to Rosebawn. She had me all dressed up and before we left the house she got down on her knees and held me against her. I felt her big breast against my belly and I cried because she was smothering me. So she let me go and then she kissed me and I wiped it off the way I always did. But I loved the nights before that when she had me on her lap at the open range. It was to get me to do a pee that would last me till the morning. I shot it away up in the air and I remember the blues and the reds and all the different colours going through the arc of it and then the straight of it and even the last dripples. And she always had this rhyme she sang when I was doing it and I thought it was great.

> *Who's at the winda who?*
> *Who's at the winda who?*
> *A wee oul man with a bag on his back*
> *To carry wee Conn away.*
> *Where will he carry him to?*
> *Where will he carry him to?*
> *Up the hill behind the mill,*
> *Far, far away.*
> *What will his mammy say?*
> *What will his mammy say?*
> *Get up wee Frankie and sweep the floor*
> *For my wee Conn's away.*